DAVID MCROBBIE was born in Scotland. He has worked as a ship's engineer, a primary-school teacher in Papua New Guinea, then a college lecturer and later a parliamentary researcher. He became an ABC scriptwriter and producer of children's radio and television programs but now writes full-time and lives in Queensland.

David has written many other best-selling books for children and young adults, a number of which have been adapted for television.

Other books by David McRobbie

A Little Drop of Wayne
The Wages of Wayne
Waxing with Wayne
The Wayne Dynasty
Mandragora
The Fourth Caution
Timelock
Prices
Schemes
Outworld
This Book is Haunted
Haunted too
Winter Coming
See How They Run
Tyro
Fergus McPhail
Eugénie Sandler PI
Mum, Me, the 19C
Strandee
Mad Arm of the Y

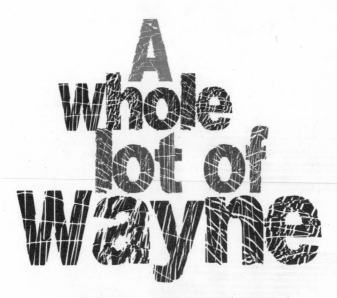

A whole lot of wayne

DAVID McROBBIE

ALLEN&UNWIN

This collection has been adapted from stories in *The Wayne Dynasty*,
Waxing with Wayne and *A Little Drop of Wayne*, published by Mammoth
Australia in 1989, 1991 and 1994.
The story 'Amy Pastrami Day', starting on page 316, appeared originally as
'Only in Wisconsin', in the collection *Celebrate!* compiled by Margot Hillel
and Anne Hanzl, published by Viking in 1996.

This collection first published in 2007

Allen & Unwin
83 Alexander St
Crows Nest NSW 2065
Australia
Phone: (61 2) 8425 0100
Fax: (61 2) 9906 2218
Email: info@allenandunwin.com
Web: www.allenandunwin.com

National Library of Australia
Cataloguing-in-Publication entry:

McRobbie, David.
A whole lot of Wayne.

For children.
ISBN 9781741752441.

I. Title.

A823.3

Cover and text design: Josh Durham, Design by Committee
Typeset by Midland Typesetters, Australia
Printed by McPherson's Printing Group

10 9 8 7 6 5 4 3 2 1

To all you good folks, young and old,

who laughed with Wayne first time around,

and generally carried on like crazy things

at a Crazy Things Convention —

don't just stand there!

Let's do it all again.

CONTENTS

Wayne, how did things start?

What things, Squocka?

You and me things. Like, how did we start?

Squocka, you should ask your mum and dad.

Don't be a dork. I mean, how did we first meet?

Oh, that sort of start?

And how did Kevin Merry come into our lives?

That's a painful story, Squocka.

One that you've never told, Wayne.

It's that painful.

Still got the wounds, eh?

And wear the bandages.

Well, let's have that story now, Wayne. Tell it now.

1 NEW SCHOOL

There I was, all those years ago, standing in the schoolyard wearing a floppy hat, grey shirt and short trousers with a heavy, new school-bag banging against my pudgy legs. I held my Mum's hand, while all around me other new kids did the same. Some cried, some sobbed, but not me. Mind you, my bottom lip made little quibber, quibber movements, so in case anyone was looking, I pretended to sing a cheery hymn. 'A-bide with me,' I went, then changed the words around to make it look like I knew the whole song. 'A-bide with me. With me a-bide. Me a-bide with.'

After five minutes, my unfeeling mum said, 'Shut up, Wayne.'

I, Wayne Wilson, was about to be plunged into Year 1 while all I wanted to do was stay home with my mother, my teddy bear and Fat Cat, my second favourite animal.

My older sister Charlene and some of her Year 5 girly mates were over in a corner, playing a jumping game that involved tangling up their legs in several metres of knicker elastic. It had very complicated rules, that game, and took all of Charlene's concentration to play

1

it, which is why she ignored me. That's what Mum said at the time, but I reckon that Charlene was scared her stuck-up friends would find out we were related, which was kiss-of-death territory.

At last an old man came to the school door and looked down at us. 'All ready for your first day?' he asked in a wheezy voice. 'How I'd like to be your age again.'

'And I wish I was yours,' a kid called out, 'then I'd stay home with my guinea pig.' The guy who made that smart remark was, and still is, Quentin Oscar Berrington, who later became known as Squocka. Don't ask me why. At the time I didn't know why I was called Wayne. Come to that, I still don't know.

The old guy rang a bell, ding-a-ling, then the older kids came running and started lining up. They were cool because they knew what to do while we new kids had our mums fussing around. I got my hat straightened forty-seven times although it was never on crooked in the first place.

'New boys and girls line up here.' The old guy pointed to a painted line and some of the mums pushed and prodded their kids into position. Jostle, jostle, elbow, poke, scratch, smack, waaa!

From the school loudspeaker came some horrible, tinny-sounding, humpty-tump music. The older kids marked time, swinging their arms and stamping their feet, then a teacher came out and uttered one fateful word: 'In.' Everyone trooped towards the school building. Trudge, trudge, trudge. To drown out the wails from us new guys, they made the music louder. Te-tump-te-diddle-de-tump-de-tump. Te-tump-te-diddle-de-boo-hoo-hoo-Mummy-I-wanna-go-home-with-you-hoo-hoo.

Some of the mothers cried too. 'Goodbye, darling.' They waved hankies. Any dads who were there went gruff, gruff, huff, huff, there now, be a man.

As I remember, it was a heart-rending scene. Some kids had to be forcibly wrenched from their parents but managed to hang onto things like wedding rings, wrist watches, bracelets and bits of dress. Me? I got Mum's handbag, but told everybody it was for carrying my play-lunch. (That handbag bit's a lie, but I did miss my mum.)

Little did I know that she and a thousand other mothers had already raced out the school gates, eager to enjoy cappuccinos in coffee shops without their offspring demanding milkshakes and teeth-rotting biscuits.

FLIGHT OF FANCY:

Mum 1: *Having another latte, Hester?*

Mum 2: *Try and stop me, Fatima.*

Mum 1: *Isn't it great. Freedom at last.*

Mum 2: *Yeah, thought he'd never start school. He's twenty-seven, you know.*

Mum 1: *I've been drinking coffee all morning.*

Mum 2: *And why not?*

❦

Grown-up people led us kids into a classroom, helped take off our sunhats and sat us at desks. We waited, most of us quietly blubbering to each other – you know, sharing our grief. Suddenly in shuffled this really old woman. She had a limp and walked with a stick. Straight off, one kid performed a protein spill (i.e. threw up). Anyone could tell this was Vampire Lady, straight out of the worst horror movie you ever saw.

'I am Miss Deeble, your teacher.' She smiled at us with her teeth. 'We're going to be good friends, aren't we, boys and girls?' It was a threat.

This was too much for Squocka Berrington. He made a bid for freedom, the first kid to crack, but Miss Deeble headed him off, spun him round and he was back in his desk wondering where he'd been. Our teacher still wore the same smile. She'd done this before. It was nothing personal.

Suddenly the classroom door barged open and in marched the guy who was destined to become my worst enemy. He wore a plastic steel helmet and carried his playlunch in a shoulder holster. 'Okay, you boofheads,' he snarled in a drill-sergeant voice. 'Who's got my chair and where's the plasticine?'

Miss Deeble looked him up and down. 'And you are?'

'Kevin Merry,' he answered. 'I can tie my own shoe-laces, see.'

Miss Deeble touched the side of her head with a finger and said, 'Haven't we forgotten something, Kevin?' He thought for a second, then the penny dropped so hard you could hear it go clunk in the bottom of his brain.

'Oh yeah.' Kevin Merry came to attention and saluted her.

'No, I don't mean that.' Miss Deeble tried again. She touched a finger to the side of her head and made a little tapping motion. She gave Kevin a grim but encouraging smile.

He thought a bit longer, then understood. 'So, you're mental,' he said. 'That's cool. Nobody's perfect.'

Miss Deeble hardened her attitude and used a voice like a spitting nail gun, 'I *mean*, when gentlemen are indoors, they remove their hats.' Miss Deeble pointed in my direction. 'There's your desk, little boy!'

Kevin scowled, then took off his plastic steel helmet and held it under his arm. Right away you could tell this guy hated being told what to do. He sauntered over with his head shaking from side to side, like he was Mister Laid-back. 'Okay, I might sit next to Boofhead here.' He sprawled into his seat, stuck out his jaw and growled, 'Who's she calling little boy?'

Miss Deeble issued big lumps of plasticine, then encouraged us to be creative. I rolled my plasticine into thin roly-poly strips, then fashioned them into a flower – stem, leaves, petals and the round yellow bit in the middle. Aw!

Kevin Merry made a stone-age club, then bashed my flower so that it finished up on the end of his club. When Miss Deeble was busy writing our names in the roll-book, he went around the room whacking everyone's plasticine creation. Soon his club was so huge he got Squocka to help carry it. No one complained. That's when I first discovered Kevin Merry had a reputation. I ended up with a blue finger from where he got me with his club.

'That's the way.' Miss Deeble beamed at us. 'You've been very quiet. Now I'm coming round to see what you have done.'

By this time, Kevin's club was two metres long. He used my name for the first time. 'Hey, Wayne, wanna have a go at my club?'

'Yeah, thanks Kevin.' I swung his plasticine creation and just missed the overhead light. Real men use clubs; wimps make flowers.

Suddenly, from behind me there came a moist hiss with spitty bits. It was Miss Deeble. 'So!' She meant me. 'Not content with your own mouldable instructional material, you have to take everyone else's?'

Kevin shook his head, drew in his breath and went tut-tut. Miss Deeble put a T in her roll-book next to my name. It meant Troublemaker. That T would stay with me for the rest of my life.

The long first day passed, then at last Miss Deeble let us out.

◆

At home Mum broke the sad news that I had to go again tomorrow – and for a few more days after that. 'What? Till Friday?' I asked cautiously.

'And a teensy bit longer.' Mum used a finger and thumb to show how long. Little did I know school would be a twelve-year stretch with no time off for good behaviour unless you pretended to be sick – and Mum was onto that!

FLIGHT OF FANCY:

Mum: *Mum, it's my leg. Ooooh-aaaah-eeeeh!*
Mum: *Looks all right to me. It reaches the ground. What more can you ask of a leg?*
Me: *No, I mean my throat. Erk, erk, erk. Croak.*
Mum: *A dose of prune juice will soon put that right. Where's the ladle and the funnel?*

❦

One of Miss Deeble's favourite lessons was the story. For this she sat us in a circle on the floor and put on a special dramatic voice. Kevin Merry kept chipping in, so a story went something like this:

'Once upon a time, there was a Lovely Princess – Kevin Merry, don't be obnoxious – who lived in a castle with her mean old uncle – Kevin, sit down – and her two repulsive sisters – look in the mirror and you'll see what it means, Kevin – and they all got on very well – and Kevin Merry will get along to stand outside the principal's office if he's not careful – until one day there came a handsome prince – I shall confiscate that until the end of the lesson, Kevin, although heaven knows who'd even want to *touch* such a thing – who had his eye on the beautiful princess – yes of course he had two eyes, Kevin, look to the front – as you can imagine the prince was a very charming young man indeed with very nice manners, not at all like Kevin Merry who has a finger so far up his nose it will come out his ear!'

We kids were confused. What exactly happened and why did Kevin Merry have such a big part to play in the story? Was Kevin going to be in every story? Had Kevin ever met Snow White? Did he know Rumpelstiltskin personally and could he get us an autograph? When would we get a chance to be in a story?

Miss Deeble always gave us a sheet of paper and crayons so we could draw a picture of the bit of the story we liked best. Everyone drew Kevin Merry wearing armour, riding a horse and poking people with a lance.

'What happened in school today, Wayne?' Mum asked at dinner one night.

'We got a story about Kevin Merry climbing up a castle wall and swinging on a girl's hair, then the girl's uncle told the charming prince to behave himself or he'd get sent to the headmaster.'

'Are we paying fees for this?' Dad frowned in my direction.

'Dunno, Dad, but Kevin Merry says the rent's due on my desk.'

Kevin told me his father owned everything in the school, which is why I had to pay rent for my desk. Not that I was taken in by this. Well, only a little bit. Seventeen lunch monies and a yoghurt.

It was not long before I discovered the benefits of sitting up straight. Do enough of it and Miss Deeble would eventually spot you and give her seal of approval. 'Wayne Wilson's sitting up nice and straight,' she'd observe to the class, and the pay-off would follow. One day, wonder of wonders, Miss Deeble spotted this nice girl called Violet Pridmore who'd been sitting up straight for as long as I'd been doing it.

Result? Miss Deeble sent us both down the corridor to get water to wash the gunk off the paint brushes. It was one of school life's little rewards, the two of us out of class, trusted to fill our water jars and carry them back without spilling a drop. Violet always did her blonde hair in two pig-tails and wore dresses with neat shoes and white ankle socks. She was my kind of girl, but then so was Rosana Conti, who wore daggy shorts and a bomber jacket that was too big for her.

I tried some conversation on Violet – man-of-the-world, sophisticated stuff. 'Violet,' I said, 'isn't that Kevin Merry a dork?'

'He's all right,' she answered primly, 'and it's not nice to call people names.'

Oops! Time to back-pedal. 'I didn't say dork.'

'You did.'

'Didn't.'

The did/didn't business went on for several minutes, then it was time to go back to the classroom with our dribbling jars of water. Violet had her nose so high in the air she took three wrong turnings before I said, 'Hoi, it's this way.'

Back in the classroom, there was Squocka, sitting up straighter than half a dozen rulers. The look on his face told me that *he* wanted to go down the corridor with Violet Pridmore. So, a rival?

When she saw us, Miss Deeble raised an eyebrow. 'What kept you so long?' she asked. 'Thought you'd run away to get married.' Everyone laughed, but Violet blushed and went back to her seat beside Rosana Conti. Squocka looked even more disappointed.

When I got back to my desk, there was a note from Kevin Merry. It wasn't in writing because Kevin hadn't learned to do that. It was a drawing of a bunch of bananas. I was perplexed. Why did Kevin draw a picture of tropical fruit? Taking the bold approach, I asked him. 'It's not fruit,' he told me, 'it's a fist with big knuckles.'

I should have known. Bananas don't wear wristwatches with fourteen numbers on them. Kevin's fist is what I'd get if I didn't stop pestering Violet Pridmore.

Me, pestering? My conversation wouldn't pester a fly, let alone Violet. Then Kevin drew another picture of me with my hair on fire. He meant business, and it told me I had another rival.

But it was too late for warnings. Even warnings from Kevin. I was hopelessly besotted with Violet Pridmore and kept trying to be her friend. One day she relented and let me carry her book home from school. It was *I Can Read – Book One*, on every page, one word, one picture – but you have to start somewhere.

Next day I waited outside the classroom for Violet,

then who should appear but Squocka Berrington and *he* was carrying Violet's book. She smiled and talked with him and he smiled back. I fell into step and said to Squocka, 'It's my turn with the book.'

'Nick off, Wayne,' Squocka responded. 'I got it first.'

'Oh, Squocka, give him a turn,' Violet pleaded.

So I carried it for a while. Then Squocka had another go and after that we carried it between us. The book got very dog-eared from all the handling. Violet said we looked ridiculous and made us walk by ourselves.

◆

In those early school days, I nursed a dark secret, one that was not even to be whispered: *I slept each night with my teddy bear on the pillow beside me.*

Everyone in the family knew that if there was no Teddy, then Wayne would not go to sleep. It was a fact of life, like the sun coming up and not going sideways.

Charlene taunted me about it. 'Wayne the Stain just *loves* his teddy bear. No Teddy, no Beddy.'

'Nerny-nerny-ner-ner,' I responded wittily.

'Wayne.' Mum frowned. 'Don't tease your sister.'

Anyway, my mother started a campaign to widen my circle of friends, and the one she had in mind for me was – Kevin Merry. 'His parents are not well off,' Mum explained. She made me invite Kevin to my seventh birth-day party and warned me not to expect a present. Just as well. I didn't get one. Worse than that, he made off with two of the ones I got from Violet, Rosana and Squocka.

Birthday party? That's a laugh. It needed a rescue party! A junior reporter was there from *The Birthday Boy Weekly*. These are the headlines:

KEVIN MERRY PLAYS PASS THE PARCEL
Parcel never seen again

KEVIN MERRY CREATES PARTY EATING RECORD
29 Sausage Rolls, Non-stop
Asks for more

KEVIN MERRY HOGS RED CORDIAL
Wayne Wilson gets Green Teeth

You'd think it had been Kevin's party. The girls were all over him like chicken pox and even Squocka joined in the fun. Kevin found my teddy bear and Squocka held him down on the floor so that Kevin could run over him with my little army tank. 'Brrrrooom!' Kevin said. 'Die, teddy bear, die! Brrrrooom!'

Okay, this didn't kill Teddy, but he lost his squeak and ended up with a surprised look on his face because one eye was up behind his ear.

Rosana laughed. 'Look what Kevin's doing to that yucky old teddy bear.'

Violet turned up her nose. 'Who plays with *teddy bears*?'

'Oh, it used to be mine,' I lied nonchalantly. 'Years ago, when I was a little kid. The cat likes to play with him.'

◆

After that I tried to keep my distance from Kevin Merry, but it was difficult because Mum's motto at the time was: Charity Begins with Kevin. 'Go on, Wayne,' she urged, 'invite him over and have some fun.'

'Is that what you call it?' I asked.

Kevin and I went into our fun-filled back garden. 'Wayne,' he offered, 'you want a haircut?'

'No thanks.'

'My dad does it at home.'

'Yeah, that's because the barber won't let you in his shop.'

'Who told you that?'

'Squocka.'

'He's dead meat!' Kevin became angry, which wasn't a good frame of mind to be in before giving me a haircut. It ended up being more than a haircut. It was a blow wave, using a box of matches and the tyre pump off my BMX.

When Mum saw my singed scalp, she was horrified, but tried to conceal her feelings. Then she gave me a balaclava to hide my fire-blackened scalp. Charlene said I looked like a bank robber who specialised in piggy banks.

'I hate Kevin,' I cried with real tears. 'He's not coming here again.'

Mum soothed me. 'Kevin just needs time to recognise the difference between social and anti-social behaviour.'

'Yeah, and cut hair in a straight line!'

Dad was sympathetic. He's a plumber and used to being revolted. 'You don't need to wear your balaclava in the house, son.' I pulled it off, then Dad said, 'On second thoughts, just keep it on it while we're eating.'

◆

Then a terrible thing happened. I discovered it when Mum tucked me in that night and heard me say my hairless prayers. 'God bless Mummy, God bless Daddy, God bless Fat Cat, GB her next door— '

'Wayne!'

'All right – God bless Charlene, and last of all, God bless – Waaaaa! He's gone! He's missing! My favouritest teddy's gone!'

Next day at school, I tackled Kevin. What am I saying? No one tackles Kevin, not without a twenty-metre start. 'Kevin,' I said, man-to-man, friendly like. 'When you were at my place yesterday, did you see an animal?'

'What colour?'

'Brown.'

'A camel?'

'No.'

'A lion?'

'No.'

'A wombat?'

'No.'

Kevin ran through ninety-two other brown animals without mentioning you-know-who. So I had to leave it there, but it was a mystery.

New School

When the afternoon bell rang, I shrugged into my schoolbag and went home. Violet didn't want to walk with me, nor did Squocka or Rosana. They all had excuses – waiting to talk with Miss Deeble, going home with my big sister, although I knew full well that Squocka didn't *have* a big sister, or even a little one. So why was I being shunned?

I found the answer when I got home. There was my teddy bear, sticking out the back of my schoolbag, with one dopey eye pointing upwards and the other looking down.

Stupid teddy bear!

I don't remember half of that first school stuff, Wayne.

I kept a diary, Squocka.

But you couldn't write.

It was a pictorial diary.

Stick figures?

Yeah.

But one thing I remember, Wayne, was when you did the big U-turn.

Yes, Squocka, another painful episode in my young life. The U-turn.

So, are you just going to stand there? Or are we going to hear it?

I'm working up to it, Squocka. Emotional stuff takes time.

Five-four-three-two-one. Time's up.

All right, here goes.

2 U-TURN

ime moved on. Miss Deeble and other long-suffering teachers taught us to write real words and sentences. Violet Pridmore created lots of poems while Squocka Berrington made up stories and even Kevin Merry executed his threats in running writing. But all I composed was lists, my favourite being – *Things I Need to Have. (Urgently)*

When Mum saw another of my multiple-item wish lists, she turned rampageous. 'Wayne, what do you think I am? A charity?'

'Aw, Mum,' I whined and wheedled, then offered to reduce my requests a bit. That didn't work. Cut it in half? No way. 'All right, just get me the top three things, and a couple of smaller ones.'

'Wayne Wilson, you've got a cash-register mind.' Mum folded my list, then doubled it over twice again and began tearing. After ten seconds she opened out my precious list to show four little impoverished Waynes with their hands out and not getting anything.

'Huh!' I said, then after a ten-minute sulk, I started writing another list.

Item one was a new bike and I couldn't understand why

my mother was against me wanting a few things. You'd have thought it was a new bike *every* week. Some weeks it was a pair of football boots, a DVD player for my bedroom or a digital camera so I could take photographs of things. Oh yes, I also wanted a computer to help me make more lists.

But did I score? Not even one item, and to make matters worse, I had to pass that bike shop twice a day.

FLIGHT OF FANCY:

Two shiny bikes in the shop window spot Wayne's face pressed against the nose-smudged glass.
Mountain bike: *There's that goggle-eyed Wayne kid.*
BMX: *Okay, look tempting. Make him drool.*
Mountain bike: *Flash your decals at him.*
BMX: *He's suffering.*
Mountain bike: *His folks can't afford us.*

All I could do was go inside the shop and fondle the vinyl seats, finger the firmness of the handlebar grips and stroke my knuckles along their beautifully painted frames. I was born to want. The shopkeeper could see this and said, 'Get out of my store and stop licking my window.'

◆

I used my clapped-out calculator to work out the sacrifices we'd have to make so my parents could afford the good things in life. 'Mum,' I suggested, 'if we did without washing powder for six months, you could afford—'

'Wayne! Will you give up?'

'Toothpaste then? We could give up toothpaste.'

'Wayne!'

'All right. We cancel the Sunday papers. Except for the comics.'

Mum stopped listening and went off to the laundry and after a minute she began making annoyed noises. 'Oh, this steam iron.' *Bang, crash, hiss!* 'There it goes again. If I'm not careful it'll have the wallpaper off!'

Charlene said, 'Mum, you should have seen what it did to my blouse.'

'Never mind, love. Maybe your dad can cough up for a new one.'

'You should send it to the museum,' Charlene added in a dark voice.

'They've already got this model,' Mum responded. 'Acquired it in 1957.'

Mothers are so full of wit and wisdom. But at that moment, something caught my eye. It was a flyer that came with this month's account from Huggets. (The Store with More, which I never got any of, so the slogan should have been – The Store with More for Everybody except Wayne Wilson.)

I sat down to read their latest brochure. Boing! That was my eyes, springing out of their sockets and shooting back in again.

NEW! HYDRAULIC STILTS. HOURS OF FUN.

With a few effortless pumps on the elbow bellows your child can elevate himself to lofty heights, see over high walls and get things down from tall shelves.

Hydraulic stilts allow your child to experience being grown up without the responsibility that goes with it.

Hydraulic Stilts. Get a pair now! Ideal for fruit-picking.

There was more! If we bought them that weekend, we could have my name embossed on each stilt in genuine imitation gold leaf! It was too good to pass up.

There was a picture in the brochure showing a kid up on his hydraulic stilts, cleaning leaves out of the gutter. His proud mum and dad stood below, smiling as he hurled down dead pigeons, handfuls of leaves and gobby stuff. His name was gold-embossed on each stilt. Malcolm Schnurd. If a drooby kid like Malcolm Schnurd could enter the hydraulic age, why couldn't Wayne Wilson?

A cunning strategy formed in my mind. The trick is, if you want something, you need to point out the advantages it will bring. Advantages first, demands second. Do them in that order and you won't go wrong.

Dad came home early, but wasn't in a good mood. 'Job was cancelled,' he snorted. 'Woman poked the drain out with a wire. Water running away like a little beauty. Is there any other work, Heather?'

Mum did Dad's books and answered the telephone because Dad couldn't afford a new mobile phone. 'No,

Bill,' she said. 'All quiet on the western front. And the eastern front too, if it comes to that.'

'What's happening out there?' Dad demanded. 'Don't people block their drains any more? I blame it on teabags. Time was when people used to chuck tea-leaves down the sink, not a care in the world. They get half-way round the S-bend, next thing you know, goomf! A blockage. Send for Plumber Bill and out he goes in all weathers with his electric eel, smile on his face, ready with a joke to take their mind off the account.'

'Yes, dear.' Mum had heard all of Dad's complaints before. He went to his workshop and banged things about.

I followed him. 'Dad,' I said.

'Yeah, mate?'

'You want to save money on bus fares?'

'How do we do that?'

I showed him the hydraulic stilts ad. 'Buy me these, Dad, and I'll walk everywhere. Take giant steps, get there in half the time.'

In deep silence, Dad read the brochure, then came the warning sign – a growl rising from deep in his throat. I didn't wait for the crescendo. My need was urgent. Fly, Wayne, fly! It was times like that you needed hydraulic stilts.

After a while, peace broke out. Church bells went ding-a-ling, doves flew away with olive leaves in their beaks and Dad landed another job. He went off happily in his Toyota truck and that night, we ate again. Bread and a carrot each. Lovely.

❦

At the dinner table two nights later, I discovered that Charlene was doing well in the local pony club. Already she could canter. Next week she hoped to do it with a horse. (That bit's a lie.) On club days, Charlene and a lot of other snooty girls went pronking over the paddocks on their hired horses. But at the dinner table that night, my parents discussed something that involved spending money. On Charlene.

'You can't keep going in jeans,' Dad told my sister. 'You need the proper gear. Jodhpurs and riding boots, spurs and a whip.'

'I'll get them some time,' Charlene agreed. 'But not all at once.'

'You definitely need a hard hat,' Mum put in. 'And not at some time, my girl – you need one *now*, before another club day.' Mum squashed a carrot with her fork. 'If a horse kicks you on the head, think of the damage it could do.'

'Yeah,' I suggested, 'the animal could end up with a broken leg.'

'Shut up, Wayne.' My parents spoke in unison.

Mum turned to Dad. 'Bill, can we do something about a riding hat before the weekend?'

'Why not?' Dad went on eating. The deal was done.

❦

At school next day, I complained to Squocka, who

22

was the only person in the world who ever listened to me. 'Guess what,' I began. 'Mum and Dad are buying Charlene horsy stuff.'

'Hay and oats? Has she gone off muesli?'

'Ha, ha. Not funny, Squocka. This is serious. I ask for one little thing and what happens?'

'You don't get it.'

'Yeah. I get threats, black looks— '

' – and the shaking fist. Do you get that, Wayne?'

'Yeah.' We spent a minute huffing and grumping over our deprivation problems, then Violet Pridmore came along with Rosana Conti. 'Hi, guys,' Violet greeted us.

'Hi, Violet,' Squocka and I answered tunefully and dutifully. 'Hi, Rosana.'

'Why the long face, Wayne?' Rosana asked.

Squocka explained, 'His folks won't buy him stuff.'

'And my sister gets *everything* she asks for,' I added. 'Heaps of it.'

'Charlene does babysitting,' Violet pointed out. 'I bet it's her own money.'

I'd forgotten about that. Just then, the bell rang and we had to go into class. Later I found Violet was right – Dad would cough up in advance, then Charlene would pay him back later. If people told me these things it would save them being embarrassed.

◆

That same evening Mum and Dad were in the lounge, which was also our dining room. Television was boring so they'd turned it off. Dad read his newspaper on an easy chair while Mum sat at one end of the table sorting through a box of old photos. From time to time I heard her say, 'Aw, little Charlene' or 'Aw, Baby Wayne. Would you look at that smile. Coochie, coochie.' It was sick-making, but that's how it is with mothers.

At the other end of the table, I tried to do arithmetic homework on a calculator which had flat batteries. 'Oh,' I groaned for the tenth time, 'this calculator's nearly dead.'

'Give it the kiss of life, son,' Dad suggested.

'Dad, it's been dead for a century.' I banged it on the edge of the table.

'Wayne,' Mum warned. 'You'll chip the veneer.'

'This calculator doesn't have veneer.' I needed a new one, so I began my campaign. 'Mum?'

'No.'

'You haven't heard what it is.'

'Something starting with gimme, gimme.' Mum shook her head. 'Get on with your homework.' Silence reigned for a while, then Mum smiled at a photograph and passed it to Dad. She whispered, 'Pity we had to give him up, Bill.'

'Yeah, wonder how he's getting on,' Dad answered in a low voice, then gave the picture back to Mum, who smiled again and sighed.

My ears went flick, flick, like radar sensors. Who did they give up? Why were they whispering? 'What's the photo, Mum?' I asked.

'Oh, nothing, Wayne,' she answered too quickly and slipped it back in the pile.

Three minutes later, Mum went out to make coffee and Dad seemed to be busy with his newspaper. I got up and went along the table and found the photograph that Mum looked at. It was one of me when I was a tiny person in nappies. But on the back of this photo it said: *Baby Shayne, aged six months.*

Dramatic music. Da-da-da-dum! Shayne? Shayne who? And why was it me?

Seconds later, Mum came in to catch me gazing at the photograph. 'Oh, Wayne!' Her voice was sharp. 'What are you doing with that?' She snatched it from me.

Dad looked up from his newspaper. 'Oh no,' he said. Both of them made dash-and-spit, botheration, that's-blown-it sort of noises. Dad was the first to recover. 'Well, I suppose he had to know some time. You tell him, Heather. Sit down, son.' I sat on the nearest chair. Dad's kindness told me there was bad news to be broken. News of great ominosity.

Mum sighed deeply. 'The fact is, Wayne, you have a twin brother called Shayne.'

Wayne and Shayne, eh? Twin brothers. No wonder he looked like me. Same nappy and everything. I guessed in those far-off days we shared them. With my luck, I bet Shayne got first go.

'We had to give little Shayne up,' Dad went on. 'For adoption.'

'Couldn't afford to keep him,' Mum added. 'Y'see,

money-wise, things were tight, they still are, but back then it was either you or him, so we kept you.'

They had my full attention.

'Mind you, we've done our best to keep in touch with Shayne's parents,' Dad said. 'Over the years, oh yes, we exchange cards at Christmas, that sort of thing, and we've had the odd food parcel from them. They are Lord and Lady Wherewithal of Spendthrift Manor.'

Spendthrift Manor? That sounded promising. My cash-register mind got working. A lord for a father, not to mention a lady for a mum. If I'd been adopted instead of Shayne, I'd be Prince Wayne or something. Duke Wayne? Better than imitation gold-embossed names on your stupid old stilts any day. At school, they'd have to bow and give me first go at the bubbler.

FLIGHT OF FANCY:

Squocka: *Sit here, Your Dukeness. Can I do anything to help?*
Me: *Strangle Kevin Merry. But only till his eyes bulge.*

'We didn't get a card from the Wherewithals *last* Christmas,' Mum pointed out. 'We usually do.'

'It's the recession,' Dad explained. 'Didn't get one from the Prime Minister either. That's twelve years in a row the PM's snubbed us.'

'I suppose Lord and Lady Wherewithal are pretty well off?' I steered the conversation around to my favourite subject.

'Oh, filthy rich,' Dad agreed. 'Loaded to the eyeballs. Wealth by the bucketful. Dripping with jewels and gold watches.'

'Shayne's got *two* bedrooms,' Mum added. 'One for himself, the other for his toys. He's got so many. And he's got *five* VCRs – one for each channel, DVD player, video camera, his very own football team to play with whenever he feels like a game. Just ring them up and along they come in the team bus.'

'They always let him win, of course,' Dad said. 'Gives him a sense of sporting achievement.'

'And bikes!' Mum rolled her eyes. 'That boy has a new one every week. He tires of them quickly, y'see.'

'Still,' Dad went on, 'you've done all right with us, Wayne. We're a nice little family unit, eh? Mother, father, one point eight children.'

In the following days, I learned new things about my lucky twin brother and the more I found out, the more envious I grew. At last, it became too much for me. I cracked under the pressure and asked Mum if Lord and Lady Wherewithal would take me as well.

'Wayne!' Mum was profoundly shocked. 'So you want to leave us?'

'Only to be with my twin brother,' I lied. 'Maybe for a holiday.'

'You sure, son?' Dad asked. This time I nodded. Already, I had made a secret list of goodies to present to

Lord Wherewithal the moment I arrived in his palace. I wondered what to call my new mum. Lady Mum? What does Prince Charles call his mother? Your Mumjesty? I would have to know these important things. Didn't want to get on the wrong side of anybody.

At last, Mum wiped away a tear, then said she'd go and telephone to see if the Wherewithals would take me as well as Shayne.

'Hello, Your Lordship,' I heard her say on the phone. Mum did a little curtsey although no one could see her. Your Dadship. That's what I'll have to call my new father. Mum was still on the phone. 'You don't mind having Wayne too, Lord Wherewithal? Are you sure? All right, you'd better give me the address.' She wrote it down on the little pad by the phone. 'Wayne'll be over soon, Your Lordship, regards to Shayne. Bye bye.'

Mum meant buy, buy! It was a warning to His Lordship. Mr Hugget, get ready for brisk business.

Hugget's Emporium. By Appointment, Wayne Wherewithal.

I planned to change my name and design my own little coat of arms. A cash register with dollar signs rampant. Violet Pridmore would be impressed.

I went to pack my suitcase but decided only to take a few things, like a T-shirt plus a couple of socks. I imagined my new parents would want to buy me new gear when I arrived. Couldn't be seen slopping around a mansion dressed like a common or garden scruffoid.

Mum looked at me, all packed for the journey. Her eyes narrowed. 'What's the suitcase for?'

'Taking some favourite things,' I explained. 'Mementoes of a happy life.'

'They don't belong to you,' Mum pointed out. 'Your dad and I bought them, remember?'

'Aw, but Mum.'

'No buts. You came to us naked, so that's how you can leave.'

'Like Lady Godiva.' Charlene had arrived home at that significant moment in my young life. She covered her eyes modestly. 'Oooh, our Wayne parading through the streets – naked!'

'Aw, come on, Heather, let the boy keep his jeans,' Dad said, 'as a farewell gift. And his T-shirt and sneakers. A going-away present.'

Mum was reluctant, but she wavered. 'Oh, all right.' She folded her arms. 'We wouldn't get much for them anyway.'

'Oh dash,' Charlene said, 'I was just going to ring the girls.'

Phew! Lucky to escape with my jeans. Dad offered to drive me to my new life and we said our farewells, then I left the house for the last time. Mum didn't even cry. You'd think she'd have shed a tear or two. Charlene was already planning to use my room as a place to keep her saddles, trophies, ribbons and stuff. Never mind. I would visit them from time to time. Me and my twin brother Shayne on *our* horses. Mine'll be called Silver Dollar and

I'll wear a mask like the Solitary Avenger. Squocka can borrow one of my bikes and be my faithful sidekick if he likes. We'll employ Kevin Merry as the court jester and sack him when he runs out of jokes.

We bowled through the streets in the Toyota and as we passed toyshops and department stores, I composed a shopping list. I'll have one of them, I thought, no, better make it two. Oh, that big one over there, the red one I think. De-luxe model, of course. We drove on. I was engrossed.

After a while, we began to travel through a seedy part of town where no one got junk mail because what was the use? I didn't mind this being a rough neighbourhood because it would be all the nicer when we got to Spend-thrift Manor.

At last, we pulled up at the daggiest, meanest, tumble-downest house you ever saw. House of the Year, 1929. The windows were covered in old bits of sacking, the door was scratched and grimy, the iron roof rusty. Behind the house an old man and woman were bent over, weeding a patch of rhubarb. 'There you are, son,' Dad said. 'Your new home. That's Lord and Lady Wherewithal.'

'Dad, where's Shayne?'

'He's working down a coal mine,' Dad informed me. 'Helping with the family finances. Didn't your mum tell you that life had changed for the Wherewithals?'

At that moment, I began to suspect certain things. 'Dad,' I said, 'can I have another think about this? At home?'

Dad gave me a long look. 'You'll have to think about *something*, son.' He put the Toyota into gear and checked the rear vision mirror before pulling away from the kerb. Then he did the sweetest U-turn I ever made.

So, you learned a thing or three, Wayne Wilson.

Yes, Squocka, and there's even more learning in the next four stories.

Starting with the almost cruel tale of Wojjer Willmott.

The same, Squocka. Followed by the fancy-dress party that wasn't.

Then the story of the haunted house.

And that wasn't either.

Wasn't what?

Wasn't haunted. It was scary, creepy, but not haunted.

Going inside that house was a bold deed, Wayne. Very brave.

Like the time I made the Wayne Manifesto. That was super-brave.

And super-stupid?

Growing up is like that, Squocka. It's a bit like falling upstairs.

You feel every bump?

You get there in the end, but it's painful. And embarrassing.

3 WOJJER WILLMOTT

t's a bad dream: I'm on parade with a long line of soldiers. We face the front, no one smiles, goes tee-hee or nudges his neighbour the way we do at Assembly. Our hats are on straight because we borrow a spirit level to get them right. They think of everything in the army. We look smart in our uniforms – polished boots and stuff. No runny noses; fighting men have no need for hankies.

Our parents are proud and line up at the barrack fence. 'Yoo hoo, Wayney-poo. Yoo hoo!' Wouldn't you know it! Mum's the only one who waves. 'That's my boy,' she tells the other mothers, who know better than to draw attention to themselves.

'Go away, Mum.' I give her my fiercest glare, the kind that's reserved for the enemy only we haven't got to that bit in the Fighting Person's Manual.

'Oh, all right.' Mum is offended and stops embarrassing me. I sigh with relief.

The drill sergeant is Kevin Merry, who barks orders in a voice like pebbles rattling inside a rusty beetroot can. 'Squad, right turn!' All he wants is for us to twirl around to the right, but the way he says it, it's death if you don't. I turn smartly and find myself face to face with another soldier. Da-da-da-dum. There's a look of horror in his eyes because he thinks he's the one who went the *wrong way. He smiles a smug military smile when he realises it's my boo-boo.*

It's too late to swing around the other way. Horrible Sergeant Merry sees me and comes stamping over on his well-polished heels. His moustache goes quiver quiver, twitch twitch. I'm for it. No pudding for a week, or peel a million spuds.

'Yew horrible little soldier, yew!' Sergeant Merry means what he says. 'Don't yew know yewr left from yewr right?' He carries a small cane and gives my knuckles a rap, first on one side, then the other. 'Left hand.' Whack! 'Right hand.' Smack! It really hurts and I want to blub, only we're not allowed to because they expect us to be grown-up about it and go out and fight people, that is, once they tell us who the enemy is and where he's hiding.

What's this? I hear you say. Has Wayne really joined the kiddie cadets?

No. The answer lies with our new teacher, Mr Dellafield, so let the story begin.

In art class one day, Squocka, Kevin Merry and I are dynamically self-expressing ourselves, painting pictures, using colours we made up ourselves – Slime Green, Flesh Wound Purple, Severely Scorched Umber and Duck Egg Ochre. Anyone who stands still for a second gets some on him. Then it happens. I knock over the jar of murky water we use for washing our gunky paint brushes.

A big dollop lands on the painting Kevin Merry is doing, a self-portrait of Squocka. The rest dribbles wetly on the floor.

Mr Dellafield hears the commotion and comes over

with a long-suffering look on his face. He suffers even longer when he sees me. 'What's the excuse, Wilson?'

'Sir, I was admiring my painting at arm's length when one of my body parts touched the jar and it went splosh.'

Kevin Merry says, 'Want me to take him outside and deal with him, sir?'

'No, Kevin,' Mr Dellafield says, 'just mop up the water before it engulfs the entire class. If you go home looking like badly done finger paintings, your mums and dads will be at me to pay for the dry-cleaning, then I'll never afford my divorce.'

He drops his gaze to my painting of a beige horse with a head at both ends because I changed my mind about which way the animal is travelling, only I haven't yet painted out the unwanted parts and created a new bottom for it. Not to mention turning the hooves to face the other way. We artists are famous for changing our minds in the middle of a painting.

The Mona Lisa started out laughing her head off, but she had bad breath so the artist did another version with her mouth shut. Michelangelo was asked to paint the floor of the Sixteen Chapel but since he'd already started on the ceiling, they didn't have the heart to tell him he'd got the instructions upside down. Those are bits of art history told to me by Squocka who has lots of stories like that. But back to the action.

Squocka growls, 'You should send Wayne to the Awkward Squad, sir.'

Oh no! Not the Awkward Squad!

Before he took up teaching, Mr Dellafield was in the army. Sometimes, to fill in the last minutes before bell time on Friday, he tells us of his experiences as a soldier. In one of those sessions, he explained the Awkward Squad.

There are some soldiers who're always long-haired and scruffy, whose uniforms don't fit, who cut themselves shaving, even with electric razors. They're late on parade, do left turns instead of right, forget their rifle or drop it on another infantryman's foot. At bayonet practice, no one goes near them in case they get seriously pronged.

The most awkward soldier of all was Private Willmott, who once got lost on a route march and was directed back to camp by three Girl Guides who were out training for their needlework badge. Private Willmott left an army jeep in a shopping-centre carpark and couldn't find it again, nor could the army. He also sewed his hat badge on upside down.

Mr Dellafield never runs out of Private Willmott/ Awkward Squad stories. In art lessons, some kids do paintings of Private Willmott and put their pictures on display for everyone to see. Friday is the best day of the week.

◆

On Monday, a new kid comes to our class, the smallest boy I ever saw. He is a muscle-free zone with white surgical tape over one lens of his glasses. You could tell this kid's just asking to be bullied. It takes a wimp to know one;

that's why I'm pleased to welcome the new guy. He'll give Kevin Merry something else to do.

For the new kid, things start badly. Mr Dellafield tells him to sit at the empty desk next to mine. 'And what's your name?' Mr Dellafield asks.

'Roger,' the new boy says, only the way he speaks makes it sound like 'Wojjer'. Some other kids giggle.

'Do you have a second name?' Mr Dellafield goes on. He has his head down writing the details in the roll-book.

'Willmott,' the new kid answers. That does it! The whole class just about explodes. Kids howl, some fall over with their legs in the air, others thump their desks and one or two even fish out their paintings of Private Willmott of the Awkward Squad and wave them aloft like banners. Poor old Wojjer Willmott doesn't know what he's done to deserve this. Nonplussed is the word.

Then Mr Dellafield raises his head from the roll-book and we can see that even he struggles to keep a straight face. But a little grin escapes so he has to go gruff, gruff, huffle, huffle and turn away. He lets the merriment go on for about thirty seconds, then shushes us. 'It's a long, long story, Roger Willmott,' Mr Dellafield says, but doesn't go on to explain it. Wojjer is just as baffled as he was before.

Wouldn't you know it, before the end of the day someone passes a note which bears the name 'Private Wojjer Willmott of the Awkward Squad'. For the rest of the week, Wojjer is too nervous to ask anyone about the way he's being treated. It's a great joke, only he doesn't get it.

By Friday afternoon, there's a quiver of excitement because this is the time Mr Dellafield gives us one of his Private Willmott of the Awkward Squad stories. But this week, he shakes his head. 'No,' he explains. 'I've run out of army yarns, so you can do private reading instead.'

'Private Willmott reading,' Kevin Merry says and gives poor old Wojjer a sulky glare.

'Enough of that, Kevin Merry,' Mr Dellafield responds.

Bang, bang, thump, thump. That's Kevin opening his desk lid to take out his favourite book: *Bullying for Boys* by Horace Stranglehold. (That bit's a lie.) He's actually reading the pop-up version of *How to be Nice*, by Percy Friendless. Kevin's shaken that pop-up hand so many times it's nearly worn out.

A silence falls in our classroom, except for the noise made by people who have to read aloud. I see Kevin Merry showing a fist to Wojjer Willmott who is to blame for us not getting an Awkward Squad story. I can't see the logic myself and neither can anyone else. But since Wojjer's here, Kevin Merry has someone else to think about.

◆

For me the next week is a breeze; not so good for Wojjer, but that's his problem. They don't call me Caring Wayne of the Kind and Considerate Squad for nothing.

Old Woj starts the second week with new white

surgical tape over one lens of his glasses and by Thursday it's dirty. Someone has drawn a big blue goggle eye on it with long girlie eyelashes. His school uniform is also grubby and his shirt pocket is ripped. His tie is pulled tight in a Boston Strangler's knot.

'How silly can you get,' Violet Pridmore says to me when she sees Wojjer going around all unkempt and battle-stained. 'How can Roger be blamed for something he doesn't even understand?'

'Yeah, tough, Violet.' I nod sympathetically.

'Well?'

'Well what?'

'Well, what are you going to do about it?'

Me? Da-da-da-dum! 'Yeah, well.' I search for an excuse. 'It takes a lot of thinking about.' I pause, then comes a brainwave. I use a big word. 'It's got implications,' I tell her.

Straight away she fires back another question. 'What sort of implications?'

'You know.' I rummage in my brainbox for an answer. 'Heavy implications.' Brilliant. I could keep this up for half a morning or more. Tick one from this list:

- ❑ **Serious Implications**
- ❑ **Grave Implications with unforeseen outcomes**
- ❑ **Ominous implications with dangly bits hanging off both ends while the part in the middle doesn't look too hot either**
- ❑ **Absolutely terrifying implications with apocalyptic overtones of violent and unsolicited behaviour directed**

against the person of myself who is already making for the nearest door

I'm not allowed to say another word. Violet stamps her foot and goes tut-tut, fiddlesticks. Before I end up totally on the outer the bell rings so I'm saved once again. When I leave school and am a man, I will come back and buy that wonderful life-saving bell. Then I'll hit grown-up Kevin Merry with it.

Meanwhile, Wojjer gets on with his sums and stuff as if nothing's happened. He's settling in well at school and on top of that, he's quite clever. I see Mr Dellafield giving him nods of approval from time to time. 'Good answer, Roger,' Mr Dellafield says. Sometimes it's 'good thinking', 'smart move', 'somebody's got his brain into gear this morning', things like that.

The more Kevin Merry does his standover act with old Wojjer, the more the girls start to rally around. They like Wojjer, only they call him Roger with an 'r'. I see him having a few jokes with the girls, sharing his homework with Violet Pridmore and Rosana Conti, their three heads together, nodding wisely over the books.

If this makes me jealous, it makes Kevin Merry even madder. The first rule of bullying is that the guy you bully is supposed to mind. He's expected to slink around looking fearful, biting his nails, swivelling his eyeballs and stuff like that. But Wojjer doesn't blub and never complains. He just takes it. It's as if he's saving up for something.

Maybe he's got a big brother who's going to enrol at the school next week – Thunderball Willmott, the one there's no stopping.

FLIGHT OF FANCY:
'Stand back, Roger, this one's mine.'
'Take him away, Thunderball.'
'How do you like this, Kevin Merry? Not so merry now, are you?'
SOCK, POW, BLAM and other hitting noises you get in American comics.

Then one Monday morning, Woj doesn't turn up. We come into class, doing the usual start-of-week things, wanting to go home and remembering the fun time we had at the weekend. Mr Dellafield is at his desk, doing the last clue on his crossword puzzle.

In comes Kevin, who sees the empty desk and demands loudly, 'So where's Woj the Wimp?'

'Woj the Wimp?' Mr Dellafield echoes the words. His voice rises higher. 'Woj the Wimp? Woj the Wimp! Who said that?' He looks everywhere but at Kevin Merry, who's beginning to regret getting out of bed this morning. 'Come on, who uttered those unwise words?'

'Kevin Merry,' says a heavily disguised voice from the back of the room. It's the Phantom Ventriloquist. The only way you can dob Kevin in – either that, or send an email from Iceland.

'Kevin Merry said that?' Mr Dellafield goes on. He

shakes his head in wonder. 'My, my, Merry. When you utter unwise words like that, you live dangerously.'

Kevin sits scowling, his eyes swivelling from side to side. He hates being the centre of attention except when he's duffing up a small kid. 'Yeah, well,' he mutters, gazing at me as if to say, What are you looking at? You wanna make something of it? Come outside and look at me like that. You and whose army?

Mr Dellafield makes a great show of turning a page of his newspaper. He starts to read aloud. 'Sports results,' he announces, then takes a deep breath. Everyone listens. 'Last night, in the International Kung-fu Tournament, Junior Fly Speck Division, Champion Roger Willmott made short work of several heavier opponents to retain his crown for yet another year.'

There's a silence. Woj is a champion kung-fuer? He throws people around. Hup, hi, hee. They fall down dead and stuff. The only sound in the classroom is a deep gulp from Kevin Merry. His jaw hits the desk.

'Come and read it for yourself, Merry.' Mr Dellafield beckons him to the front.

'Yeah, well.' Kevin slouches out to Mr Dellafield's desk. His eyes follow our teacher's pointing finger as it moves along the line of print. Kevin nods with deep understanding. Everyone knows he can only read pictures. 'Kung-fu, eh?' he says.

'Ties people in knots,' Mr Dellafield agrees, 'and you call him Woj the Wimp?' He whistles admiringly. 'I've got to hand it to you, Kevin, you're a brave, brave man.

Woj, as you call him, is no wimp. He's actually a seething bundle of tightly controlled killing power.'

Mr Dellafield is so carried away with these words he has to walk around the room, flexing his muscles, breathing in and out through his nose. He grabs a whole stick of chalk and with a single snap, breaks it in two. Everyone flinches and goes, 'Oooh!'

This is not the Woj we know. Pull the head off daisies, yes, but a killer who snaps sticks of chalk in half, no way.

Kevin says, 'I was only joking, sir. Honest, sir.'

As the day's work starts, we are very thoughtful. Later in the afternoon, Mr Dellafield warns us not to say anything to Roger when he comes back to school tomorrow. 'Like most champions, he's modest,' he explains.

'Can we ask Roger for a look at his medal?' Kevin Merry asks.

'No, Kevin,' Mr Dellafield advises kindly. 'Roger is sensitive about his sporting achievements. I'd just steer clear of him.' He smiles at Kevin, then frowns at the rest of us. 'And for heaven's sake, don't any of you let slip what Kevin called Roger. That's in the past; it's forgotten. Settled. Buried. Rest in peace.'

'Amen,' says Kevin with an expression of sad desperation in his eyes.

◆

Next day Woj comes back with a new white surgical tape over the lens of his glasses. His mum must buy it by the twenty-metre roll. Roger can't understand why everyone's so respectful all of a sudden. Normally he's pounced on as soon as he walks in the gate, but not today. He's baffled all over again. But Roger's new reputation contains a bonus for us guys: the girls are not into violence, so they drop Roger like a schoolbag for Mum to pick up later. It gives me a chance to worm my way back into Violet's good books. 'Hello there,' I greet her in my dark brown Mr Cool voice. 'Long time no see!'

'Get lost.'

Oh well, I can be patient.

Later, oh later! Oooh! Da-da-da-dum! This is where the plot takes a twist and a turn. I am doing homework, lying on the carpet in front of our television, which is broken because my father decided it was just a fuse that had gone only it wasn't and there is now a screwdriver butt-welded to the chassis plus melted plastic dripping down one leg of the TV stand.

Charlene comes in with her friend Alisha who does ballet. Charlene wants to do ballet, as well as horse riding but not at the same time. Charlene shows Mum a newspaper with a photo of Alisha doing a dance routine. It's in one of those local papers they throw over the fence for nothing. Dad usually throws it back; two points if you hit the guy who delivers it. But this newspaper's from the part of town where Alisha has her ballet lessons. 'Oh, lovely,' Mum says.

'Can I learn ballet too, Mum?' Charlene goes grovel, whine, coax and sweet-talk but Mum's not opening her purse, so no ballet career for Miss Wilson.

As part of my sister's cunning scheme, she leaves the newspaper lying about for Dad to see because he's easier to get around, not to mention having scorched fingers from where the television reared up and got him. Later, I look at the photo which shows old Alisha pronging around on tippy-toe, looking dainty.

The newspapers shows lots of other kids doing ballet and – Doi-^{ing}-$_{ing}$-^{ing}-$_{ing}$! That's my eyeballs falling out and wobbling on little springs. There's a photo of Wojjer. The caption underneath says: *Roger Willmott and Tanya Dunn, two of the young pupils at Miss Millsort's Ballet School going through their paces.*

Woj holds Tanya who's in a fluffy tutu. He's not wearing his one-eyed glasses because that would spoil the effect, not to mention making it hard to focus if Tanya should do one of those great flying leaps across the stage. 'Roger – I'm over *here*!' Crash. There goes the scenery. (That bit's a lie.)

My eyes narrow. I have already put two and two together. Woj does ballet, not kung-fu! There's nothing wrong with guys doing ballet. In fact, I've often fancied myself in a pair of tights. Mum says I've got the legs for it and I'd be good at catching hurtling girls. Pity about the face. But how can old Woj fit in ballet *and* kung-fu?

The penny drops. He doesn't. None of us *saw* Mr Dellafield's sports report, so for some reason, he's been spinning a yarn, making fabrications or telling down-right lies. My eyes narrow even more until they're closed entirely. Silently my family enter, eat dinner, then clear the table and I miss out on my evening meal. (That bit's another lie.)

Since the newspaper is due to be recycled, I take it to school, but don't show it to anyone. It is dynamite. Ka-boom!

My plan is to tax Mr Dellafield with his fiblications, but before that happens, I make a serious error of judgement during our Japanese lesson. Next thing you know, I get fifty lines and have to stay back after school and write: *Sony Minolta Toshiba Mitsubishi Toyota Sansui Honda is not a proper Japanese sentence.*

Mr Dellafield keeps an eye on me in case I form an escape committee and smuggle myself over the wall. Scribble, scribble, goes my pencil. Scratch, ooops, rub out. So it goes. 'Mr Dellafield,' I begin.

'Yes, Wilson?'

'Um, about Roger Willmott doing kung-fu?'

'Yes.'

'This newspaper shows him doing something else.' I give it to Mr Dellafield.

'Hmm.' He nods for a long time. 'Hmm.' He says that bit twice. 'Well, Wilson, sometimes those in power have to bend the truth a little— '

'To help someone out?' I use my sympathetic understanding voice.

'You've got it, Wilson.' He tears up my newspaper, then asks, 'How many lines have you done?'

'Ten, sir.'

'All right. Forget the rest. How about you just write out five reasons why we should keep that bit of information to ourselves. Agreed?'

I grin. 'Piece of cake, sir.'

4 FANCY DRESSING

ique toque, tique toque, the French clock that Dad won in a raffle moves on, as does the calendar. Days and months fly past on wild, carefree wings. I'm older now, and wiser, which is just as well because the world's full of people who think they're smarter than everyone else. One of these is Rupert Pringle, a rich kid whose parents own a mansion, which makes Rupert think everyone else is a peasant.

Charlene's heavily into pony club, so her bedroom's full of weird horsy gear, strange gadgets, plus cans of hoof polish and tail stiffener. One day she'll talk Dad into building a tack shed, then all her stuff can be moved out or better still, taken to the dump.

My sister reads tales of Jill the Laughing Stable-maid. There's a whole series of these books and Charlene's got them all. 'Ha, ha, ha,' Jill cackles insanely, then canters across the misty moors on her Welsh mountain pony, Taffy Timrock. 'Ho, ho, ho. Hee, hee, hee. Har, har, har! Wild as the wind, that's me!'

I reckon she's escaped from somewhere.

One day after school, I pop into Charlene's bedroom and hear her sigh, 'Oh, I'd love to be like Jill.'

'What?' I ask. 'Off her head? Laugh a lot?'

'No, stupid,' Charlene snaps. 'Because whenever Jill wants, she can jump on Taffy Timrock and go for a gallop.'

'So, what's stopping you?'

'Can't afford to hire a pony this week.'

'Aw, Charlene, that's really tough.' I pile on the sympathy. 'If I had the money, I'd give it to you. Well, *lend*.'

'Thanks, Wayne.' Charlene sighs.

I sigh with her. 'So we've both got problems.'

My sister looks at me. 'What's yours?'

'It's this map, for homework. I've got to put in cities and rivers and stuff.'

'Let me look.' Charlene takes my assignment and says, 'M-mm.' She makes up her mind. 'Okay, clear off and let me do it.'

'You will? Oh, thanks, Charlene.' I go to my room. Piece of cake. Homework done by an expert.

❖

Next day, Mr Dellafield holds up Charlene's map for everyone to see. 'Wilson has created a brand-new country,' he tells the class. 'The Democratic Republic of Velcro. The capital is Emulsion, which stands on the Gummygoo River. Principal towns are Splatt, Splott and Splurt.' Several kids die laughing and I get fifty lines: *I must study geography, not create it.*

'How was your map, Wayney-poo?' Charlene inquires

sweetly when she sees me that night suffering from writer's cramp and squinty vision.

'Huh,' I say. 'Jill the Laughing Stable-maid wouldn't do a thing like that.'

'No, for what you said about her she'd just clock you one.'

◆

That weekend, the pony club holds a gymkhana. We take a picnic lunch and go trooping along with all the other families to watch snooty kids make their horses roll over, sit up and beg and do other undignified stuff. Charlene hires a pony for the event, not the rampaging stallion she'd like to ride but a small beige one called Bunnykins.

'I never knew they did horses this size,' I remark.

My sister snaps, 'Go play with your map!'

Mum, Dad and I sprawl under the shade of a tree while Charlene and other kids sit on tired-looking horses in the middle of a field. There seems to be some sort of event taking place, but it's not action-packed. Animals loiter about looking droopy, then every so often one of them ambles a few metres and stops.

A red-faced man sits near us. He wears a tweed coat and a flat cap and seems to know what's going on, so everyone waits to see what he does before joining in with nods of approval. One of the horses moves a bit, then stops. 'Jolly well done.' The man claps loudly. 'Did you see that, eh?' he demands. 'What horsemanship.'

'Horsemanship?' Mum challenges. 'It was a *girl* did that.'

The red-faced man goes harrumph, harrumph as if to say what do you know about it anyway? Mum ignores him.

'What did the girl do?' I ask Dad, because this horsy stuff's a mystery to me.

'Didn't fall off,' Dad responds.

Suddenly, to brighten all of our lives, who should come on the scene but Rupert Pringle. He strides along in a no-nonsense fashion, pulling a horse by the reins. The animal has its neck stuck out in front while the rest of it trails behind. Give it half a chance it would resign from the pony club and eat grass all day. Rupert comes into the shade of our tree and hands the reins to me. 'Hold her while I go for a snaffle.'

I point. 'Toilets are that way.'

Rupert gives me a look that would wither a plastic shrub and marches off. His horse seems friendly.

FLIGHT OF FANCY:

Me: *Hello, horse.*
Horse: *Good afternoon, Wayne. Got any food?*
Me: *Hungry, eh?*
Horse: *You kidding? I could eat a horse.*
Me: *Okay. Let me consult my parents.*

'Give her an apple,' Dad suggests. Since we've eaten most of our picnic lunch, I feed the leftovers to the horse, apples and cake mostly. The animal can't get enough of them. Its mouth is big and soft, and as long as I keep up the supply of goodies, Rupert's horse is my friend for life.

Other parents produce carrot cake, more apples, lettuce sandwiches, which the horse devours with great seriousness of purpose. It's like a conveyor belt. I'm offering a bag of Cheese Twirls, which is about all the animal can fit in, when there comes a bellow of anger. 'You idiot,' says this rampageous roar. 'You buffoon! Don't you know any better?' The question comes from Rupert Pringle.

Parents pull back and shake their heads at my ignorance. The red-faced man joins in. 'Feeding a horse before an event,' he says. 'Bad show.'

Rupert snatches the reins from me. 'If I'm disqualified, it's your fault.' He gets on the saddle and gives a kick with his heels, then canters off. Pfft, pfft, pfft. With each lumbering step, his horse emits a cloud of noxious apple gas. Anyone lights a match round here, Rupert'll do his next event on the moon.

SPACE FLIGHT OF FANCY:

Me: *Hello, is that NASA?*
NASA: *Yes, this is NASA. What do you want?*
Me: *I've just discovered a new rocket fuel.*

I see Rupert, several metres away, pointing in my direction. Other kids go Tut, tut, Never! He didn't? Some people! Should be horse-whipped! Charlene has gone red in the face. Rupert's voice comes curdling across the meadow. 'Anyone know the twit?'

'No.' Charlene blushes even redder.

At last, the horsy day comes to an end and kids turn their tired ponies loose to gnaw the stubbled grass. Mum, Dad and I go to help Charlene undo the saddle, but it's easy to see my sister is upset. 'Mummy, Wayne just spoiled my entire day.'

'Wayne was here all the time,' Mum answers. 'He didn't do anything.'

'Except upset Rupert Pringle,' Charlene flares. 'Who's not speaking to me.'

According to my sister, the entire Wilson family is deep in the social black books. It's the end of our life as we know it. We'll have to move to a new neighbourhood, make new friends, start life afresh and put my error behind us.

For the rest of the week, Charlene sighs and wilts. She vows to burn her pony books, destroy the horsy things, resign from the pony club, then grow up and become a nun. Dad says she can nun all she likes but we're not moving. Charlene sighs again.

❧

Then two letters arrive, one for me, the other for Charlene. She grabs hers and races upstairs. Mine is an invitation to Rupert Pringle's birthday party. Fanfare! Whistles, hooters, fireworks! Did you get that? I am no longer a peasant. Let hymns of joy ring throughout the land! Sing along, but only if you know the tune.

Hymn of Joy
Oh joyous day, oh wondrous day,
Our Wayne has made the grade.
He's scored a precious invite to
The party of the decade!

I guess that Charlene got one too, so she'll stop sulking, read horsy books again and withdraw her pony club resignation. She's been forgiven for having Wayne Wilson for a brother. Rupert has also forgiven me for sabotaging his horse.

But wait, there's more. Rupert has written on the back of my invitation:

Dear Wayne,
    It was nice meeting you at pony club. I look forward to having you at my party, which is fancy dress – Mother forgot to put it on the invitation, so come as something way-out and original.
Rupert

'Mummy, Mummy!' Charlene screams her way downstairs. 'I've got an invitation from Rupert Pringle and it's fancy dress!'

'Rupert Pringle,' Mum says. 'That's nice, dear.'

'Nice? Mummy, it's wonderful.'

Mum sniffs. 'Of noble birth, is he?'

Charlene ignores Mum's remark and races to consult *Every Girl's Book of Expensive Costumes*. 'What can I go as?' She flicks the pages. 'Let me see, let me see – ballet dancer, milkmaid, Cinderella, Joan of Arc, can-can dancer, Lady Godiva – whoops! Blushes!' Her ecstasy knows no bounds. 'What about – a slave girl?'

'That comes *after* you're married,' Mum says.

I take it with a touch of cool. 'I might go as a gorilla.'

Charlene lets out a gasp of great gaspiness. 'You?'

'Yeah. I'm invited.'

With a look of anguish she grabs my invitation. 'Oh Mummy, no! My life is in tatters! Shreds! Fragments!'

'Don't be so dramatic,' Mum says. 'It's only a boring old birthday party.'

'Only a boring old birthday party?' Charlene's voice goes so high you need special electronic equipment to decipher it. 'It's only *Rupert Pringle's* Birthday Party.'

'Oh, I remember,' Mum says. 'He used to be a frog, until someone kissed him.'

Charlene rants and does emotional stuff, but in the end I'm still going.

❧

Mum looks through the old clothes bag and decides that one of Dad's vintage singlets is not going to make a costume for me. It's nothing but some holes held together by stringy bits. I could paint myself silver and be a fish caught in a net, or dab some brown on and go as a bag of onions.

Charlene has looked out a little nurse's outfit she got when she was seven and somehow manages to struggle into it, then make her delicate way downstairs where she stands red-faced, holding herself in, not daring to breathe. Mum puts her nose to one side of her face, then announces the costume's too brief to be seen in public.

To disagree with Mum's opinion, Charlene needs to take a deep breath. Wrong move! Zzzzzzzzip, rrrrrip, snap, twang; the seams fly apart in different directions. Being sensitive, I hide my eyes as Charlene flees for her bedroom.

There's nothing for it but for us to hire fancy-dress costumes so Mum promises to take us to town on Saturday, to visit Mr Patel in his Imperial Joke and Novelty Emporium.

*

Mr Patel has spent too long meeting cheerful, effervescent people who plan to have a good time at a fancydress party. He's not happy about missing out on all that fun over the years. 'Oh goodness, no,' he greets us. 'Here is another assortment of would-be revellers.'

'Costumes,' Mum says shortly. 'For these two.'

'What is wrong with the garments they're wearing?' Little joke there from Mr Patel, but we let it pass. 'There's been a run on costumes their sizes,' he goes on. 'Big party this weekend. Everything is out, don't you know?

Then on Monday it will all come back covered in gravy stains, cordial down the front, sausage roll in the pockets, not to mention tomato sauce— '

'Have you finished?' Mum cuts him off.

'And the excuses,' Mr Patel ignores Mum and imitates his loyal customers. 'Oh, Mr Patel, I fell on the barbecue plate. The birthday boy started a fight. The dog went for me. My wig fell in the soup. I sat on a plate of curry.'

Finally, he shows us a rack of droopy-looking costumes. I pop into the change room and emerge as a boy fairy, a gorilla, a spaceman, then Albert Schweitzer. Every time I appear, Mum shakes her head. None of the costumes is me.

Eventually I settle for clown costume – baggy pants, conical hat, orange wig, red nose and a big plastic hammer that goes 'Tweep' when you bop another clown with it.

Charlene has found a badly patched blow-up plastic horse with a hole in the middle. She slips the horse over her waist, blows it up, then arranges a little pair of legs to hang down each side with feet in the stirrups. There's a cap and whip as well as a jockey's outfit to wear on top. It looks great only Charlene can't breathe. 'How will I get to the party?' she gasps. 'Can't get in a taxi wearing this.'

Mum has an answer for everything. 'You can go on the back of Dad's truck.'

'No way!' Charlene makes a vigorous protest. She doesn't explode, but the plastic horse does. Pop!

Pshooooo, flubber-flubber-flubber, then ploof. It hangs from her waist like a wet flag on a school day.

'Oh, how enervating.' Mr Patel surveys the damage. 'I have mended that poor animal sixteen times. And you have perpetrated the biggest hole yet.'

◆

On the day of Rupert's birthday party, two clowns come twinkling up the driveway of the Pringle mansion. One of them swings a plastic bopping hammer and the other clown carries two wrapped presents for the birthday boy.

It is at this stage that warning bells begin to tinkle.

Warning Bell One. ✔

 The driveway has flowerbeds on each side. An aged gardener picks weeds from the lawn, but looks at us and seems puzzled. 'You're the last to come,' he says.

'We got held up,' Clown Charlene explains.

The gardener goes back to work and mutters, 'Didn't know it was fancy dress.'

Warning Bell Two. ✔

Worried, we move on. As we pass the front window, we see signs of party activity inside. No one is in fancy dress. 'Charlene,' I whisper. 'Are you thinking what I'm thinking?'

Warning Bell Three. ✔

Rupert flings open the front door. 'Har, har, har,' he goes. 'Har-de-har-har-har!' Rupert wears a blue shirt and tailored pants.

So this is Rupert's revenge. The joke of the century and it's on us. He takes the presents from us. 'You two look a sight. Har-de-har-har!' Some of the other guests hear his demented laughter and come into the hallway. They're dressed in ordinary gear, so the joke's not on them either. They laugh, wipe away tears, point fingers and go on for what seems like a century.

Then three things happens. Thing One: Mrs Pringle emerges from a room across the hallway.

Thing Two: Rupert stops laughing.

Thing Three: the party guests disappear into the front room. This is Rupert's private joke – they're all in it, we're not.

'Ah, the entertainment's arrived.' Mrs Pringle greets us kindly. 'You're earlier than I expected, but never mind. The children are in there, and I must say, they're *very* bored. A typical Rupert party.'

'Oh, Mother,' Rupert protests, 'that's not fair.'

'Rupert, stop your odious cackling,' she says, 'and for heaven's sake remember it's the anniversary of your birth!'

Charlene and I follow Rupert into the party room. A cheer goes up. I recognise some of the kids from the pony club gymkhana.

The kids are still laughing, which gives me a chance to hiss instructions to Charlene – but she already knows what to do. This is my sister we're talking about. The one who put the Democratic Republic of Velcro on the map. Charlene regards Rupert Pringle as just another homework assignment that has to be done, only this time I'm here to help.

When the noise subsides, Rupert comes and stands between us. He's about to give the game away by saying who we are. 'Hey, everybody,' he announces. 'Guess who this— ' Tweep! I get him on the back of the head with my bopping hammer. Everyone laughs. First bop of the day! Tweep! I give him another one on the left knee for luck.

Brilliant! All we need to do is keep up the clown act and we'll get away with it. What do clowns need? A straight man, a stooge, a foil, a dummy. Someone to get sprayed with water, bopped with a plastic hammer, knocked over or in other words – be made a fool of.

That someone is Rupert Pringle. When he tries to reveal that we are Charlene and Wayne Wilson, something happens to him. Rupert opens his mouth. Charlene plugs it with a lamington.

He is not enjoying his own joke but the guests love it. Rupert drops bits of lamington on the carpet and bends over to pick them up. His bottom is a lovely target. Tweep! Couldn't resist it. Tweep! Charlene's eyes go wide, then she inspects Rupert's rear portion and takes a look at my hammer. Where's that tweep noise coming from? To check, she borrows my hammer and hits Rupert on the bottom with it once more. Tweep! Now she's satisfied. Rupert has a squeaky bottom. Charlene holds up one thumb to the audience. They cheer. As Rupert is recovering, Charlene gives me my hammer then solemnly picks up a big, soft runny custard tart sort of thing.

'Ooooh!' say the guests. They can see what's coming. Charlene has found something to lubricate the squeak. She gently presses the tart into Rupert's bottom and gives it a good smear around.

'Yuk!' Rupert says, then walks funny. There's more where that came from. Ice down his shirt front – ooooh, shivers! More fun with custard, not to mention trifle, which is very colourful.

Charlene whispers to Rupert, 'I hope you're enjoying your trick.' My sister dips a Cheerio in tomato sauce, then paints a round target on his forehead. At that range, I can't miss. Tweep! Nice one, but we're only warming up.

❧

Much laughter later, Rupert surrenders. 'All right,' he gasps, 'I apologise.'

'Accepted.' Charlene keeps her voice low. 'Now pretend you've been in this from the start.'

'You mean, that it was all my idea?'

'Well, it was, Rupert, wasn't it?'

'Oh yeah.' He smiles in relief. Rupert looks pretty daggy, what with tomato sauce, custard and other party fare all over him. All three of us join hands and make a low bow. 'Give them a big hand.' Rupert grins and leads the applause. The party guests like him.

'Time to go, Wayne,' Charlene says, then we make for the door.

Rupert comes to see us off. 'Hey, see you at pony club, Charlene?'

Charlene considers. 'Yeah, okay.' We make a final bow then leave Rupert with his guests who congratulate him for being a good sport.

Mrs Pringle meets us in the hallway. 'From what I heard you did well,' she observes. 'Not my son's usual affair. He's such a boring little blemish. Still, I suppose some girl will make something of him one day.'

'Yes,' Charlene agrees in her carefully disguised clown's voice. We edge to the front door.

'Let me pay you then.' Mrs Pringle holds out an envelope. Charlene takes it and we make a bow, then we're off.

Outside, we see a taxi drawn up at the front door. Oh no! A sad little Pakistani clown has just got out. He's the real entertainment and we've used up the squishy food and done the funny routines plus invented new ones. 'Here, what is the meaning of this intrusion?' the clown demands in a bad-tempered way. His brother runs a fancy-costume hire business.

'Wrong party, just leaving,' Charlene tells him. She gives the clown the envelope from Mrs Pringle. 'It's money up-front here.'

FANCY DRESSING

We pile into the taxi and Charlene tells the driver our address, then settles back as we sweep down the driveway. She turns and gives me a hi-five.

My sister, eh? There are times I'm really proud of her!

5 THE MINISTER'S CAT

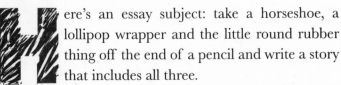ere's an essay subject: take a horseshoe, a lollipop wrapper and the little round rubber thing off the end of a pencil and write a story that includes all three.

Give up? So do I, but that's the kind of problem I meet every day in my young and tender life. Well, not every day. It comes once a week when Mr Dellafield gets in an evil mood.

You can tell he has something on his mind because he lurches up and down the classroom with his shoulders shaking in silent laughter. Every now and then he leers at us, scratches his chin and says, 'Now, my little chickadees, we'll soon see what's what.' He's either going to make us run around the school ten thousand times, picking up litter as we go, or he's got an impossible assignment for us.

Mr Dellafield's got a book of ideas in his desk. I saw it when he was taking out his high-pressure water cannon to quell a riot in the canteen. A kid found a fly in his gravel sandwich and complained. The volume in question is *Ivor Wrangle's Book of Time Fillers for Busy Teachers* (3rd edition). Thought you'd like to know. (That whole bit's a lie, but

Mr Dellafield does give us really difficult assignments.)
'Right, you lot,' he announces. 'It's essay time and today
I have for you a fabaloosie!'

'A fabaloosie?' says a small boy. 'Oh no! Not a fabaloosie!'

'Oh yes,' insists Mr Dellafield. 'A one hundred per
cent fabaloosie!' The small boy silently dies. Funeral
Wednesday. I get his yo-yo. 'This week's topic is . . .' Mr
Dellafield likes to drag it out but he always gets to the
point well before bell time.

'Yes, yes?' we say.

'Is . . .' Mr Dellafield repeats himself.

'Yes, yes?'

'. . . you have to write a story in which these three
items appear: a house brick, a postage stamp and a used
teabag.'

'Oh no!' There are groans of anguish. Kids faint or
turn pale. One group organises an escape committee
and makes a ladder out of glued-together rollerball pens.
(Another lie.)

'Enough!' says Mr Dellafield. 'Write at least a page,
watch your spelling, punctuation and write neatly. And
Wilson, do not slobber!'

I write swiftly: *I went to my Dad who is in the Royal Canadian*
Mounted Plumbers and wears a postage stamp on his hat and asked
if I could borrow his house brick to flatten my used teabag.

I sit back with a sigh of relief. That's it for another
week. But Mr Dellafield has snuck, sneaked or snack up
behind me to read my essay. 'I said a story, Wilson,' he

snarls, showing his tooth. 'Not a sentence. Write more. Tell me why your father wears a postage stamp on his hat. Is he going to send it somewhere?'

'No sir. He does it because he's an individualist.'

'Well, tell me that, boy. Also, tell me why you want to flatten your used teabag with the house brick.'

'I'm making a used teabag mosaic, sir.' Other kids look at me strangely. Some move their desks back several metres.

'Those are interesting ideas, Wilson,' Mr Dellafield goes on, 'so put them in. Make a story of it. Let your imagination run wild. Go on, write more.'

So in goes all that rubbish and before long, there's so much nonsense it takes up three pages. Mr Dellafield reads my essay and wears half a leer, half a smile and half a scowl. That's three halves on one face, but he's that sort of man. Suddenly, it's bell time and we can go home. Oh, relief.

◆

On the way home, I pass the Witches' Den. It's a big old house with a tall fence to keep people out or to keep the witches in.

There's only one witch left now – even so, all the kids hurry past, especially at Hallowe'en and on dark, windswept, rain-lashed nights when bats and owls do flit, tu-whit, tu-whoo. Atmospheric, eh? Spooky? Read on.

I get home and drop my schoolbag and see what's for eating. No one's home but Mum has stuck a note on the fridge door because she knows it's the first place I'll look.

Waynee-poops (Mum calls me that when she wants me to do something for her), *I want you to do something for me. Go to Miss Ridley's and do a couple of odd jobs for her.*
Love Mum.

Oh no! Mum, what have you done to your little Waynee-poops? Miss Ridley's the one remaining witch and you want me to enter her front gate, and maybe even go inside her brooding old house? It means I'll see her book of spells, hooked nose, pointy hat, wand and who knows what else? I forget about eating and head off to the Witches' Den with my feet like lead.

◆

There's a rusty front gate which squeaks when you open it – a witch/spooky house giveaway if ever there was one. The garden path hasn't been weeded for years and there's an old falling-down porch full of pot plants. The grass has been left uncut for centuries, but the front doorbell is polished and gleaming. I give it a pull.

Dang, dong, says a doom-laden bell somewhere deep inside the house, then at last the door creaks open and there's the witch, looking down at me. 'You must be Wayne?' she says.

'Must I?' I'm not giving anything away here.

'Mrs Wilson's boy. Come to do a couple of things for

me. That's kind.' She doesn't look very witchy but that's only a front.

'Just a couple of things,' I agree. It turns out the witch only wants me to fix a fallen shelf in her kitchen. A screw has come out of the wall so it's only a couple of turns of a screwdriver to get it back in.

The other job is to file the edge of a door that doesn't close properly. The witch gives me the file and I set to work. Rasp, rasp, scrape, scrape, I go, all the while looking around to see what she's doing behind my back. I keep remembering what happened to Hansel and Gretel – and there were two of them.

Miss Ridley is pleased with the work: the shelf is back in place, the door closes properly and I've left everything neat and tidy, the way Dad taught me. I'm about to head off and see what there is to eat back home, but Miss Ridley has read my mind. She has a plate of cakes and a can of soft drink.

I try to say no, no, that's all right, but you know how grateful people keep forcing you to eat. Anyway, as I sip the soft drink, it's easy to see this place needs a *thousand* odd jobs done. Instead of stopping myself, I offer to cut the grass out front.

'I'd appreciate that, Wayne,' says Miss Ridley. 'It hasn't been cut since Sister Willie's funeral. Your father came over and did it.'

I don't remember Dad doing that! And what sort of woman is called Willie?

At home that night around the dinner table with my

warm little family, Mum explains. 'Willie's name was Wilhelmina. Then Miss Ridley, the one you met today, she's called Frederika.'

'There was one before that,' Dad puts in. 'Her name was Alexandra.'

'Funny names,' I say.

'Well, that was the fashion in those days,' Mum goes on.

Charlene sighs. 'Wish I had a name like Frederika, or Wilhelmina.'

Mum responds, 'There's nothing wrong with Charlene.'

Charlene just sighs again and pushes her food about the plate.

◆

On Saturday, I ask Dad for the mower, then trundle it over and trim Miss Ridley's front yard. After it's done, she's pleased to find a garden hose that's been missing for ages plus a long-lost deckchair.

FLIGHT OF FANCY:

A jungle explorer emerges from the wilderness. He's been trying to find the way out, but with the grass cut, he can now see a landmark. He encourages his bearers.

Explorer: *Come on, lads. Milk bar's this way.*

Bearer: *Thank you a million times, Wayne.*

Explorer: *Yes, goes without saying. Muchas gracias, Waynee-poops. Now, lads, the jellybeans are on me.*

Bearer: *Ooh, bags I the pink ones.*

Miss Ridley offers more cake, then we sit on the porch and talk. She tells me how it used to be when they first moved into this house. Her father was a minister, so they all went to church three times on Sunday to hear his sermon and set a good example.

Miss Ridley never gets the chance to talk these days, so I listen politely and try not to be bored. After a while, it's not boring and she makes me laugh about the antics of the Ridley sisters. She shows a photo of them when they were teenagers. I recognise Miss Ridley straight away. 'This is you?'

She nods and smiles. 'That's Alex, and the one in the middle's Willie.'

'And you're Fred?'

'That's what we called each other.' she sighs. 'Oh, I miss them. Dear Alex and Willie.' Miss Ridley has a tear in her eye, which puts a damper on things. There is one of those silences that come when people don't know what to say.

'How about I weed the path next Saturday?' I offer, and that cheers her up.

After the usual protests, we make an agreement for next week. As I wheel the mower home, there come thoughts about growing old and being left alone.

◆

The very next week, old Dellafield puts on his I've-got-something-for-you look. He pins a paper on the class noticeboard, then perches on his high stool to tighten

70

the bolt in his neck. Crick, crick, crick. 'Ah, that's better. Must get a washer for this bolt.' For Christmas, we're buying him a couple of wing nuts so he doesn't need to use the spanner all the time. (That bit's a lie.)

The notice says:

STORY COMPETITION
Write a short story
and win a spectacular prize
Topic: An Animal Friend

There once was a student at our school who actually learned something. When he left, he became a gazillionaire. Every year, he donates a prize for the best short story so no one will ever forget him, but I can't remember his name.

The good thing is, the topic's an easy one. None of Mr Dellafield's include-these-three-items-in-your-story routine. At least, that's what I think.

'An animal friend,' I say to Squocka later. 'What'll you write about?'

Squocka thinks hard. 'My goldfish.'

'Is he friendly?'

'Only to lady goldfish.'

Trouble is, I haven't got an animal friend either. Fat Cat's only friendly when he wants something.

FLIGHT OF FELINE FANCY:

Fat Cat: *Lie down, Wayne.*

Me: *No way. You only want to sleep on my head.*

Fat Cat: *All right, open the fridge and get out the tuna and a dollop of cream.*

That's not what you call friendly. He doesn't catch mice or do what he's told. He won't fetch sticks or scare off burglars. In fact, he's useless.

Me: *You're only an ornament, Fat Cat. You know that. An ornament.*

Fat Cat: *So what are you going to do about it, Half-a-Brain Wayne? Now, I'm going to purr and rub myself against your leg.*

The more I think about it, the more I can see that this is a very difficult topic.

Kevin Merry's got more to write about. He had a pet fly that used to follow him everywhere, then one day his mum sprayed it with something toxic and the wee beastie was never the same any more. Everyone said she was aiming for Kevin.

On Saturday, I weed the garden path as promised. Afterwards, Miss Ridley and I sit in the shade of the mountain of dead vegetation. Later I'll put a red light on top to warn low-flying aircraft. Miss Ridley talks about how she and her sisters passed the time when they had no television or radio.

'We read or sang songs around the piano,' Miss Ridley tells me, 'and sometimes we played parlour games.' She laughs as she recalls one of them. 'Willie could never get the hang of a game we often played. It was "The Minister's Cat".'

It's a game where everyone thinks of an adjective to describe the minister's cat. They start off with words that begin with 'A' – the minister's cat is an *angry* cat, the minister's cat is an *active* cat, and so on. Then they start on the letter 'B'.

'The trouble was,' Miss Ridley goes on, 'Willie never knew what an adjective was so she was always wrong.' She laughs fondly as she remembers the gentle times they had together, Willie, Alex and Fred. I leave her on the porch with her memories, smiling to herself.

As I walk home, the short-story topic is still a problem. If it were one of old Dellafield's three-item jobs I'd do it in a flash. Suddenly, it hits me. It *is* a three-item job! I've got my short story.

I can almost hear old Dellafield say it: 'Write a story in which these items appear: one, three sisters; two, a parlour game; and three, a cat.'

At home in my room I get out some paper and a pen and write:

THE MINISTER'S CAT

Once, there were three sisters called Alex, Willie and Fred who lived all alone in a big house. Their father had always admired emperors so he named his daughters after three of them: Wilhelmina, Frederika and Alexandra (or Willie, Fred and Alex, for short).

Next door to the sisters lived the local minister. He had squeaky shoes and kept a large marmalade cat that was shiftless and lazy.

The sister named Willie quite liked the minister's cat and often left out bits of meat for him, a piece of fish or saucer of milk. This caused the cat to spend a lot of time in the sisters' garden, where Fred and Alex were forever saying 'shoo' to him. It didn't do any good because the cat's name was Wellington.

'The minister's cat is worthless,' said Fred.

'The minister's cat is lazy,' Alex agreed.

It was these complaints that gave Fred and Alex the idea for a new parlour game to be called 'The Minister's Cat'. The rules were that the players should take turns at making up a sentence containing a different adjective starting with 'A', then working through the alphabet.

That very evening, they played the new game for the first time.

'The Minister's Cat is an awful cat,' said Alex. 'Your turn, Fred.'

'The Minister's Cat is an artful cat,' said Fred.

Then it was Willie's turn. 'The Minister's Cat is – an architect!'

Fred and Alex shook their heads. 'No, Willie,' they said. 'It can't be a noun, it has to be an adjective!'

'All right,' said Willie. 'The Minister's Cat is an adjective.'

Fred and Alex looked sad. They tried again, but poor Willie just couldn't think of an adjective that began with 'A'.

She ran through words like armadillo, artist, Acapulco, aye aye Captain, axe, and actually. For the 'B's', the best she could think of was banana.

'It's not much good trying to play the game with only two of us,' Fred complained. 'It's like playing ping without the pong!'

What the sisters didn't know was that Wellington, the real minister's cat, had jumped up on the windowsill to have a look into the room. After all, people were talking about him, so he wanted to hear what was what.

Alex and Fred couldn't see the minister's cat because they had their backs to the window. But Willie saw him and the cat noticed the unhappy look on her face.

Besides being awful, lazy and worthless, Wellington the minister's cat was also wise, wily and quite clever. In the cat world, he was a well-known actor and gave frequent performances on Saturday nights to packed back yards.

He stood up and gave the show of his life. Willie saw him in action at the window and cried, 'The Minister's Cat is an active cat!'

'She's got it!' said Fred. And so the game went on. When they came to the letter 'B', Wellington pulled at his fur and made himself untidy and dishevelled.

Willie was triumphant. 'The Minister's Cat is a bedraggled cat!' she called. The real minister's cat acted out more and more adjectives until Willie got the idea, by which time Wellington was quite exhausted, so he slumped down and went to sleep on the windowsill.

'The Minister's Cat is a tired cat,' Willie said, and the others agreed she'd done very well. The three sisters were tired too, so they all drank cocoa, then went to bed, and that's how the parlour game The Minister's Cat was played for the very first time.

I check my story over for spelling mistakes and read it again. It's a bit of fact, a bit of fiction and it's about an animal friend, so that's okay.

On Monday I hand in my entry and forget about it.

●

Next weekend, I spend an hour at Miss Ridley's house

doing little things here and there. She tells me the batteries on her radio are dead, but she's bought new ones for me to put in for her. I take the back off. Not only are the batteries dead, they are decomposed. Gooey stuff runs out of them and the whole radio has that I-will-never-work-again feel. 'When did you last use this, Miss Ridley?' I ask.

'It was working a month ago,' she tells me, 'but it was very faint.'

'Looks like you'll have to buy another radio,' I say in my professional voice. 'Or look at television.'

'I haven't got television, Wayne,' says Miss Ridley. 'It's a pity about the radio because I like to hear the news and enjoy a classical music concert.'

I do a few other jobs around the place, then go home.

*

At school next day, Kevin Merry enters with a large scrap-book sort of thing and flops it on his desk. It is very daggy, this scrap-book, with bits of paper sticking out of the pages, but Kevin seems proud of it.

'What's that, Kev?' I ask, friendly-like.

'It's my story,' he answers, 'for the competition.'

'Where are the words?' Squocka asks. 'A story's got to have words and sentences and stuff. Phrases.'

'I did it without words,' Kevin answers. He flicks the pages for us and all we can see are pictures and photos cut out of magazines and newspapers – dogs, cats, tins of pet-food, a butcher's shop, then a ball of wool. Kevin explains, 'It's the life bicycle of a family friend, only I couldn't find a kitten or a pet cemetery.'

Squocka and I try to keep straight faces, but they're not straight enough. Next thing you know, Kevin's in the huff with us and a battle starts. His scrap-book gets in the middle of it, then Mr Dellafield enters. 'Stop!' he says.

We stop. Bits of torn-up paper flutter down from the ceiling. We look sheepish. Mr Dellafield glares, then it's fifty lines all round, and Kevin's not allowed to do his in pictures.

◆

The following Monday, Mr Dellafield points to me with a severe, you're-in-trouble look on his face. 'Ms Dillon wants to see you, Wilson,' he announces. Oh no! Ms Dillon is the Principal.

Trudging to the door on feet of heavy metal, I receive looks of sympathy. Violet Pridmore waves her hanky and cries, 'Stay brave and true, Wayne.' (That bit's a lie.)

The trouble is, I can't imagine what I've done wrong. Was it the battle with Kevin Merry, or has she got wind of my plan to take over the state? But it's nothing like that. 'Congratulations, Wilson,' Ms Dillon says. 'You've won the short-story prize. Well done. Now get out.'

That's it. I'm a celebrity. Old Dellafield must have known what it was about, because he's got a smile on his face starting at one ear and going round to the other.

'Little winner, are we, Wilson?' he says, then tells the class about the story as if he'd written it himself. Well, in a way he did, because if it wasn't for his three-item trick I'd never have thought of writing that way.

Mr Dellafield presents me with the prize. It's a voucher for a radio-CD combo plus a choice of ten CDs.

●

Tony Parianos, the man in the electrical store, knows me well. 'Guess what, Wayne?' he says. 'We've got the latest Melvin Dole CD.'

Melvin Dole and the Nose-pickers happen to be my favourite group, but they can wait. There's only one thing on my mind. 'Tony, where's your classical stuff?'

'Classical?' cries the man. 'You gone crazy, Wayne?'

I pick ten CDs – *Blue Danube*, *Four Seasons*, Mozart, Beethoven and Schubert and some others like that. Then it's a quick check of the radio-CD combo to make sure batteries are included.

I explain to Miss Ridley that the Wilsons already own a radio and a TV and I have a CD player in my bedroom. 'Besides, I got the story idea from you.' I explain. 'So the prize is yours as well as mine.'

It takes some persuading before Fred agrees to keep the new radio-CD combo. But she's only going to 'look after it' for me. She's very excited about the classical CDs and puts one on straight away and lets music fill her house.

Best of all, Miss Ridley reads my short story, which

makes her laugh. 'You know, Wayne, she says, 'that's just how it happened.'

Fred asks me to choose something of hers for me to look after, so I go home with the photograph of the teenage Ridley sisters to hang on the wall of my bedroom.

Every time I look at those three faces, I see another story.

⑥ THE WAYNE MANIFESTO

'm sick of meeting the demands of parents, sister, aunties, uncles and teachers. Add to that list the requirements of a certain fat animal of the feline variety who expects me to open doors and windows to let him in or out when there's a cat flap through which he can come and go. Thank you. (That bit's a lie. He never says, 'Thank you.')

But does Fat Cat come in that way? No, not he!

That is just one of the things that makes me unhappy. A lot of other events do not meet with my approval. For example, I'm fed up being the youngest in the family and people using this as an excuse when they want anything nimble done, like getting up and turning down the volume on the television or answering the telephone. 'Change to Channel 2, Wayne,' Dad orders weakly as he slumps in his comfortable chair. 'Your legs are younger than mine.'

What garbage! Of course they are! If I had the money, I'd shout him a leg transplant so he'd never be able to say that again!

FLIGHT OF FANCY:
Plumber Receives New Legs in Transplant

'It feels good to have young legs again,' said grateful plumber William Wilson, after receiving the legs of a glamorous New York fashion model in the world's first controversial double limb transplant.

'My mates all take the mickey,' Mr Wilson said. 'They keep asking me to hitch up my overalls and show a bit of leg but that is only because they are sex-mad. I'm looking forward to trying out some of those stockings with little flowers up the side.'

So I change the channel, then wait for the next demand from my family or the cat, or some distant relative who's dropped in for a cup of tea and can't reach the biscuits.

❖

We're in class one Friday afternoon doing an A & E session which means we can ask Mr Dellafield questions about Anything and Everything, which is a good way to end the week. In this A & E session, Squocka wants to know about *The Communist Manifesto*.

'Where did you hear about that, Berrington?' Mr Dellafield asks.

Squocka explains that he wrote to the Russian Embassy asking for pictures of people doing that dance where their bottoms are very close to the ground. Instead, the embassy sent him *The Communist Manifesto*, but he couldn't get past the first sentence because it contained more big words than his meagre brain could handle plus it was in Russian.

Mr Dellafield tells us it was a public declaration that helped guide the destiny of the Soviet people. *The Communist Manifesto* described what things had been like in the past and let everyone know what was going to happen in the future, but after seventy years it hadn't worked, so they scrapped it.

This information sets me thinking that a manifesto is what I need. It would say what used to happen in the Wilson household, then how things would be from now on. The school bell rings and I go home with ideas bubbling in my mind.

It takes me all weekend, then at last it's finished:

THE WAYNE MANIFESTO

(1) **I will enjoy showers** for as long as I like.

(2) **I will not collect the morning paper** when the newsboy hurls it under the big bush in the front garden.

(3) **My room will look like a rubbish dump** until I tidy it up.

(4) **I will not answer the telephone** while watching television.

(5) **I will play CDs loudly** in my bedroom.

(6) **I will not get up** to change channels on the television.

Squocka is the first to read it and he thinks Wayne Manifesto sounds like a Corsican rugby halfback so he goes on like a radio commentator. 'And Wayne Manifesto scoops up the ball and oh, he drops it! Good thing the game hasn't started yet or that could have been a costly error on Manifesto's part.'

'Just you wait,' I tell him. 'You'll see some big changes around here.'

Fastened to the fridge door with a magnetic moon and a little plastic clown, my manifesto looks very impressive. I can't wait for Mum to see it and be one amazed mother. 'Our Wayne's got a manifesto,' she'll tell the neighbours. They'll not know what it is, so they'll shake their heads and say, 'What next?' and 'Young people today,' or 'Our Gerald's got a Suzuki.'

None of that happens, and Mum doesn't say *anything* about my six points. Mothers can be maddening at times.

◆

Next morning is day one of *The Wayne Manifesto*. I stand in the shower, then face this way and that while the bubbles wash my body. Luxury! Then it happens. The water turns icicle cold! Freezing hailstones pelt my skin while frigid shafts drum upon my bottom. I spring from under the shower spray and go, 'Yoobba, yabba, ye!' Strange words from a long-lost language which mean, 'What's with the hailstones?'

Wrapping my freezing, soapy person in a towel I pad out to complain about the plumbing. 'Shower's gone c-o-o-ld, Mum.' An icicle dangles from my nose and my goose-pimples are like watermelons, except not green. (That bit's a lie, but it was cold.)

'That's because I turned off the hot water.' Mum calmly drops the key of the water-heater cupboard into her pocket in a way that tells me she's not going to bring it out again.

'But what about my manifesto?' I say. 'Point One – long showers.'

Mum consults my manifesto. 'Says nothing about *hot* showers.' She turns away to make some toast.

'But, but— '

My mother's not listening. 'Oh, are you still here?' Her toast pops up. She hears my pleas, then nods wisely. 'So we make a compromise, Wayne.' Mum takes a pen and changes Item One until it says, 'I will enjoy *hot* showers for *three minutes*.'

'Aww, Mum.'

Mum lets me have another two minutes in the shower to wash off the frozen soap and bubbles.

Later, I hear Charlene spend five minutes in the shower. She sings a whole song right through, then starts another one. She's got her guitar in there too! (That bit's a lie.)

I complain to Mum, who says Charlene's a girl and she's older than me so there's more of her to wash. While getting dressed, I make plans to raise this question during Mr Dellafield's next A & E session. In the end I chicken out because she's my sister after all and I don't want her to be the subject of classroom discussion.

◆

I come down for breakfast and find Dad already at the table. He issues his first order of the day. 'Wayne, nip out and get the paper.'

Outside I find that the newsboy has struck again! The morning paper lies beneath the big, spreading bush in the front garden. There are two lots of nauseating doggy poo and a dead frog under there. The fact that Kevin Merry is the newsboy explains everything. I return to the break- fast table without the newspaper. 'Sorry, Dad. I refuse to crawl under that bush. See Point Two of my manifesto.'

Dad swings round and consults the manifesto, then sniffs. 'Looks like there's room for a bit of give and take, Wayne.' He changes Point Two to read: 'I will collect the morning paper *with the long garden rake* when the newsboy hurls it under the big bush in the front garden.'

I try to argue, but Dad tells me the rake's in the shed with the garden tools, so I go out grumbling. Mum gives Dad a smile. That's one good thing to come out of my manifesto. More people should compromise. It brings families together and makes parents smile at each other in the morning.

Later, I hear Mum on the telephone telling Mr Teeth the newsagent she is not happy with the delivery arrange- ments.

'Is that so, Mrs Wilson?' Mr Teeth says on the tele- phone. (I can hear this because of my super-sensitive hearing and by listening on the extension.) 'Well, I don't know how I can improve it, Mrs Wilson. If you don't like the service, you know what to do.'

'Fair enough,' Mum says. 'I'll do that, Mr Teeth. Remember, you need me. I don't need you.' Clunk. That's telling him. Mum folds her arms and waits by the telephone and sure enough, after twenty-five seconds, it rings.

Mr Teeth is super-grovelly. 'Let's not be hasty, Mrs Wilson.'

'Oh, I'm never hasty, Mr Teeth.' Mum is full of charm. She tells him about Kevin Merry and his lifelong feud with me. Mr Teeth promises the paper will be delivered on our doorstep from now on, or Kevin Merry will know the reason why.

Even Mr Teeth's compromising and doing it Mum's way. To protect his identity, I've not used our newsagent's real name, but call him 'Mr Teeth'. Since he got a family discount at the orthodontist, Mr Teeth and his kids smile so much his customers have to use sunglasses. (That bit is not quite true.)

❧

Back to the manifesto and the episode of my untidy bedroom.

I go to school one morning, leaving a few things scattered around the floor, plus a pair of underpants hanging from the overhead light fitting. They got kicked up there when I was aiming at Fat Cat and missed. Stupid animal never stays still when you want him to.

When I come home, I find the contents of the kitchen tidy on the floor of my room. Not only that, there's a bunch of old newspapers in a corner. Dad has left some things on my bed – an old fishing rod, a basket and an ancient, smelly gumboot. Charlene's old love-lorn magazines and empty make-up bottles litter my desk. They're using my room as a rubbish dump! Next thing you know, the council will be at it too!

All right, if they want to play it tough, then so can little Wayne. I ignore the rubbish and say nothing. But as the days pass, my loving family dump more and more stuff in there until I have trouble finding my bed. This is too much.

I go downstairs and inquire of my female parent what is going on with all the rubbish in my room including the contents of the kitchen tidy. Mum consults my manifesto. 'I thought you *wanted* your room to be a rubbish tip, Wayne.'

'But only *my* rubbish!' I say.

Mum takes up her pen. 'Shall we find the middle ground?'

A few minutes later, Item Three of the manifesto reads: 'My room will look like a rubbish dump until I tidy it up, *which will be sooner rather than later.*'

When I look at the mess, I think not only is it unfair, it's also unhygienic. Mum assures me it's a good compromise, so I start to clean up my room and before long, Dad wanders in with a big garden rubbish bag, then Mum arrives to help out. Charlene removes her stuff too and before you know it, my room is spick and span, but nobody spots the underpants on the light fitting.

Then comes one of those moments of sheer horror, a time in a boy's life when he wishes the floor would open up and swallow him and not spit out the pips. We are watching television, taking turns at saying, 'Ar, would you believe it,' and, 'It's time we got a new one, Dad.'

The reason for these outbursts is that our television set is very old. The repair man has told us fifty times the picture tube will go any day now. As we watch our gripping serial, the telephone rings. 'Get that, Wayne,' Dad says. He's trying to be engrossed in the flickering action.

'What about my manifesto?' I remind him. 'Point Four.' The phone rings on and on and no one moves.

'Might be for you, Wayne,' Mum says.

'Could be for Charlene,' I point out.

'Not expecting anybody,' Charlene replies. 'I told the girls not to call me during the serial.' The phone still rings, so Mum finally gets up and answers it.

It's a triumph! The manifesto works. I have made a stand and declared independence.

'Hullo,' Mum says into the telephone. Then she hardens her voice. 'Wayne says he doesn't want to talk, so you'll have to wait till tomorrow.'

'Looks like it's for you, Wayne,' Dad murmurs.

'Who is it, Mum?' I start up to take the receiver, but Dad restrains me.

'Let your mum handle it,' he says. 'She comes from a long line of diplomats.'

But whoever's on the phone has made Mum angry. 'Listen, Fish-features!' she snaps. 'My boy doesn't want to answer the phone, and that's all right with this family, you got that? Drain-brain!'

'Mum!' I say in some alarm. This could be embarrassing, but there's no holding my mother.

She goes on, 'Oh yeah, well, Wayne'll see you tomorrow!' She hangs up and storms back to her chair. 'That Kevin Merry! What a nerve!' She puts on a Kevin voice. 'I just want to apologise, Mrs Wilson. For the newspaper under the bush.'

Dad passes Mum the box of jellybeans. 'Yeah, Heather, far too late for an apology.'

Charlene asks, 'Can we watch the serial?'

I completely forget the stupid TV with its non-colour, rolling-over images and rotten sound. Because of my manifesto, I've got a duel to the death with Kevin Merry. 'Erm, Mum, maybe I should ring back or something.'

'No, don't bother, son.' Mum pats my hand. 'You sit there and enjoy yourself.'

Later, we agree to more compromises. The manifesto now reads: I will *take my turn at answering* the telephone *like everyone else in the family.*

◆

Next day at school, I tippy-toe through the gates and try to make myself very small. In fact I make myself so small the Year 2 teacher thinks I'm one of her kids and rosters me as goldfish monitor for August.

But Kevin Merry is not in a bad mood. In fact, he's absorbed in his yo-yo, but he makes a wrong move and the thing swings around and clocks him on the back of the skull. He sees me and grins, then says, 'Tricky, eh?'

What's going on?

At home I corner Mum. 'Who *was* on the phone last night?'

She smiles a secret smile, then picks up the telephone receiver and presses her finger to hold the cradle down. 'Listen, Kevin Merry,' she snarls into the mouthpiece. 'I want you to stop bugging my boy, Wayne!'

'There was nobody there!' I say with a huge surge of relief.

Mum puts the telephone receiver down and smiles a sweet mumly smile. 'They hung up just as I got there, so I thought I'd have a bit of fun.'

Then we get talking about my manifesto. 'Y'see, Mum, I just want to do my own thing.'

'I wish I could do *my* own thing,' she sighs. 'But I've got to think of other people all the time. But one day, when I'm really old and there are no family members for me to care for, I'll do my own thing.'

Afterwards, we're sitting at the table having tea – just we three, Mum, Dad and me. Charlene is out with her friends. Mum raises the idea of me wanting to do my own thing.

'You *can't* do your own thing,' Dad says. 'Because you've got to come and go with other people.'

This is a very profound thing for my father to say,

so I ponder it awhile as I take the last sausage from the serving plate. 'How do you mean, Dad?'

'You've got needs, son,' he says, 'a place to sleep, a roof overhead, tucker in your tum and pants on your bum!'

'And the love of a good partner,' Mum adds, not in the least shocked at the language Dad uses at the table. Good thing Charlene's not here, otherwise Mum would have to join in with the shock-horror routine. Dad reaches for the last sausage and finds I've got it. We compromise and he gets half. Well, five-eighths of it.

'You need other people to buy what you sell,' Dad goes on. 'Whether it's the work you do, something you've made or something you've grown. We're like a lot of little cogwheels, all spinning like billy-oh and all turning because our neighbours are turning. Try doing your own thing in there and you get spat out of the system. Bang! You end up bruised and whimpering with broken teeth.'

'What your dad means is you can only do your own thing to a certain extent and at certain times,' Mum explains.

'You mean on holiday and at weekends?' I ask.

'Something like that, Wayne,' Dad agrees. 'But even then there's rules and regulations so you can't go dancing on the tables.'

Pondering upon my father's profound utterances, I go to my room and play a CD very loudly. No compromise here, I declare. This is my room, my personal space, these four walls and built-in wardrobe are my territorial boundary. This floor and this ceiling and light fitting with a pair of underpants still on it, they make a private world where I can be myself and do my own thing.

Fat Cat springs up and curls around my head. When he dies I will have him made into a furry set of stereo headphones.

The door of my private space opens and in glides Charlene, filled with fun and good humour, having arrived home after being out at a movie. 'Wayne, that noise is a bit loud,' she says sweetly and turns the sound down, then with her fingernails, lifts the volume knob off the CD player and drops it down the front of her blouse.

There's no answer to an action like that. My volume knob has found another private space!

Charlene refuses to give it back, so I have to compromise some more. Item Five on the manifesto now reads: 'I will play my CDs as loudly as I can *without the volume knob.*'

However, there is light on the horizon. Charlene says I can get my knob back by promising to consider the feelings of others, especially my sister. I don't think I want it back, knowing where it's been, but I promise anyway.

◆

There's an air of a mystery in the house. Dad and Mum are excited about something. They whisper furtively, but when I come into the room, they stop and look airy and innocent. Something is going on.

After homework, we watch television and as usual, I'm the one who has to walk around the room holding the aerial to get the best reception. Ha! That's a laugh! Once I actually climbed out the window and stood in the front garden while everyone inside said, 'That's fine, keep it there.' It was pouring rain at the time and I hoped I wouldn't be struck by lightning or spotted by Violet Pridmore or Rosana Conti.

Anyway, I find the right position on top of a pot plant, then we watch a program about new technology and television sets of the future. After our evening's viewing, Dad groans and grunts and looks as if it's hard to get out of his chair. 'That's it for tonight,' he says. 'Time to shut off the old telly.' He looks so ancient and sad, with his back bent and his brow furrowed.

I take pity on him. 'I'll switch it off, Dad.'

'No, let your dad do it,' Mum says. 'You just sit there, Wayne. After all, you've got your manifesto. Item Six!'

I nearly forgot, in fact, I'm getting fed up with my manifesto.

Dad limps towards the television. He switches it off, pulls out the wires at the back, picks up the whole box of tricks and marches out with it. My eyebrows rise a millimetre. Mum just looks at the *TV Times* and pays no attention.

Out in the yard, I hear a sudden crash and a tinkle of breaking glass as something gets hurled into the back of the Toyota. My eyebrows go up another millimetre. Dad comes in and sits down again. 'That's that, Heather,' he says. 'No more television. No more fighting and bickering or asking Wayne to get up to change channels. Just peace and contentment and conversation as a family.'

'Well done, Bill,' Mum approves.

'Dad, that was a bit *drastic*!' I protest. 'I *offered* to switch it off.'

'Oh no, son,' Dad soothes me. 'It wasn't your turn. Besides – you've got your manifesto.'

'Yeah, but we don't have a TV any more!' I am devastated. But this is where Mum and Dad break out in big smiles. Dad gets up and goes to the front room and rolls in a brand-new wide-screen job on little wheels. It's got a remote control! Oh, joy of joys!

I go to my manifesto and make another compromise. Item Six now reads: '*Wayne will work the remote control.*'

Dad inspects what I've written. 'I think we'll negotiate a bit more on that one.' He scores out 'Wayne' and writes 'Dad' instead.

Wouldn't you know it!

You want to hear a terrible story, Squocka?

Can I give it a miss?

Not really.

Okay, so let's hear it then.

It's the awful, dreadful tale of – Harris Weed.

Your cousin?

You got it, Squocka. My cousin, Harris Weed. A blight and a blemish. A stain and a pain.

And a guy called Wayne.

Thanks, Squocka. I appreciate your support.

7 HARRIS WEED

y cousin Harris is eight years old, going on twenty-six. He knows everything and will tell you about it if you give him half a chance. He's a weedy little genius with round glasses who asks 'why' all the time.

Privately I call him Harris Weed.

He's come to stay at our place for a fortnight, which does not please me in the extreme. (That's one thing I know that he doesn't.)

Harris's mum has come to stay too. She's my Aunt Irene, who is Mum's big sister. It seems that back in the olden days, Dad started out being keen on Irene. At that time, Mum was going to business college but flunked the course when her hair got caught in an electric typewriter or something. When Dad saw Mum's new short hair-do, his eyes went zonk and it was goodnight, Irene.

Just imagine if Dad had married Aunt Irene! I might have ended up with Harris Weed for a brother instead of being landed with Charlene for a sister. Take your pick.

Charlene thinks Harris is charming. Such a well-mannered little boy who says please and thank you without being reminded. He opens doors for people even when they don't want to go out and replaces the cap on the toothpaste as well as putting the toilet seat down after he's had a go at it. Harris is also a better aimer than me, she says.

He thinks he's the berries because his dad's a chartered accountant and mine is a plumber. I don't know what a chartered accountant does. Maybe people charter them like aeroplanes.

BUSINESS-CLASS FLIGHT OF FANCY:

Me: *Fly me to the Bahamas, Mr Chartered Accountant.*
Chartered Accountant: *Right sir, hop on my back and hold on. Here we go! Up, up and away!*
Me: *Never mind the in-flight conversation. Just fly.*
Chartered Accountant: *Yes sir.*
Me: *And mind that cloud!*

Harris would tell me what a chartered accountant does, but that would only give him another chance to be superior, the way he is about Dad's car, for example. Actually, Dad drives his clapped-out old Toyota truck and Harris's Dad drives a Saab! I make a joke at the dining room table one night and ask, 'Is that an Indian car?' (Saab = Sahib. Get it?)

They don't get it either. Some of my jokes take time. Aunt Irene looks at me through glasses that glint in the light. Later, I hear her asking Mum if I'm all right. 'Not backward at school, is he, Heather?'

Later, Mum and Aunt Irene have a private and serious conversation during which my keen ears pick up a word here and there. 'Why can't you have him?' Mum protests.

'We've got the overseas trip coming up, haven't we, Heather?'

'We don't have much room,' Mum says. 'It would be hard fitting him in.'

Are they talking about Harris Weed? It makes me so troubled, I need to find Squocka and see what's on in the world of cool people. 'See you, Mum,' I announce.

'Take little Harris,' Mum says.

'Take him where?' I reply, being smart.

'Take him *with* you.' Mum uses her gritted-teeth voice, for my eyes and ears only.

'Aw, Mum!' I protest, but she smiles sweetly and shakes her head, which means I can plead till my ears drop off but it won't make a difference.

I ask Harris Weed. 'You don't want to come, do you?' He wants to come.

Aunt Irene springs into action. If Harris is going out, he'll need to be rugged up. She spends an hour kitting him out for the South Pole. He wears little yellow wellies, a rain-hat and oilskin coat so he looks like a teddy bear you wouldn't want to cuddle.

I offer to fill a hot-water bottle but Mum shushes me. Aunt Irene wraps a scarf around Harris's neck and we're ready, although it's nearly bedtime. (That bit's a lie.)

'Bye, bye, darling.' Aunt Irene sees us off. 'Oh, they're

such a pair of little men, going out together,' she says. She waves as we go down the street. I try to hurry but Harris finds it hard to move with all the swaddling clothes he wears.

Wouldn't you know it, by the time we get to Squocka's place, he's already gone out. 'He waited ages,' Mrs Berrington says, 'then went to a movie with his cousin.'

Then it's brainwave time. We'll go to the pictures too. Might even run into Squocka, who was keen to see *The Brain Who Walked*. I've seen it three times. It's about this scientist who lives in a spooky castle and keeps a brain in a jar of chemicals. Suddenly, it becomes really gross. 'Look! Der brain grows der little stumpy bits down the bottom,' the scientist says to his mad assistant. 'What you tink zey are, eh?'

The mad assistant grunts and hops up and down, pointing to his big black boots. 'Schnegg, schnegg,' he screams in his obscure language.

'Ja! Is what I am tinking,' the scientist agrees. 'Zey look like legs. Zis is a profound ting to happen all of a sudden.'

Later, the brain escapes from the jar and goes looking for its body, which is a bit decomposed and that's when the movie becomes truly gruesome. Just the thing for Harris Weed to see. Put him off going with me for life, and it's only day one!

I buy half-price tickets, and we're just about to go into Cinema Five when a voice says, 'Hoi!' It's the manager. 'Where you think you're going?'

'To see *The Brain Who Walked*.'

'You're both too young for that movie,' says the manager. 'If I let kids in, people will write letters to the newspapers.'

'It's true, Wayne,' Harris Weed pipes up. 'Daddy's always writing letters about litterbugs and people who're late for appointments, women who smoke in the street, de-sexing dogs and other important subjects.'

Next thing you know, we're in Cinema Two with a lot of little Timothys and Edwards where we see *The Princess and the Pea* in glorious yucki-colour with comical villains who bump into each other and crash through doorways at the same time. It's got the rottenest theme song you ever heard and they put the words on the screen with hyphens and a little pea bouncing along to help the little kids in the audience keep time:

> *Oh, the Prin-cess and the Pea*
> *Is a won-der-ful thing to see.*
> *It's so full of joy and sweet-ness*
> *It's just right for you and me.*

I grind my teeth and the little kids think there's a wild dog on the loose. The manager comes and says if I don't stop he'll put a muzzle on me.

Going home, Harris Weed wants to take my hand while we cross the road. Squocka *never* takes my hand!

◆

In the living room, Harris Weed teases Fat Cat, who bites him on the finger. How I love that animal! Aunt Irene rushes to the aid of her stricken son with bowls of hot water, bandages and tubes of ointment. She checks her medical insurance and fixes an intravenous drip. Aunt Irene tells Mum she should have that vicious creature put down.

ANOTHER FLIGHT OF FELINE FANCY:

Fat Cat has overheard this fatal remark:
Fat Cat: *Is she serious, Wayne?*
Me: *'Fraid so, Fat Cat. Looks like curtains this time, boy.*
Fat Cat: *Oh, well, hasta la vista, Wayne.*
Me: *How about we have you stuffed?*
Fat Cat: *She's a determined woman, so I'm stuffed already.*

What a way to spend a holiday. Every move I make, Harris Weed is on to me. When we go out, Aunt Irene makes me wait while she gets him ready for another great adventure.

I have to go everywhere with a ladder in case he falls down a pit or something, then I'll be able to get him out without calling the police or the Deep Hole Rescue people. (That bit's a lie.)

If it looks like rain, Aunt Irene makes sure he has three umbrellas and a portable canoe. She gives him a label to tie on his coat in case he gets lost. The label gives me ideas. If I could afford the stamps, brown paper and string, I'd send him somewhere.

A PHILATELIC FLIGHT OF FANCY:

Postmistress: *Wait a minute. This parcel moved!*
Me: *I didn't see it move.*
Postmistress: *It moved when I hit it with the postmark stamp.*
Me: *Well, hit it up this end.*
Postmistress: *THUD!*
Me: *There you are. It's not moving now!*

◆

I keep missing Squocka and think I'll never see my human friends again. But that night, after a boring day with Harris, I escape and telephone Squocka to have a civilised conversation.

Squocka is cool and distant. 'What's wrong? Are you giving me the swerve?'

'No, Squocks. My cousin's come to stay, that's all.'

'That's no reason for keeping away.'

I'm just about to tell Squocka that he wouldn't want to *know* my cousin, when Aunt Irene comes to look up a number in the White Pages. She guesses I'm talking about her precious darling, so I have to make up a lie. 'We sort of enjoy doing things together,' I say into the phone. 'Just the two of us.' Aunt Irene beams with pleasure.

'Huh. I get the picture,' Squocka growls. 'Well, if you want to play it that way. My cousin's here too, so we could team up, all four of us. But never mind. I might see you around.' He hangs up. End of friendship. I've got to do something!

My plan is to occupy Harris's mind, which will let me

go out without him. But Mother Nature takes a hand and sends rain in buckets and cauldrons. So whatever trick I use, it'll have to be an indoor one. It's okay for me to sneak away, but Harris would need so much wet-weather gear it would take all day to get him ready for the great outdoors. I show him my Melvin Dole CD, then act nonchalant and chew pretend gum plus snap my fingers as if I've got rhythm. I go dooby, dooby-do and make musical noises. 'Hey, kid,' I say in cool language. 'You into MD and the Patients?'

'I beg your pardon?'

'It's a rock group,' I explain. 'MD and the Patients used to be Melvin Dole and the Nose Pickers but changed their names. They got Craig Cyst on drums, Johnny Bedpan, lead guitar, Madeleine Transplant, vocals and Melvin Dole on keyboard and scalpel. They were trying for a new musical style, not quite heavy metal, more sort of medium plywood. MD and the Patients is the kind of music you can listen to most of the time. Well, some of the time.' Actually, not at all, but the CD might keep Harris Weed amused, or he could use my headphones and fry his brain.

He doesn't like the music and gives a superior sneer. I try another approach, this time with my plastic constructor set. But wouldn't you know it, he wants *me* to make things. Ages ago I gave up playing with bits of plastic that connect to other bits of plastic and make objects that don't look like anything. To humour him, I join in and make a thing he invented. He won't tell me what it is, but gives orders for me to put that bit there or join the little blue ones together. He says my plastic constructor set's not as good as the one his daddy brought back from a business trip to Schnurdland.

We play Ludo, which I've outgrown. When he goes, I'll destroy the board and melt all the counters and flush the dice down the toilet. So passes another day.

◆

That night, Mum and Aunt Irene hold another secret debate of great intensity that is not for my ears.

Mum: *We couldn't fit him in here.*
Aunt Irene: *But we'll be away six months. World trip. Remember?*
Mum: *How could I forget. You keep telling me.*

It's very worrying, especially if Harris Weed plans to put down roots here.

In the middle of the night comes a plan! It's so fiendish, Aunt Irene will never let Harris go out with me again. With a smile on my face, I fall asleep, then would you believe it, he's even in my dreams!

I am doing well, impressing Violet Pridmore when Harris Weed ambles along and impresses her even more. Violet admires guys who wear glasses. I wear contacts but she says they're not the same. Violet and Harris Weed go off together, leaving me to call, 'Violet, Violet, I can stand on my head if you'll hold my legs up!'

I wake up to find my father staring at me strangely. 'Wayne, it's half-past seven. You're going out with Little Harris.'

'What's new, Dad?' I ask, but he goes off to plumb the depths of something.

At least I've got my cunning plan. Fortunately the sun shines, which is good because to work properly, this plan needs the great outdoors. I give it to Harris straight, using my tense voice. 'I've got dangerous stuff to do.'

'Dangerous, eh?' His eyes grow wide.

'Yeah, I got to pass a bravery test, to get into the Junior Pee-wees.'

'Oh, exciting.'

'But don't tell your mother, she'd only worry.'

'Righty-oh, Wayne. Just wait till I get dressed.' He already *is* dressed, but he means to add his junior suit of Tudor armour plus other bits and pieces – first-aid kit, global positioning system, emergency beacons including a direct line to the rescue helicopter. It all adds up. Never mind, when my plan works, I'll be a free man.

We sneak out of the house like conspirators, except that Aunt Irene says to Mum, 'Oh, there they go together. Wayne's got a secret assignment this morning.'

'Harris,' I frown when we're out of earshot, 'you blabbed.'

'It's not blabbing, Wayne, it's common sense to tell grown-ups in case we get lost.' Harris wears my padded parka and looks ridiculous.

'Okay,' I growl, then start softening him up. 'I'll try to protect you, Harris, but don't blame me if you get your legs ripped off by a Doberman.'

'We've got a Doberman, Wayne. They're nice. Very expensive, so they're not for everybody.'

There's no crushing this kid. 'Well, try to keep up.' Off I go at a brisk pace with Harris Weed trotting alongside.

My feet lead me in the direction of a pine plantation where trees grow close together and in rows. A sign on the barbed wire fence says KEEP OUT but it doesn't mean me. I duck under the wire fence, then a few seconds later I hear the very satisfying sound of clothes ripping. Someone's having trouble with the barbed wire, I smile. My face turns sour. Harris Weed only ripped my padded parka in two places. 'Where are we, Wayne?' he asks.

'In a spooky forest,' I tell him. 'So stick with me, kid, or you'll get lost forever!'

I set off with Harris following behind. Bits of white stuffing fall out of my padded parka. As we get deeper into the forest, it becomes darker and scarier. Oooh, shadows.

Finally, I call a halt. 'This is where I perform my test,' I tell Harris.

'To get into the Junior Poo-poos?'

'Pee-wees.' I correct him. 'It's a private moment, so you stay here because no one's allowed to watch me do what I have to do.'

'So how will the Junior Pee-wees know you've done it?'

'They have ways.' I head off.

Harris Weed calls, 'Good luck, Wayne.'

My plan is to leave him for a while until he's frightened and thinks he's lost. He'll complain to Aunt Irene and she'll never let me take him out again. I'll be in trouble with Mum, but it'll be worth it. Half an hour should do it. I take a left turn in the forest, then a right and double back, turn around and go down that way, turn left, turn right, think of the number I first thought of, then head back to Harris Weed.

He's not there. Silly boofhead!

I told him to stay in one place. I call his name and run around looking for him. He really is lost! I go in search, but one tree looks like another. What's more, the forest is spooky and silent.

It is not the place to be, so I decide to run home and get a search party, but I can't remember which way is out. Worse than that, this place looks different and I can't even see the barbed wire fence. I am lost too. 'Oh no!' I wail in a brave manner and think terrible thoughts. When they cut down the trees in twenty-five years, they'll find two little skeletons. One will be Harris Weed and the other me. Our meaty bits will have disappeared, so they'll only recognise my skeleton by the brave smile on my skull. And my DNA.

Squocka will be grown up and married with kids. He'll take advantage of my disappearance and marry Violet Pridmore. When he sees my bleached bones he'll feel remorse and put up a memorial stone so he'll never forget me. 'What was his name again, Violet dear?'

I lie on the ground and wail, then beat my fists on

the forest floor. 'What a way to die!' I howl. 'Alone. I will starve.'

Just then, someone pats my head. Who is it? A passing woodsman? The rescue party? A hunter? No, it's Harris Weed. 'Don't cry, Wayne,' he says.

'I wasn't crying,' I tell him. 'There's a pine needle in my eye.'

'But you're crying out of both eyes.'

'Okay, so it's *two* pine needles!' Getting angry with Harris Weed makes me tough again.

'Well, let's go home,' he says. 'It's this way.' He points to the trail of white stuff that fell out of my padded parka.

'Very clever of you to spot that, Harris,' I say, leading the way out of the forest.

Harris Weed promises never to breathe a word about me being lost and emotional. In return, I'm to take him everywhere I go for the rest of his visit.

For the rest of *my life* if he comes to stay! That spectre still looms before me. That night, Mum and Aunt Irene have another private confab in hushed whispers behind closed doors. I can listen to this because of an ear-level keyhole someone provided for just such a purpose. 'It's not fair,' I hear Mum say. 'You've got a bigger house.'

'Of *course* we have a bigger house, Heather dear,' Aunt Irene says patiently, 'and staff. But he'd be lonely if we left him there for a whole six months. He'll be no bother. You'll see. He's very clean and quite amusing.'

'Oh well,' Mum growls. Aunt Irene sounds pleased.

If it's Harris Weed, I'm leaving home. This last fortnight has been a lifetime!

◆

At last, departure day arrives. A taxi comes and Aunt Irene and Harris Weed get in and with much blowing of kisses and cries of 'Bye bye', they disappear. I bet he tells the taxi driver I got lost in the pine forest and he rescued me!

Aunt Irene leaves us a gift – a lump of lurid pink pottery with red, orange and purple bits hanging off it. 'What's it supposed to be?' Charlene asks doubtfully.

Dad inspects the thing. 'Looks like something they cut out of a racehorse.'

Later, Mum and Dad talk privately about Aunt Irene's visit. 'I suppose we *could* take him, Bill,' Mum says. 'Be a bit of a squeeze.'

'It's up to you, Heather girl,' Dad responds. 'Wayne likes him.'

Father, how could you? The telephone ring signals the end of another mystery conversation and gives my ears a well-earned rest.

◆

A couple of days later, I catch sight of a downcast figure with a tragic look on his face. It is Squocka, walking to the bus station, carrying a suitcase. 'Hi, Squocks,' I greet him in my bright voice. 'What's up?'

'Saying goodbye, Wayne. That's what's up.' Squocka

sighs a deep sigh. Just then, a girl comes out of the news-agent's with a magazine under her arm. She's about our age, with long dark hair and deep blue eyes. My eyes go zonk! The girl runs to catch up with Squocka to help with her suitcase.

'Who's your friend, Squocka?' she says in a voice like tinkling bells, making my schoolboy heart go thunkity-thunk.

I put my eyes back in and say, 'My name's Wayne.'

'Hello and goodbye, Wayne,' the girl says.

Squocka sighs again and they walk on together into the bus station.

A few minutes later, a bus emerges and heads in an out-of-town direction. At one of the windows, I catch sight of the vision, waving goodbye to Squocka. Then she's gone.

Squocka comes to join me. 'Cousins, eh? I had such a great time.'

What are you writing, Wayne?

A poem, Squocka, in honour of my grandpa.

Let's hear it, then.

I've only done two lines.

Two lines, eh? Not a lot of honour in two lines.

I'm still composing it, Squocka. It might have six lines. Or seven.

So, am I going to hear it, or what?

Right. Here goes. Don't laugh.

As if.

**'What a wonderful man is my grandpa.
Then one day he came to stay.'**

That's not a nice thing to say about your grandpa.

It's what I thought at the time. Give me a chance to finish it.

How about: 'He helps me with my problems, and gives me good advice.'

Yeah, I like that, Squocka. So, what rhymes with 'advice'?

Rice.

That'll do: 'He eats his own weight in pizza, and invented fried rice.'

Now that's a man I could honour, Wayne.

8 You Can't Take Him Anywhere

aynee-poops,' Mum says in the voice she uses when she wants me to do something I'm not going to like. 'I've got a little problem.'

'Oh yes,' I say in the voice I use while waiting to hear what it is before getting enthusiastic.

'It's like this— ' Mum drags it out ' – your Grandpa Dawson's sort of getting on a bit, isn't he?'

'Yes.' I nod slowly. 'Last time I looked he could give the Pyramids a run for their money. And the Sphinx.'

'Don't be smart. It will stunt the growth of your pocket money.'

'Sorry.'

'So, Grandpa needs someone to look after him,' Mum goes on. 'Agreed?'

'Yes.' It's my turn to drag it out, except you can't drag 'yes' out for more than a second or two unless you turn it into a hiss.

'The other night,' Mum goes on, 'he fried some chips and nearly set fire to the net curtains.'

For me, little alarm bells start to ring ding-a-ling. (No,

they're not fire bells!) 'You don't use net curtains to cook chips,' I point out cautiously. 'You use a wire strainer sort of thing.'

Normally Mum would just cut off my food supply for making a remark like that but for some reason she wants to butter me up so smiles a patient, mumly smile. 'The thing is, Wayne,' she explains. 'We thought he should come here for a while.' Little pause, then emphasis where indicated. 'That is, your *father, Charlene* and *I*, thought *we* should have him with us.'

'And I bet Aunt Irene thought that too.' I remember all the not-quite-secret conversations during her recent visit, which I will not forget in a hurry.

'We won't go there, Wayne,' Mum says. 'It's true Aunt Irene did happen to mention it while she was staying with us.'

So, she *didn't* come to see Mum, Dad, Charlene and little me; she came to lumber the Wilson household with Harris Weed for a fortnight and Grandpa for ever. How unbelieviously devious!

It's a relief that it's not Harris Weed who's coming, but only Grandpa (who is Mum's father). He used to be a music-hall comedian, then because of TV, the world became swamped with stand-up comics. You couldn't buy a bus ticket without the driver trying one of his jokes on you. Old comedians had to learn new routines, but Grandpa gave up and retired to a boarding house with some elderly actors who shuffled around in carpet slippers laughing at each others' ancient jokes. Then came the chip-frying routine that was nearly Grandpa's final curtain in more ways than one.

He's not a bad old stick, so why should I mind him coming to stay? And why should Mum have to butter me up? I become manly about it. 'It'll be fun having him here, Mum,' I say. 'We'll make him welcome. Grandpa will be all right with us.'

'That's a generous attitude, son.' Mum pats me on the back. 'So you won't mind giving up your bedroom?'

Da-da-da-dum! I didn't know about *that* bit!

My room is special. It's decorated the way a boy's room should be and has my personal things in it, which I check off every week:

A plastic shrunken human head with eye sockets that light up as long as you put batteries in. ✓

A cricket bat with autographs of the entire Australian team, forged with different colour ball pens. ✓

Ninety-seven glass marbles, no longer round on account of the vigorous playing I did in my younger days. ✓

Mum says she'll show me a large plastic box to put them in. Little Mum joke there. She means the wheelie bin! Ha-ha. I'm not laughing.

Charlene doesn't mind Grandpa coming to stay – after all, she's not giving up her bedroom.

Mum makes preparations for Grandpa's 'visit', as she keeps calling it. She buys him a reading lamp and a little hand-bell to ring if he needs help. 'Why not get him a direct line to the fire brigade?' I suggest.

'Wayne,' Mum says. 'Remember all the brownie points you got for the generous sacrifice of your bedroom?'

'Yes, Mum.'

'You're using them up fast, so watch it.'

Mum buys Grandpa a pillow filled with hops so he can get a good night's sleep. All these years *my* pillow's been stuffed with broken vinegar bottles and barbed wire! (That bit's a lie.)

Gradually, I get oozed out of my bedroom and have to put my things in a cupboard and take down my poster of MD and the Patients, which was coming off the wall anyway, but I don't tell Mum that.

*

Grandpa comes in a taxi, with his possessions in twenty-six brown-paper parcels tied up with hairy string. 'Hello, Heather,' he greets Mum. Grandpa still tries to be independent and insists he's only staying until he's fixed himself up with a flat and a floozie.

He seems bewildered and forgets to take his hat off, but Mum does it for him and fusses around until the six o'clock news comes on television, then he's on his own. Dad gives up his favourite chair for Grandpa, but at the dinner table it's me that has to sit on a miniature stool so that my nose only reaches the edge of the table.

Then at bedtime, I go out to the back verandah where Mum has made up a small, creaking camp bed for her darling son who's been so nice about the whole business of having Grandpa to stay. I bet Harris Weed's laughing his fool head off and only went overseas to Tasmania or some place you don't need a passport.

The deep freeze is on the back verandah and when it switches on during the night it makes a 'clunk' noise, then vibrates the verandah. When it switches off, it goes 'da-da-da-duh', followed by a long, breathy sigh. During that first lonely night, my imagination gets to work. There are frozen things inside the deep freeze that speak to me in ghostly whispers.

FLIGHT OF FRIGID FANCY:

The lid of the deep freeze slowly lifts. Snap-Frozen Asparagus Man peeps over the side, wrinkling his long green fingers to shake off the icicles.

SFAM: *Wayne, come in and join us. In here it's c-o-o-l.*

Me: *Go away, Snap-Frozen Asparagus Man.*

SFAM: *Come on, Wayne. You can scrape the ice off the sides and make snowballs.*

Me: *I'll end up deep-frozen, like the broccoli and turkey drumsticks.*

SFAM: *It's lovely this time of year. A Winter Wonderland. Come on.*

In the morning, Charlene Wilson finds her brother inside the deep-freeze.

Charlene: *Mum, Wayne's in the deep freeze.*

Mum: *How's he looking?*

Charlene: *Stiff.*

Mum: *Well, shut the lid. We don't want the fish fingers to go off.*

I don't get a lot of sleep, but eventually fall off, then climb back into the camp bed to massage my bruises. A sudden loud scrunching disturbs the silence of the night. It sounds like an iceberg breaking apart, but it's only Fat Cat having a midnight feast. His food bowls are on the back verandah so he won't disgust the family while he eats.

Fat Cat then has a go at my toes, which stick out the end of the bed. He gives them a lick and sometimes a nibble, depending on his mood. Personally I wouldn't touch my feet with metre-long chopsticks, but that's cats for you. While all this is going on, Grandpa is upstairs with his head resting on a new hop-filled pillow, snoring on my Wonder-slumber mattress.

◆

Next morning, I eat a bleary-eyed breakfast, but cheer up when I remember it's Saturday, so freedom yawns before me. Until Mum says, 'Wayne, get me a few things at the supermarket, and take Grandpa with you. Make sure he doesn't get lost.'

My tired eyes go pop. *Make sure he doesn't get lost?*

Here I have to recount a small piece of Wilson family history. There was a time when Grandpa took *me* out in my stroller when I was a tiny, bouncing baby, wearing pink bootees that once belonged to Charlene but had a bit more wear in them.

As Grandpa wheeled my stroller, I said, 'Abba dabba ooble dobble ubble.' At the time it was as far as my language had developed. (Some words are verbs, some adjectives, sort them out for yourself.) As Mum told the story to me, Wonder-Gramps popped into the betting shop, where he met Archie McGangle and got talking. Gramps emerged and toddled home, forgetting me altogether as I sat outside going, 'Gooble nubble peeble niggle blong and poop,' to anyone who listened. (I also blew fascinating bubbles.)

I filled my nappy three times over and maybe experienced some discomfort, but then in the gathering dusk, Mum collected me. And so began the legend of *How Grandpa Went Shopping and Forgot Baby Wayne.* See it at a cinema near you!

Since I am to look after Grandpa, the bootee is on the other footee! With an evil leer, I suggest it's time for another legend, but Mum warns me to bring him back in one piece. 'Which piece do you want?' I ask, but Mum gives one of her heavy-duty frowns, designed to quash me for the rest of the week.

We set out and Gramps tells me to slow down because he's not as spry as he used to be. He uses old words that I have to translate for the guy at the supermarket checkout. Grandpa still talks about pounds of sugar, pints of milk and ounces of tea. Then he forgets his walking stick and nearly crashes a trolley into a tall tower of tinned tomatoes. It wasn't even his trolley.

◆

After shopping, we take a rest on a park bench on the

cycle path by the river, when all of a sudden, two jogging young women approach. Their long manes of golden hair stream behind them as they flow along in running shorts, white shoes and brown legs. My eyes go zonk while strange chemicals chase themselves around my body and do mischief to my woobly glands.

Early in my young life, I worked out there's a difference between boys and girls. There are helpful books on the subject, e.g. *You are a Boy*. I also had a squint at *You are a Girl*, which was much more interesting. In case Violet Pridmore caught me reading this stuff, I hid it inside a bigger book called *The Golden Age of Liquids*.

Being cool, I pretend not to notice the jogging women, but Grandpa's not like me. 'Cor!' he says in elderly rapture and rises to his feet as the women bounce closer. He waves his walking stick in the air. 'Go on, girls!' he cries. 'Shake them fetlocks!'

'Pervert!' the taller woman snaps. She frowns at me. 'Keep him under control!'

'Boy, I wish I was seventy again!' Grandpa sighs, gazing after the receding women. 'Pair of corkers if ever I saw them.'

'Grandpa,' I protest. 'You can't *say* things like that. It's embarrassing.'

'Go on, they love it. I bet right now they're laughing about it.'

'Yeah, all the way to the nearest cop.'

Grandpa promises he'll behave himself, then comes an incident so embarrassing it could have stunted my growth and made me a hermit. Worse than zits. I stand up and say, 'Okay, Grandpa, let's go home.'

'Yeah, boy,' he responds, then, 'Ka-choonka!' My grandfather sneezes loudly and possibly wetly, but I'm upwind so that doesn't matter. Nothing wrong with a hearty sneeze, I hear you say. It's part of the human condition. But how many of us sneeze our false teeth out?

And guess who has to get down on hands and knees and look for the expelled dentures because Grandpa has not brought his reading glasses?

I search under a bush amongst the overflow from a nearby rubbish bin, while Grandpa gives me encouragement. 'Hurry up, lad. There might be shome more of them corkersh coming thish way. Don't want them to shee me with a faish like thish.'

'My name's Wayne, Grandpa. Not "lad".'

'Can't shay Wayne wishout my teesh in.'

'Gotcha!' After several minutes, I find his dentures and scoop them into an empty hamburger carton.

But is my Grandfather pleased? No, he's not! 'Oh, you've shmashed them, lad. There'sh a bit mishing!'

Just then a little dog runs along, wagging his terrier tail all ready for a game with someone or something. He goes snuffling amongst the rubbish and next thing you know, he's got the other half of the false teeth! 'Good dog,' I say. 'Give it here, boy.'

Wheedling, coaxing noises make no difference to this animal. He tosses the bit of denture into the air and catches it so the teeth stick out of his mouth. He looks sinister, then sprints back to his owner, who's sitting on another park bench along the cycle path.

Grandpa looks at me, then nods in the direction of the leering dog and his buck-teeth. 'Go on, boy. I'll shtay here.'

I approach the owner of the dog. Horror of horrors! It's only Mr Dellafield. He sits reading a paperback. The dog drops the teeth at his feet and goes 'Wuff!' Absently, Mr Dellafield picks up the object and throws it away. The dog hares after it.

If Mr Dellafield knew what his pet's been handling, there's no saying how things might pan out. I decide to get after the dog, but being more spry than me as well as having four legs, he gets Grandpa's teeth first and tosses them triumphantly into the air, then taunts me with them. I try to corner him, but he dodges past and scampers back to Mr Dellafield, then sits up and begs, with the false teeth still showing.

'Write an essay,' Mr Dellafield will command when we get to school on Monday. 'Stranger than fiction – what happened to me on the weekend.' I'll have a head-start on the whole class, and the story's not told yet.

This time, Mr Dellafield looks down, then recoils in horror at the sight of his toothy terrier. 'What on earth– ?'

It's time for me to come forward. 'Good morning, Mr Dellafield.' I take the direct approach. 'Your dog's wearing my grandfather's false teeth.'

Mr Dellafield looks at me as if madness runs in my

family, then makes the dog spit out the teeth. 'Wilson,' he says, 'I'd hoped to finish this chapter in peace, but now I'll have to take my dog for a tetanus injection.'

'Sorry, sir.'

'One day we'll laugh about this, Wilson. But this is not that day.' He goes. I'll never live it down!

By this time, the false teeth are severely dog-bitten and chewed, plus there are bits of grass and spittle on them. I find a fast-food box and take the teeth back to Grandpa.

He joins a queue of sweating joggers at the water bubbler and gives the two bits of false teeth a rinse to make them hygienic. Some faint-hearted yuppies mutter, 'Yuk!' but Grandpa ignores them. I suffer terminal mortification and observe things from a distance.

'Thish looksh like a job for an exshpert,' Grandpa says as he tries to fit the two broken parts together. He uses his penknife to smooth down the bumps where the dog's teeth bit into the plastic parts.

Then it's brainwave time. I trot off to the newsagents and buy a tube of superglue, or as Gramps would say, shooperglue, but we'll have that fixed in a couple of squirts.

I explain to Grandpa that superglue is a wonder of modern science they didn't have in his young day. I put a few dabs on each side of the false teeth, then show him how to hold them together until the glue sets. There's no way I'm going to be seen holding a set of false teeth! But wouldn't you know it, Grandpa moves the two bits of teeth so any second now, they'll set crooked. I make a grab to straighten things out, then discover we're both joined together, both forefingers on the same bit of false teeth.

Warning it says on the superglue tube, *Do not allow glue to come into contact with fingers.* Now they tell me!

'Well done, boy,' Grandpa says in a fine-mess-you-got-me-into voice.

If those two female joggers see me stuck fast to my grandfather and his false teeth, I might as well put my gooly glands back in their box and abandon all thoughts of puberty.

When the bus driver sees us stuck together he laughs so much he forgets to tell a music-hall joke. It takes him half an hour before he's in a fit state to move away from the kerb. Every time he lets passengers on, he tells them about us two back there, sitting side by side, forefingers in the air looking both toothy and sheepish. I gaze out the window as more and more smirking passengers join the bus. Word gets around and before long there are people hanging onto the sides of the bus as well as lying on the roof trying to peer inside. (That bit's a lie.)

Dad's home when we get back, so he takes over. With a straight face and a sharp blade, he sets us free without drawing blood. Then Dad takes Grandpa to a specialist false-teeth repairer to fix the dental damage and somehow it's all my fault because of the superglue suggestion.

❖

Later that night, in my narrow camp bed on the spooky, draughty, cat-ridden, deep-freeze-sighing, back verandah, I am totally dejected. Being dead tired I fall asleep and sink into an uneasy dream where I'm chased by long-legged blonde Brussels sprouts from the freezer. They snap their big false teeth as they come to get me!

Suddenly, there's a crunching noise as if someone's chewing coal. It is Fat Cat at his biscuit bowl having a midnight beano. I lie listening to the noises of the night. Among them are voices in the kitchen. I roll over in bed so that my ear is against a little crack in the adjoining wall.

Grandpa and Dad are talking seriously. Grandpa says it's about time he went into a retirement home.

Dad's a bit embarrassed, I can tell. He makes cheer-up conversation. 'You'll get decent chips there. Without setting fire to anything.'

'Yeah, and not be a bother to anyone.'

'You're not a bother.' (Speak for yourself, Dad! I think.)

'It's what I feel,' Grandpa goes on, making me regret my mean thought.

Dad goes on to say that Grandpa can share his time between us and Aunt Irene.

'Not going to her place!' The words explode from Grandpa. 'Rather live in a wet cardboard box with no lid on it.'

'Won't come to that,' Dad assures him. 'We'll get you a dry one.'

'Can you imagine yon pimple of a son of hers – what's his name again?'

'Harris,' Dad and I say together, except I say it under my breath.

'Yeah, him,' Grandpa goes on. 'Can you see him searching under a bush for my false teeth the way Wayne did?' Here he starts to laugh, then goes on, 'I tell you Bill, I wish I'd had a routine like that when I was on stage. It was hard not to laugh.'

'Yeah, it must have been funny,' Dad agrees.

'That's what I like about being here, Bill,' Grandpa says. 'Being around that Wayne lad of yours, especially when he blushes. And he's got a lot more left in him.'

'Yeah, fair enough.' Dad encourages Grandpa to drink up his cocoa so they can get some sleep.

I roll away from the crack in the wall and start to think about the day. Before long, I'm laughing too and have to put a hand over my mouth in case Snap-frozen Asparagus Man hears me being jolly and springs out for a frigid frolic.

If the false teeth business cheered Grandpa up, then what's a bit of terminal embarrassment? I can always change towns, or live in a damp cardboard box. It made an old man's day, so that's got to be worth something.

On top of that, there is now a *new legend* – even better than the one about me being left behind in my stroller! The Legend of the Super Sneeze.

With a smile on my face, I roll over in the narrow camp bed. The deep freeze cuts in with a click and a shudder. In the darkness, Fat Cat sinks his teeth into my big toe.

Want to come to a party, Squocka?

What kind of party?

Birthday.

No, thanks, Wayne.

Come on, mate. A party's a party.

No it's not.

All right, when is a party not a party?

When it's Reuben Partridge's party.

Oh well, Squocka, just thought I'd try.

Yeah, nice one, mate. And if you want to know the reason –

Just turn the page. It's called Reuben.

⑨ REUBEN

t is September the fourth, one of the calendar's most special days, an anniversary to avoid. On this date falls Reuben Partridge's birthday. He is six, and a bit of a dork.

For a present, I'm giving him a dork's outfit. I pop along to Mr Patel's Imperial Joke and Novelty Emporium, which also sells whoopee cushions as well as hiring and selling tatty fancy-dress costumes. We have already met Mr Patel, the ever-amusing proprietor. (People call him Laugh-a-minute Charlie because of his sense of humour.)

FLIGHT OF FUN-FILLED FANCY:

Me: *Excuse me, Mr Patel. Do you have a dork's outfit in stock?*
Mr Patel: *What does a dork's outfit resemble?*
Me: *It's like the one you're wearing. Boo-boom!*
Next thing you know I'm out in the street, rolling in the gutter with the bus tickets and orange peel, wondering what happened. Some people just can't take a joke.
Me: *Squocka! Take this joke.*
Squocka: *Where will I take it?*
Me: *To Mr Patel. I want my money back.*
Squocka: *No way, panti-hosé.*

See what I mean? Even Squocka can't take a joke.

Anyway, it's Reuben Partridge's birthday this coming Saturday afternoon, and his mother cannot cope. Mrs Partridge has never been able to handle things, not since day one. She's always coming to our place with an 'I can't manage it' look on her face, then she slumps. Her shoulders drop down to where her elbows should be and Mum says, 'There, there, what is it this time?'

On this occasion Mrs Partridge can't deal with the prospect of her son's birthday party. An assortment of kids are coming and Mrs Partridge is not sure if she can put up with them running around the house and doesn't know any party games to amuse them, plus she's just finished having the carpets cleaned and new drapes installed and oh, just everything. Not to mention the Blind Venetians. She slumps.

'Never mind,' says my smiling mother. 'Wayne will help out, won't you, Wayne?' The smile is for Mrs Partridge. For me Mum's look says: *If you know what's good for you.*

'Of course I don't mind popping over, Mumsy darling.' That's my Wayne-the-Good-Neighbour voice. 'For a minute and a half or ninety seconds, whichever is shorter.'

'Wayne would *love* to *spend the whole Saturday afternoon* at the birthday party,' Mum says. 'He knows *lots of party tricks and games*, don't you, Wayne?'

'Yes.' I fix my lips in a dazzling smile, which means I show all my teeth at the same time.

Mrs Partridge takes this as a sign of sincerity and un-slumps, then springs joyfully homewards. Later she rings to say her washing machine's overflowed and the repairman can't make it until the first week in the New Year. Mum convinces her that I'm no good with washing machines and Dad's out on a job with his electric eel stuck up a drainpipe and looks like having to dig it out.

◆

What can I say about Reuben? Apart from it being a good name for cough mixture. Couple of swigs and you'll soon be laughing your head off.

> **COUGHS AND SNEEZES?**
> Get some Reuben and laugh them away.

Ha ha, hee hee, ho ho! There you are, you're better already. Reuben – in your pharmacy now!

If your name's Reuben then don't take that advertisement personally. If it *really* offends you, then get a pen and change the name to Frank or Joe, but only if you actually own this book. If it belongs to the library, then behave yourself and get on with the story, otherwise you'll end up in court with all the other Reubens.

FLIGHT OF FELONIOUS FANCY:

There's a special day for it every year. The Judge walks into the courtroom, adjusts his wig, then catches sight of many little boys lined up waiting for justice. He clutches the doorpost for support.

'Oh no!' he says. 'Don't tell me it's Naughty Reuben Day!'

''Fraid so, Your Worship,' says his clerk. 'Twenty-seven of them on book-defacing charges and twenty-seven librarians eager to give their side of the story.'

The librarians sit in a row doing knitting and laughing the special librarians' laugh they keep for book-spoilers who're about to get what's coming to them.

So put up with it. It's nothing personal. Now, on with the story.

Being a sharing kind of guy, I try to get Grandpa to enjoy the Saturday-afternoon fun. But he already heard Mum lining me up for the Partridge birthday festivities, so went sneaky-sneaking upstairs to fling himself on my bed.

'Gramps, do you want to come to a party?'

'Snore,' he fibs. 'Oh, snorey, snorey, snorey snore.' He soaks the pillow with his slobbers, so I retire in frustration and disgust.

It's brainwave time. Who better to share an afternoon of Reuben and his slumping mother than my good buddy, Squocka?

'Guess what, Squocka,' I say on the telephone. 'We've been invited to a fabulous birthday party.'

'You get an invitation?'

'Yep.'

'How come I never got one?'

'Your name's on mine,' I lie, then grab a bit of paper and make invitation sound effects on the telephone. He falls for it and doesn't ask who, when and where questions.

'Will there be girls there?'

'Wall-to-wall, mate!' I give Squocka the address, tell him the time and hang up. He'll really enjoy himself once he gets there. Squocka loves parties.

❧

Knockity, knock, I go at the front door. Mrs Partridge opens it and her face shows relief when she sees it's not one of the guests. 'Oh, thank heavens!' she cries.

I follow her inside where Reuben gives me a baleful look and fingers his South American Indian plastic blowpipe. Each dart is tipped with imitation poison and spittle plus goobly bits left over from breakfast. *'He's* not coming to my party, is he?' Reuben demands.

'Be quiet, dear,' Mrs Partridge sighs. 'Go and wait for your guests to arrive. They should be here any minute. If I got the day right.'

Mrs Partridge sets me to work writing nametags for the guests. I have a bottle of gold ink, so taking great care I print Leroy, Enzo, Reuben, Amanda, Leland, Chauncey, Giovanni and George. Looks like Squocka's going to miss out on the girls since Amanda's the only one coming, unless George happens to be one with a tomboy name.

Reuben thinks the tags are yucky and doesn't like the kakky yellow colour, like poo-poos. That sets me wondering what they eat at their house. He says he wants them done in red with drips on them to make them look like human blood. His mother tells him to be quiet, so he goes and kicks the wall. Reuben is not in a party mood, and it hasn't even started.

Squocka turns up, dressed for a teenage affair, hair slicked down, sneakers, jeans and T-shirt with the words *Girls, Queue Here* on his manly chest. He has a gift wrapped in Christmas paper with holly on it. He explains it's suitable for boys or girls – a unisex present, plus multi-seasonal.

On hearing the magic 'gift' word, Reuben races to the door, grabs the package and rips the wrapper off. He holds up a small pencil-sharpener. If he is disappointed, Squocka is treble miffed. 'You mean, it's *his* party?'

'Yeah,' I laugh my bright, whoop-it-up laugh. 'Didn't I say?'

'No, mate.' He doesn't laugh his let's-have-fun chuckle. 'You didn't. And I bet the girls are his age as well.'

'Only some of them.' I happen to know Amanda's just five. 'Anyway, now you're here, you might as well hang around and help out. We can play a few games, grab a bite to eat, then go down the mall, see what's what, hang out.'

'Huh! Homework never looked so attractive.' Squocka is a complete downer. He takes wet-blanket lessons from a correspondence school.

Mrs Partridge gives him the job of blowing up balloons while Reuben gets in some South American Indian poison-dart practice. The result is only three balloons survive and they're all blue ones.

I sprinkle the hundreds and thousands on the iced biscuits, then stick six candles in the cake, which is made in the shape of a boot with windows in the side and a chimney on top with cotton-wool clouds of smoke. I'm having fun already.

The first guest is Leroy Merry who is a junior thug, younger brother to the famous Kevin. Even Leroy's cat is a thug who gives Fat Cat a rough time when all he wants to do is go for a quiet wander in the garden and chew the heads off Mum's carnations.

Leroy the Thug carries a long, thin parcel under his arm which I think might be a meat cleaver. Reuben rips it apart to reveal a coat-hanger-cum-backscratcher with a little hooky gadget for doing up zips on the backs of ladies' evening dresses.

Reuben scowls the scowl of the deeply disappointed. Never mind, there are more guests to come. Leroy doesn't get anything to eat so he sits in a chair, swinging his short, pudgy legs, wondering which part of the house to vandalise first.

Ding-a-long says the doorbell and guest number two is Chauncey! His mum and dad are rich so this is Reuben's opportunity to make it big in the gift department. Yes, yes, under his arm, Chauncey has an exciting-looking parcel. He passes it over and mutters, 'Ha'ey Bir-gay, Roog.'

'Yer, fangs ver much, Chonks.' Rip, rip, shred, tear, destroy, and the parcel's open. It is bingo time! Chauncey's gift is a postman's outfit. A hat, a badge, a shirt, a bag with little letters in it plus a stick for beating dogs over the head. Reuben is in rapture. 'Oh, oh, fangs, Chonks.' He puts the hat on. It is too big for him so he has fun turning around quickly leaving the hat still facing where it was in the first place.

Soon guests begin to arrive thick and fast. Reuben greets them in his postman's outfit. George's look says he didn't want to come to this dumb party in the first place and no way he's going to enjoy himself anyhow. He demands to be allowed to watch television, but Mrs Partridge can't cope with the noise. George sticks out his lower jaw and kicks the china cabinet, leaving scuff marks on the veneer. He's got Reuben's gift hidden up his jumper and won't part with it.

I leave that challenge to my mate. 'Go on, cheer him up, Squocks.'

'How?' he demands. 'Strangle the birthday boy, so we can all go home?'

Reuben is doing better with the presents. From Amanda, he receives a plastic golf set with little putters and three orange balls. The instructions are in Japanese, Finnish and English and say: *To enjoy the golfing, stand with your legs in different places.*

Golf and confined spaces do not mix. Whack! There goes another shinbone.

Squocka coaxes George into giving up his gift. It is a pair of green socks that glow in the dark. Giovanni has brought Reuben a board game in Italian.

'Aren't they marvellous gifts?' Mrs Partridge cries. 'Now,

let the fun begin! We'll play a game first then we'll eat.'

Amanda says she ate already and has been warned not to touch the sausage rolls. 'No, no, let's have games!'

Noble Squocka springs into action. 'Yes, let's have a game. Everyone get in a circle.'

A circle is difficult because it means two kids have to sit next to Leroy so Squocka makes Leroy sit between Amanda and Enzo with a gap between them and a promise from Leroy not to be obnoxious. So after ten minutes, we have a circle.

The game is one where you stick the outer part of a matchbox on the end of your nose, then pass it around the circle from nose to nose while music plays. When the tune stops, the one left with the matchbox is out. Last one without the matchbox is the winner and the prize is a sausage roll, which you don't stick on your nose.

I get to work the ancient cassette player, track three: *The Teddy Bears' Picnic*. The music plays and the matchbox goes from nose to nose. Leroy pokes Amanda in the eye with the matchbox and she belts him with the golf putter. George takes the opportunity to have a fight with Giovanni, while Chauncey goes to check out the toilet and see if the water is blue like at home.

We decide the game is over when the matchbox becomes sopping wet, and Squocka declares it a health hazard.

'Who won, who won?' They clamour for a prize.

'Everybody wins!' declares Mrs Partridge. 'Come and eat.'

'Ya-ay! T'riffic!'

Mrs Partridge gives each of the kids a small party hat, which is held in place with elastic. I become a little policeman and Squocka is a nurse with a red cross on his hat. We look ridiculous, especially Squocka.

See one birthday party table for six-year-olds, you've seen the lot. The trick is, no one ever eats a whole thing. They take a bite, leave the rest then start on something else. Take a swig of cordial, munch a few lollies, then look for something they haven't tried. There's not much conversation except about food. 'Mrs Partridge, how come I've got red cordial and Giovanni's got blue cordial?'

'Blue cordial makes your teeth yicky.'

'I don't like squishy cake. I hope it's a hard cake.'

'The jelly went up my nose.'

'Put some red cordial in with blue cordial and you get grey cordial.'

Mrs Partridge is coping well. She hasn't slumped once, but there are still two hours of party time to go. She announces that they'll have the birthday cake later when Mr Partridge gets home to share in the joy of it and make a video, which I bet they'll never look at again.

The party-goers all scamper away from the table, except for Leroy Merry who is looking a bit green. 'Do you want to go home, Leroy?' Mrs Partridge asks him.

'Me too?' Squocka's voice is hopeful.

Leroy stays at the table while Mrs Partridge offers us sandwiches, iced biscuits with hundreds and thousands on them, sausage rolls and Cheerios. We are saved from having to put the stuff in our mouths by a strange and wonderful event.

Plop! A sausage roll comes through the front-door letterbox and lands on the hall carpet. Mrs Partridge sees it and begins to slump.

'Oh, my, my,' I say in my party-spirit voice. 'Look what Postman Reuben has brought us. All the way from sausage-roll land.'

There is a little tee-hee of laughter from the other side of the front door and I wonder what else Postman Reuben has in his bag. 'Quick, Squocka!' I hiss. 'Nip round the back way and get him!'

Plop! A wriggling goldfish comes through the letter-box and lands on the carpet. Its goggle eye pleads with me to give it the kiss of life. It has hundreds and thousands stuck to it with a dollop of tomato sauce. 'Oh thanks, Wayne,' says the goldfish. 'In the nick of time.' (That bit's a lie.) I lob him into a tank, where instantly a Siamese fighting fish goes for him. Ooops! Wrong tank! I belt the Siamese fighting fish with a plastic deep-sea diver, then rescue the goldfish and put him into his own tank. I have to walk him around a bit until his little tail begins to waggle, but he'll live to tell his grandchildren how he was saved from a cruel fate.

By this time, Squocka has collared Postman Reuben. He opens the door and puts on his hearty voice. 'Look who's come to visit us. Ho, ho, ho. It's Postman Reuben, with a bag full of wonderful things, including a coat-hanger with a hook and backscratcher, three golf balls, luminous socks and other stuff.'

We usher the kids into the lounge and Squocka leaves the front door open, which turns out to be a big mistake.

We play other games, then Mrs Partridge goes to check on poor little not-feeling-too-well Leroy. She rushes back into the lounge room with a tragic look on her face. There's no way she can cope with this one! 'He's gone!' She has to lean against the doorpost to keep from slumping senseless to the floor. 'Leroy's gone!'

We rush to see for ourselves, noting the open front door as we go. It's not only Leroy who's gone; so has the birthday cake!

We do a check of the house and he's not in any of the rooms.

'He must have gone home,' Squocka says.

'That takes the cake,' I say, thinking to make light of it, but Mrs Partridge wilts and does a lulu of a slump because she has committed the kids' birthday party no-no. She has lost a guest. To make it to the big time in the kiddies' birthday party circuit, you've got to end up with the same number of guests you started with, preferably the same kids.

'Never mind,' I sound just like Mum. 'Squocka and I will look for him.'

'Oh, I must come too,' Mrs Partridge says. 'What will people say?'

The problem is, if we all go, who's going to mind the

kids in the house? The goldfish doesn't think it's a good idea to be left alone with Postman Reuben and he comes to the wall of his tank and goes gloop gloop and makes a praying gesture with his one remaining fin.

'Let's *all* go,' says Reuben and before we can stop them, the kids scamper for the exit. Reuben leads the way in his postman's outfit with the others strung behind. Squocka and I and Mrs Partridge race after them.

We find Leroy sitting in a bus shelter sharing bits of cake with big brother Kevin and a derelict who got thrown off a bus for making a political statement about homelessness. Luckily, Squocka and I get there first so we manage to rescue the cake and keep the others from taking their revenge on Leroy and Kevin, who claims he was only waiting for another bus when this kid turned up and force-fed him birthday cake.

'A likely story,' says Squocka.

Triumphantly, we march back to the house but get lots of funny looks from Violet Pridmore and Rosana Conti when they see us with little kids in their party gear. Not to mention our own funny hats which we forgot to take off. We'll never live it down.

Back at the house, we play another endless game while Leroy looks sick again. Mrs Partridge repairs the damage to the cake and calls us all to the table.

We try to light the six candles, but everybody blows them out as fast as we can get a match to them. With success at last they all sing a birthday song, which Reuben can't hear because he's got a peanut stuck in his ear. Mrs

Partridge runs with the tweezers. Reuben makes a wish, then wants to attack the candles with his golf putter. Mrs Partridge encourages him to *blow* them out, but he makes as much moisture as an amateur fireman bringing a burning warehouse under control.

'I won't have any cake,' Amanda says politely. Wise move! Squocka and I also decline.

Then, wonder of wonders, the mums and dads arrive and one by one, whisk their kids off to be sick in the loving comfort of their own homes.

Mr Partridge never actually made it to the party. He rang in to say something urgent just came up. I bet it was an afternoon movie he just had to see. Mrs Partridge gives us each a little parcel of leftovers, a few sausage rolls, some sandwiches and a slice of cake. Squocka gets the bit of cake with the licorice bootlace.

Mrs Partridge has hope in her eyes. 'Same time next year, boys?'

Squocka shakes his head. 'Sorry, Mrs Partridge. I'm going overseas,' he lies through his teeth. 'But Wayne'll turn up. Won't you, Wayne?'

I do a private slump.

Oh look, Wayne, isn't that Kevin Merry?

Where? Where?

Fooled you. It's only his little brother.
So come out from behind that wheelie bin.

Ha, ha. Not funny, Squocka. Anyway, who's scared of Kevin Merry?

Give me a minute and I'll think of somebody. But tell me, Wayne, does your dad still collect used toilets?

That's a sore point, Squocka. Very sore.

As well as the talk of the whole neighbourhood.
There was junk from one end of the street to the other.

It wasn't our junk, only some of it.

But what junk it was, Wayne. Historical junk. In more ways than one.

Then we both went leaping here and leaping there—

It wasn't the leaping that bothered me, Wayne. It was the landing.

After that, Squocka, we had a magic moment. But first, a Wayne's gotta do what a Wayne's gotta do.

10 A Wayne's Gotta Do What a Wayne's Gotta Do

'Yip-pee! Triffic! Wayne's the one!' a small boy from the junior school yells one bright morning as I walk through the gates. 'He'll do it!'

Do what? I am mystified at the fuss and smile on the small person. After all, I was his age myself once, but now I've graduated from Mr Dellafield and the primary grades. Little kids are still around because seniors and juniors attend the same school.

I move on to find Squocka checking out Violet Pridmore's homework without showing he hasn't done much himself. In fact, he hasn't done *anything*. His hungry eyes gobble up the information while his compliments make Violet blush. 'Yeah, Violet,' he says greasily. 'Question Five *was* difficult, but you spotted the trick straight off. Smart work.'

'Oh, do you think so, Squocka?' She's eating out of his hand.

'Yeah, bottler, Violet.' He copies her work as fast as his pencil can scribble. 'Is that a seven or a nine?'

I join them, but just then another group of small

boys from the Year 3 come past and give me four cheers. 'Wayne's the One!' they cry. It's like I'm standing for election or something, so I ask Squocka what gives with this sudden junior enthusiasm for me. He's still copying Violet's homework, but takes time off to say casually, 'They want you to sort out Kevin Merry.'

'Oh, is that all?' I remark. 'Sort out Kevin? Piece of cake.' On the outside I'm cool, but inside, it's a different story. My knees turn to jelly, angels blow trumpets and sing that well-known hymn, *RIP Wayne*. I shiver and shake, tremble and quake, get hot flushes and cold palpitations, but keep my cool exterior. After all, Violet Pridmore's watching. (In return I've been watching her, but that's another story.)

'Oh, you guys!' She tuts and stamps her sensible shoes. 'Always into violence!'

'Yep, a Wayne's gotta do what a Wayne's gotta do,' Squocka drawls, taking aim at a make-believe spittoon and going 'ding' with his mouth.

'Violet, it's nothing to do with me,' I protest.

Squocka ignores this. 'Thing is, Violet,' he goes on, 'the little guys are sick of aggression so they picked Wayne to stop it once and for all. Wayne's the One. Sort out Kevin Merry, end of story.' The way he puts it, it's beautifully simple.

'Oh really?' Violet gathers her books before Old Squocks can copy the last two answers. She huffs away with her nose in the air.

A small boy hears Squocka's bold words on my behalf

and goes screaming across the playground, 'Wayne declares war on Kevin Merry!'

Kevin's only about my height, but he has a terrible reputation, plus a gang of four hench-boys who all look mean at the same time, which makes a lot of mean. They've got tough nicknames and keep changing them so it always seems there's more of them. Last week they were Donny, Spoon, Strangles and Beat-up.

In his schoolwork, Kevin's a bit slapdash, more slap than dash. He gets everything wrong, can't spell and even makes blots with a pencil. He's not one of our home-room teacher, Ms Dinmore's, favourite scholars, so he makes up for it by bullying smaller people. That way he's good at something.

Kevin just goes up to a little kid and his gang gathers around and looks tough. The kid gives up his bus money or lets them have a free dip in his lunchbox. To make up the shortfall, some kids tell their mothers they've developed a huge appetite and ask for extra lunch. Kevin even puts in his order the day before. 'Make sure there's ham on my sandwiches tomorrow.'

'But, Kevin, my family's vegetarian.'

'So make it vegetarian ham.'

Some small boys wear nappies so Kevin will think they're too young for violence, but it makes no difference. Kevin's gang steals their safety pins! (That bit's a lie.)

Their favourite trick is to keep little kids out of the toilet block during recess time, so when they're back in class, boys ask to leave the room straight away. 'Why didn't you go when you were outside?' their teacher demands.

'Please miss, there was a horrible hairy monster in the toilet, with ten legs.'

'Oh, come on, I don't believe you.'

'It's true miss,' the little boys insist. 'We saw them.' (Kevin + four gang members = ten legs.)

As I wonder how to withdraw my declaration of war on Kevin, the man himself arrives with his gang. They have changed their names again and are Knuckles, Eyeball, Killer and Throttle. They look mean.

Before I can stop him, a small boy moves to a safe distance and shouts, 'Kevin Merry, you're for it! Wayne Wilson said he's gonna sort you out!'

There comes a thundering silence, except for the patter of the small boy's feet as he sprints away to disguise himself as a shrub. Kevin and his gang saunter over, chins first. Kevin plants himself in front of me, nodding his head and doing the sizing-up bit, although he knows how big I am. He speaks first. 'Wayne Wilson, eh?'

'Yeah, Kevin Merry.' I nod my head the way he does.

'Little Wayne-ee Wil-son.' He draws it out.

'Yeah, Little Kevvie Mer-ry.' I play for time and wonder how to keep the conversation going. Does he have a middle name? Can I bring his dog into it?

'You and me gotta get a couple of things straight.' Kevin pretends to chew gum.

'Such as?' I'm cool on the outside. Inside's another story, but you know that bit.

'Such as you saying you're going to sort me out.'

The little kids creep closer to watch and take notes. With such an audience, I can't pretend it's a misunderstanding. Nor can there be any peace offerings. Not this early in the war. Instead I say, 'You heard right,' and hope it sounds aggressive.

'Any sorting out's gonna be done by me,' Kevin goes on.

It's my turn in this conversation, but suddenly, my life is saved by a wonderful woman. It is Ms Cook, our drama teacher, who takes in the entire scene: aggressive Merry, peace-loving Wilson. She holds up one finger and in two words beckons Kevin Merry to join her. 'Merry! Here!' She points to a spot in front of her feet where she wants him to stand. I wish I could do that!

'Yes, Miss,' Kevin says.

'Merry,' Ms Cook begins. 'I hope I didn't hear what I think I heard you say.'

'No, Miss.' Kevin looks sheepish.

'Kevin would never say a thing like that, Miss.' Knuckles shakes his head.

'A thing like what?' Ms Cook snaps.

'A thing like what you thought you heard him say,' Killer offers.

'And what was that?'

'Dunno, Miss,' Killer goes on, 'but it's what he didn't say.'

This exchange takes time, then the bell rings. Saved! Ms Cook goes away. Kevin and I drift off in different directions, giving each other the special look that enemies keep for times like this. 'Oh, I was ready for him,' I whisper to Squocka.

'Yeah, next time, mate,' Squocka says. 'He'll keep.'

'We'll get him, Squocka, old buddy.'

'Correction. *You'll* get him, Wayne. Violet hates punch-ups.'

End of round one.

◆

Round two comes as I head home after school, using back streets, shortcuts and little-used byways. I turn a corner and there's Kevin and two of his gang. We exchange words, then promise to meet tomorrow afternoon behind the toilet block, a traditional battleground. Before going, we have a brief skirmish in which I break his HB pencil and Kevin tears the pocket off my school shirt, leaving a hole.

At home, I go in by the back door to avoid Mum, but mothers have a sixth sense where torn school clothes are concerned. She pounces. 'What's this? New shirt, only worn sixteen times and now look at it!' There's no point pretending it's normal wear and tear because Mum's on to that one. She demands to know how it happened.

I go 'um' and 'er', but have to come clean. 'We were fooling around,' I confess, 'and it got torn.'

'Who is "we"?'

When Mum hears the name Kevin Merry, she's all

for marching round and sorting him out there and then. End of Kevin, end of me! Having your mum fight your battles is the true road to being an instant outcast!

FLIGHT OF FANCY:

Boy 1: *Know what? Wayne Wilson's Mum went round and sorted out Kevin Merry, the Terrible, Ruthless Bully.*

Boy 2: *His mother? How could she? And how could Wayne let her? Beating bullies is men's work!*

Boy 1: *He's weak. That's what's wrong. Wilson is weak.*

Boy 2: *I hope poor Kevin gets over it soon.*

Boy 1: *Should we send flowers?*

Boy 2: *Some grapes would be nice.*

I assure Mum it was an accident, stressing words to sound more sincere. It was really *my fault*. Kevin only happened to be in the *same street* at the time. In fact, he was at *one end* and I was at the *other* and somehow my shirt got in between us and next thing you know, a hole appeared, just like that. *Kevin had nothing to do with it.* Mum backs off with her threats.

Phew! Narrow escape but Mum tells me to wear the offending shirt at dinner so that when Dad sees it he'll become rampageous. For me this spells Doomsville, but it's sausages for dinner so that's a good thing.

◆

At the dinner table Dad is all ho, ho and jolly and doesn't spot my torn shirt. It's Charlene who discovers my left nipple peeping out of a place where shirt should be. (I have got a few hairs near my nipple, so I am growing up.) 'Must Wayne come to the table half undressed?' she asks. 'It's offensive.'

'Haven't you seen a bloke's tit before?' Grandpa asks, but Charlene ignores him.

Dad demands, 'Wayne, who tore your shirt?'

Then my sad story comes out. How the little kids talked me into sorting out Kevin Merry who's a bit of a bully. Even Charlene turns sympathetic. 'Kevin's older brother, Arthur, is also a lout,' she tells us. 'He once turned up at pony club wearing a motor-cycle crash helmet. They wouldn't even let him *near* a horse dressed like that.'

'Arthur wasn't there for the horses.' I try to change the subject. 'He was only collecting dung – manure.'

'Not at the table!' Charlene informs me.

Somehow I convince my caring family that Kevin is my problem to sort out.

Dad relaxes and Mum promises not to go and see Mrs Merry, so we all get on with our dinner. Charlene doesn't complain when I slap the bottom of the tomato ketchup bottle and the sauce squirts on the tablecloth. I offer to lick it up and my sister says, 'Grow up, Wayne!'

※

That night, I lie awake on the back verandah wondering how to deal with Kevin Merry and his four thugs. In the next room, the television blares and I hear gunfire as people like Kevin Merry get what they deserve.

FLIGHT OF FICTIONAL FANCY:

'Blam! Blam! Come out with your hands up, Kevin Merry!'
(American cop show)

'Whoa there. I thought I fixed you once and for all, Kevin Merry. Looks like I'll jes' hev to do it all over agin.' (Western)

'Hullo, hullo, hullo, what's all this then? Why, it's Kevin Merry. Just come with me, my lad.' (British police drama)

'Ah, so, Merry San. Hi! Ha! Hup! Hee! Ho!' (Kung-fu movie)

'Nurse, this patient has the Kevin Merrys. We'll need to operate. Prepare him for surgery.' (Hospital drama)

'Well-known bully Kevin Merry finally met his match today when popular Wayne Wilson gave him what for.' (ABC late news)

It's easy on television. No one gets hurt. At the end of the show the actors go home in one piece. Finally I drop off to sleep and, in my dream, you-know-who is there again, wearing a Dracula outfit. He wants my blood.

❖

Next morning, Charlene is in a hurry but has time to give me a sisterly smile and hopes I'll be able to deal with my bully and keep all my teeth. Then she flies off to work on her broomstick. (Actually she rides a pushbike and I'm looking for a frog to put in her saddlebag.)

After Charlene's gone, I search through her wardrobe for an old headscarf. The plan is to put my arm in a sling. After all, who'd attack an injured man? Kevin Merry would, so I abandon that idea.

Dad has gone to work and Mum irons my second-best

shirt. She goes bang, bang, bang with the iron, making puffs of steam fly everywhere. It's her way of telling me I should do my own shirts because I am big enough now and have been able to look down on the ironing board for the last two and a half years.

She is not sympathetic about my fateful meeting with Kevin Merry, the Famous Bully. In fact, she says it would be a good idea if he gave me a good biff for her while he's at it. She even says she'll get on the phone and put him up to it. I think Mum is joking but I am not sure, so don't press my luck.

Grandpa is available for a bit of sympathy and advice. He's also trying to pick winners on the horses. He has been trying to do it for the whole of his life and some instinct tells him the next bet will land the big one and we'll all be on Easy Street. 'Today's the day, Wayne boy,' he says.

'Yes, Grandpa.'

'Ten minutes past three, and it'll all be over.'

'Yeah, Grandpa,' I say. 'That's when I'm meeting him.'

'Oh, you mean the bully fella,' he says. 'I was talking about the three o'clock race at Eagle Farm. Got a little certainty running.' Typical. He's forgotten already. Grandpa rustles around in his Multi-Bran then pours on some milk. 'What I always say about bullies is— ' He sneezes, then gets up and wanders around looking for a tissue. I wait for his words of advice but when he gets back to the table, he can't remember what he started to say. In our house, a conversation sometimes takes a whole week. I remind him he was in the middle of saying something. 'Bullies are cowards,' he picks up where he left off. 'They only take on people who are weaker than they are.'

'That's true, Grandpa. Like me for example.'

'Rubbish! You're as big as he is. Give him a taste of his own medicine and he'll soon stop his nonsense.'

'Yes, Grandpa.'

'And another thing, Wayne,' he adds. 'When you finally sort out a bully – always leave him with his self-respect.'

'You mean don't flatten him completely, Grandpa?'

'You got the idea, lad. Use enough pressure to do the job, no more, no less.'

Easy to say, hard to pull off. I sit poking at my Corn Flakes, wondering what to do. Grandpa reminds me it's time I went to school, then he spots another sure thing in the paper and wanders off.

❦

With feet of lead I walk to school, composing a sad and lovely poem.

Lines written before a battle

Oh, bury me deep in the schoolyard,
Beneath my favourite tree.
Upon the trunk just carve these words:
'He met the school bull-ee.'

Not bad for a young man about to face an uncertain future. I will dedicate it to Violet Pridmore and make Squocka furious.

At school and before things start, there's no sign of Kevin Merry and his gang. Squocka arrives, then comes Violet Pridmore and he pounces. 'Carry your homework book, Violet?' He never misses a chance, even at times like this. One day the penny will drop with Violet: Squocka only likes her for the homework. And while he's so engrossed, he doesn't spare a thought for me, or my looming battle.

◆

Somehow I get through the day, then it is afternoon. Three o'clock and all roads lead to the rear of the toilet block. About three hundred small boys gather there in festive mood. It's like it's a holiday, but there's still no sign of Kevin and his reinforcements. The small boys grow restive as they wait for The Fight.

'Wayne's the One!' a boy chants and others take it up. I smile a sad smile – and then – Oooh! Put ominous music on your CD player, for it is Kevin and his back-up. They come jaws-jutted round the corner of the toilet block, looking for me.

It would be nice if, by some miracle, Ms Cook came on the scene, but I can't think of a reason why she'd want to come behind the toilet block.

'Let's get this show started,' Kevin shouts.

Then a miracle *does* happen. The small boys crowd

around to carry me forward until suddenly, there we are, face to face, me and Kevin, plus all the little guys. There's no escape.

'You're going to get it, Kevin Bottom-Face!' A small boy has suddenly discovered bravery. 'Wayne's going to crunch you like a Rice Flake! Chomp, chomp!'

I tell the little boy not to be so definite about it as Kev and me still might work something out. But the other junior kids become bold and start making terrible threats about the things I'm going to do. 'You're going to get what's coming to you,' another kid says to Kevin's knee-cap. He's a *very* small boy but he talks big. 'You dirty nappy!'

Kevin's gang becomes uneasy with all the small boys milling around. First rule of bullies everywhere: Bullying is fun when it's three against one.

Knuckles gets the message and prepares to leave the scene of battle. 'See ya, Kev,' he lies. 'Gotta go. I promised Mum no fighting. Bruises are bad for me complexion.'

'Yeah, sorry I can't stay and help, Kev.' Throttle pretends he's got a sore leg and limps off into the crowd. Suddenly, all four of his gang have gone and it's just Kevin left to face me, well *us*, if you count a hundred little guys.

'Look, Kev,' I begin.

'Yes, Wayne?' He's polite and attentive.

'The little guys don't like being pushed around.'

'That's telling him, Wayne,' says a small boy with white surgical tape over one lens of his glasses. 'Saves me sorting him out myself!'

'Well, why didn't they speak up, Wayne?' Kevin asks.

Seeing he's about to crumble I become bold. But not too bold. Grandpa's words come back to me: *Use enough pressure to do the job, no more, no less. Leave him with his self-respect.*

'Okay,' I say, 'let's call it quits, then. So that's the end of it, eh, Kevin?'

'Yeah, fair enough, Wayne.' He seems relieved.

We shake hands, then go our different ways and the little kids stream home, cheering and laughing.

Kevin comes to school a bully and goes home nice. Not a bad day's work, a piece of cake in fact. One day, the junior kids will realise they had the numbers all the time, so it was their own doing. But until that day comes, I'll enjoy their cheers.

Next day at school, Violet smiles at me, but Squocka's too busy copying her homework to say anything.

The gang go back to their old names: Patrick, Habib, Trevor and Mario. Kevin stops bullying, but claims it's only to see how he likes it. If being a bully is really his thing, then he'll go back to it. 'Yeah, sure, sure, Kevin,' we all say. He begins to do better with his schoolwork and even beats me for forty-ninth place in the October Spelling Contest, which is taking niceness too far.

11 JUNK

t's Friday night and Aunt Wilma is round at our place complaining to Mum about Uncle Robert. 'Heather, he's so short-sighted,' says Aunt Wilma. 'He'll smash the car one day. He ran into a supermarket trolley in the carpark. This woman was unloading things into her boot, then wham! She turns around to see her groceries all over the bitumen. Robert gets home with a frozen chook stuck on the front bumper bar.'

Mum makes sympathetic noises. 'It's time he gave up his licence, Wilma,' she says. 'He's a danger to himself.'

Uncle Robert is Dad's brother. He calls me Maxwell, so that proves he's short-sighted. I don't look a bit like Maxwell. Come to that, I don't even know who Maxwell is.

Suddenly, we hear the sound of my un-short-sighted dad arriving home in the Toyota. 'Dad's home,' I announce, just like I did when I was little. In those far-off days, Dad would bring a chocolate for us kids and something for Mum. Once he brought us ice creams but they melted before he got home. 'Never mind,' Mum said, 'it's the thought that counts.' Charlene and I went to bed and cried ourselves to sleep.

Even now, on Friday nights I look forward to the sound of my homecoming Dad. Mum also cocks an ear to the back yard. She's listening too, but for another sound. Bloonk! That's the one.

Mum purses her lips and snorts, 'Not another stupid toilet!'

''Fraid so,' I say and wander out to help unload the Toyota.

As I've said before, Dad likes flush toilets and thinks they're the invention of the century. He knows all about the inventor – a man named Thomas Crapper. 'What a benefit Crapper brought to plumbers and the human race,' Dad says. 'His name ought to be a household word.' Whenever Dad installs a new toilet, he checks out the old one to see if it's a special rarity, like from the turn of the century or one that came to Australia with the Seventeenth Fleet or something. When he brings one home he expects me to admire it. 'Look at that, Wayne,' he says proudly. 'You're looking at a genuine Scottish "Willie Waterfall", with original kilt adjuster and sporran hook.' Dad walks around to view it from another angle. 'And a wee stand for your cup of tea and digestive biscuit.'

I pretend to be impressed, but to tell the truth, I've run out of surprised-sounding words to describe Dad's toilets. Together, we go 'oomph' and 'hup' and 'steady' and make worker-like noises as we manhandle the Willie Waterfall off the truck. 'Thank goodness it's not the reclining model,' Dad says conversationally. 'They're *really* heavy.' We wrestle it round the back of the workshop and find a place for it with all the others – the Potter Stand-easy, the Barker Aim-well and the Lucknow Commemorative.

'Dad,' I ask, 'why do you collect toilets and not postage stamps or beercans?'

'Well, Wayne,' he says, father-to-son. 'One day some-one's gonna start a National Museum of Toilets. When that time comes, I'll donate my entire collection plus my vanity basins, bidets, ballcocks, grommets, my adjustable wrench, the lot.'

It was a relief. For a while I thought he was planning to bequeath them to me.

We go inside to wash up and Mum gives Dad a look with her nose on one side of her face.

'Another used toilet?' Aunt Wilma whispers. Mum nods grimly.

'It's a beauty,' Dad says.

❖

Saturday morning, bright and early, I work outside in the fresh air, wind and rain. There's a rule in our house that says 'No work – no pocket money.' So I tidy the front garden, pulling weeds and gathering rubbish. I find a bit of paper lying in the long grass under our mailbox. It says:

COUNCIL RUBBISH COLLECTION
Leave your unwanted rubbish
in front of your property for free collection.
Old bikes, used tyres, packing cases
and similar rubbish will be removed.

I show the paper to Mum. Her eyes light up and little snorts of steam come out of her nostrils. 'This is my chance!' Mum hides the paper. 'Don't breathe a word about this, Wayne!'

'Oh, all right, Mum.' I speak in the whiney voice I use to get out of performing strenuous effort and work. I collect my pocket money, clean up and go in search of Squocka to tell him I am free. 'I'm free! Free!' I sing as I walk along. 'Free as a bird!'

An old lady looks at me as I go past her front gate. She thinks I'm an escaped convict, so takes in her washing and the milk bottles. (That bit's a lie.)

I wander off and do something else which I cannot now remember, which is the nature of boyhood: here one day, gone the next, unless you write it down, which I didn't because I did not have a pencil with me at the time. Or paper.

Starvation drives me home where I find my mother has something on her mind. She consults the calendar and marks crosses on it and counts on her fingers. A plan is hatching. So far, I'm not involved. When I ask Mum what's what, she just says 'Che sera sera' in French and acts mysterious.

❀

Later, Mum, Grandpa, Charlene and me are having dinner when Dad comes home and announces there's going to be an interstate plumbers' convention. He's got the latest edition of *The Gurgler*, the plumbers' journal with the details in it. It's to be a whole week of copper pipes, electric eels, shower fittings and plungers, plus all the latest hints and tips about free-flow treble-flush cisterns connected to double bypass back-flip relief valves with enzymes and multi-vitamins.

Dad is full of it and at mealtimes from then on, he keeps telling us what's in store for the lucky plumber who can find the money for a whole week of it plus airfare. Then he becomes sad. 'Don't suppose I can afford it, though,' he says, looking at Mum, who is the one who knows whether he can or not.

'I don't know, Bill,' Mum says. 'It would do you good to get away. You'd learn new things to do with your blowlamp and you'd soon make up the cost of it.'

'Yes, Daddy,' Charlene says. 'I'd love you to go to a convention. Then I can tell everyone at school.'

'Look, Bill, why *don't* you go?' Mum smiles. 'You need a break to take your mind off things.'

'Things like toilets,' I say and Mum, with that smile still upon her lips, reaches me under the table with a well-aimed foot. I will have trouble walking in future, not to mention trusting my mother.

'Go on, son,' Grandpa covers the moment. 'Take the plunge, lad!'

Dad's mind is made up. 'Okay, I'll go, but I won't take my plunger.'

❖

In the days that follow, Mum gets him ready for the big trip, and since there's to be a posh dinner at the convention, she rings Aunt Wilma to see if we can borrow Uncle Robert's evening suit. Uncle Robert brings it around in the car, only he runs into the driveway of the house next door and gives our neighbour a kiss on both cheeks and a gent's suit smelling of mothballs.

After Uncle Robert's gone, Mum soothes our traumatised neighbour, takes the suit and sponges the gravy off it from the last time it had an outing. Mum reminds me that I must not mention toilet collection and council clean-up campaign while I am under her roof or even in the garden. In fact, in my father's presence I am to remain silent. To drive the message home, Mum adds, with a tight-lipped blackmailing smile, 'You want to see your next six months' pocket money, don't you?'

'You mean all of it? Now?'

'No – over the next six months!'

I agree to co-operate.

Dad tells us there's a Plumbers' Convention Song they sing at the opening ceremony. We keep nagging him and coaxing him until he shows us the words and music in *The Gurgler*. Grandpa goes to the piano and we gather round and sing the song to give Dad a bit of practice.

A bold young plumber lay dying
Upon his sad death-bed he lay,
He propped himself up on one elbow
And these are the words he did say:

'Oh don't you lads ever forget me,
Remember bold Danny McGrew.
I'm the one they called out to a job –
a job that no one would do.

It happened one fine Easter Sunday,
They were going to pay double time
The job was only a leaky old pipe
And that sort of work suits me fine.

I got out my tea-can and blowlamp
And opened my lunchbox with care.
I struck my last match that Sunday
The result is I lost all my hair.

That pipe it was flowing with petrol
A fact I'd neglected to view.
Pay heed to the dangers around you
Or end up like Daniel McGrew.'

It is a jolly evening.

◆

The big day arrives. A taxi comes and Dad gets in, then tries to play with the radio but the driver smacks his hand.

'Bye, bye.' Mum waves and blows kisses. As soon as the taxi is round the corner, Mum turns to me. 'Right, Wayne. Your father's toilets! Hop to it!'

'Oh Mum!' I protest. 'Dad's proud of his collection and says he's sending it to the Frankfurt Toilet Fair. And

Bologna.' I add the Bologna bit to impress Mum but she's not having any of it.

'I want them all outside on the footpath for the Council to collect.' She uses her hard-as-iron voice. I grumble and mumble but it doesn't do any good. I can't stand the sight of a woman carrying a toilet so I have to do it and Grandpa helps. Traitor! You'd think he'd be more loyal, but he knows which side his crusts are spread with margarine.

As we work, neighbours pass and ask what we're doing. I resist being smart and just tell them it's a Council clean-up and show them the notice. 'Good-oh,' they say and before long, piles of rubbish begin to appear up and down the street. None like ours, though. What with all the white and multi-hued porcelain gleaming in the morning sun, it looks like a miniature Taj Mahal out front, only made of toilets.

Mum is very embarrassed about it so we get some old timber and canvas and try to make them look decent, but people can still recognise by looking at them that they're toilets. Some people are sharp that way.

Grandpa suggests we gift-wrap them in brown paper and string but Mum says the paper would get wet if it rained. So Grandpa sighs and shuffles off again. 'Nobody ever takes my advice,' he says. 'I've got a great wealth of experience but does anybody listen? I entertained troops in Italy and Korea.'

Mum gets him to peel the potatoes and he feels useful again.

By moving things around and taking up more space, I make a small cave of all the toilets. Squocka comes along and names it Dunny Grotto, and so ends day one of my father's absence.

◆

Day two, I'm pulling weeds by the front gate and Squocka is sitting inside Dunny Grotto having a think about things when along comes Rosana Conti. Squocka decides on a bit of a lark. 'Helloooo, Rosana Conti,' he says through one of the toilets so that his voice sounds deep, hollow and eerie.

Rosana stops dead and looks at the toilet. 'Hello. Is anyone in there?'

'Yes, my name is Potty William,' says Squocka. 'I am the Spirit of the Toilet.'

'Oh, fancy,' says Rosana who is something of a romantic. 'What do you do, o spirit?'

'I tell your fortune for a small coin,' Squocka responds.

'Here you go then.' Rosana drops five cents down the S bend.

A second later, the coin comes hurtling up again. 'Not that small,' says Potty William, so Rosana drops ten cents down instead. 'For ten cents I will give you one of my cheapie forecasts,' says Potty William. 'What is your star sign?'

'I'm a Virgo,' says Rosana, as if it's something to be proud of.

Squocka's got last week's Sunday paper with him, so

he turns to the horoscope pages. 'Wait, my little Virgo, while Potty William looks inside the Deep Puddle of Knowledge,' he intones. Squocka finds the page in the paper and reads Rosana's horoscope. 'You will have a tedious week, little one. You will know frustration and monotony but do not let it get you down. Avoid arguments, especially with members of the opposite sex, i.e. Boys. Lucky numbers two and seven.'

'Hang on,' says Rosana. 'That's *last* week's horoscope!' She spots a familiar leg sticking out of Dunny Grotto, then grabs hold of it and drags Squocka out and beats him about the ears with one of those floating ball things you get inside toilet cisterns. 'I knew it was you all the time!' she snaps.

'Then why did you give me ten cents?' Squocka asks.

'I was just leading you on, Squocka Berrington!' she says in a voice dripping with Virgoan scorn. 'Wait till I tell the girls how you pass the time, *Potty William!*' He'll never live it down!

Rosana goes off in the huff and I keep on with my weeding. I pulled the same weed twenty-five times that afternoon.

The days pass and Mum becomes anxious. Reason: Dad is due home and the Council has not taken our junk away.

◆

Da-da-da-dum! Ominous music. We have not had a family row recently and this looks like being a biggie!

I piece things together later, but as the story goes, comes a taxi, bearing my father, fresh from his interstate convention. It's night time and dark and, as the Spaniards say, Dad's a bit *El Squiffo*. As he pays the fare, he suddenly spots porcelain gleaming whitely in the pale moonlight. 'Hang on a minute,' he says to the driver. 'Put your lights on high-beam, mate.' Suddenly there is Dunny Grotto in all its shimmering magnificence. Dad recognises some famous toilet models. 'Stone me,' he says. 'This is a Californian Thunderer. And if I'm not mistaken, that's a Willie Waterfall.' Dad staggers back to the taxi driver and says, 'I've got a benefactor. Somebody has bequeathed to me a whole collection of sanitary history. If I give you another five bucks, will you help me round the back with them?'

'You gotta be kidding, mate.' The driver shuts his door and departs.

Dad spends several more minutes out front admiring and mentally cataloguing these new additions to his collection, then he rolls into bed a happy man.

❧

In the morning it's a different story. Dad storms back inside and demands to know what these rare items from The Wilson Collection of Antique Sanitary Ware are doing on the footpath.

Mum explains that they are vermin-infested rubbish, awaiting collection by the Council to which we pay rates for just such a purpose. At times my mother can be very grammatical.

Is that so, says my male parent, and my mother confirms that it is indeed so. I am all agog. I have not been that much agog for a long time.

Mum says she has had enough clutter in her life. She recalls some other incidents in her action-packed marriage that she allowed pass at the time, but the hurt still runs deep. She remembers a birthday when she received a new motor-bike tyre as a present, her husband claiming it was for the back wheel, therefore for her own safety and comfort as well as being for the part of the bike upon which she sat. My mother is adamant she is not going to lose this latest struggle – it is the toilets or the marriage. Take your pick, William.

Dad says he'll think about it.

The toilets stay out front, so it is round one to Mum.

Dad is very grumpy and frowns a lot and then comes the incident of the thief in the night. Da-da-da-dum! More dramatic music.

I've gone beddy-byes when I hear a noise at the front of the house. 'Bloonk', it goes. A familiar sound. Old keen-ears Wayne knows what that means. A pilferer is at the toilets. I sneak out in the cold night air and see a dim figure trying to pull the Barker Aimwell out from the bottom of the pile. 'Stop, thief!' I yell, and the dark figure makes off toilet-less. Dad comes grumping out in his dressing gown and I tell him what I did, brave little lad that I am.

Mum is unimpressed. 'Wayne,' she says in a voice reserved for addressing simpletons. 'As far as I'm concerned, he can take the lot! That is what they are doing out there.' She wraps her dressing gown around herself, then steps into the street and bellows after the fleeing villain. 'Come back! Bring your thieving mates and steal the entire collection!'

Dad is embarrassed and drags Mum back inside but by this time, Grandpa is awake and Mum leaves Dad to explain things to him and goes to bed. I sneak off to the back verandah and more beddy-byes as Dad puts on a pan of milk for Grandpa's cocoa.

●

Days pass and the toilets remain. The weeds come up so I have to trim round a dozen S bends. Dad says I need to be careful and not do any damage.

Squocka comes with his guitar so we sit inside Dunny Grotto and compose a song. We sing like we're a couple of laid-back hippies from a commune:

Me: *Now ah got a worry an' ah got a care*
and that's no good unless you share
so gather round and listen to ma song.
Squocka: *Yeah man. Listen to Wayne's song.*
Comes straight from the heart, man.
Me: *I ain't a whinger and I don't whine*
but it's all about some trouble o' mine –
The Council Rubbish Man sure done me wrong!
Squocka: *Yeah man. Done him dead wrong.*
Me: *Oh the Council never took ma junk away.*
Squocka: *No sir, not them.*

Me: *Ah put it out the front one day,*
on the grassy bit like the notice say.
But the Council never took ma junk away.
Squocka: *No sir. Not them. That Council never took*
his junk away.
Me: *Why the Council never drag ma junk away?*
After all the lousy rates we pay?
Ma Maw complains, an' ma sister too
But the Council never cart ma junk away.
Squocka: *No sir. Not them. Stiff cheese there, boy.*
That old Council Man, he sure giving you
the big ignore and that's for sure.
Me: *It stand in the boilin' sun all day.*
The grass grows tall and the weeds all sway,
But the Council never take ma junk away.
Squocka: *Come on, Council, come and give*
them flamin' weeds a spray.
Me: *It starts to smell but I know dam well,*
Ah never put no dead thing in that junk.
So Council Man, can't you hear ma plea –
Squocka: *Very sad, man. Sure rends ma heart!*
Me: *So come and drag ma flamin' junk away.*
Squocka: *Yeah man!*

It doesn't do any good. The junk stays. Mum becomes rampageous because some neighbours are getting sniffy about us having toilets and them only having decent things like bald tyres, old washing machines and cricket pads and stuff. Our junk is not as good as their junk.

To make things worse, Grandpa starts going on nocturnal fossicking raids, coming back with other people's junk. He has a baseball catcher's mitt and in his words, a cage for a parrot with no bottom. I don't get involved in that one.

Mum marches off to the Council, where the man takes a look at the clean-up notice and laughs drainfully. 'That's an old one,' he says. 'Must have been there since last clean-up. There won't be another collection for seven long months.' He enjoys the little exchange of fire. Mum retires to lick her wounds.

As she reaches home, who should come hurtling around the bend in his car but Uncle Robert. He has come to collect his dinner suit because the Bowls Club is giving him a send-off. They asked him to leave because he was bowling east to west when everyone else was doing it north to south. He also caught a lady bowler a painful one in the knee with the little white ball when he lobbed it down.

He mistakes Dunny Grotto for the entrance to our driveway and screams straight in. Bang, crash, wallop and kadankie. Tinkle, Tinkle. Porcelain everywhere! 'Oh no,' says Uncle Robert as he surveys the car and the damage. 'Bill's toilets. How will I ever pay for the ruination of them?'

Mum takes him aside kindly and tells him to give up his licence, or get new specs and everything will be all right. (One round to Aunt Wilma.)

Mum organises shovels for the men in her life and we

heap the shattered remains of the Lucknow Commemorative and the Chesterfield reclining model on the back
of Dad's Toyota, then with a sad face he drives off to
the dump. His dream is like his toilets – in a million little
pieces.

Mum doesn't tell the neighbours about my mistake
with the clean-up notice. 'I'll give them till the end of the
week,' she says, 'then complain about their junk lowering
the tone of the street.'

12 Look Before You Leap

t's Saturday, so I leap out of bed, then in five seconds, I've washed, combed and brushed – all the Mum-pleasing things. I don my debonair T-shirt, jeans and matching sneakers and a horrible thought hits me, like when you step on the head of a rake and the handle flies up and whacks you between the eyes. I have no money.

How can this be? Answer: I spent it all. Receive it Thursday, gone by Friday. Too much week left at the end of my money.

I politely and respectfully enter the kitchen where Mum enjoys toast and jam. Charlene reads a glossy magazine, as she nibbles some hydroponic girly cereal off the tip of her spoon. I say, 'Good morning, Mother, and Charlene.'

Charlene grunts but Mum answers, 'Good morning, Wayne. Better hurry. Don't want to be late for school.'

My eyes go pop. Have I made a mistake? But it's Mum's idea of a joke, so I bung on a hearty guffaw that puts her in a jolly mood. Not exactly an opening-the-purse-strings one, but cheerful enough. When it comes to moods, I don't want *good*; I'm aiming for *generous*.

I show a sad face and go, 'Mum, there's a hole in my jeans and I lost all my money out of it.'

'That's a shame,' Mum responds. 'They're your expensive new ones too.'

Bad sign. Mum thinks it's a shame about the pricey jeans, not my fictitious loss of money. Time to move on. 'What I was wondering was— '

'Not a cent till Thursday.'

'A loan?'

'You couldn't afford the interest.' Mum takes a sip of tea, then adds, 'You could always *earn* some money.'

Earn? That's like work? I protest. 'Mum, I've got plans.'

'You could help your Auntie Edna at the fete this afternoon. You might score a bit that way. Mind you, it's a *charity* fete so why you should *expect* payment— '

But I've already switched off and turn to see what's for eating this fine morning. Saturday is no-porridge day, which makes it all the finer. Porridge is compulsory for growing lads. Gobble, gobble, munch, munch, there goes the tablecloth plus Charlene's bowl of girly cereal and eating tools. Charlene says, 'Do you mind? I was using that spoon. Not touching it now.' (That bit's a lie.)

As I prepare to leave the house, Mum forestalls me. 'Give your mother a kiss, and the saying of the day is: "Look before you leap".'

Mum's got a desk calendar with a different motto for each new day. Yesterday's was, "Many a Mickle Maks a Muckle". No one in the family understood it.

'I'm not leaping anywhere,' I respond to this new saying. So we settle for a kiss, then I'm off into the wide blue yonder, a smile on my face and nothing in my pocket except a fabricated hole. Squocka will have money, so I turn my feet in his direction.

Coming along the street is Violet Pridmore, who trundles a squeaky old English-style pram with big wheels. Violet is accompanied by her friend Rosana Conti and both wear a girls' club uniform with hundreds of badges embroidered on each sleeve, yet with all that weight their arms do not droop. When the girls draw near I see the pram is full of old clothes. Violet greets me warmly and Rosana joins in. 'Wayne,' they say together.

'Just the man,' Violet adds. I like this. It must be my debonair charm.

'We're taking these old clothes to the fete,' Rosana explains.

'To earn our good-deed badges,' Violet adds, 'and what we were wondering, Wayne, was— '

My eyes narrow. I have heard that expression before. But I listen to what the girls were wondering. They only want me to push the squeaky-wheeled pram, which is a bad look. Being seen out and about with Violet and Rosana is okay. Being out with Violet and Rosana in their girls' club uniforms with sleeve badges is borderline okay. Throw in a squeaky-wheeled pram and it's a definite no-no. 'I'd do it in a flash,' I assure them, 'but I've got urgent plans.'

They go, 'Aw' and 'Oh, well,' then they squeak-squeak away with their pram. If I were in a boys' club I'd get my liar's badge for sure. Also one for avoiding work and another for being a late riser on school days. Much relieved, I go to Squocka's place.

I get there just in time to see him hurtling out the front door showing the fearful whites of his eyes. His mother's voice sails after him, 'You're nothing but a scrounger!'

'Whew,' Squocka says. 'Escapes don't come any narrower than that one.'

There is no need to ask. I recognise the signs of acute boyhood poverty. So what we need is a plan. 'Any money-making ideas?' I inquire.

'We find lost golf balls,' Squocka answers. 'Sell them, fifty cents each.' It's the idea of the century, out in the open air, fossick, stoop, lift, sell and we're in the money.

Experience has taught us the place to find lost golf balls is the golf course. I once tried looking in the school library and found not a single one. In fact, I got banned for a month for being smart.

FLIGHT OF UNABRIDGED FANCY:

Librarian: *What are you doing, Wayne Wilson?*

Me: *Looking for lost golf balls.*

Librarian: *Are you trying to be funny?*

Me: *Not at the same time.*

Librarian: *There are no golf balls in here. Kindly leave.*

Me: *Can I change my library book?*

Librarian: *You just took it out. What do you want to change it for?*

Me: *A golf ball.*

I was lucky to escape with only a date stamp on the end of my nose. It said 15 Jul. Another date to remember.

✦

We arrive at the golf course and scale a low wall, then begin our search. Minutes pass and there isn't a single ball to be seen. Reason? Kevin Merry's got there first and has a bag of balls. 'Wanna buy one? Sixty cents each or two for a dollar forty.'

'The going rate's fifty,' Squocka tells him. There is no deal. Kevin slopes off to find a golfer who's not good at mental arithmetic.

If Kevin has cleaned out the obvious places, it means we'll have to venture right into the golf course. So, trudge, trudge, we go across the fairways. Squocka complains it's a waste of time and he's growing hungry. We climb a small hill and there before us is a feast of golf balls. And they are all lost.

'Excuse me, golf balls,' I call. 'Are you lost?'

'Yes, Wayne,' they chorus ventriloquially. 'We are very lost, and a nasty man hit us with a stick.' There you are. That's evidence for you.

The rule amongst lost-ball-gatherers is to count ten before you pick one up. That gives an owner time to get to where his ball came to rest. So I chant one-two-five-nine-ten, then start to gather the balls. Squocka joins in with a will. There are dozens of them – green ones, yellow ones, blue ones and orange ones as well as the traditional white. We begin stuffing them in our pockets and before long, we look like winter squirrels who've had a good morning at the nut-gathering.

It's not pockets we need, it's a wheelbarrow. We stuff them down the neck of our T-shirts. At fifty cents apiece, we could be millionaires by lunchtime. As we collect the last ball, another one sails over the hill and lands with a plop at Squocka's feet. 'Thank you,' he says and adds it to the spherical bundle inside his shirt.

At last, and looking distinctly bulgy, we waddle off to find a cashed-up golfer. 'Remember, we don't take cheques,' I remind Squocka. It's nice to be rich. Potentially.

Suddenly, there comes a roar. No, make that a bellow! 'Hoi!' it says.

At the top of the hill are three electric golf carts silhouetted against the sky. They start rolling in our direction. A trio of red-faced retired colonels have us in their sights! 'That man there!' one of them uses a commanding-officer voice. 'Stand where you are!'

The three retired colonels gain speed as they charge downhill. 'Put down our property, you rogues!'

They split up and come at us from different directions. To them it's a military operation. To us it's scary. We run, but that makes the colonels more livid. 'Stop, thief!' one bawls, then all three put their feet down. The golf carts make angry hornet whines. Trouble is, we can't run very fast with our pockets and T-shirts full of golf balls.

When you read this bit, put some fast diddley-dum music on your CD player, because that's what it's like: converging colonels and fat Wayne and Squocka waddling away as fast as we can go.

We began discarding golf balls, which lets us run faster but leaves a trail for the colonels to follow. Their carts scream around bunkers, charge down hills, skirt greens and bounce over hillocks, but all the time they're getting closer.

One of the colonels throws a golf club at us, so we dodge and run and chuck out handfuls of balls. What with running, dodging and discarding, we begin to weaken. Voom! A three-iron misses me by a centimetre. 'They're within range!' one of the colonels yells. 'Fire!' Ping! A tee ricochets off Squocka's head. Thank goodness it wasn't a nine-iron!

Ahead of us is a clump of undergrowth and a small creek. Around here the ground is muddy so the golf carts can't follow. We are safe and ford the creek without taking our sneakers off, then leap over a stone wall and make soft, slow-motion landings. Very soft. Right in a heap of bio-degradable material that cows leave behind. Yecchh!

Two narrow escapes in one morning. Only this one's narrow and *smelly*.

We're covered in the organic stuff, but there is no sign of the colonels. In the distance we hear them retrieving their golf balls. They huffle and gruffle about court-martials and field punishment being too good for us.

FLIGHT OF FANCY:
Corporal Berrington and Private Wilson face their military accusers.
Colonel 1: *How do you plead?*
Me: *Guilty. And may I say –*
Colonel 2: *No, you may not.*
Squocka: *Can I escape with a small fine? And time to pay?*
Colonel 3: *No, you are both hereby sentenced to a painful twanging.*
Colonel 1: *Sergeant-major! Bring forth the heavy-duty elastic twanger.*

With the coast clear, we stand up and let gooey stuff drop off in gollops. It makes a filthy squelching noise. At the small creek we say, 'Excuse us, fish,' then rip off shirts, jeans, sneakers and socks and let the flowing water do its cleansing work. The fish hate us and make rude remarks about our underwear. (That bit's a lie.)

We spread our clothes to dry on some convenient branches. 'I've had better mornings,' Squocka observes.

'Come on, Squocks. Look on the bright side.'

'There isn't one,' he responds. Then we hear it: squeak-squeakity-squeak-squeakity-squeak. It's Violet and Rosana's pram. I'd know that squeak anywhere. We can't be seen like this, so we duck out of sight. The squeak-squeakity stops and we hear girlish voices exclaiming and wondering. Then the squeak-squeakity goes on and disappears. 'Third narrow escape,' Squocka says. 'I'm not ready to be seen in my underpants.'

Violet, Rosana and the pram have gone. So have our clothes, but not our footwear. 'That's a plus,' I tell Squocka. 'We got our Z-fronts and sneakers. Could be worse.'

Then two things happen. On the deserted road beside the golf course I spy a yellow charity bin. The second thing is that a van draws up. The driver has come to empty the bin. I do some thinking. Charity bins contain clothes. We need charity. Squocka and I draw lots to see who goes to find out what's what. Squocka loses. He disappears and in three minutes he's back. 'The guy wasn't there, so I helped myself. There's big pile of stuff next to the bin.'

'I hope you left him a note, Squocka.'

'Of course,' he assures me. 'I always carry writing gear in my underpants.'

I check to see what he's got for me. It's a T-shirt with *Girls, your luck's in* on the front and a kilt. The alternative's a pink eiderdown. 'A kilt, eh? A Scottish frock?'

'Says on the label it's Robertson tartan,' Squocka tells me.

'Well, that's all right, then. You can go anywhere in Robertson tartan.' Squocka's got baggy shorts and a football jumper. At least he looks human. We don our charity clothes then set out for home. Squocka marches ahead of me making bagpipe noises.

Then comes a sound of a different kind. 'Coo-ee! Wayne!' says this female voice.

There is only one person in the entire world who says,

'Coo-ee, Wayne.' It's my Auntie Edna, Dad's other brother's wife. There's no escaping Auntie Edna, for once she has you in her sights, she'll keep calling, 'Coo-ee, Wayne' until you turn around and say, 'Hullo, Auntie Edna,' or something civil. Then she's quite nice. On one occasion I ignored Auntie Edna for thirty-seven hours and all that time she kept calling, 'Coo-ee, Wayne'.

I wrote to *The Guinness Book of Records* to claim a world first for ignoring an auntie but they weren't interested. They'd just received a claim from a woman who called out, 'Coo-ee, Wayne,' non-stop for thirty-seven hours, which was the sort of feat they were looking for. (That last bit's a lie, but Auntie Edna does call out, 'Coo-ee, Wayne.')

'Hullo, Auntie Edna,' I say. My aunt is loaded down with plastic food containers. She also has armfuls of other stuff like ladles and spoons and squirt bottles. 'I'm going to the fete, Wayne, and do you know what?'

'What?'

'I would *love* you to help me carry all my bits and pieces.'

I am caught. Squocka starts to edge away, pointing to his jumper and muttering about football practice he has just invented, then Auntie Edna turns her attention to him. 'And coo-ee, Squocka.'

'Yeah, coo-ee.'

'Would you like to help me too?'

Next thing you know, we're all marching together towards the fete. Squocka and I carry the containers and squirt bottles. 'What are you doing at the fete, Auntie?' I ask.

'I'm running a chicken stall,' she says. 'I do it every year.'

A great one for chicken is Auntie Edna. At the fete she finds her stall, then we help her lay out a container of strips of chicken meat which she cooked this morning. All she has to do is put some rice into a bowl, add a ladleful of chicken, squirt on the right sauce and that's Chinese chicken.

Auntie has a blackboard with the menu on it:

> **Chicken Chow Mein**
> **Chicken with Almonds**
> **Chicken without Almonds**
> **Chicken Salmonella**
> **Sweet & Sour Chicken**
> **Sweet Chicken**
> **Sour Chicken**
> **Funky Chicken**
> **Chicken Little**
> **Ordinary Chicken**
> **Chicken With Rice**
> **Chicken Without Rice**
> **Chicken With Noodles**
> **Curry Chicken**
> **Chicken Milkshakes**
> **Vanilla Chicken**
> **Vegetarian Chicken**
> **Boiled egg**

Just as we are about to leave Auntie Edna at the stall, she slaps her forehead and says, 'Silly me.'

Uh-oh. A bad sign. Auntie Edna has forgotten the almonds. Which is why Squocka and I find ourselves in charge of the chicken stall while my coo-eeing auntie hotfoots it home.

◆

It seems on this fete day, no one wants to eat chicken. On the other hand, I'm hungry because a lot of running around gives me an appetite. So does a lot of sitting down, standing still and lying about. In fact, everything I do gives me an appetite. So I delicately pick out some chicken and hold up a long bit and pop it in my mouth. Yum! Squocka does the same. Yum, yum.

A Japanese tourist comes by and watches us, then asks, 'What you eating?'

For a laugh, I tell him it's a witchetty grub. Genuine Australian bush tucker. I show him a piece and tell him I've cut off the leggy bits. From a distance, who can tell what they are? Besides, I've got an honest face. The tourist takes a photo of this kilt-wearing youth eating a witchetty grub, then calls to his mates. They talk to each other in Japanese and all we can hear are the words, 'Witchetty Grubs'. They consult guidebooks and look wise. Ah so.

Before long, they want Squocka to eat a grub so they can get a picture for the folks back home. We tell them it's for charity and they say, 'How much we pay?'

'A dollar for every witchetty,' I reply. They produce wallets and travellers' cheques.

For the next few minutes, the air is filled with the sounds of cameras going click, flashbulbs going flash and Squocka and me going munch. The money in the till mounts up and I think we're on to a good thing. This charity I like. We eat, they pay. Before long, a crowd gathers, mostly with money. They want us to eat more witchetties. The Japanese tourists demand to be photographed next to us as we down yet more chicken strips. One sumo-wrestler has a movie camera and ten dollars in his hand. 'Eat witchetty,' he says. 'Ten dollars worth!'

To tell the truth, we've had our fill of chicken. Squocka whispers that he's eaten enough to last the rest of his boyhood. Any more and we'll start to cluck or lay eggs. I become desperate. What can I do? I slip my chicken-bloated brain into gear and say, 'Sorry, we're closing for lunch.' The crowd's not having it.

'Eat witchetty!' says the sumo-wrestler. 'I make video.'

The Japanese look at each other and mutter baleful things in their own language. The only word I can make out is 'ratbags', so they've been learning our language.

Right! If they want to play tough, so can we. Sort of accidentally-on-purpose, I upset the container of chicken, which tumbles to the ground. Squocka treads on it and makes it muddy and unfit for human consumption. 'Sorry, folks,' he says. 'Come back tomorrow. We can't eat food that's been on the ground. Even witchetties.'

The crowd becomes angry. They shake their fists and we take the money and make a slender escape out the back of the stall. Then I hear, 'Coo-ee, Wayne.' Auntie Edna has returned with the almonds. We give her the money and she's delighted because it's more than she'd have made on her regular bowls of chicken with squirt-bottle sauce.

We leave Auntie Edna to clean up the wreckage of her stall and head off home. There's still the problem of how to explain to our parents where our gear went. As Mum is fond of saying, jeans don't grow on trees.

'They do if they're cotton,' I'm equally fond of reminding her, but always manage to duck before retribution comes my way.

❖

Then we see something terrible. There is a second-hand clothes stall and who should be running it but Violet and Rosana, the badge ladies. What's worse, they have our gear on display. What's double worse is that Kevin Merry is buying our jeans. Before Squocka and I can reach the stall, Kevin has paid up and disappeared into a crowd of argumentative Japanese tourists. 'Violet,' I say, 'they were my jeans you just sold.'

'And mine,' Squocka adds.

Violet and Rosana look at us, but mainly at me. 'It's the Highland Laddie,' Rosana says. 'Are you guys a novelty act or something?'

'Ha, ha,' Squocka and I laugh. It's good to get on the right side of women. It sometimes helps.

By now Violet has read the slogan on the front of my T-shirt. 'Tacky,' she says with a distant sniff.

Quickly we describe our ill-fated golf-ball-collecting expedition, the run-in with the unfriendly colonels, our flight to safety, the manure heap leap, the hygienic wash-up in the creek, then the brazen daylight theft of our garments. Violet mellows to some extent, but not a lot. She tells us they gave Kevin Merry a discount because the jeans he bought were still soaking wet. Helpfully, Violet points, 'He went that way.'

Since they still have our T-shirts on display, we ask if we can have them. Rosana is all heart and agrees to hand them over, in return for us taking their pram to the dump. Then it's squeak-squeak-squeakity-squeak and we're off in pursuit of Kevin Merry who has our moist jeans. The pram contains some clothing that is so old, moth-eaten and mildewed it is only fit for the dump. 'It's a long time since I felt so ridiculous,' I confess to Squocka.

'Oh, I don't know,' he responds. 'What about that time you— '

I cut him off before he becomes personal. 'Look!' It's Kevin Merry, and he has our jeans slung over his shoulder. Squik-squik-squikity-squik. That's us going faster as we get after him. 'Kevin,' I make with a friendly greeting. 'Kevin, old buddy.'

'How's the golf-ball business?' Squocka adds.

Bad news. Kevin won't part with our jeans. We walk alongside him, squeaking, pleading, squeaking, cajoling and begging, but he says no way. Then it's Squocka's turn to have a brainwave. 'Kevin,' he whispers. He also makes his eyes roll to show lots of anxious white. 'There's a big guy watching you.'

'What big guy?' Kevin goes to turn around.

Squocka frowns a warning. 'Don't look! He'll see your face.'

Kevin knows about keeping a low profile, as well as aliases, alibis and character witnesses. 'Who is the guy?' he says out of the side of his mouth. I look, but can't see any guy, big or little.

'He's the greenkeeper from the golf club,' Squocka tells him. 'Looking for kids who nick golf balls. You better hide, Kevin.' Naturally, Squocka suggests Kevin hide inside the squeaky-wheel pram. There's enough room in it under our convenient pile of pre-owned clothing and a Robertson tartan kilt. We don our jeans and push the pram for a minute or two more, then it's hi-five time and we head home, walking funny because our jeans and T-shirts are still damp.

That night, Mum announces that it's chicken pie for dinner. Wouldn't you know it! Mind you, she was wrong about one thing. I didn't have to leap all day.

Or did I?

13 NOW YOU SEE IT, NOW YOU STILL SEE IT

One bright and glorious holiday morning, I find Squocka in my back garden wearing a pointy hat and waving a black-painted stick at Fat Cat. 'Ally-kazoop!' Squocka gestures. Fat Cat ignores him. Squocka frowns and consults a tattered old book that lies open on the laundry table. He tries again, but Fat Cat is busy washing his tail.

'What are you up to, Squocks?' I inquire.

'What's it look like?' he snarls. 'I'm making Fat Cat vanish.'

'Why not say "Go away" or "Shoo"?' I'm at my most helpful, but Squocka only sneers a superior sneer.

'Can't you see I'm learning conjuring?' he demands as if talking to a simpleton. He shows a copy of *Every Boy's Book of Magic*. It has this really old-fashioned guy on the cover with a wand in one hand and a worried-looking pigeon in the other. 'We could learn some of the tricks and put on a show.' I note his use of 'we' and raise an eyebrow. 'They're really easy,' he adds.

'Like making Fat Cat disappear.' I am sniffy about the whole idea because he thought of it first.

'The book's great,' Squocka encourages me. 'Second-hand, only one owner.' Before you know what's what, I get involved and we try one of the beginner tricks. Squocka puts five cents inside a matchbox, gives it a shake, then opens it to reveal twenty cents! 'See, it works!' he says.

'You sure know how to hook a guy,' I confess.

Squocka tries another trick. He fans out a pack of cards, then offers it to me. 'Take a card, Wayne.'

'Where to?' Can't help being smart.

'Just take one, sonny, or I'll wave my wand and give you a nuclear wedgie.'

'Ooh, listen to the man of magic!' I take a card.

'Not that one,' Squocka warns. 'It's got jam on it.' I take another card. Squocka fumbles and mixes it with the rest of the pack. He brings a card out and says, 'Viola!'

'Who's she?' I ask.

'It's a word we magicians use.' Squocka shows my card. 'That's yours.'

'No, it's not,' I lie.— ?'

'Has to be,' he says. ''Cause they're all the same. Ta-ra!'

●

After a couple of weeks, Sqocka can do ten tricks, including one where he wraps his thumb in a hanky and hammers a nail through until real blood appears – only it's orange-coloured. I pretend to faint. He produces a flat parcel, mysteriously tied up with brown paper and string. He goes to open it, but pauses. 'You won't laugh, will you?'

'Me? Laugh?' I say. 'Go on, give us a look.' Truth is, I'm keen to see what it is.

He starts undoing the string, then says shyly, 'Wayne, I'm ready for the big time.'

'The big time?' I ponder deeply. 'Does that mean you're trading in your teddy-bear watch and buying a grown-up one?'

'No, Wayne.' His voice is troubled. 'I'm gonna do my act in front of an audience.'

'What? Real people?' I ask. 'This is a big step, my son.'

'I've made up a stage name,' he goes on, 'and printed it on cardboard.' He takes the paper off and shows me the sign:

THE AMAZING LESTER SQUOCKINGTON
MAN OF MAGIC

'Lester Squockington, eh?' I die of inward mirth but keep a straight face.

'What do you reckon?' he asks.

'It's great,' I say. 'Simple and elegant.' 'Elegant' is a word I saw on the cover of Charlene's girly magazine: *Why not be elegant this season?* 'Why not go around with a paper bag over your head?' I suggested at the time and was lucky to clear the back yard fence just as my sister turned terminally bitter.

Squocka is relieved. 'Yeah,' he breathes. 'That's what I thought. Elegant.'

'When are you putting on this show, Lester?'

Squocka seems to like me using his stage name. He puffs up and grows two centimetres. Then he deflates. 'That's the trouble, Wayne,' he confesses. 'I need an assistant – one who wears a short skirt and helps with my act.'

'Why the short skirt?'

'It's traditional. Plus spangles, and she's gotta smile a lot.'

We consider all the available girls. Apart from Violet Pridmore and Rosana Conti, who wouldn't be in this sort of thing, none of them is ready to share the glory of Lester Squockington, Man of Magic, in his premiere public performance. What I'm actually getting around to suggesting is that Wayne Wilson, Undiscovered Talent, be his assistant. No, he will not don the short skirt and spangles. There is a better idea.

Half an hour later, Squocka is nearly convinced it will work. The act will now be:

> **LESTER SQUOCKINGTON**
> **MAN OF MAGIC**
> **AND HIS**
> **CRAZY ASSISTANT**
> **GLOOPEN-FANKEL**

I demonstrate how Gloopen-fankel will perform. In a black suit with tight pants that are too short and big boots, I drag one foot behind me and make slobbering noises.

I stick out my tongue and show off my horrible teeth. Squocka says he's got a relative who looks like that without even trying.

I convince him it is really *me* he needs to give his act pizazz and zing and other stuff. So he agrees, as long as I hurry up and limp quickly, and don't slobber or wave my arms while he's doing his magic bits. I promise to be the complete professional, and so we make plans for our show.

Note that if Squocka can say 'we', I can say 'our'.

❧

In the next few days, I polish my performance while Squocka fumbles trick after trick. 'Oops,' I say in the voice of Gloopen-fankel. 'You drop-ped it, master.'

'Don't drool so much,' he responds in the voice of Lester Squockington, Man of Magic. 'It's unhygienic.' Already we are professionally jealous of each other.

We dig out a battery CD player, then choose suitable music, as well as curtains and two poles to hold the string. The first performance is to be outside the shed in Squocka's back garden, where there's room for the audience to come and go without scaring his mum's chooks.

Squocka puts the word around at school that Lester Squockington, World-renowned Magician, is his uncle from Paraguay who has come to stay. He will give one performance only for some special friends. Invitation only. Bring a silver coin and expect to leave without it.

'They'll bring five cents,' I point out. Squocka changes the invitation to read: Bring a *large* silver coin!

Squocka can now do twelve tricks without looking at the book. He can do another one if everybody turns away and gives him time to stick a golf ball up his sleeve.

Gloopen-fankel is a touch of genius. One day, I go home in my disguise and when Mum sees me, she drops the frying pan. Sausages all over the kitchen floor but we pick them up and wipe them clean before Charlene catches us at it. Narrow escape.

At home, there's some sad news. Matron McTavish from Dwell-a-Wee Retirement Home has phoned to say there's a vacancy for Grandpa. 'We can take him in any time,' Mum whispers to me, then sighs because she's the one who has to tell Grandpa the news.

'Oh well,' he says when he finds out. 'This is it, then, isn't it?'

That night, it's extra gloomy around the Wilson dinner table. Grandpa doesn't eat his sausages so I score one and Dad has the other two but our hearts are not in it so we eat slowly. To cheer up my family, I try my Gloopen-fankel act and Charlene says, 'Yuk! Gross!'

They're not ready for such a powerful performance. Maybe the Hunchback of Notre Dame got the same from his sister.

FLIGHT OF FRENCH FANCY:

The Hunchback of Notre Dame and his family eat their midday meal.

HBND: *Mama. Pass my luncheon, sil vous plais.*

Mama: *Here you are, mon petit son. Un luncheon coming up!*

HBND: *Merci very much, Mama.*

Sister: *Mama! He ees so gross et gruesome. All I can see are le eyebrows, le bald patch et le hump. Can't we give him un cushion or something to raise him higher?*

HBND: *Snuffle, grunt, squish, chomp, slurp, chew, burp.*

Sister: *On second thoughts, Mama, never mind. He will also eat le cushion!*

Even Grandpa isn't interested in Gloopen-fankel. Normally he'd give me some old jokes to use. But on the night before he goes into Dwell-a-Wee, he's very subdued. 'I don't want a big fuss tomorrow,' he tells us. 'Just grab a taxi, go myself.'

'My father will do no such thing.' Mum is very firm.

'You'll go in style,' Dad says. 'In the truck.'

⬤

Next morning after breakfast, we take a farewell of Grandpa. Mum, Dad, Charlene and I are all out at the front gate. Grandpa's not going very far away, but he won't be under our roof, which is the sad part. He makes the best of it and stands by the Toyota, declaiming like an actor on stage. 'The curtain's come down, the crowd's gone home, the greasepaint's off, so let's away!'

'You don't have to go,' Dad tells him.

'No, we've got plenty of room,' Mum adds.

Grandpa ignores this. 'They do ballroom dancing every Thursday. Call themselves the Dwell-a-Wee Hoofers. One-two-cha-cha-cha!' He does a few steps, then tries to take Mum as a partner, but she's not having it.

'You were happy here.'

'I'll be happy there. Move it, Bill!' Grandpa climbs into the cab.

Dad gets behind the wheel and starts the motor. 'Hang on to your hat, Grandpa.'

'Haven't worn one since I quit showbiz.'

'It was a figure of speech, Grandpa,' Charlene says.

Mum's unhappy but tries not to show it. 'This is no time to make figures of speech.' She climbs in beside Grandpa.

He gives Charlene and me a final wave goodbye. 'I might even take Spanish lessons,' he calls. 'Always wanted to do the fandango.' Then they're off.

'That's very sad,' Charlene says to me.

'Yeah, and I get my bedroom back.'

'Huh, talk about unfeeling!' Charlene stalks off and shuts the front gate so that I have to open it if I want to go in the house. To show that I don't care, I vault the gate, except I'm not very good at it and go crashing to the ground. 'Serves you right,' my sister says.

I am uninjured. Except in the pride department. And gravel rash.

For the next few days without Grandpa, things are

really sad around the house. Even Charlene misses him and Mum feels guilty and visits every day, taking small things that he likes.

I spend a happy hour or two unearthing all the things I'd put away so Grandpa could have my room; my models, my posters, my books and my cassettes, although I've gone off most of them. But it's fantastic to have my own bed back. I stretch out full length, then Fat Cat comes in and snuggles at the end so I can feel him at my feet.

At night, I dream about being Gloopen-fankel the World's Greatest Clown and nobody knows it's really me, schoolboy Wayne Wilson in disguise.

◆

At the weekend, Mum and Dad go to visit Grandpa and when they get home, Mum is mournful. 'He's not happy there, Bill,' she says. 'He hates it.'

'Give him time, Heather, love,' Dad soothes. 'He'll get used to the place and soon make friends. That's all he needs, a couple of mates and he'll be set like a jelly.'

'He's missing his own people and things around him,' says Mum.

I remember how it was when I couldn't take all my stuff down to the back verandah. How would it be if I never saw my things or my room or Mum, Dad and Charlene again? Then it hits me: that's what Grandpa's feeling. It makes me think about growing old, but as Grandpa says, life goes on. I put the sad thoughts aside.

There are other things to think about, such as Lester Squockington's first performance, ably supported by his Crazy Assistant, Gloopen-fankel.

❧

We get eight people in the audience, including Violet and Rosana, plus William and his small brother, Kenneth from over the back fence. Five of the magic tricks don't work because the audience is too far away to see what's going on. Another one bites the dust because even Kenneth can see how it's done. The rest of the show is successful and everybody laughs at Gloopen-fankel the Crazy Assistant so when Lester Squockington's busy, I put in a few extra slobbers and eye-rolls behind his back.

'Now,' says the Man of Magic in his phoney Paraguayan accent. 'Regardez-vous! I hef here, one small golfie ball.'

I butt in with some dialogue we didn't rehearse. 'He puts zee golfie ball in zee little baggie, so! Viola!'

Squocka hates this. 'Okay, Gloopen-tangle, now go fetch ze little hammer.'

'It's Gloopen-fankel,' I whisper, then shuffle over to get the hammer, glowering and slobbering until my chin is wet.

'In Paraguay,' Squocka tells the audience, 'we would not hef such a stupido assistant as this lunatic. But you hef to mek do wiz what you ken get.' (We didn't rehearse this bit either.)

'Iz zat so?' I slobber. 'Hokay, der next trick iz gonna be a lulu!'

'Zere is no next trick, Gloopen-pongel,' snarls Squocka. 'Zis is zee last one.'

He takes the hammer and proceeds to belt the little baggie which bounces up and down because it has a little golfie ball in it. With a note of triumph, Lester Squockington sticks his hand in and brings out Rambeau the white mouse which was up his sleeve all the time. He flicks the bag to show it's empty and even I have to say it was a good trick, although we never found the golfie ball again. How's that for a disappearing act?

When we count the takings, Squocka is dismayed to find only forty-five cents. We think of posting the money to charity but since a stamp will cost more than we got, we drop the coins into a blind man's collecting box instead. 'Thank you, Madam,' he says. We are totally depressed.

❖

On Saturday Mum gives me a bunch of grapes and a tomato and sends me to visit Grandpa in Dwell-a-Wee.

'Hullo, Wayne boy,' he says. 'How's tricks?' He tries to smile but he's lost the knack.

'Not bad, Gramps.' Over in one corner, there's a guy playing the piano while some old women join in with a sing-along. They croon, 'Daisy, Daisy' and other ancient songs whose words are lost in the mists of time.

'That fellow comes in now and then and gives the

old biddies a tune,' Grandpa sniffs. 'Passes the time for them, I suppose.'

'How do you pass the time, Gramps?'

'Watch television, read and sit,' he says, which doesn't sound like a ball of fun. 'Can't even put a bet on here.'

'Have you made any pals yet?' I ask.

'No – they're all old in this place,' he growls. 'I don't feel old.'

I sit listening to the guy with the piano. 'He's not bad, Grandpa,' I say.

'He *should* be good,' Gramps tells me. 'He's Lester Dorrington. Plays in the Theatre Orchestra. I knew him when he was only a lad. Just starting out in show business.'

Lester Dorrington – Lester Squockington. It's such a coincidence. I tell Grandpa about our magic act and he laughs for the first time. (Genuine laughter, showing his false teeth. I will report to Mum.) 'You should put on your show here,' Grandpa says. 'Liven the place up.'

We talk a bit more, then it's time to go. We've eaten all his grapes anyway, so I give him a big hug and tell him I'll see him again soon.

◆

Squocka likes the idea of putting on our show in Dwell-a-Wee, but says we'll need to rehearse harder than ever if we're to perform in front of grown-ups. He's borrowed a racing pigeon from the guy next door and plans to produce the bird from his sleeve, then make it disappear again. He's full of confidence, is Squocka, you have to give him that. Since Fat Cat introduced himself to Rambeau, the white mouse lost his enthusiasm for the show.

I concentrate on being the Great Gloopen-fankel, Man of Mirth, using some white make-up in Charlene's beauty box. With that all over my face, Gloopen-fankel looks better than ever. I wonder if I can stick a bolt through my neck but decide not to because the ones in Dad's workshop are rusty and I don't know how to make the hole without killing myself. Lester Squockington and his Dead Assistant.

We rehearse until we're perfect, then take the bus to Dwell-a-Wee, where Grandpa has already put the word around that a magician is coming to entertain them.

We arrive in good time and Matron McTavish shows us where we can change into our costumes. Squocka now wears a false moustache and has bought a proper plastic wand from Mr Patel's Imperial Joke and Novelty Emporium. With his cape and black jeans, Squocka looks quite good, but he won't beat me in my Gloopen-fankel costume.

Dressed for the show, we present ourselves to Matron McTavish, who sniffs when she sees Squocka. 'What are you supposed to be?' she grumps. 'A waiter?' I do a small inward chuckle. Quite a sense of humour has old Matron McT. She should go into showbiz herself. When she looks at me her eyes go all wide and circular. 'And what are *you* supposed to be?'

'I, madam, am the famous Gloopen-fankel, Crazy Assistant to Lester Squockington, Man of Magic.'

'I can't have you caper about in front of elderly residents looking like that.' Her voice crackles with finality. 'You look like a corpse!'

I plead, I reason and promise to polish her car but she shakes her head. Finally, I have to go and wash off the white make-up. I become, Wayne Wilson, Ordinary Schoolboy and Un-crazy Assistant, with neither limp, drool nor slobber. Squocka is ready to go on in his full Lester Squockington glory, moustache included. It's not fair. He has a large grin on his face, but he'll keep.

Matron McTavish takes us to the common room where there's a small stage. The old people have already gathered round and two of them start to applaud, then stop when they realise we're not the bringers of tea and biscuits. Squocka bows and waves his cape in my direction. I bow too. If I'd been Gloopen-fankel, I'd have treated them to a good old slobbering.

Grandpa hasn't made any friends, so he sits all by himself at the back of the room, which makes me sad.

The show begins and Squocka does a few simple tricks while the audience talk amongst themselves and some of them knit things. One nods off. The show bores on, trick after trick and nothing goes right. Squocka drops things and fumbles his props; he can't get anything to come out of his sleeve; he taps the tumbler too hard with his magic wand and water spills everywhere.

The final trick is the racing pigeon one, which

Squocka gets wrong in a big way. The bird slips down one leg of his jeans and starts to panic, wings flapping, claws scratching. Squocka tries to pretend everything's okay. He smiles at the audience but hisses in my direction. 'Wayne, it's pecking me!' This is something we didn't rehearse.

Squocka tolerates it for a few seconds more, then gives a mighty kick and the pigeon comes out the bottom of his jeans and flaps away to disappear out an open window. Squocka tries to hide the fact that he has a severely pecked inside leg.

None of this has any effect on the audience. Apart from Grandpa, no one is paying the slightest attention to us. Our show is in ruins! Careers too, come to that. We bow low and Squocka mutters sheepishly, 'Thank you very much, ladies and gentlemen.' We shuffle off and there's no applause. The audience is busy talking to each other and knitting bootees. They don't even know we've finished. Maybe they never noticed we'd started.

Grandpa comes to the dressing room and sits for a full minute. He looks at Squocka's pile of tatty props, then shakes his head. 'Terrible,' he growls at last. We just nod. There's nothing else to say. After the build-up I gave our act, I've let him down.

The door opens and a woman comes in and laughs when she sees us looking so sad. 'Never mind, boys,' she says. 'You're not the first act to die on stage. I've seen dozens of them go flop.'

At these theatrical words, Grandpa sits up and takes

notice. 'Wait a minute!' He recognises the woman. 'You're Dottie Fingleton, the singer!'

She looks at him for a few seconds. 'And you're Ray Dawson, the comic.' It turns out they knew each other in the old days when they were on stage.

They start talking together, remembering the old times and the people they used to know. Grandpa's eyes light up and he's smiling genuine smiles for the first time. Squocka and I sit and watch and it's like we're at the tennis with the theatrical talk flying back and forth between them. Then they remember we're still there.

'Here,' says Dottie. 'You boys don't want to waste time on that corny old magic act. You haven't got the knack anyway. Come, I'll show you an idea.'

We troop along the corridor with Dottie and she's got her place done up like a dressing-room from the theatre. There are old posters on the walls, a couple of masks and a big feathery hat. There are photos of Dottie when she was young and a real knock-out. Grandpa's in wonder-land.

Dottie finds some make-up and soon has me looking like a ventriloquist's dummy with red cheeks and a big ginger wig. I learn how to move in a jerky fashion while Dottie makes up Squocka as the ventriloquist with a thin black moustache and his hair all plastered down on one side.

Grandpa starts reciting some jokes and patter we can use. As the dummy, I sit on Squocka's knee and he puts his hand on my back as if he's operating my jaw.

'Now, off you go and work up a routine like that,' says Dottie. 'It's more your style.'

And so we leave Grandpa and Dottie in Dwell-a-Wee, talking about old times in the theatre. Now I've really got something to tell Mum. Best news in weeks.

On the bus, I sit on Squocka's knee and say, 'Gottle of Geer.' Several passengers roll their eyes and get off even though it's not their stop. Squocka does not enter into the spirit of it, but sits looking out the window.

One thing's for sure – if he's to be my assistant, he'll need to work a lot harder!

Wayne, how come you don't like pizza anymore?

Don't mention that word, Squocka.

What word? 'Anymore' or 'pizza'?

The second one. It's because of a certain disaster in the kitchen.

Pizza burn your mouth, did it?

No. It got stuck, Squocka. In several places. So the 'P' word is out.

Well, what about the 'B' word? As in – birthday. Charlene's birthday.

Yeah, the time she put her foot right in it.

I thought it was both feet.

And guess who saved the day?

*No. Wayne, can't think who that could be.
Racked my brains and nothing came out.*

I'm not surprised. Anyway, moving right along, as they say in show biz, what about your angelic on-stage performance?

I was a legend, Wayne. Everyone talked about me.

And since you unkindly mentioned the 'P' word, as in pizza, I've got one for you, mate – pantihose.

Oh, no! I'll never live it down. Okay, cop this, Wayne! Pizza! Pizza! Pizza!

Pantihose! Pantihose! Pantihose!

Wayne, Violet Pridmore's looking at you – rather strangely.

14 PIZZA

he blue Volvo guy is back. Five times a day he turns up outside our place, does a very slow and careful three-point turn, then heads off along the street again. He is Rupert Pringle and a learner driver; this you can tell from the L-plates and his white-knuckled mother in the passenger seat beside him. Charlene notices Rupert too, in fact, every time he turns up outside our place, my sister springs to the front window, hides behind the curtains, then looks and sighs pensively.

From the depths of those sighs, Mum can tell what's what. She teases Charlene, 'I'm going out there to tell that boy to do his three-pointers somewhere else.'

Charlene colours red. 'Mum, you wouldn't!'

'Well, why don't you go and say hello or something?'

'I can't do things like that!' Charlene blushes pink. 'Not with his mother in the car.'

Mum goes away and Charlene settles down to await Rupert's sixth visit. So that's how things stand: Rupert and Charlene can't break the ice. If the rest of the world's population went on like them, the human race would die out. Mind you, last occasion we clowned with up-market Rupert Pringle, it didn't start out well. But as Mum is fond of saying, time forgives many things.

So, that night, the four of us in the close-knit, loving Wilson family sit round the dinner table and I reveal my brilliant plan. 'Charlene,' I begin, 'how about, next time Rupert Pringle comes around in his car, I pretend to be injured or something.' I clutch my arm and make realistic urk and ark noises.

Charlene is not impressed. 'And what will *that* do?'

'You come running out with bandages and iodine, then say hello to Rupert. Easy.'

'How do you know I *want* to say hello to Rupert?' Charlene snaps. 'Nong-brain. Hyperactive.'

Mum comes to my aid. 'Now Charlene, your brother's not hyperactive.'

'Yeah,' Dad adds his bit. 'And he's not going to pull any medical stunts either.'

Mum and Dad warn me in frown-language not to come up with another stupid plan; especially not one that involves Rupert Pringle. Charlene is very mopey and pushes her sausage around the plate, surgically trimming a tiny bit off one end and placing it between her lips, then nibbling slowly. My parents shake their heads at this performance.

◆

Comes Saturday afternoon and Squocka turns up at my place in a seriously starving condition. We have the house to ourselves because everyone else is out shopping or clearing drains. More importantly, we have the kitchen to call our own, which is where we assemble. Squocka calls this place Food-a-rama and rolls up his sleeves. 'Ever made a pizza?' he challenges.

'It's my middle name,' I tell him, but he claims to have won medals for it. The game is on. In a flash, we lay out the ingredients – flour, butter, eggs, cheese, milk, lemonade and tomatoes. Squocka sets to and before long, he has a large dollop of dough slopping about in Mum's mixing bowl.

He's been too generous with the eggs and other liquids so the dough's a bit runny. It drips through his fingers like pancake mixture. 'No worries.' He talks like a TV chef with an international audience and a range of designer cookware. 'When I do the tossing up and spinning bit, it'll dry out.'

'You reckon?'

'Yeah. Centrifugal force. Works every time.' Squocka takes up two handfuls of dough and squeezes out the juice, then gets ready to do the spinning thing like they do in the pizza shop. He hurls the dough upwards and three things happen, all of them ominous. One bit lands in Fat Cat's kitty litter, another chunk ends up behind the stove but the biggest, wettest wodge of dough sticks to the high ceiling. Thud, it says and stays up there, taunting us. Nerny-nerny-ner-ner! We watch that dough in awe. 'It'll come down again soon,' Squocka tries to comfort me. 'You get the oven on.'

'Oven on nothing!' I protest, then, as they say in musical circles, I become agitato. 'Squocks, we've got to get that stuff off the ceiling before Mum gets home.'

'Nah, it'll be cool.'

'What if it fell down here when Mum's reading a recipe or something?'

'It'll stay up there, so maybe she won't notice.'

'You're talking about my mother,' I remind him. 'A woman who can tell the state of my underdaks through three pairs of trousers and one thick bedroom door.' We poke at the dough but the ceiling's a high one and nothing reaches it. I get up on the kitchen table and try swiping with Charlene's hockey stick, then the broom. No go. Then it's brainwave time. I get out the vacuum cleaner and stick the extension tubes together, but still can't reach that ceiling.

I may or may not have told you that I come from a long line of inventive Wilsons. My ancestors were the guys who discovered fire, the wheel and anti-wedgie underwear.

Problem: Vacuum cleaner tubes won't reach.

Solution: Join on more tubes.

Our house sports an elegant set of door chimes that go 'ding-dong' every time somebody pushes the button at the front door. The tubes are made of tasteful anodised aluminium in copper bronze finish. The long one, technically known as the dong tube, is just what we need to reach the ceiling. Squocka switches on the vacuum cleaner and I aim the nozzle end at the pizza dough.

It works. As the sloppy dough comes surging off the ceiling, it makes a squoddle, squoddle, squoddle noise while the tube jumps and twists like a no-appetite python being force-fed two soccer balls. We are winning the battle, with most of the dough removed except for the stain. Then with a noise like 'goomf' or 'goomph', the electric motor gums up. 'I'll fix that later,' I tell Squocka. Our first priority is to get Mum's dong tube back where it belongs.

Problem: Dong tube is now stuffed full of pizza dough.

Solution: Poke dough out with long, thin object.

For the poking operation we choose Mum's purple feather duster and after five minutes expert prodding with the stick end, no dough emerges. What is worse, we can't get the feather duster out. The dough has set hard and a big gollop of it has extruded from the end opposite the feather duster.

It is Squocka's turn to have a brainwave. 'How about we *flick* the dough out, like we're fly fishing?' His demonstration nearly has the door off the microwave.

'Watch it, ning-nong,' I warn him. 'Mum wants *some* of her kitchen left. We gotta eat dinner tonight.' At Squocka's place they only have one meal a day and dinner's not it. (That bit's a lie.)

We go into the back yard, because there's less chance of being seen by nosey pedestrians. Squocka does three mighty flicks and the situation does not change:

Purple feather duster still sticks out one end. ✓
Dough remains firmly jammed in anodised dong tube. ✓
Wayne still desperate. ✓

My fire-inventing ancestor had less trouble than this.
The number one worry in those far-off days was the lack
of a fire brigade. I take over with the fly-fishing operation and flick so hard the entire dong tube slips out of my
grasp. It sails over the roof of the house, then we hear it
land with a metallic thud.

'You hit something,' Squocka points out needlessly.
We sprint around the front of the house just in time to
see a blue car make off from our place at high speed.
The dong tube is stuck fast to the boot lid and the purple
feather duster waves us a jaunty farewell as the vehicle
disappears along the street.

Our door chime plus duster also waves to my mother
and sister who are returning from their shopping expedition. It is slack jaw time all round. Mum sees me out the
front and becomes rampageous. 'Wayne, are you irre-
sponsible for this?'

I make some rapid-fire explanations: we were making
a pizza and things got out of hand.

'Out of *Wayne's* hands.' Squocka uses his not-getting-
any-on-me voice. That's it! No pizza for him! (What am
I saying? No pizza for anyone!)

Mum takes charge. 'We'll have to get our property
back,' she says. 'That stupid brown tube thing, whatever
it was.'

I'll tell her later. Right now we have other concerns. Before we know it, Squocka decides he's needed at home, then he's off like a scared rabbit, hands over his head in case my mother's aim is good with whatever tinned food's in her shopping bag.

Mum issues orders. Charlene and I are to *find* that car, *apologise* to the driver, then Wayne is to bring home the tube thing. As Mum gives these crisp instructions, she keeps a face so straight you could rule lines with it.

Charlene parts with her shopping, then we set off. Strangely enough, my sister knows exactly where the car driver lives. She probably knows his inside leg measurement and pet budgie's star sign. Charlene walks so fast I can barely keep up. Conversation is kept short and insult-free. I'm out of breath trying to keep pace with my enthusiastically loping sister. Then, da-da-da-dum! We are there.

The blue car is a Volvo. It's parked in an open carport and the dong tube is still in place, purple feather duster undulating gently in the breeze. 'What say,' I whisper to Charlene, 'what say I grab the tube, then we head off out of here?'

'Are you mad?' My sister's eyes are wide with outrage. 'I must apologise.'

Even before I've plucked the tube off the car, Charlene is going knockity-knock at the front door of the house. No anodised door chimes for them, I notice.

Since I'm at a distance, the door-opening moment is hard to hear. But yes, it's Rupert Pringle himself and there are smiles all round, a lot of apologetic arm-waving from Charlene as she points at me. I hear her say the words, 'training', 'athlete' and 'Commonwealth games' and guess that she's coming up with an excuse. To support my sister's lie, I try to look athletic.

Rupert smiles at me and calls a question. 'Javelin?'

'No, dong tube,' I reply. Next thing you know Rupert's smiling mother's on the doorstep too, inviting Charlene inside.

But first Charlene comes to me. 'Wayne, get lost.' Her lips move not a millimetre. 'They'll drive me home. Tell Mum I'll be back later.'

'What about driving *me* home?' I ask.

'Walk. It's only four hundred metres.'

Huh! That's it. I slink off and leave her. The good thing is I'll be able to tell Mum Charlene has made contact with Rupert. This might even take the heat off the pizza mess. And the dong tube.

◆

As it turns out, I'm wrong on both counts and what's worse, the dong tube no longer makes its musical note. The doorbell now goes 'ding-clack', with a little bit of powdered pizza dough falling out the bottom every time. Dad swaps the dong tube for a length of galvanised water pipe. The chimes now go 'ding-poop' and my mother is not pleased. By a process of transference, Dad gets some of the blame so it's not all bad news.

On the Charlene/Rupert front, it looks rosy. For one

thing he doesn't need to do three-pointers outside our place any more. That was a little trick he invented so he might catch sight of you-know-who. The Council came and fixed up the road where his tyres left big ruts. (That bit's a lie.)

Even better news is that Rupert got his licence and now he can come visit Charlene, where Mum makes him welcome. Rupert has grown up to be a bit wet, but you can't have everything.

So at the Wilson house, things go well. Rupert visits more often and Mum likes to see the Volvo parked outside our place. Dad's been warned on no account is he to try to interest Rupert in toilets. 'What about bidets?' Dad asks.

With a single glare from Mum, my father is frozen solid.

◆

Peace reigns. Rupert comes to dinner, which is a plan Charlene's been hatching for a long time. So, we sit down to eat and Charlene makes sure Rupert is as far away from me as possible. She hangs on every word he says and laughs at his not-funny jokes. He must have bought the same Christmas crackers we did.

Since everyone ignores me, I stick a bread roll up the back of my shirt and pretend to be a snuffling mongle-troid. I crouch low to the table so that Rupert can only see my face over the food on my plate. I become an obnoxious, javelin-hurling Olympian hyperactive and make with a big scowl. Rupert doesn't know where to look.

I trail my knuckles on the carpet and fossick in my plate, looking for morsels among the gravy.

'Rupert, pay no attention to the gory object along there,' says Charlene. 'It's my brother, Wayne. He's hideous.'

I look up and catch sight of Dad staring down at me. He's been watching my performance and is not amused. 'Wayne,' he says, drawing out my name so long and putting such a growl into it, the neighbours think there's a bear in there. One growl is all I need.

Finally, there comes a lot of shuffling from Mum and some heavy grunting and harrumphing from Dad. Mum announces, 'Charlene, dear, why don't you take Rupert into the front room – we'll stack the dishwasher.'

'What dishwasher?' I say and Dad growls with his eyes. Only parents can do that.

The problem is, nobody tells me what's going on. They know what's to happen next but I've got to guess and if I ask an innocent question, Mum tells me to see my father, it's his department. Dad says I'll find out about it when I'm older. Once I waited a whole week then went to Dad and reported I was seven days older. All he said was, 'Give us a hand to sling this old hot-water tank on the truck.'

Together we went, 'One – two – three!' At which point I threw my end of the hot-water tank on the truck. Did I do well? Nope. Dad tells me I should wait for the 'hup.'

'Remember that, Wayne. One – two – three – hup! It's traditional.'

And I never found out what I wanted to know. And anyway, I forget what it was.

In our house the colour television is in the front room, where Charlene and Rupert have all the space in the world. The small back room, where we are forced to cram ourselves, contains a tiny black and white TV. On screen, it is very difficult to tell which team is which, so I complain. 'Can I watch in the front room, Mum?'

'No!' Okay, family, don't all speak at once.

Dad's fast asleep. Mum's knitting. Everyone is enjoying themselves except Wayne, who is thoroughly bored with life. Suddenly, Charlene appears at the door with her little foot going tappy, tappy, tappy. 'Mummy! Someone is in the front garden making a disgusting hooting noise!'

'It's not me,' I tell her. 'Not a single hoot has passed out of my body.' Charlene ignores this.

Just then, the doorbell goes 'ding-poop'. 'Oh, Wayne!' Mum hisses. 'That doorbell!'

It will follow me all my life.

It turns out to be Squocka at the front door, wearing a bandsman's uniform and carrying a trombone. He has been to band practice. The uniform's too big for him and his trombone is bent and in two pieces.

'It was *you* out there,' says Charlene. 'I might have known it would be one of *his* gruesome friends!' She flounces back to Rupert.

'Yeah, Wayne,' Squocka says. 'Got me trombey damaged, see.'

'How?' Mum asks.

'I was practising walking and blowing at the same time, Mrs Wilson, and I poked the glockenspiel player with it and he cracked a hairy. I was wondering if Mr Wilson could fix it for me.'

At the mention of his name, Dad wakes up and becomes all professional. 'Oh, right, Squocka, the instrument's bent just there by the saliva drain,' he says. 'I'll whip that bit off, put an elbow in the grease trap, solder it up there and put a grommet in that bit and a new ballcock in the bypass, work a plunger up and down from this side and put a female socket in there, and that should do it.' I love technical language.

So Dad wanders off to the workshop with the main part of Squocka's trombone while Mum goes to make coffee for Charlene and Rupert.

'There's a dirty big Volvo parked out the front,' Squocka says.

'Belongs to Rupert Bear,' I tell him. 'He's chatting up Charlene in the front room.'

'How he's going to drive home then?' Squocka asks. 'Without any wheels.'

I do a deep gulp. No wheels? Rupert *must* have had them when he arrived. Squocka and I go out front, casual like, and sure enough, the Volvo's resting on the round things that are left when you take the wheels off.

'He'll still have the spare,' says the ever-helpful Squocka.

I sidle back to Mum in the kitchen and whisper the bad news. 'Oh no!' she says. 'Go get your father.'

Dad is not amused. 'We'd better call the cops.'

'Police?' Mum protests. 'Are you mad? If they come with their siren and blue light, Rupert will *know*. How about we borrow the wheels off your truck?'

'Different size,' says Dad. 'Besides, I need 'em.'

'Talking of wheels,' Squocka puts in, 'I saw the Merry brothers rolling some along. You know, along the ground.'

'How many?' says Dad.

'Two of them. Jim and Trevor.'

'No, how many *wheels*?'

Squocka counts on his fingers. 'Oh, one – two – three – four. Yeah, it was four.'

'Right!' Dad becomes purposeful. 'We'll get 'em back before they flog 'em.'

Mum will keep Rupert in the front room with Charlene while we go after the missing wheels. 'How about I play Rupert a solo?' Squocka asks.

'Don't reckon that'll work,' Dad says. 'Might make him want to leave early. Besides, there's bad news about your trombone, son. Tell you as we go.' Dad climbs into the truck. Squocka and I follow.

◆

If something goes missing in our neighbourhood, the Merry brothers are the first port of call. They're the older brothers of the famous Kevin and have been in and out of the police watch-house so often they're thinking of putting in revolving doors and an escalator up to the nice bedrooms. (That bit's a lie, but around our way everyone locks things up in earnest.)

When we get to their house, we see them sitting on the verandah working out an alibi. Squocka still has the bell part of his trombone so he uses it as a loud hailer. 'Okay, you dirty rats!' It sounds musical.

'Is that Mister Whippy?' Trevor Merry cocks an ear to the street.

Dad pops up from behind a hedge. 'What have you guys done with the wheels?'

'Wheels?' Jim says. 'What wheels?'

'The ones you nicked tonight, you dirty rats,' Squocka bellows through his trombone only it sounds like he's playing *I Tot I Taw a Puddy Tat*.

Anyway, they know the game's up when they see Dad. As we load the Volvo wheels on the truck, Dad says stern words to the Merry brothers, calling them low-lifes and other words he learned from Charlene.

Trevor cringes. 'I can't get a job!' he whines. 'No one'll trust me.'

'*I* don't trust you,' his brother says.

'I need a couple of hefty blokes to dig a ditch to-morrow,' Dad says. 'It's hard yakka with a seven o'clock start and a hairpin bend. Bring your own spades.'

Jim and Trevor Merry clutch each other for support but say they'll be in it.

When we get back home, Dad sends me inside for a quick reconnoitre. Mum is still pouring coffee into Rupert, who's a trifle edgy and showing signs of caffeine overload. He's keen to get home since he promised his mummy he'd have the Volvo back in good time. To keep him glued to the sofa, Mum shows him photos of Charlene when she was a fat little podge with no teeth. Charlene protests, 'Mother!' and tries to cover the one that shows her bare botty.

The thing is, Charlene doesn't know about the missing wheels, so even she is wondering why Mum's using all these delaying tactics.

I report to Dad how things stand with Rupert. Any second he'll be out here ready to make a dash for it. We find the nuts, spanner and jack and soon have the wheels back on the Volvo so that everything's fine. Then we sidle into the front room and give Mum a wink to report a job well done.

But when we see each other in the light, it's a different story. We're a bit grubby from all the muck off the wheels. Hands, faces, T-shirts – you name the place, we've got the dirt. Charlene recoils at the sight of us. She makes several kinds of frown which lets us know we have done a bad thing. Rupert sees this as an excuse to make for the door and a minute later, the Volvo tail lights wink at us from the end of the street as he heads for home.

Charlene blames me for spoiling an otherwise lovely evening. She calls me a misfit, a dropout, a fringe-dweller and a creep, in that order. I protest to Mum who says,

'Let it go, Wayne! And don't you ever breathe a word about those wheels.'

Right! Charlene Wilson, you'll keep! You owe me big time, only you don't know it. When I grow up and write my memoirs, then you'd better look in the index, my girl!

That's all I say.

15 THE HARDER THEY FALL

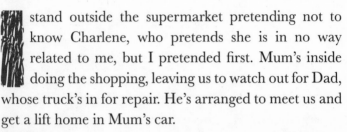stand outside the supermarket pretending not to know Charlene, who pretends she is in no way related to me, but I pretended first. Mum's inside doing the shopping, leaving us to watch out for Dad, whose truck's in for repair. He's arranged to meet us and get a lift home in Mum's car.

What we don't know at this stage is that my father has had a piece of good news and stopped off to celebrate, but kept going too long. He arrives at the supermarket in a taxi and is afflicted with that ancient Spanish condition known as *el Squiffo*. Charlene is the first to recognise the fact. She goes board stiff. Her eyes blaze twin warnings.

'Hello, darling,' Dad greets her with arms wide. 'How about giving your old father a big, smoochy-smoochy kiss?'

'Oh, Daddy.' Charlene tosses her hair as only a wounded heroine can. 'In front of all these people, how could you embarrass me?' She collects an Oscar for over-acting, makes a low bow to the audience, then runs to break the distasteful news to Mum.

'Hi, Dad.' I'm more forgiving than my sister.

'Wayne.' He rewards me with half a bag of prawns he

won in the pub raffle. Dad dropped the other half on the floor of the taxi. 'Where's that little wife of mine, eh?'

'Mum's inside,' I say and try to warn him with my eyes that his wife will not be as thrilled to see him as he thinks. But being *el Squiffo* means my father is not his usual wide-awake self. Instead he sees one of those stupid rocking grey dolphin things that little kids like to sit on as they lick their ice creams to death.

'Come on, Wayne, have a go on this contraption although I can't think why anyone would want to sit on an ocean-going mammal.' I don't want to either. People are looking at Dad but I don't mind. He ain't heavy, he's my father. He puts a coin in the rocking dolphin thing and it starts to sway up and down. Dad watches it for a second or two then has to look away because he's suddenly seasick. 'Oh, bilious,' he says.

Mum arrives to take in my teetering father and the undulating dolphin. I don't know why she bothered because Mum doesn't want to have a conversation with her husband, but simply desires to check that Charlene got the facts right. 'That's it,' Mum snaps, 'make a spectacle of yourself.' She storms back into the supermarket.

'You say spectacle?' he calls after Mum. 'I haven't even started.' My father is not a man to be easily put down.

I crouch behind the shopping trolley to await developments. Dad comes over, gives me a wise wink then starts inspecting the things in the trolley. 'Dad,' I warn, but my father cuts me off.

He drags out several metres of thin sausages, strung together. 'Mm,' he says. 'Looks like Mum's having a barbecue for the footy club.' He decorates himself with the sausages then starts juggling with three eggs. Oops. Correct that – *two* eggs. To make his act even more spectacular, he balances a two-litre soft-drink bottle on his head then goes over and gets up on the seat at the bus stop. 'Look, Wayne,' he calls. 'A tightrope walker.'

'Yes, *very* tight!' Mum has emerged again at this critical moment with Charlene who pushes a trolley full of things. Mum gathers me into her care and heads for the carpark, leaving Dad standing on one leg atop the bus seat with the bottle now balanced on his swaying foot. Waiting passengers think he's been sent by the Council to take their minds off the rotten bus service.

'Mum,' I say. 'How come we've got a trolley full of things and Dad's got a trolley full of things?'

'Your father is full of surprises.' Mum strides on.

I look back and see my father now down on the footpath doing a dance with a mop. Cha-cha-cha, he ruffles its white stringy hair and sings, 'Darling, you dance divinely,' he says.

'I have made up my mind,' Charlene announces. 'I want to divorce my father.'

'You can't!' Mum heads off to find the car. 'That privilege is mine alone.' She opens the door of a car and flops into the front seat, then pulls the lever to release the boot lid. Charlene leaves me with the shopping and flounces in beside Mum.

As I survey the contents of the boot, alarm bells ring ding-a-ling. 'Mum,' I say, 'there's something you should know.'

'Just put the shopping in, Wayne,' Mum tells me. 'And don't argue the toss like a typical male.' I do as she says. After all, parents know best, except Dad of course. I load the shopping, slam the lid shut then slink into the back seat of the car while Mum fumbles to get the key into the ignition. 'Now this idiotic key won't fit,' she snaps. 'This is the stupidest car. Nothing ever works.'

'It's all your husband's fault,' Charlene puts in her bit. 'I mean who'd be seen dead in a smelly car with tatty old seats like this?'

Mum snorts agreement and adjusts the rear-vision mirror but it comes off in her hand. She tosses it out on the ground where the glass breaks. Seven years bad luck, back-dated from the moment Dad turned up *el Squiffo*, if not before.

'Typical,' she says. 'The number of times I've asked your father to fix that mirror. All it wants is a dab of glue, but oh no, he prefers fondling other people's groceries and dancing with mops. He leaves his precious little family to drive about in a stupid car with bits flying off every time we go round a corner. It's nothing but a box of spare parts on wheels.'

'And look at this,' Charlene says. A bit of the dashboard fabric has come loose. She tugs at it and it tears a little. Mum grabs the bit Charlene has torn and yanks a one- metre strip off and hurls it into the carpark.

'Cheapjack rubbish,' she says. 'But I suppose it's the best he could afford.'

Inside the car it suddenly becomes dark. That is because a large lady is blocking all the light. She stands by the driver's door, tapping her foot while looking down at my Mum. She's Kevin Merry's mother and a very big lady. In fact she is the biggest mother in the world and we are in her car, making rude remarks about it, not to mention ripping bits off and throwing them away.

'Oh,' Mum says, then in the same breath, 'Wayne, get our stuff out of the boot.'

But soon we get everything sorted out and drive home in our own car which now has two large bottom-shaped dents in the bonnet from where Mrs Merry gave it the double-buttock treatment because she doesn't have a forgiving nature like mine. It's then I realise Dad's half bag of prawns is lying somewhere. Never mind, they'll turn up before the end of summer.

❧

After a while, like about tea-time, Dad arrives home to find two non-speaking female icicles moving frigidly around our kitchen putting plates and cups away. The refrigerator is turned off because for the time being, we don't need it. Dad sums up the situation expertly and speaks exclusively to me since I am the only un-frigid non-icicle in the house. It takes one to know one.

'Wayne, that woman with the shopping trolley was an old school mate of mine,' he says. 'Remembered me from

Year 9 and was *very* understanding about what happened with her groceries. Lovely lady.'

'That's great, Dad,' I say. 'And you'll never guess in a million years what happened to us. We all got into Mrs Merry's car by— ' But before I can utter another syllable, the larger of the two female icicles freezes my lips solid so I'm unable to speak. 'Oop, oop,' is the best I can do because my mother also has me by the throat. Mum wasn't really an icicle. That was only a literary figure of speech I used to describe how cool she was. (Did you spot it? Good. Give yourself a tick. ✓)

'Oh, lovely lady, is she?' Mum snarls at Dad. 'Understanding was she? Well I hope she's understanding enough to get you something to eat.'

'No need for that,' my father says cheerfully. 'We shared a pizza.'

I'll say this about Dad: for a man in his condition, he sure knows how to duck.

◆

What with the coolness, the sighing and the sad looks from Mum and Charlene, old Dad doesn't get a chance to tell his good news. It takes several days of bringing flowers, chocolates and perfume as well as sleeping on the couch in the lounge. It all adds up. Then comes a thaw and he tells Mum he's landed a big plumbing contract with Joe Sartori, who's building a row of upmarket townhouses. Dad will connect showers, baths, basins, sinks, toilets and bidets, as well as water taps.

That afternoon, Mum, Charlene and I hit the shops again, this time mainly to buy Charlene a new dress for her sweet-sixteen birthday party. Only the best people are invited and I'm being sent to the movies. We have to pick Dad up since his truck's still not fixed because the mechanic's away on six months holiday. Five if he behaves himself. He got caught re-spraying a car that belonged to someone else.

With Charlene's birthday shopping out of the way, Dad turns up in a playful mood. He guides Mum and Charlene to the right car, carefully checks the number plate to confirm it's ours, then inspects the boot to make sure everything in there belongs to the Wilson family. 'Jack, tool-bag, box of tatty old magazines,' he ticks them off. 'Right, Wayne, this is our car all right.' Mum is amused and goes along with the joke. Dad slams the boot lid, then sees Joe Sartori coming our way.

'Hi, Bill,' Mr Sartori greets Dad. 'Next month okay for you to start work?'

'Yeah, fine, Joe,' Dad agrees and introduces Mum to Mr Sartori but he wants to talk technical with Dad about grommets and greebles.

Charlene hasn't paid any attention to this meeting. She's keen to get home to try on her new dress, so fidgets by the open car door, then sees someone she knows coming along the line of parked vehicles. 'There's that Angelo Sartori,' she hisses to Mum. 'He's in my class and he's no angel. Keep an eye on our hub caps, Mum.'

'Charlene,' I whisper urgently. 'Belt up.' I make my

face a sad clown shape and shake my head, but my sister ignores me.

'We did a book review last week,' she goes on, 'only Angelo did it in three words: "This book sucks." He spelt it with an x.' She laughs. Angelo comes in our direction and smiles. Charlene snarls privately for all the world to hear. 'Well, you obnoxious loony, who are you grinning at?'

'Hello, Angelo,' Mr Sartori says unexpectedly, although I expected it. So did Mum and Dad. My parents wince and wait for the outcome.

'Hi, Poppa,' Angelo greets his father, and wonders what's going on.

'This is my son.' Mr Sartori is very serious all of a sudden. 'Angelo's a good boy. Never says a bad thing about anybody.'

'This is my daughter,' Dad says. 'She's got a mouth on her like a deep, dark tunnel.'

Charlene goes bright pink to match her birthday dress. Keep this up and Mum won't need to buy her any accessories.

On the way home in the car, Dad makes Charlene suffer. 'It was going to be a big job, Wayne.' He shakes his head and goes tch, tch. 'If I don't get Joe Sartori's work, we'll be out in the street eating grass sandwiches.' Dad pauses. 'That's if we can afford the bread. But we'll definitely have to eat margarine from now on.'

'Oh Bill, what a disaster,' Mum sighs.

'Oh Daddy, I feel dreadful.' Charlene dabs at a tear.

'Wayne, tell your sister she feels dreadful because she *is* dreadful,' Dad says. 'She needs taking down a peg or three. Tell her that as well.' We drive on in silence.

At home, Mum does a lot of tutting and sighing while Charlene flops on her bed, biting her bottom lip. She wants to make plans for her birthday party, like how the symphony orchestra's going to fit into our lounge room, but she's not game to raise the subject because it'll start Dad off. He makes her suffer. Every time he sees Charlene, he's got something new to say.

Monday: There'll be no more birthday parties in this house. Ever.

Tuesday: We'll have to take in washing, ironing *and* mending.

Wednesday: Wayne, get the tent out for an airing, in case we get evicted.

Thursday: Wayne, you'll have to leave school and get a job!

Friday: The cat will have to go Ta-ta Bonk!

Ta-ta Bonk is Dad's delicate way of saying Fat Cat will have to be p-u-t d-o-w-n or executed. We can't afford to feed useless animals. It would be different if the cat did the washing up or mowed the lawn, but he's too old to learn.

On Saturday we're having dinner around the table in our kitchen. To save money, Dad has turned off the lights so we use a candle. In the dimness it's hard to find my peas, but I don't like them anyway so it's a good excuse.

230

'The shape of things to come,' Dad reminds us. 'Poverty staring us in the face. Never thought I'd see it. P-o-v-v-e-r-t-y.' Charlene would like to tell him that's not how you spell it but a sixth sense warns this is not the time or place for uppity behaviour.

'Bill, have you tried apologising to Mr Sartori?' Mum suggests. Charlene looks up, hoping for some good news, but there's none.

Dad shakes his head. 'I think the man's avoiding me,' he says sadly. 'Can't blame him. I mean, if somebody came out with an unfeeling remark like that about our Wayne, well— '

Charlene wonders what that's got to do with anything.

◆

But every cloud has a silver lining and in this case, it is me. Yes, it's SuperWayne to the rescue! Charlene put her foot in it, so Charlene is the one to make things right. My idea is so brilliant we'll be able to see without the candle. I explain it in seven words, two quotation marks and a full stop. 'Invite Angelo Sartori to the birthday party.'

Thud. That's Charlene's jaw dropping on her plate. Peas scatter in all directions and knock one of the flying ducks off the wall. Two ducks to go and she's got the set.

'M-mm.' Dad considers my suggestion. It is the longest m-mm in the history of parenthood. It goes five times up and down the scale, plays two pop tunes and the national anthem before Dad runs out of breath. (That bit's a lie, but he does say M-mm.)

Mum takes over. 'Well,' she says. 'That *might* do the trick.' Charlene hasn't had time to think of a reply. All she can do is sigh, then get up from her place and leave the kitchen. She pauses with her hand on the doorpost for a final tragic pose, looking like one of those long-haired ladies who get tied to a tree to wait for the local dragon to drop by for lunch. Nobody pays any attention. Mum and Dad discuss the pros and cons of my suggestion while I remind them who came up with such a brilliant idea. Dad even lets me switch on the kitchen light so my parents can see the hopeful expression on each other's faces.

The invitations go out and Angelo's name is on one of them, written in Charlene's blood. Two days later, Mrs Sartori rings to say her boy would love to come to the party. A day after that, Dad comes home smiling to say he got the installation job after all. We can turn the lights on again, eat proper food and ban margarine. Charlene's the only one who's not happy about it.

❖

On the big day, my stocks are still high, which means I get to go to the birthday party. If I push my luck a bit more, maybe I could invite Violet Pridmore, Squocka and Rosana Conti, but I decide not to go there. Instead I stand by our front gate to watch the guests arrive. At three o'clock, a line of majestic cars start dropping off

Charlene's friends – Sharon Collins, Ailsa Watson, Emily Spurgeon, all in their pretty dresses.

Then come the boys, who wear brown shoes, white pants and blue shirts each with two breast pockets buttoned down. They are Mousewald Dunfermline, Webster Lexicon, Rupert Pringle, Dudley Worcester and Dingwall Orkney. Say their names one after the other and it sounds like a list of places you might visit on a holiday to Britain.

It's a small party, just the right number. One and a half boys for every girl. From time to time, Charlene comes out front with her binoculars to look anxiously up and down the street. There's no sign of Angelo Sartori. Maybe he mistook the date or went to the wrong city.

But no, her hopes are dashed. A black car cruises to a stop at our front gate. Da-da-da-dum! Even the car windows are black. The engine cuts and four doors open at the same time. Click, click, click and clump. (Need to get that one fixed.) *Four* guys get out, not just one. They're dressed head-to-foot in black leather and have silver studs all over their clothes. They wear earrings, sideburns and scowls. At the front door Mum greets them.

'G'day, missis,' Angelo grunts. 'Brung me brothers. They got the wheels, see.'

Mum's smile of welcome remains fixed. 'Come in, Angelo. Say hello to the birthday girl.'

The newcomers fill the room with their dark tallness. Charlene recovers and introduces her friends, who seem very small.

'G'day,' Angelo greets them. 'I'm Angelo, dis is Fabiano, dis here's Rufino and over dere's Tomaso.' Angelo's really putting on the ethnic with the 'dis' and 'dere' routine. After introductions, no one knows what to say until one of Rupert's friends rises to the occasion.

'Isn't it funny,' Dingwall Orkney remarks, 'how all your names end in o.'

Fabiano looks him up and down. 'Wanna make somethin' of it?'

'Well, no, actually. I was just struck by the coincidence, that's all.'

'So, what kind of name's Dingwall?' Tomaso sticks his chin out. 'Sounds like an accident at da line dancing. Oh deary me, me partner just dinged the wall.' Nobody dares to laugh.

'Anything to eat, missis?' Rufino asks Mum. The four guys produce bottles of wine. 'Don't worry about drink, just bring on the tucker.'

'We were going to play some games first,' Mum says. 'But maybe I'll get the food.' Dad's in the other room having a snooze. 'Bill, Bill!' Mum disturbs him. 'The Sartori boys have brought – gasp – wine!'

Dad's very calm. 'Italian kids are used to a bit of plonk.' He rolls over.

Back at the party, Angelo pulls the cork from his bottle and pours a glass, then gives it to me. 'Drink, kid,' Angelo growls. It's an order. I take a sip. It's cola. Angelo gives me a private wink. I like him. Charlene and her friends look on in horror.

'Dese games,' Tomaso says. 'Dey got any kissin' in dem?'

'Kissing?' Rupert Pringle repeats the word as if he's been slapped.

'Yeah, you know, with da females – bit of da old clinchin'.'

'Well, no, actually,' Rupert replies. 'We're going to play charades. There's no kissing in charades. Not unless you were to represent Henry Kissinger or someone like that, but it would only be a small kiss.'

'Yes, a *token* kiss,' Mousewald Dunfermline confirms.

The four Italian guys take a sausage roll and munch silently as they consider this information.

'We gotta split,' Angelo says after twenty minutes of manful brooding. 'Thanks for the tucker, missus.' As they file out, each of them produces a parcel and gives it to Charlene. By the time they reach the front door, they're all laughing their heads off.

Charlene comes back from seeing them off. She sighs and the girls sigh with her. It's as if the lights have been turned off.

'Weren't they *exciting*?' Ailsa Watson's eyes shine.

'Flair,' Emily Spurgeon breathes, 'they just *have* it, don't they?'

The boys who are left at the party stick out their two-pocket chests and try to look resolute.

'So, what about these charades, then?' Rupert demands but Charlene gives him a withering look and sighs some more. All of a sudden, things have become very dull.

Later, when I tell Dad what went on in the party room, a big smile comes across his face and he puts a warning finger to his lips. 'Wayne, not a word to your sister.'

'What?' I ask. 'You mean, the whole thing was a set-up?'

Dad taps one side of his nose, gives me a wink, then rolls over and goes back to sleep. But as he lies there, his shoulders start to shake.

16 SHOW BIZ

'm sitting in the front row of the circus, being mildly amused at the antics of a bunch of guys in baggy pants, big feet and red noses. The audience laughs as the clowns fall about, break things, throw pies at each other and generally do childish stuff. I have seen better clowns. What am I saying? I've *been* a better clown. So has my sister.

Squocka likes them and kills himself with laughter. He can be very immature. It's no good pretending we don't know each other because he keeps digging me in the ribs and screaming out, 'Oh, look at that one, Wayne!' Then he pokes his handkerchief into his mouth to stop the excitement spilling out.

'Act your age,' I growl. The strong man was funnier, especially when he dropped an iron bar on his foot, then pretended it didn't hurt. After a while the clowns collect their gear and run off, blowing kisses at the audience who cheer like mad things at a Mad Things Convention.

Squocka blows kisses with both hands. 'Blow kisses, Wayne,' he says. 'Go on. Blow kisses!' Smack, smack. He makes that noise.

'I will not blow kisses,' I snarl through gritted teeth. 'Get real! They were totally unfunny!'

Suddenly, in comes this very small clown who walks around the empty ring with his big feet going flap, flap. He gazes at the audience with a sad look on his face, then uses an outsize megaphone to make an announcement. 'Somebody no laugh at my big brudders,' he tells the audience. 'Itsa very serious when you no laugh. So who's the guy who no like da show?'

'Not us, not us!' The audience show how enthusiastic they were. The little clown walks around sadly staring up into the faces, looking for the one who didn't laugh.

Before I can stop Squocka, or strangle him, he's on his feet pointing at me, shouting, 'He didn't laugh.'

The little clown strides across the ring, kicking up sawdust. 'So! We got a no-laffer, eh?' He looks at me, then says, 'Why you no laugh at my big brudders?'

'Well, I *smiled* a bit. In fact, I smiled a lot.'

Squocka dobs me in even more. 'You said they were totally unfunny.'

At this, the little clown starts to cry and the audience goes, 'Oh!' in one big breath. Somebody hisses, 'Shame.'

'Orright,' says the small clown. 'We work our fingers to da bone, sit up late at night, needling da costumes, putting on da funny noses, practise with da jokes and stuff – and dis guy no laugh!' The audience are enjoying this. Squocka thinks it's the joke of the century, but on the way home he might fall off the bus, then we'll see who laughs with a mouthful of road gravel. 'Right! Mister Miserable who no laugh,' the little clown goes on. 'You come down here and help me shift da scenery.' There's no scenery. Only a chair.

'I've got a bad leg.' I tell him and pretend to have a limp, but it's not something you can do sitting down.

'Liar!' says Squocka. 'Go on, give the little guy a hand.'

The audience begin to chant, 'Go, Mister Miserable! Go, go, go!' They are not taking no for an answer. I stand up and the chant turns to cheers, so I go out in the ring. A spotlight picks me up. So much for keeping a low profile.

'You pick up a da chair,' the small clown orders. Before, I can pick up a da chair, there comes a roll of drums, a crash of cymbals and the little guy does a somersault and ends up sitting in it with his tiny legs waggling like an egg-beater. 'Dat's a funny, eh?' he says and I have to nod agreement. Scale of 1–10, about a 6.

The audience laugh and cheer. The clown falls off the chair and rolls in the sawdust as if he's hurt. He points to me as if I'm to blame.

'Aw!' roar the audience, 'pick on somebody your own size!' They boo and hiss while the little clown runs off wailing like a baby. Seconds later he's back with the strong man who wears a leopard skin and has arms that bulge with rippling muscles. With purpose in every stride he advances towards me.

The audience think this is the funniest thing they've

seen. Squocka must have died of terminal amusement because all I can see are his two legs sticking up in the air.

If I can reach the exit, there might be an early bus, so I sprint. Too late! A bunch of other clowns come on and head me off. They carry blunderbusses, cutlasses, spears, planks of wood with nails through them and a telescope. They've got a barrow full of custard pies and buckets of water. Little clown gets a one-wheel bike and he begins to chase me. The strong man comes after me with a club while the orchestra joins in with a fast, merry tune. Merry for them, not so cheerful for me.

Custard pies on my left, strong man on my right and little clown to the rear and me flat out around the ring. The audience love it; they hoot, clap, shout, snort and so on. Best belly laugh they've had in years. When it's over, I get to take a bow with the strong man and the clowns. The little one presents me with a red nose to wear whenever I need cheering up, like now, for example.

On the way home in the bus, Squocka urges me to wear the red nose, but he's had his ration of jollity for the night. 'It was embarrassing and juvenile,' I say, 'and will make me become a hermit or something lonely.'

'Well, can I have your red nose?'

'You've already got one.' So on that bitter note, we part company. No more show biz for me. Definitely, never again, no way.

❖

Next day at school, thanks to Squocka putting in overtime as a juvenile reporter and circus critic, everyone knows about my performance. Wayne Wilson's show-biz fame has spread far and wide.

Anyway, the fun dies down to be replaced by another sensation. In the hall outside our classroom, a large notice greets my eyes.

BE IN THE CHRISTMAS PAGEANT!
Talented Volunteers needed!
Your chance to show off,
to strut your stuff and make
everyone agog with wonder.
Sign up today.

Our whole class is already agog, except me. Kevin Merry asks, 'Are you agog, Wayne?'

'Yes, Kevin, fairly agog.'

Kevin thinks for a second. 'Wayne, what's a gog?'

'A little wheel like you get inside a clock.'

'You mean, a gog wheel?'

'That's the one.'

Ms Cook is agog in a different way. 'I need you all to be in the pageant!' she declaims dramatically, waving her arms about. 'It's in the New Civic Theatre, with a *huge* stage so we require lots and *lots* of actors to fill it. Wilson, I hear you starred in the circus last night, so put your name down.'

Yeah, sure Ms Cook? After my experience? No way. Everyone else rushes to sign up, but I keep my distance.

A couple of days later, Squocka tells me he's going to be in the Christmas pageant. 'I got a part, Wayne.'

'What? A spare part? A mudguard?'

'Ha, ha, ha. But can I borrow your protractor because I'm gonna be an angle.'

I look at the bit of paper with his part on it. 'That's an *angel*, you dill!'

Squocka is to be the angel who brings the good Christmas tidings and stuff, and there's more. He's to wear a large pair of wings plus winged sandals. I warn him not to jump from great heights because there's no guarantee his flying equipment will keep him suspended in mid-air. Don't try this at home.

Suddenly, Violet Pridmore confronts me, holding the list of names in her hand. 'Wayne, yours isn't here,' she points out. 'The only one in our class.'

'Dah, um, sorry, Violet,' I blush, shuffle my feet, then mumble, 'acting's not my scene.'

'That's cool,' she says. 'I'll put you down as stage manager.'

'Okay, Violet. I'll do it.'

'Check.' Violet ticks my name off the list. 'Rehearsals start Monday.' She smiles warmly, then goes away and my thoughts go with her even more warmly.

What has happened, I hear you ask? Why the change? Don't ask me, but in the last few weeks I've been noticing Violet more and more. I make excuses to talk with her, although usually it's just to listen and look. I give my teeth an extra brush in the morning, comb my hair, stuff like that. In front of my mirror in the privacy of my bedroom, I rehearse cool, sophisticated things that I'll say to her when we meet, but then it's mostly just 'Dah,' and 'Um.' I do a lot of umming and feet shuffling, but so do a thousand other guys, so I guess there's a queue, although I saw her first – way back in Year 1.

The long and short of it is I'm to work backstage, changing scenery and organising props for the actors. This involves operating the machine that makes angel Squocka fly across the stage.

●

The New Civic Theatre is all pine wood, varnish and blue drapes. Trouble is, the place is so brand-new no one quite knows what's what or where anything is. Some cast members run this way, others clump upstairs, then come clumping down again. Everyone talks at the same time, two teachers faint, building workers go on strike, the caretaker has a lie-down and the president of the Amateur Dramatic Club writes a letter to the newspaper editor complaining about the theatre of hooliganism.

The flying machine has a sign on the controls that says: DO NOT TOUCH. MACHINE NOT TESTED. So, it looks as though Squocka's going to be an earth-bound angel. The angel who catches the bus. We find a quiet moment for his rehearsal in which he strolls on stage, points one finger, then proclaims, 'Behold!'

I consider his performance. 'M-mm, looks like you're

about to do the Pull-My-Finger Joke. And angels don't slouch.'

Squocka holds up his pointing finger, inspiration-style, and suggests, 'How about, to take their minds off me not actually flying, I say – *three* words?'

'Such as?'

'Behold, you guys.'

'Nah. It's not biblical. Stick to the script.'

There's a full dress rehearsal in which actors run around looking like plum puddings and chickens. They get mixed up with other actors dressed as Roman legionnaires who go about poking the puddings with their lances and swords. Three swineherds have a fight with a shepherd, who knocks over a small boy who's supposed to be a cherub except he wears football boots.

Unhappy Squocka turns up in his costume. In addition to his feathery wings, he wears a long white nightie sort of thing plus a halo made from cooking foil. It twinkles in the light. 'Wayne, I'm gonna look a real dill,' he growls. 'Walking on stage like this.'

'Well, ha-de-ha-de-hah!' I laugh without mirth. 'Remember the circus? Who made *me* look like a dill? Squocka Berrington, that's who! The angel who can't fly.'

'And whose fault's that?' he accuses in a hoity-toity voice. 'Fine stage manager you are. Don't know how to work the flying machine.'

I am wounded and take my turn at being hoity and toity. 'So that's all the thanks I get? Work my fingers to the bone, organising this, fixing that— '

'Huh! You sound like the little clown guy,' Squocka tells me, then gathers his nightie and stalks off with his nose in the air.

All right, I can take criticism. Even unfair criticism. If Squocka wants to fly, then fly he will.

◆

The man in charge of the machine is the caretaker of the New Civic Theatre. He's in his office and has a cold, so he takes a generous swig of cough mixture. 'Ish all too mush for me,' he cries squiffily. 'Kidsh everywhere, dreshed as Shanta Claushes or Jelly Trifles or Mince Pies. If I see another Robin Redbreast on a Yule Log shinging *It all began on Christmas Day*, I'll need another bottle of this stuff!' Swig, swig.

'Er, I was wondering if we could use your flying machine?' I ask. 'Please?'

'Flying machine?' the caretaker echoes carelessly. 'Didn't even know we had such a thing.' He rummages in his desk and finds an instruction book, then with a wave of his hand, sends me away.

The instruction book is in German and it's for the air-conditioning.

The first thing I do is remove that stupid DO NOT TOUCH notice from the flying machine control panel. It looks straightforward. There are four buttons marked:

0 ⇑ **UP**	0 ⇐ **LEFT**
0 ⇓ **DOWN**	0 ⇒ **RIGHT**

To operate this baby will be a piece of cake. With the stage to myself, I push the Down button and the hook descends from somewhere up high. So far so good. Hanging nearby is a harness with a metal eyelet on it.

At that moment of discovery, Squocka turns up, still dressed in his angelic nightie and winged basketball boots because he hasn't got sandals. When he sees me in charge of things his eyes shine like his cooking-foil halo. 'You got it to work, Wayne?'

'Of course.' I'm still sniffy about his insults, but will let him stew for a while.

He puts the harness on under his nightie and I click the hook onto the eyelet, then hit the Up button and hold him a couple of metres above the stage. Squocka dangles like the angel he's supposed to be. His feet hang down, looking a bit odd with the winged bootees. 'How do I look?' he asks.

'M-mm,' I consider. 'Try it with your undercarriage up.'

Squocka makes a creaking sound effect as he slowly raises his winged bootees until they disappear under his nightie. 'How's that?'

'Okay, fly with wheels down,' I tell him. 'And skip the sound effects.' It's great giving orders.

◆

Meanwhile, you have to be really lucky to avoid getting a ticket to the Christmas Pageant, like being out of town on business. Mum and Dad turn up with Miss Ridley and Aunties Wilma and Edna who have heard about me and the flying machine. Auntie Edna calls me 'the daring young man'. When it comes to getting hold of the wrong end of the stick, Auntie Edna's the one to do it. Charlene and Rupert arrive, Auntie Edna calls him Rudolph, which gives him something to think about. Does she think he's a reindeer, a ballet dancer or a great lover?

Back stage I help Ms Cook assemble little kids and make sure their costumes are on the right way round. In the background Squocka tingles with nervousness, awaiting his death-defying appearance on the flying machine.

Act One is the Sugar Plum Fairies who come on stage shyly, then prance about in time to a Christmas carol. The CD gets stuck and plays the same musical phrase over and over. The S P Fairies swivel their eyes, then go boing, boing, boing on the spot until Ms Cook gives the CD player a slap on the side. By this time, the kids have lost the beat, so they flap around in confusion. Two kids start crying. Mums and dads say, 'Aw', then it's out with the big hook and the 'Psst' to encourage the fairies off stage.

Act Two is a story called 'A Christmas Feast' in which little boys and girls come on dressed as items of festive cheer. The hero of this piece of fiction is Jack Sparkins, who eats too much, then instead of throwing up like everyone else, he has a dream where his Christmas dinner comes back to haunt him and tell him what a fat, greedy pig he is.

During this drama, Squocka approaches me. 'Wayne,' he whispers. 'We only tried going up and down on the flying machine. What about going across the stage?'

'So let's have a try-out here,' I agree.

Squocka already wears the harness under his nightie so he hooks himself on, then signals OK. I press the ⇑ **UP** button and lift him off the floor. I press ⇒ **RIGHT** and he moves away from the stage. The problem is Squocka has got his harness on backwards so he's flying the wrong way round, i.e., face up.

'Bring me back,' he whispers, 'then lower me so I can fix the harness.'

I press ⇐ **LEFT**. The button gets stuck and next thing you know, Squocka is hovering above Jack Sparkins head. Jack is lost for words. This is not in the script.

The audience lets their jaws hang slack at the sight of a weird angel floating across the stage on his back. 'Behold!' Squocka declares. At least he didn't forget his word. I press ⇒ **RIGHT** to bring him back. 'That was a close one, Wayne,' he mutters. 'Don't think anyone noticed.'

'Well, apart from Jack Sparkins and three hundred mums and dads.'

Meanwhile, Jack Sparkins has been put right off his stroke. He was expecting a succession of Stuffed Tomatoes, Jelly Trifles, Plum Puddings and Mince Pies, but no angel. He forgets the rest of his lines and a little Plum Duff has to sneak in and jab him with some festive holly to bring him to his senses.

So we move on to Act Three. It's the Hootenpaffen Triplets with *Der Karols aus Deutschland*. They come bouncing out in matching dirndls and do a knee-slapping dance, then get on with the karols.

Meanwhile, Squocka puts his harness on the right way round, but has another problem. He's supposed to make his entrance from the other side of the stage. I press the ⇑ **UP** button and take him very high so the audience can't see him because of the curtain, or, as we say in show biz, the proscenium arch. Then I push the ⇐ **LEFT** button to transport him to the other side of the stage.

Oops! There's a big spotlight in his way so I stop and press ⇓ **DOWN** to lower him gently, still hoping the audience won't see him. The button gets stuck again and Squocka floats down until one of the Hootenpaffen Triplets catches sight of him out of the corner of her eye. The audience spot him too and their jaws fall open again. It's a great night for slack jaws. No one can believe it.

'Good evening,' Squocka says and raises his halo. Everyone checks their programs to see where this bit fits in.

I press the ⇐ **LEFT** button and he sails off backwards. The Hootenpaffen Triplets don't miss a beat. That's professionalism for you.

Squocka is now on the other side of the stage, where he's supposed to be. He gives me a thumbs-up to signal: 'Mission accomplished.' Then I see Ms Cook approach him. She is not amused. I lip-read and guess that Ms Cook's saying something like, 'Tell Wilson to stop messing about!' She departs with little puffs of smoke emerging from her ears. That mad, eh? And she's not acting. Squocka signals me to bring him back across.

I signal to him, I just delivered you over there.

Nevertheless, he flashes back in sign language, I have an important message for you from Ms Cook. It can't wait.

There's a button at the side marked ⇒⇒, which means double speed. So I give it a push and Squocka skims towards me with his winged bootees trailing on the stage. At this precise moment, The Hootenpaffen Triplets are into *The Lonely Goatherd* so as he hurtles past, Squocka joins in with, 'dooly-oh-le-dooly-oh-le-oh'. Great timing, wrong key. Black mark for Squocka, who says when I let him down, 'Ms Cook wants you to stop messing about. Now, take me back over the other side.'

'No way, my little seraph,' I tell him. 'You *walk* back. I'll send the hook over for you. They'll never see it.'

Squocka, disconnects himself, then goes to march across stage but just in time I show him the back way, behind the scenery. He's done enough damage for one night.

The Hootenpaffen Triplets finish up with a flourish, make a sweet, smiling bow, then come off stage and pass me. 'You're dead, Wilson!' Gerda snarls.

'Yeah, curtains!' snaps Irma.

'It'll be you on that hook next,' Eva adds.

'Love your work, girls.' For my encouraging words I receive a trifecta of glares.

The show goes on. Act Four is kilted and bonneted Squeamish McSporran doing a bagpipe solo entitled *A Scottish Christmas Amang the Heather*. He and his pipes have reached the dying-cat stage when I decide to send the hook across to Squocka. With all that noise and red-faced movement on stage, who's going to see a little hook?

QUICK QUIZ

On its way across the stage, what does the hook latch onto? Tick one.

Squeamish McSporran's kilt?   ❏
Squeamish McSporran's bonnet?   ❏
Squeamish McSporran's bagpipes?   ❏

If you ticked Squeamish McSporran's bagpipes, then give yourself a pat on the back. But Squeamish has a good grip on them and puts up a fight. 'Come back an' behave yersel'!' He struggles to keep the wind in the instrument. But it's a losing battle and Squeamish has to run after his floating bagpipes. Once he's off, he takes a fit of the huff and darkly refuses to go back on. 'Ahm gonna tell ma faither on ye.'

Suddenly, Ms Cook breathes down my neck. 'You have done enough for one night, Wilson,' she intones. 'Touch not a single button until the finale. Got it?'

'Yes, Ms Cook.'

So I watch the rest of the acts – What Santa Wants for Christmas, the Skaters Waltz without skates, Christmas Around the World and then the finale – the First

Christmas. Scruffy Roman legionnaires test their spears on each other, shepherds look for their missing flocks and other kids wrestle plywood cows on stage while Squocka waits to do his big act. 'Excuse me,' he asks Violet. 'What's my word again?'

'Behold, you turkey!'

'That's three words.'

'Behold!'

'Behold. Yeah, got it.'

The curtains draw back, the shepherds watch their flocks and I push my buttons. Angel Squocka gently lifts, then floats out on stage where a spotlight picks him up. 'Behold!' he says. The shepherds look where the angel points. They see the star. Violet leads a choir of small voices on stage, singing, 'While shepherds watch their flocks by night'. In the audience, there are some wet eyes.

I get a lump in my throat. The spotlight fades and I push a button and quietly slide the angel out of the darkened scene. Ms Cook nods, but doesn't say anything. Perhaps she's feeling the way I do.

17 SPECIAL OPERATIONS

t's late Friday afternoon and I'm sharing quality time with my loving family as we wait for the potatoes to boil and the smell-free cabbage to become tender. Mum reads the local paper, Dad does his accounts, Charlene is on her mobile phone murmuring to Rupert while I simply observe the passing scene, making notes for my memoirs.

Suddenly Mum breaks the silence. 'Ooh, what a lot of Saturday specials.' Dad ignores this and keeps counting aloud on his fingers, Charlene makes kissy-kissy noises into the phone mouthpiece while the vegetables bubble merrily in their assorted pots. My mother rubs her hands in delight. 'Specials,' she breathes again.

'Yes, Mum,' I respond dutifully because everyone else has ignored her.

Saturday specials, in case you don't know, are what supermarkets put on to attract customers through the turnstiles. They advertise on a Friday so that shoppers can make plans, then fight and claw each other to bits as they fill their weekend shopping trolleys. The ads say encouraging things like 'Red Hot Bargain', 'Rock Bottom

Prices' or 'Unrepeatable Offer', as if they won't do it all again next Friday.

The Saturday specials that Mum likes best are the ones that warn in stern words: '**L**imit **O**ne **P**er **C**ustomer.' It stands to reason if they say that about an item, then it must be a phenomenal bargain. My mother ticks off six LOPCs, then swings into action. 'Right, tomorrow we're doing a raid on the specials.'

Dad dives for cover, making a don't-involve-me sort of grunt that translates as, 'I've got an emergency ball cock to fit.' He's excused because plumbing comes first.

The usual thing is for Mum to muster her forces and involve the entire family in a strategy that is unbelievably cunning. The idea is for the Wilsons to turn up at the supermarket early on Saturday morning, pretending not to know each other. Everyone has a list so we know what to buy, then afterwards we meet in the carpark like conspirators with our trolleys full of LOPC loot – multiple packets of steel wool, soap powder, cat food, Brekkie Bits plus tubs of margarine, or whatever.

Meanwhile, Charlene is still on her mobile, talking to Rupe Baby and hasn't heard Mum make her plans. Charlene and Rupert are at the compromise stage in their relationship. 'We could do that,' I hear my sister purr. 'But what would *you* like to do, Rupert?' She takes a pause. 'I mean, not just to please me?'

Mum has ideas for this pair. In a stroke of parental genius, she calls to Charlene, 'Is that Rupert on the phone?' (As if we didn't know.)

'Yes, Mum.'

'Look, why not ask him to drop round tomorrow morning,' Mum says. 'We haven't seen Rupert for oh, ages and ages.'

Charlene is thrilled at the suggestion and tells Rupert the good news. She likes to think her boyfriend is flavour of the month in our house. 'He's coming,' Charlene reports with her eyes glowing.

'Tell him to get here good and early,' Mum smiles.

'Many hands make light work,' I add, 'and we need his Volvo.' Luckily Charlene doesn't hear this but with a single glare, my mother renders me speechless.

Mum also rings Squocka's mum, Mrs Berrington, and they compare notes on the Limit One Per Customer specials. Mrs Berrington agrees to be in it too and Squocka will lend a hand.

It's like a military operation. With Charlene still blissfully unaware, Mum prepares shopping lists for four people, then counts out sums of money. To be honest, we don't really need these LOPC specials. I think my mother's just a born organiser and likes the thrill of the chase. If she'd lived in prehistoric times, Mum would be out there with the men of the tribe, hunting down a woolly mammoth.

FLIGHT OF FANCY:

Scene: A prehistoric woodland clearing. A dead woolly mammoth lies on its back with all four feet pointing skywards. My prehistoric mother wears fashionable furry garments and carries a spear and flint knife. Other tribesmen congratulate themselves on their hunting skills.

Mum: *Stand back, you tribesmen. I get first whack. Gotta family to feed.*

Man: *We've all gotta family to feed.*

Mum: *But my family's got Wayne in it.*

Man: *Oh, sorry, I forgot that, missus. Go on, you can have first whack.*

◆

On Saturday morning, Rupert turns up bright and early. Charlene goes to meet him. 'Oh Rupert darling, you got here safely.' They've made it to the darling stage, which I find vomitous, but there it is. She brings him inside.

'We've got an exciting adventure today, Rupert,' Mum tells him.

'Oh, yes?' Rupert looks wary, as well he might.

'We're off to the supermarket to do some shopping,' Mum adds, then she remembers something. 'Oh no, that's done it! Dash and spit!'

'What's wrong, Mum?' I act all concerned, playing the part we rehearsed until we've got it down pat.

'Your dad's got the car so we can't go!'

'Oh no,' I cry, then make it sound like the *Titanic* Disaster of the Week. 'I really wanted to go shopping, Mummy!'

We draw deep sighs of anguish and disappointment, look meaningfully at Rupert, then swivel our glances to the keys of the Volvo, which he foolishly tossed on the coffee table. Try to impress us, eh?

'Oh, well, I suppose— ' Rupert begins.

'Yes? Yes?' I encourage him.

'You mean, we can go in *your* car, Rupert?' Mum can hardly believe this stroke of good fortune.

'Oh, that's so kind of you, Rupert.' I sag with relief. 'Isn't it, Mum?'

With the snow job over, Mum gathers shopping bags. 'I'll explain what to do as we go, Rupert.'

◆

In the Volvo, Mum fills us in on the details.

> **We're not supposed to know each other. ✓**
> **Enter by different turnstiles, use individual trolleys and go separate ways. ✓**
> **If we pass each other in an aisle, on no account do we smile or make remarks. ✓**
> **Any problem: see Mum, speak in a low voice, use one side of the mouth. ✓**
> **Look out for Under-manager Clancy, who is down on LOPC abusers. ✓**

Mrs Berrington and Squocka have their own rules and they don't know each other either and I don't recognise Squocka and he's not acquainted with me, so with that sorted, we start by entering the supermarket in small groups. I scamper around the aisles and get nearly everything on my list, then catch sight of Charlene with her trolley and Rupert with his. They walk along together, looking into each others' eyes – *and holding hands.*

This could threaten the entire mission. Mum's in the next aisle so I slither around to report. 'Mum, Mum,' I whisper, pretending to be interested in a packet of starch on the shelf. I give her the bad news.

'Leave it to me.' Looking as if she's hunting for vanilla flavouring or something, Mum nudges her trolley forward and disappears around the end of the aisle.

With my good deed done for the day, I saunter on and see Squocka in the gardening section, fingering the plastic hoses with brass nozzles. I amble up to him and examine a packet of fertiliser which promises to do wonderful things for your hollyhocks and lupins. 'What you doing, Squocks?' I whisper furtively, using the right side of my mouth because the left is tired from overuse.

'I'm looking for a beige hose, size ten,' he mutters without moving his lips.

'Hoses don't come in beige,' I tell him. 'They only do green ones.'

'It's gotta be beige.' He looks around surreptitiously to make sure we're not being spied upon by Under-manager Clancy, then shows me the list his Mum wrote. It says: *P-hose, size 10, beige.*

'P-hose. That's pantihose, you numbskull!' I mutter under my breath. 'They're in the women's underwear aisle.'

Squocka forgets our urgent need to keep a low profile. 'What? You mean – like knickers and things?' he blurts out. 'I'm not going there. How would it be, me swanning through the checkout with knickers? I'll get a reputation.'

I tell him to keep his voice down. 'They'll be in a packet, mate,' I say. 'The girl's not going to wave them about or anything.'

'Yeah?' Squocka looks doubtful. 'It'll be just my luck for her to sing out, "Look, everybody! Squocka Berrington's buying knickers!"'

'Be a man, mate,' I tell him. 'Be brave. Go on, women's underwear's that way.'

'Well, you come with me.'

Long-suffering, I agree. Squocka leads the way, muttering, to the aisle where the pantihose are.

Wouldn't you know it, we find ourselves in an Aladdin's cave of pantihose. This place has got them in all sizes, colours and shapes from dumpy to lamppost. They've even got ones with three legs. She'd be a whiz at soccer. As we finger the various packets to sort out which is which, who should come around the corner with a trolley full of LOPC specials but Violet Pridmore. 'Hi, Wayne, hi, Squocka,' she carols brightly.

Any other time and any other place I'd be happy to see Violet, but not here in this aisle. Squocka and I stop fingering and looking, then say, 'Hi, Violet,' at the same time. We try not to look guilty.

'What are you guys doing here?' she asks. 'Did you take a wrong turn?'

'A short cut,' Squocka explains, then he's off like a startled rabbit.

Violet's eyes light on my LOPC specials and my eyes settle on hers. 'So,' she accuses, 'you're on a special raid?'

'I won't tell if you don't.'

'Deal,' she responds. Next thing you know, we're walking along the aisle together, talking about this and that and it's very fantastic. When Violet's not looking, I filch a packet of p-hose, size 10 in beige, and slip them between two king-size boxes of cornflakes. Squocka owes me big time.

I'm on the point of suggesting we turn about and go back the other way when my mother comes on the scene to hiss at me, 'Wayne, you got everything?'

'Nearly, Mum.'

Mum swings her surreptitious attention on Violet. 'Saw your mother over in knitwear, Violet.'

'We're pretending not to know each other,' Violet answers.

'Special raid?' Mum asks.

'You bet.'

'How devious,' Mum responds and heads off.

Since we've both got more things to get, Violet and I part company. I ooze past Under-manager Clancy who has already confiscated two trolleys full of LOPC specials. Since I'm feeling impish, I find six LOPC specials and add them to an unattended trolley which contains someone else's shopping. It might create a useful diversion at the checkout.

Squocka is grateful when he sees the p-hose, size 10,

beige, and, for the sake of his blushes, hides them beneath a frozen pizza. Cold stockings. Exotic, eh?

We stroll past a rack of woolly cardigans when there comes a voice. 'Psst!' it says. 'Psst, psst!'

'Sounds like steam escaping.' Squocka looks around but can't see a boiler or anything high-pressured.

'It sounded like a voice,' I tell him, 'going psst.'

'In here,' says the same hissing speaker. We investigate the rack of cardigans. 'Yes, come closer, Wayne. I'm in here.'

Squocka examines a grey bulky-knit job with long sleeves. 'It's this one,' he says with relief, 'and it seems to know you, Wayne.'

'I need your help,' the voice goes on, 'so stop messing about, you knuckle-head!'

'Who are you insulting?' Squocka is offended. 'Like, you're not even pure wool.'

'Belt up, Squocka.' I move closer to the rack, then ask with a note of wonder in my voice, 'Rupert, is that you hiding in there?'

'It's what I've been trying to tell you,' Rupert hisses. 'It's a long story, but the thing is, Wayne, I haven't got any trousers on!'

I roll my eyes at this information. No trousers, eh? What sort of man has my sister got tangled up with? 'Er, how did this come about, Rupe?' I inquire cautiously, keeping my voice low as instructed by Mum.

'I went to try on a pair of work trousers,' says Rupert's voice. 'You know, for when I polish the Volvo. Went into a cubicle, tried a pair on, didn't like the colour, whipped them off and found some swine had pinched mine when I had my back turned.'

'Well, you could have worn the work trousers,' I say.

'Thought of that,' Rupert responds. 'But someone nicked them as well! So I hid in here and thank goodness you've come.'

'Want me to go and get Charlene?' I ask. This is a meeting I'd like to see.

'No, don't do that!' The rack of cardies starts to shake with emotion. 'It would be too embarrassing! Let's keep this between us three guys!'

'What? Like including me?' Squocka backs away.

'Stay where you are, Squocks,' I order. 'Remember who got the p-hose for you.'

'Yeah, okay. You're a hero.'

'Leave it to me,' I assure Rupert. 'I'll get another pair of work trousers and you can wear them. What's your waist and leg length?'

Rupert tells me his size, then I stroll off to the rack of work gear and select the worst colour I can find, making sure the pants are two sizes smaller in all directions. Sometimes a little imp gets into me.

Rupe is grateful, then grunts and pants behind the rack of cardigans and finally emerges but walks with his toes turned in and his eyes watering. 'Oh,' he groans. 'Talk about tight!'

'Okay, it's checkout time.' I nudge my trolley forward to join the Saturday morning throng of baleful and ill-mannered shoppers, all trying not to catch the eye of Under-manager Clancy who's on the prowl. Rupert lines up behind me.

Just then, from the adjoining queue, Charlene sees Rupert in his glorious trousers and the love light fades from her eyes. 'Rupert Pringle!' she snaps. 'What are you wearing?' Still pretending they don't know each other, they have a muttered lovers' tiff.

'I say, Charlene-poops, steady on!'

'Steady on nothing. You're a juvenile exhibitionist!'

'Mum, Mum,' I whisper out of the side of my mouth to my mother who is in the next queue. 'Charlene and Rupert are at it again. They'll blow our cover for sure!' Mum sails along and non-verbally converses with her daughter by means of raised eyebrows, grimaces and head tosses. It has the right effect. Charlene's high temperature reduces to a low simmer. Rupert will keep.

As I go through the checkout, wouldn't you know it, Auntie Edna has just finished her shopping and rolls up the docket. She spots me. 'Yoo-hoo, Wayne Wilson,' she greets me in that musical auntie voice that goes from deep note to high and two times up and down the tonic sol-fa scale.

'Hello, Auntie Edna,' I answer cautiously.

'Doing the Saturday shopping?' she goes on.

'Um, yes.' *No, Auntie Edna. I'm up in a hot-air balloon. Can't you see?* But there's worse to come.

'And you're getting some specials?' Suddenly, Auntie Edna spots Mum who's in her own checkout queue.

'Yoo-hoo, Heather. Specials are good this week, aren't they?' Auntie Edna spots Charlene. 'And yoo-hoo, Charlene. The whole family's here. That's nice.'

For a group of close relatives who're pretending not to know each other, this is not good. Our cover is blown. Under-manager Clancy suspiciously makes a move in our direction, withdrawing his barcode scanner from its holster. But before there comes a showdown, we're saved by an amazing circumstance.

Rupert has reached the checkout where the girl at the till finds *six* specials in his trolley. How did they get there?

'Greedy, eh?' snaps the girl. 'The limit is one per customer!'

'Oh, sorry,' says Rupe. 'Take five of them back.'

'I will!' The girl's voice is full of menace. 'I've met your type before.' Now that she's got Rupert cowed, she calls Under-manager Clancy through the microphone. Her words are amplified over several suburbs. 'Customer here's got six LOPC specials.'

'Come on, sir,' says Under-manager Clancy who rolls up as if he's on little wheels. 'Play the game.'

'Sorry,' Rupert whispers. The girl scans his legitimate items, then takes his money with a smug sneer. Rupert limps away with his trolley, wishing he'd gone jogging instead of getting involved in this humbling business. Suddenly an alarm goes and security people run from all directions.

Rupert has only forgotten to pay for the garish trousers

he's wearing! They've got an anti-shoplifting thing stuck on one of the very short legs. Well, how could he pay for them? He couldn't say casual like, 'Oh yes, and these trousers too.' Then what happens? Is the checkout girl to lean over and consult his bottom to get the price off the ticket? Or worse still, will Under-manager Clancy make him sit on the glass window that reads the bar code? No, it was an honest mistake on Rupert's part and I leave him to sort it out.

'Shoplifter! Shoplifter!' the checkout girls scream and point to the offending Rupert.

'Oh, doesn't he look the type!'

'Shifty eyes!'

'You can spot them a mile off!'

Under-manager Clancy thrives on events like this. Shoplifters make his day. But then comes a second amazing face-saving occurrence. A tall and majestic man approaches. He doesn't have a trolley, so he's not a shopper. No, he's better than any supermarket frequenter; he's the owner of the place. 'Rupert!' he greets his son.

'Dad!' Rupert responds.

This is a turn-up. Under-manager Clancy backs away. Rupert and his father have a huddled conference with Mr Pringle saying 'M-hm' and 'I see'. Charlene comes through her checkout and goes to the side of her man. Rupert's father recognises Charlene, so she's included in the conference. Mum emerges from her checkout and Rupert calls her over to introduce Mr Pringle.

'Pleased to meet you all,' Rupert's father says as we

drape ourselves unnaturally over our trolleys to conceal the LOPC specials. We chit and we chat for a while then go our separate ways, with Rupert leading the procession out to the Volvo.

'Why didn't Rupert say something?' Mum hisses at me.

'Don't know, Mum,' I answer. 'Maybe he didn't like to.'

'I'm so ashamed,' Mum goes on. 'It's as if we've *stolen* from them.' Knowing Mum, I bet she's already thinking it would be no bad thing for Charlene to go out with the son of a supermarket owner. Play her cards right, Dad could get the plumbing maintenance contract too!

Anyway, all's well that ends well and we go to the Volvo with our bags full of LOPC specials. What a morning!

When we get to the car, Rupert points out that the keys were in his trousers, the ones that were stolen.

Five of them manage to squeeze into Mrs Berrington's Mini, with Squocka sitting on Rupert's knee. Everyone knows Squocka's mum's a rotten driver! Corners like a maniac!

Me? I offer to find my own way home. As the Mini scoots off into the traffic, I look over to the corner of the carpark where Violet Pridmore loads her shopping into the boot of her mother's car. She sees me and beckons. 'Wayne, do you want a lift home?'

Smiling, I go to her with my plastic bag of shopping banging against my leg. A trip home in the car with Violet? Now that *is* a Saturday special, with me the only customer.

As her mother steers out of the supermarket carpark, she says, 'What do you think of Violet going to America, Wayne?'

Thud! That's my jaw falling on the floor. Violet picks it up and clips it back in place. 'America?' I echo.

'Yes,' Violet rattles on, 'big country, across the Pacific Ocean, otherwise known as the United States. I'm going there.'

'So what do you think, Wayne?' her mother asks.

'Terrific.' I force a smile. 'Yeah, really terrific.'

No it's not. It's the most un-special news in the world.

In this next bunch of yarns, Wayne's mad sister, Charlene has a bust-up with her demented boyfriend, Rupert Pringle—

Hang on, Squocka. You're treating my family like a soap opera.

Well, soap comes into the story. And rope, and violence.

So, nobody's perfect.

Then we turn to the wonderful work of work.
The unpaid variety. Also known as 'work experience'.

Squocka, did you know it's how they built the Sydney Harbour Bridge? They got all these kids out of high school and said, 'Go on, you'll love it up there. Don't forget your spanner.'

That bit's a lie, Wayne.

But paid employment wasn't much better.

Yeah, babysitting!

And who had time to sit? Answer me that! It should be called, 'Baby-dodging!' Or 'child-avoidance'.

Still, we got out in one piece.

Well, two pieces, since there are two of us.

But only one piece of soap, Wayne.

That's all it took, Squocka. One piece of soap.

18 Soap

One moonlit night, a taxi arrives outside our house, and since Mum's expecting Charlene home, she cocks an ear in that direction. 'Doesn't sound like the Volvo,' she observes. Mum can tell the difference between Rupert's mother's car and one like ours. She flings open the front door and in sweeps Charlene, who wraps herself around my mother's neck in a dramatic way. 'Mummy, it's all over!' she sobs. 'It's all over!'

Dad gets up from his chair in front of television and goes to see what the drama is. 'All over where?' He looks out in the street, but there's no answer to his question.

'*It's* all over, Daddy,' Charlene cries with real tears. 'Would you pay the taxi, please?'

Numb with worry, Dad goes out to fix up the cabbie. 'Thirty-seven dollars!' He recoils. 'Where'd you pick her up, mate? Alice Springs?'

'She howled all the way home,' the driver explains, 'so I bunged on a bit for the emotional stress. It's me soft heart, see.'

Grandpa has come to stay for the weekend, so rouses himself and slippers his way to the front hall to take in the scene. 'What's the matter?' he demands.

'I really don't want to talk about it, Grandfather,' Charlene responds.

Grandfather, eh? So it's serious. Charlene's not up to rending her garments because it took her three weeks to sew the little number she's wearing. (Vogue pattern 1863, in case you want to run one up yourself.)

Meanwhile we males mill around helplessly, wondering what terrible thing could have caused all these tears. Behind Charlene's back, Mum gives a silent this-is-women's-business signal for her menfolk to go away. We make harrumph, harrumph and other manly noises as we stagger around feeling utterly useless.

Television is no longer exciting, not when we have a real drama going on in our kitchen. After a while, we're joined by Mum and red-eyed Charlene, who dabs at her tears with a tissue in each hand.

'Better now?' Dad asks cautiously.

'Oh, Daddy,' she sighs. 'It's all over.'

'Did Rupert hit a cat?' I ask, thinking he might have run over one and it's that kind of all over. 'Or was it a dog?'

'Shut up, Wayne,' one of my elders tells me.

Then slowly, tearfully, Charlene reveals the cause of her angst. She's had a major row with Rupert and it's all over. Da-da-da-dum!

Mum is unhappy because Rupert was a good catch as a potential son-in-law, plus it's nice to see the Volvo parked out front. (Neighbours might think it's ours.) Nearly every time Rupert visits our place, he's good for a small offering from his dad's supermarket: shop-soiled perfume for Mum, executive mustard for Dad and false-teeth cleansing powder for Grandpa. The fact that Rupert is a drop-kick doesn't come into it, but nobody listens to my opinions.

From what Charlene says, I reconstruct the dramatic events of that evening.

Scene: A patch of waste ground overlooking the town, known locally as Lovers' Lane or a good place for dumping old car bodies. Time: A moonlit night.

[CHARLENE AND RUPERT ARE IN THE BACK SEAT OF THE VOLVO. IT IS VERY ROMANTIC. THEY SNOG VIGOROUSLY.]

Rupert: *Oh, Charlene-poops!*

Charlene: *Oh, Fairy Floss!*

Rupert: [SNOG, SNOG, SNOG, PAUSE FOR AIR.] *I say, I've just remembered something, Pretty Princess.*

Charlene: *What is it, Sweet Romeo?*

Rupert: *I've got a present for you.*

Charlene: *A present, Rupert Bear? But it's not my birthday.*

Rupert: *Being heir to a supermarket means not having to wait for birthdays, my little Passion Fruit. It's in the glovebox.*

[CHARLENE OPENS THE GLOVEBOX AND TAKES OUT A BOX. SHE TEARS IT OPEN TO REVEAL A CAKE OF SOAP ON A WHITE ROPE. HER DISAPPOINTMENT SHOWS.]

Charlene: *Aow! It's soap!*

Rupert: *It's called 'Scrub for the Tub', Charlene Charmalot. A new line in Dad's store. When you're in the shower, you won't need to fumble for the soap.*

Charlene: [FROSTY] *I'll thank you not to imagine me in the shower.*

Rupert: [ENTHUSIASTIC] *It's very convenient, little Pollywaffle. It leaves both hands free to wash yourself.*

Charlene: *How dare you suggest I need a shower?*

Rupert: *I didn't. You've always struck me as a pretty clean sort of girl.*

Charlene: *So why give me soap for a present?*

Rupert: [CORRECTS] *'Scrub for the Tub', Charlene-poops!*

Charlene: *If I'm so smelly, Rupert, you won't want to sit with me.*

Rupert: *Oh, Charley Barley, it's just an old bit of soap.*

Charlene: *Well! You have it!* [SWINGS SOAP, HITS RUPERT ON NOSE.]

Rupert: *Oooh! I say! I'be got a bloody node. It'll be all ober Mubby's Bolbo!*

Charlene: *I'm waiting for an apology, Rupert.*

Rupert: *Apology nudding! Look at the bess on the theet!*

Charlene: *So use Scrub for the Tub to wash it off.*

Rupert: *Ungrateful febale! You wash it off.*

Charlene: *So that's your attitude, you chauvinist! You expect the woman to do all the cleaning and drudgery. I'm going home. Don't bother to drive me, I'll get a taxi.* [GETS OUT AND WALKS AWAY, EXPECTING RUPERT TO RUN AFTER HER AND SAY HE'S SORRY.]

Rupert: *Too jolly right you will! Here, take your soap!* [THROWS SOAP OUT AFTER CHARLENE.]

Charlene: [PICKS UP SOAP AND SWINGS IT ROUND HER HEAD AND HURLS IT BACK, HITTING RUPERT ON THE FOREHEAD. CONCERNED, SHE GOES TO THE CAR WINDOW.]
Oh, Rupert darling! Did that hurt?

Rupert: *Of course it did, you maniac!* [HE COWERS IN THE CORNER.]

Charlene: *Rupert darling!* [TRIES TO GET IN BUT HE LOCKS THE DOORS.]

Rupert: *Get away from me, you mad, violent woman! I don't want to see you ever again!*

Which is why Charlene came weeping home in a taxi for thirty-seven dollars.

◆

The next few days are tender and delicate with everyone tippy-toeing around trying not to upset Charlene, who has a long face and does a lot of sighing and wilting.

Poem
Oh what can ail thee, Sister Dear,
Our sweet and lovely daughter?
Yon scoundrel Rupert laid thee low,
The dirty stinking rotter!

When the telephone rings, Charlene asks somebody to answer it in case it's you-know-who. She's given us a list of replies in case Rupert does ring: she's indisposed, has gone away to become a missionary, recently married the postman, become a nun.

Rupert doesn't ring. Charlene checks with the phone company three times a day to make sure our telephone is working. When she's out driving in her Mini and catches sight of a Volvo, she slams on the brakes and has another weeping fit. So that other motorists give her a wide berth, we get her a sticker for the rear windscreen:

At the Sight of a Volvo, Driver Becomes Emotional

(That bit's a lie.)

No one mentions soap, rope or Rupe in Charlene's hearing. You have to think before you speak. For a joke, I plan to refer to him as Ropey Rupert but decide not to risk it. You never know with romantic disintegrations.

Mum neglects the menfolk and fusses around her daughter, offering words of sympathy and appetite-tempting goodies. Charlene toys with the food, sighs, then scrapes the lot into the pedal-bin.

I ask why doesn't Mum put Charlene's meals straight in the garbage and save all the walking in and out with them. For my trouble I receive a barrage of motherly scorn. 'Just wait until you're emotionally shipwrecked. We'll see how you like it!'

Meanwhile, old Rupe Baby is definitely in the wrong. From the injuries he got from the flying soap, he's probably needed a head transplant or something. We could have passed him in the street a dozen times and not recognised him with his new head, but he is *definitely in the wrong!*

Charlene spends hours on the telephone speaking with girlfriends, giving different versions of 'That Night'. After each call, Charlene reports to Mum, 'Mummy, Ailsa agrees that Rupert was totally insensitive.'

'Oh yes, love,' Mum confirms. 'Men are all the same. For a present, your father once gave me a new rear light for a motor bike.'

'You never had a motor bike, Mummy.'

'But *he* did.' Mum smiles at the memory. 'Said the

light went on the back, the place where I sat. They're all the same, men. Big kids, really.'

So there you are – a family poser. One heartbroken sister, daughter and granddaughter, and life is not the same for the men of the Wilson household.

I miss the cheery way Charlene used to snarl and tell me not to be obnoxious. I yearn for the frivolous way she found fault with everything I did and how she used to turn up her nose when Squocka came around to visit and scrounge food. *I* turn up my nose at Squocka but he's my mate, so I'm allowed.

Now that Charlene is in the market for sympathy she's super-sweet to me. 'Oh, here is my dear brother Wayne,' she sighs from her sofa where she's rapidly fading away to nothing. 'How did you find school today?'

'Just went along the road,' I reply warily, 'turned left and there it was.'

'Oh, a little joke,' she dabs at a tear. 'It's easy for you to be funny, Wayne dear, but I'll never laugh again.' Tragic, tragic, sigh, sigh.

●

The following Saturday afternoon, Grandpa's home from Dwell-a-Wee, and in the kitchen, doing the young lovers' crossword from one of Charlene's vomitous magazines for the incurably lovesick. [*Appetite – The Magazine for the Young and Lovelorn.*]

'Tell you what, Wayne boy,' Grandpa says. 'I've had a basinful of that sister of yours. Mournful Maggie.'

'Yes, Grandpa. She can be hard to take.'

He concentrates on 23 down. The clue is: 'Such sweet sorrow.' He writes 'farting'. Charlene will be amused. 'I feel like banging their heads together,' Grandpa goes on.

'Rupert won't like that,' I say. 'It's where Charlene got him with the soap.'

'In a manner of speaking, I mean,' he growls. 'If they're to spend the rest of their lives together, they can't flare up like a bushfire when one of them says a wrong word.'

'She does a lot of that, Gramps.'

'*And* she's as miserable as a wet holiday,' Grandpa adds. 'And so is he. They only have to pick up the phone and say sorry and it's all fixed.'

'Yes, Gramps.'

'Time we did something, Wayne boy,' he goes on. 'Put them out of their misery.'

'How?' It sets me wondering. I'll need to know this if Violet Pridmore and I become long-distance lovers.

Grandpa turns to the advice column in *Appetite*. No young woman has written into the magazine to say she's recently clocked her boyfriend with a swinging cake of soap and he's not speaking any more, so there's no help from that direction.

Then that very same evening, Grandpa does something mysterious. He wears a raincoat, shoes and socks, but no trousers! Da-da-da-dum!

What's going on? He opens his coat to reveal an

ancient pair of running shorts and a singlet. He puts his cloth cap on backwards. 'I'm off jogging,' he says. Oh no! I remember what happened last time we were involved in such physical activity. The memory of those jogging women and their stinging rebuke will stay with me for ever.

'You can't jog at your age!' I protest. 'I'll tell Mu— ' Before I can utter the rest of that word, Grandpa claps his hand over my mouth and frowns at me not to tell a soul, especially not my mother.

We go on the bus and people give us strange looks. I try to tell them he's only going jogging but cannot think of a way to open a conversation with so many people at the same time. Perhaps I should just stand and make an announcement.

FLIGHT OF FANCY:

'May I have your attention, ladies and gentlemen, boys and girls? This is my grandfather, who's a harmless old stick, but a bit batty. This evening he says he's going jogging. Yesterday he wanted to wrestle steers, so who knows what tomorrow may bring. Thank you for your kind attention. Now look to the front and enjoy the rest of your journey. Next stop is the abattoir.'

The bus trundles on until at last we get off at the bicycle path along the river. Grandpa sits on a park bench and inspects the joggers pounding and panting their way through the balmy evening air. He's looking for somebody.

'So what about this jogging?' I ask.

'Mind your own business,' he says. He looks left and right, then springs up, throwing off his raincoat. Grandpa takes half a dozen steps before faltering with a cry of 'Oooh!' He sinks to his knees. I go to him and he gives me a wink. Just then, a young male jogger comes along and yes, yes, yes, it is Rupe Baby, completely recovered from his soap-induced injuries. 'It's my grandpa,' I say to Rupert, pretending to be overwhelmed by the seriousness of it all. 'He's done it this time.'

Rupert helps Grandpa to his feet and we shuffle together to the bench where he sits and shakes. 'Me old ticker,' Grandpa says. 'Looks like I'll have to slow down a bit. Not do so many kilometres.'

Then Rupert recognises me. 'Wayne.'

'Rupert,' I respond. 'Fancy meeting you here.'

'Yes.' He gazes down at his sneakers, looking as if he's got something on his mind. He tries to be offhand. 'How is Charlene?'

'She's fine,' I reply.

'She's gone out tonight,' Grandpa lies. 'With a fella. What's his name, Wayne?'

'Gregorovich Rasputin,' I say.

It means nothing to Rupert. He ponders deeply. Ponder, ponder, think, think, gloom, gloom. I can read it in his eyes. 'Well, if you're all right,' he says at last. 'I'll get on. But you should give up jogging.'

'Me? Give up jogging?' Grandpa is offended. 'I'll jog till I die. I ran the marathon in the Helsinki Olympics.

They can't keep me off the track. What's a few palpitations, a heart murmur and a gammy leg? Off you go, young fellow, I'll keep pace with you.' Grandpa struggles to his feet, wheezing loudly.

'Look, Wayne,' Rupert hisses. 'Your grandfather's not fit.'

Grandpa gives another wheeze. A real death's-door job. 'Oh, where's me last will and testament? The light is fading, oh dear, so this is it. The curtain's coming down.'

'I'll get a taxi.' I speak urgently. 'Or an ambulance.'

'Better than that,' Rupert says. 'The Volvo's over there. I'll fetch it.'

Off he trots, the sucker, while Grandpa stops acting and sits with a smile on his face. 'Phase one,' he tells me with a wink.

❖

Phase two is when the Volvo comes to rest at our front door and Mum bustles out to help Grandpa into the house. She spends her time telling Grandpa what an old fool he is and thanking Rupert for his Good Samaritan act.

Just to make sure Rupe Baby comes inside, Grandpa throws another wobbly and has to be helped through the front door and into the living room.

Then – Da-da-da-dum! Charlene comes on the scene. She is not out with Gregorovich Rasputin. That's a little lie we made up. (Did you spot it?)

'Hello, Charlene,' Rupert says formally.

'Yes, hello, Rupert,' she answers. 'Have you been keeping well?'

'Never better.'

Grandpa collapses in his chair in front of television. Rupert makes to leave, but Mum is not letting go. 'Have a cup of coffee, Rupert,' she offers.

He dithers, then Grandpa makes up his mind for him. 'Of course he'll have coffee. Charlene, coffee for this lad who saved my life.'

'Oh, all right. Coffee, thank you.' Rupert says, then sits gingerly on a chair beside Grandpa. 'I'm a bit sweaty. After jogging,' he tells us. 'Seven kilometres.'

'I did ten,' Grandpa lies.

'Why not have a shower, Rupert?' is Mum's brainwave.

'Well, yes,' Rupert decides. 'My tracksuit's in the Volvo. To change into.'

'Wayne, fetch Rupert's tracksuit,' Mum says. It goes like a well-rehearsed script. Everything falls into place.

'Charlene!' Grandpa shouts. 'Rupert's having a shower. Get him a towel!'

Charlene comes in. She doesn't like being spoken to like that, but this is as close as she's been to Rupert since That Night. 'I'll put one in the bathroom for you.' She pauses. 'And a fresh cake of soap.'

It's Rupert's turn to pause. He grins, then asks, 'On a rope?' There's another really long suspension of conversation, then Charlene smiles. Rupert laughs and she laughs too. I have a bit of a grin on my face because it's better this way.

'Harrumph.' Grandpa rises from his chair. 'I've got to rinse out me singlet for tomorrow. I'm pumping iron.' He shuffles out, followed by Mum who drags me by the ear, leaving Charlene and Rupert who're already making hot, R-certificate glances.

'There you are,' says Grandpa as Mum closes the door. 'Piece of cake. Now we can get some harmony in the house.'

Dad comes home and Mum fills him in on the details, using a special language that parents have developed for times like these. Hand signals from Mum and grunts from Dad.

Half an hour later, Charlene comes out dragging Rupert by the hand. Her eyes are shining, while he's got a sheepish look on his face.

'Mummy, Daddy, Grandpa, Wayne,' Charlene announces. 'We've got something to tell you.'

'I suppose I should speak with Mr Wilson first,' Rupert hesitates.

'Don't worry, Rupert. Mr Wilson won't mind,' Mum gives Dad a nudge in the ribcage to make sure he doesn't.

'Thing is,' Rupert goes on. 'Charlene and I would like to get engaged.'

'Well, *that's* a surprise!' Grandpa gives me a big wink. Then there's kissing, hugging and handshaking all round, general clucking and going on.

Much later, after Rupert has had his shower and the
hubbub has died down a bit, we're all sitting around
feeling good about being part of this little family, when
who should arrive but Squocka, my old buddy and best
friend, got up in his best jeans and sneakers. He congrat-
ulates Charlene and Rupert, then casually lets drop that
he's dressed so sharply because he's on his way to a
birthday party given by one Rosana Conti.

'How come I didn't get an invite?' I inquire of my
chum.

'Oh yeah,' he says. 'You *did* get one. Rosana asked
me to give it to you but I forgot to take it out of me shirt
pocket and Mum put it in the wash and ruined it, so I
didn't like to say.'

'I see.' I'm emotionally shipwrecked, but don't let it
show.

'I got Rosana a present.' Squocka produces a parcel
wrapped up in gift paper.

'What did you buy her?' Mum asks.

'Something nice?' Charlene is her old self again
and only needs to let fly at me with a couple of insults
and she'll be fully restored. 'Not Scrub for the Tub?'
There is a tense moment, then everybody smiles.

'Scrub for the Tub?' Squocka can't believe such an
idea. 'That would be tacky and insensitive! Who'd give a
woman soap?'

Rupert says 'ahem' and looks away. Charlene smiles even more.

Squocka shows his birthday parcel. 'I got deodorant and toothpaste.'

Rupert puts a man-to-man arm around Squocka's shoulder. 'Let me give you some advice, Squocka. From an expert.'

Squocka is all ears, the rat!

19 Work Experience

t is dark in my bedroom because it's half-past five on a winter holiday morning. I'm fast asleep like a good little human being, dreaming of Violet Pridmore in the United States, when suddenly, there comes a voice that says, 'Wayne Wilson. This is your big day. Time to join the workforce!'

It sounds like my father and when I prop one eye open, it *is* my father and he has a large ear-to-ear kind of grin on his face. Oh no! I remember. It's work experience!

A few days before this slumber-shattering event, Dad said, 'It's time you had some work experience, Wayne. I'll have a word with the foreman at the building site. He'll give you a week of it.'

I tell Dad that holidays are more my line of work, but he ignores that and says how good it'll be for me. He's got a list of benefits: it will put muscles on my thin frame, make me realise what goes on in the workplace, teach me how to be punctual, how to take orders and work as a member of a team. Every time Dad sees me, he adds more to the list. Work experience has lots of pluses.

The opposite of pluses is minuses and I forgot to ask about them. There's a big one. You don't get paid. Since

I believe in spreading good fortune around, I ask Dad if he can arrange some work experience for Squocka. 'Yeah, why not?' Dad agrees. 'Make sure his mum and dad are okay with it and I'll fix it at the workface end.'

My cunning plan is that with two of us on the building site, I'll only have to do fifty per cent of the work. Squocka gets the nod from his parents and it's arranged. On this bout of work experience, we're to be junior labourers. 'Not so much labourers,' Dad explains. 'You'll be go-fors. You know, go for this, go for that. Fetch and carry, shift that rubbish, polish that doorknob.'

'You mean labourers, Dad?'

'Nothing wrong with labour, lad. It's noble. Sweat on your brow, a pick and shovel in your hands.'

'What! At the same time?' Squocka protests. 'I'll get blisters!'

'It's good experience.' Dad reassures us. 'You start at half-past six on Monday. I'll give Wayne a call an hour before so we get there in good time.'

◆

Morning one of our work experience falls in the coldest day of winter. At half-past five it's still dark and a freezing wind blows. Dad is hale and hearty as he clumps about the kitchen making tea and frying things, telling me to eat up. He cuts huge slices of bread and spreads things on them to make our lunch, then at last it's time to go.

Outside, the wind takes a big bite out of me and I'll never be the same again. We have to roll-start the truck because Dad doesn't like to disturb Mum and Charlene, so we trundle down the street past all the houses where our lucky neighbours are in beddy-byes. The truck starts and we're off. Brmm, brmm. That's the engine. Chatter, chatter. That's my teeth.

At Squocka's place, the front door opens and a padded zombie appears wearing a bobble hat. It is Squocka himself who is being pushed out into the cold by his mum, who wears a chenille dressing gown, so I know where she's going as soon as the front door shuts. She doesn't even take in the milk!

Squocka climbs into the truck. 'Morning, Mr Wilson, morning, Wayne.' Already he's moaning. 'Why did I say yes? I'd jump out and run home except Mum's locked the front door and hidden my bed.'

Dad becomes robust and enthusiastic. 'Think of the good things, son.'

'And the money I'll earn,' Squocka says.

Apart from the brmm, brmm noise from the engine and the sound of icicles dropping from the cab roof, there's a sudden silence until I go, 'Ahem,' and break the bad news to him gently. He faints and needs to be fanned with his empty wallet.

Early in the morning, building sites are grey. Technicolour doesn't happen until the sun gets up. If it rained overnight, building sites are grey and muddy. If there's a cold wind blowing, they are grey, muddy and freezing cold, like this one.

Workmen walk around carrying long things on their

shoulder or wheeling short things in barrows. Everyone greets everyone else. 'Morning, Trev,' Dad says to Trev and Trev answers, 'Morning, Bill.' Then it's, 'Morning, Sam, morning, George, morning, Enzio,' until there's no one else to say 'Morning' to. Then after lunch they start all over again with a different time of day greeting.

I reckon workmen spend too much time saying, 'Morning', 'Afternoon' or 'Cheerio' to each other. (Some say, 'Hoo-roo' or 'What? You here again?') Think of the time they'd save if they wore message buttons and pointed to them as they walked past each other.

There's a small blue-painted shed with a portable toilet next to it. The shed stands beside a newly completed house that's waiting for the owners to move in. 'Foreman's in that shed over there,' Dad says. 'He'll show you what to do.' My fortunate father goes off to put in vanity basins or something elegant where he'll work inside, sheltered from the wind and freezing cold. We trudge across the soggy ground, then see another disadvantage of work experience. It is Kevin Merry, trundling a new red wheelbarrow with a long-handled shovel bouncing in it!

'I'd turn my feet the other way,' Squocka mutters, 'only I can't get them out of this mud.'

Kevin wears overalls and at first doesn't see us because he's concentrating on steering his wheelbarrow. Then he raises his eyes and stops. 'Hey, you guys! Don't even *think* of going in that toilet.'

'Wasn't going to,' Squocka tells him. 'I've sworn off

toilets. Went yesterday and that's me for the rest of my days.'

'Yeah, well that's your problem. That dunny belongs to Doctor Death,' Kevin informs us.

Doctor Death, eh? What have we let ourselves in for? But that's only Kevin's nickname for the foreman and we're not to use it, and not to mention who made up the name in the first place.

'Thanks for the tip, Kev,' I say.

'Okay, gotta get on.' Kevin uses his gruff workforce voice. 'Things to do, places to be.' He struggles on across the muddy field with his wheelbarrow.

Doctor Death comes out of his shed. He's a tall man wearing a hard hat and immaculate overalls and shaggy eyebrows that do most of the talking for him. 'Work experience, is it?' he snarls and his eyebrows meet in the middle of his face, somewhere above his nose. 'Right, no mucking about, be punctual, do what you're told and you might learn something.' He sounds like Dad with his list of benefits, only from this fearsome man they sound like punishments. He gives us our first job. 'I want you to go for a long stand.'

'How long?' I ask.

'They only come in one size,' Doctor Death snaps. 'Long.'

Squocka wants to argue the point, saying that if you have a long stand, then you need to have a shorter one otherwise how will you know that the long one really is long. It might actually be a short one because there could be longer ones somewhere else, like in the storeroom or in a mail-order catalogue. You never know with long stands.

'You finished?' Doctor Death asks in tones of great ominousness, his eyebrows disappearing under his hat. He's not interested in Squocka's logic. 'Go and ask Percy to give you a long stand.'

'Where's Percy?' I ask. Doctor Death points in a direction away from his shed and private toilet. We trudge across the mud, looking for a helpful sign that says:

> **PERCY THIS WAY ➜ ➜ ➜**

Eventually we find the man. Percy is a carpenter with grey hair, thick glasses and a nervous habit of hammering nails into things. If it doesn't move, then bang bang, in goes a nail. 'What do you boys want?' Percy demands.

'The foreman says you'll give us a long stand.'

'Right, go and stand over there.' He indicates a place. 'I'll fix you in a minute.'

We stand where he tells us while he gets on with nailing things to other things. Workmen walk past and ask us what we're doing. We tell them we're waiting for a long stand, which makes them go away sniggering and guffawing. It's very jolly on a building site, only we don't get the joke.

Squocka finds an empty oil drum and sits, but Hammering Percy frowns in his direction. 'Hoi, you! The foreman said a long stand, not a long sit.'

Clang! The penny drops. We've been on-site entertainment! That's why they've been strolling past, then killing themselves with merriment.

FLIGHT OF FANCY:

It is very tense in the coroner's court.
Coroner: *How did this workman die?*
Witness: *He laughed himself to death.*
Coroner: *What was the joke?*
Witness: *The one about sending two kids for a long stand.*
Coroner: *Oh I remember that one. Very funny. Causes lots of deaths, that does.*

Percy starts to wheeze and turn purple. Maybe he's about to die too, but no, it's a form of silent, shoulder-shaking laughter we've not seen before. He cackles so much, he bangs in a nail, which bends. This makes Squocka laugh. Percy sees it as an insult and glares, then picks up two claw hammers and swings them like he was doing Kung fu.

Building Site Rule Number 1: *Victims must not enjoy the joke.*

We return to Doctor Death, who's in his blue-painted shed sharpening his teeth and practising intimidation and browbeating. He asks, 'Did you get a long stand?'

'Yeah, it's outside,' Squocka says nonchalantly. 'Where do you want it?'

This does not please Doctor Death, and we learn Building Site Rule Number 2: *Victims are not allowed to make their own jokes.*

The idea is to let them have a chuckle at our expense. One day, we will get a chance to be cruel and hurtful to newcomers, then we'll have a giggle too.

●

Time rolls on and our next assignment is to see what the men want from the Shop.

Near every building site there is a Shop where workers buy things like sticky buns, soft drinks, cartons of peculiarly flavoured milk, pies and sausage rolls.

The men give us their order and money, writing what they want on bits of paper, cardboard, planks of wood, house bricks and a dozen other things. We'll have trouble carrying them and feel sure we'll get it wrong. The men are good-natured about it and say no, no, it's a piece of cake. Dead simple. Even a nong can get it right.

It's brainwave time. We approach Kevin Merry, who lovingly polishes his red wheelbarrow, which is spotless and unused. 'Kevin,' I tell him, 'Doctor Death says we're to use your wheelbarrow to go to the Shop.'

'Use my wheelbarrow? Use my wheelbarrow?' Kevin's voice goes so high it can only be heard by dogs. 'No way.'

'Okay,' Squocka adds to my lie, 'we'll tell Doctor Death you said no, right?'

Kevin hums and haws. His bottom lip drops. He grits his teeth then slowly, slowly lets go of the wheelbarrow handles. 'All right. Take it, but you're not using my shovel.' He grabs it and holds it close to his body.

'We're only going to the shop,' I tell him. 'Not a polar expedition.'

We trundle the wheelbarrow off the site, while Kevin watches us with shoulders slumped so low it looks like two long-handled shovels standing side by side. The wheelbarrow is great fun. The rubber tyre bounces bouncily over every little cobble and bobble on the ground. We find the Shop and pile all the orders on the counter. They make a stack so high the shopkeeper has to stand on a chair to see us. (That bit's a lie.)

Soon we head back to the site with the wheelbarrow full of steaming hot pies, sausage rolls, peppermint milk and cold cans of Fizzy Slush and Squidgy-Fruit. It is not long before we realise we're lost. We ask passers-by if they've seen a building site and they say smart things like 'Where did you leave it?' and 'Which way was it going?'

It starts to rain and the lunch orders get wet, so we hurry. It is a rule of nature that if you move faster than a walking pace with a bouncy-wheeled wheelbarrow, it bounces even higher. By the time we find the building site the starving workmen have lost their good-natured, cheerful high spirits. They hurl insults at us and snatch up their damp lunches, then for a moment or two there is a grudging silence until they pop their cans of fizzy drink. As the over-stimulated cans rip open at the same time there comes such a bursting and swooshing it's like an underwater fireworks display. The entire site and its workforce becomes drenched in multi-coloured liquid. The stuff drips from noses, eyebrows and other facial features. Some houses won't need to be painted.

To make things worse, the hot pies and sausage rolls, said to be filled with mouth-watering prime minced beef and flavoursome gravy, are now a soggy mass of frozen fat and gristle you wouldn't give to a dog. That's what super-bouncy wheeling in the rain does for you.

After a while the 'Yechs' and 'Yuks' of disgust from our work colleagues become too much to bear, so we wander off while the going is good.

◆

Later, Doctor Death blames us for putting his lads in a bad temper. We are Marked Men who didn't have lunch either. As punishment, we get to work with Hammering Percy, who has blue fizzy-drink stains on his overalls. He growls, then snarls, 'Go to the store and get me a pair of sky-hooks.'

We trudge off, but Squocka has twigged. 'This is another joke, right?'

I agree, 'It's like the long stand, tartan paint and a left-handed screwdriver.'

'Or a new jackum-flip for an oglibob,' Squocka suggests. 'Or thrupple nuts and double-headed split-pins.'

Our idea is to say the store was out of sky-hooks so we decide to look for an ordinary ladder. Not only will it fill in time, it's also well-known that if you walk about carrying something, it makes you look busy. We find a convenient ladder leaning against a half-built house and carry it to Percy, who doesn't die laughing so we saved his life.

Tragedy strikes. The ladder we took belonged to some roof tilers who were stranded up there. They were spotted by the pilot of a low-flying airliner who advised the authorities. (That bit's a lie, but the roof tilers are angry and blame Percy for taking their ladder.) By this time we have moved on to seek fresh work experiences.

'Psst,' says a familiar voice. We look and see Kevin Merry lurking behind a tin shed. 'Guys, come and see this.'

We move around the shed and see that Kevin has got the long-handled shovel to stand up vertically in his wheelbarrow. Squocka has a note of wonder in his voice. 'How'd you do that, Kev?'

'I spilled a can of Speed-fast glue,' Kevin explains, 'then tried to scoop it out, only me shovel got stuck.'

'It looks like a yacht with one mast and no sail,' I tell him.

'Yeah, you should fly a flag on it,' Squocka suggests. 'Show a bit of patriotism.'

We're enjoying this, but Kevin's not. 'Very funny,' he says. 'So what are we going to do about it?'

'We?' Squocka puts a hand to his chest and takes a step back. 'You said, "we", as in Wayne and me?'

'Well,' Kevin points out reasonably, 'you guys were last to use the wheelbarrow, so you'll get the blame.'

'Oh, charming,' Squocka says. We inspect the disaster, pushing and pulling the handle of the shovel, but it's not going to budge. But something else has budged. It is Kevin Merry who is nowhere to be seen. Even his foot-prints have gone. Typical! Turn your back and he's off. Now it *is* our problem.

'Any ideas, Squocka?'

'How about we hide it?'

'Good thinking. Hide it where?'

We look around the building site, wondering how we can camouflage a brand-new red-painted wheelbarrow with a long-handled shovel sticking up in the air. Stroll-ing about casually, we find that all the best hiding places are full of other items that men have hidden in the past, like snapped-off shovels, bent crowbars, a damaged anvil and two vanity basins that accidentally fell off a truck. 'What about a hole?' Squocka asks.

'Where are we going to put it?'

'In the ground,' he responds.

'It'll have to be a big one,' I say, 'and besides, we can't go digging deep holes in a building site. There might be drains and stuff.'

'Yeah, and if Doctor Death spots us, he's going to ask what we're doing.'

'So let's get someone else to dig it for us. Like him.' I point.

There's a Lebanese guy sitting in a backhoe with nothing much to do. He seems fairly happy-go-lucky, the kind who might enjoy a joke. We sidle up to him and say, 'Psst!'

The backhoe driver's name is Ahwad. We explain

everything: Kevin Merry – tin of Speed-fast glue – long-handled shovel sticking up like a rude finger – need to hide the damage, deep hole-wise – what about it?

Ahwad thinks it's the funniest thing he's heard and agrees to dig a quick hole and he'll even fill it in for us afterwards.

We do a rapid check to make sure Doctor Death isn't about, then choose a spot in front of the newly finished house and stand aside to admire Ahwad's workmanship. With the coast clear, we trundle in the wheelbarrow and its tell-tale long-handled shovel. A few quick scrapes of the backhoe and the hole is filled in.

This is when two tragedies strike.

Tragedy One: The hole isn't deep enough to hide the handle of the shovel. It sticks out of the ground like an accusing finger. We try to break it off but it's made of good Australian hickory. We beg Ahwad to snap the handle off, only to witness:

Tragedy Two: Ahwad reverses carelessly away from the scene and his backhoe knocks over Doctor Death's private toilet.

'Okay, you guys,' he says. 'I'm out of here!' With a voom the backhoe disappears, and we're on our own.

'We need a saw,' Squocka snaps. 'Hammering Percy's the man. Let's go.'

Percy hates us for what we did to his Blue Passion Fruit Pulp at lunchtime, not to mention the ladder dispute with the stranded roof tilers. We decide on a softly, softly approach. 'Percy,' I begin in a wheedling voice. 'We'd like to cut off a bit of wood, so can we borrow a saw?'

'No,' he snarls and bangs in a nail.

'Oh, please, Mister Percy,' Squocka pleads. 'How can we learn if you won't let us saw a bit of wood?'

'Everyone reckons you're the best carpenter on the site,' I add.

Percy weakens. He likes that kind of talk. 'So, what sort of saw do you want?'

'A sharp one.' Squocka almost blows it.

'They're *all* sharp!' Hammering Percy snaps. 'When I say what sort, I mean do you want a cross-cut, a tenon, a rip-saw or what?'

Squocka says, 'It's for cutting the handle off a shovel.'

Percy becomes suspicious. 'A shovel, eh? Where do you want to cut it off?'

'At ground level,' Squocka tells him. That does it! Percy will have no part in it, so we go away saw-less.

We return to the spot where we buried the wheel-barrow to find that something wondrous has happened. Doctor Death stands with folded arms, looking down at Kevin Merry. He indicates his private toilet, which is lying on its side. 'Kevin Merry, did you do this to my restricted-use executive convenience?'

'No, sir.' Kevin shakes his head in wonder.

'Right, I'll get to the bottom of it later,' Doctor Death growls. 'Just at this moment I've got a job for you, lad.'

Along comes Sue the Architect in her hard hat and fashionable steel-capped boots. She's the one who designed the house and has brought the new owners to inspect their property. They're young newlyweds, which makes Doctor Death go soft and mellow. The new owners' idea is to plant a tree in what will be their front garden. Since this is the first house completed on the site, other workmen gather around to watch the planting ceremony.

Gallant Doctor Death produces a spade, then asks the couple where they'd like the hole for the tree.

'Here,' says the husband, and points to a spot in the ground.

His wife adds, 'Someone's already put a stake in. How thoughtful.'

Kevin Merry wears a look of horror because he recognises the stake for what it is. Doctor Death gives him the spade and says, 'Dig right there, Kevin. The ground's nice and soft.'

Everyone stands back to watch Kevin, and I whisper to Squocka in a not-our-fault sort of voice, 'Who'd have thought work experience could be so fascinating?'

20 WE BABYSIT ANYTHING

There's nothing worse than not having a lot of money, apart from not having any money. We face terminal poverty and the school holidays yawn penniless in front of us. To make things worse, Violet Pridmore hasn't sent me a postcard from America. The good news is she hasn't sent one to Squocka either. He doesn't seem to care very much. His main complaint is about being a member of the cashless society. 'Wayne, I gotta have bread,' he wails. 'Give me bread.'

'Multi-grain? Hi-fibre? Wholemeal? Gluten-free?'

He responds in a half-baked way. 'This is not the time for stale jokes.'

'Okay, hand me the bread-knife and I'll slice them in half.'

'Come on, Wayne. We need to earn a crust.'

'I thought we'd stopped making bread jokes?'

'Ha, ha.' Squocka laughs a mirthless laugh.

But suddenly, I'm on a roll! Eureka! The idea of the century. 'Squocks, old buddy, what say we go into business?' I sketch out my money-making scheme.

'Babysitting?' he echoes. 'You mean, looking after little kids?'

'No, we look after *other* things. Babysitting's only a concept.' I get out some cardboard and Charlene's felt-tip pens that she hates me using and print a notice.

WE BABYSIT ANYTHING - ANYTIME - ANYWHERE
Two careful, respectable young men will look after
anything that needs looking after
Animals, pets, gardens, plants, children
Moderate Rates

Squocka looks at my effort, then holds up a wait-a-minute finger. 'I reckon you should say we're *desperate* young men.'

'Nah, that's negative. They'll think we're criminals.'

'Would it be negative to say you forgot a name and telephone number?'

'No, I'm still deciding where to put them.' I scribble in my home number and name, then roll up the cardboard before Squocka has a go at my hyphens.

We go to the supermarket and ask Mr Briscoe, the manager, if we can stick our poster on his community noticeboard. 'It's very big, isn't it?' he sniffs as we unroll it. 'Like, huge.' He's a sad, nervous, nail-biting little man who keeps glancing over his shoulder as if they're after him. 'Biggest notice I ever saw.'

'First rule of advertising,' I tell him. 'Get their attention.'

'That ad could get attention from outer space.' Mr Briscoe hums and haws for a while, then agrees, 'Okay, it can stay for a week. Best I can do.'

We borrow forty drawing pins from him and put up our eye-catching notice, then go home to await results.

◆

We're in the middle of a boring computer game, chasing Mad Dr Zoompimple through a cavernous maze of dripping slime urdles, when the phone rings. 'Wayne!' Mum calls. 'It's Mrs DeWinter from along the street looking for careful, respectable Wayne Wilson. Will I tell her she's got the wrong number?'

'Mum, you're such a joker.'

Mrs DeWinter is a friend of Mum's and says the regular babysitter has let her down and since she already knows the Wilson family, she'll trust me to look after her little Carrington. She adds, 'He'll be no trouble.'

Ten minutes later, we're at the front door. Knockity-knock.

The house is full of books, and little Carrington looks as if he's read them all. A three-year old with reading glasses is a strange sight. 'If he gets bored,' Mrs DeWinter advises, 'just play a game or tell him a story. I'll be back in two hours.'

'No worries, Mrs DeWinter,' Squocka says in his best caring and respectable manner. 'Just leave Carrington to us while you head off and have a good time.'

Mrs DeWinter pats his hand gently. 'I'm going to a funeral.'

He doesn't do it very often, but this time Squocka manages to look embarrassed.

Five minutes pass and things are going well. Carrington sits looking at us and we sit looking at him. So far, so good. Only an hour and fifty-five minutes to go and we've got this job licked. But after another three minutes of sitting and looking, Carrington breaks the silence. 'Is that all you're going to do?' he demands. 'Stare at me?'

'We're just sizing you up,' Squocka says. 'So what say we play a game?'

'Right,' Carrington agrees. 'Trivial Pursuit? Monopoly? Chess? Bridge?'

'What about we play *Here We Go Round the Mulberry Bush*?' Squocka suggests.

Carrington is puzzled. 'Why?'

'Well, it's fun, good exercise and – um – other grown-up reasons.' Since this is Squocka's idea, I let him run with it. See how far he goes.

Carrington persists. 'Why would you go round an imaginary mulberry bush?'

'One of the imaginary berries might drop off,' Squocka snarls desperately.

'Mother's only been gone ten minutes,' Carrington says, 'and I'm bored already.'

The mulberry-bush argument occupies a moment or two longer, then I spring to the rescue before it's a complete disaster. 'What say I tell a story?'

'You mean, to him?' Carrington indicates Squocka.

'No, I'll tell you one.'

'Well, if you must.' Carrington sighs and folds his arms.

'Here we go, then.' I invent furiously. 'One day, Billy Bluetongue, the friendly lizard, met Kevin Koala, the cheerful koala bear— '

'Koalas are not bears,' Carrington points out.

'And they're not cheerful,' Squocka adds smugly.

'Excuse me.' I glare at Squocka. 'What is this? Gang-up-on-Wayne time?' I huffle and puffle for a bit, then pick up my tale where I left off. 'They went to the super-market to buy flour and eggs to bake a cake— '

Carrington interrupts. 'Koalas eat eucalyptus leaves. Not cake.'

'I didn't say they're going to *eat* the cake. They're just going to *bake* one.'

That doesn't stop the little smarty-nappy. 'They're wildlife, not pastrycooks.' Carrington puts me in my place. 'It's a silly story. Where did you get it?'

'I made it up.'

'I thought so.' Carrington sniffs. Just our luck to have a three-year-old know-all as a first customer.

Squocka has recovered from his mulberry-bush disaster. 'Would you like me to read to you?'

'No thanks,' Carrington says. 'I can read for myself.'

Then it's brainwave time again. I am learning that to deal with the infant species of the world you have to be smart. I put on a scoffing voice. 'What? A little guy like you? Reading? Don't make me cackle?'

'Watch this.' Carrington sprints on his chubby legs to the bookshelf and hauls out an encyclopedia that's twice as big as he is. With a grunt he drops it on the carpet, then opens it. 'Ready? Here I go.' Carrington starts to read aloud and before long he's droning on about rhomboids, rhubarb and ruminants.

'We're getting bored with cattle and stuff,' I inform him. 'What else you got?'

Carrington dashes off and drags out another volume, then reads aloud while we sit marvelling at how brainy he is. 'You could go on TV.' Squocka ladles on the praise. 'Win sideboards and stuff.'

But Carrington has the bit between his tiny-tot teeth and wants to show off. In meeting this challenge he drags out so many heavy encyclopedias that before long he's exhausted. His eyes droop. He sinks into a chair and falls asleep.

'Easy as tripping over a log,' Squocka whispers. 'Now, Wayne, tell me about Billy Bluetongue and Kevin Koala.'

◆

For a while there's a job drought, followed by a work down-turn plus an acute employment famine, then Mr Mellifont rings from the Doggy Hotel. Can we look after the place, two days tops, while he goes into hospital for a small operation?

Squocka says he reckons one of the dogs has sunk his teeth into Mr Mellifont and won't let go so the animal has to be surgically removed. I tell him in my naughty-naughty-smack-smack voice not to make silly jokes. Working with kids gets to you in the end.

As soon as we walk in the gates of the Doggy Hotel I feel a sense of rising apprehension. The thing is, when I was two, a small fluffy spaniel used to follow me everywhere, until I worked out how to untie the string that fastened him to my nappy. But that's another Charlene story.

Mr Mellifont only wants us there during the day as his wife will look after the place at night. He's written a list of duties, which includes morning and afternoon feeding and watering arrangements. Most of the dogs are on diets so they have special food:

Kennel 17	**Great Dane**	**Nothing fried**
Kennel 23	**Skye terrier**	**Keep away from postmen's trousers**
Kennel 7b	**Pekinese**	**No ice cream or donuts**

Mr Mellifont teaches us about flea powder and how to deal with pooey substances. I leave that to Squocka, who is not as sensitive as I am. We also get the key to the bulk supply of dog biscuits and the squishy brown stuff that comes in cans. They advertise it on TV just when you're sitting down to a plate of Mum's wholesome squishy brown stuff and you get to thinking.

Then we're on our own – just me, Squocka and thirty-seven dogs. They are no problem, except they bark a lot. Woof-woof, waff-waff, wuff-wuff, weff-weff and wiff-wiff. (That's the Pekinese.) When they all go off together it sounds like this: Woof-waff-wuff-weff-wiff!

We go along the line of kennels and pull out the feed

bowls, check the list and give each dog its food and a drinkie. 'This is a piece of cake,' Squocka says.

'No cake, Squocks!' I say. 'They're on a diet.'

'Ha, ha.' Squocka's insincere laughter sets the dogs barking again so I don't make any more feeble jokes.

Mr Mellifont's instructions say we should be friendly with the dogs. *They come from loving homes where they're used to being talked to, petted, pampered and treated as members of the family,* he writes. *Spend time talking with each animal, pat it and make it feel at home.*

'Quite right,' Squocka approves. 'This is not a doggy jail.'

'Apart from them being locked in cages,' I say. But we talk to the dogs.

Conversation:

Me: *Good morning, Great Dane. Isn't it a lovely day?*
Great D: *Woof!*
Me: *Do you think it will rain?*
Great D: *Woof!*
Me: *Yes, that's what I think.*

Then calamity! After a whole day of devoted doggy-watching, Squocka makes a terrible discovery. There's a sheet of instructions we haven't read. *Make sure each animal has some daily exercise,* it says in Mr Mellifont's hand-writing. *A half-hour walk is all that's required with the dogs on a leash.*

Squocka finds the leashes. About fifty of them,

ranging from dinky little tartan jobs to huge, thundering, clanking chains that would moor a battleship alongside a wharf. 'Walkies!' he announces to the canine world in general and the dogs go mad with desire to get out of captivity. O trees! O lampposts!

FLIGHT OF FANCY:

'Just my luck!' the Skye Terrier thinks. 'The postman's finished his rounds! Never mind, I might get a chance with a policeman.'

The woofs and waffs can be heard on the moon. I get eighteen dogs and Squocka has the rest.

'Squocka, what say we just take one or two at a time?' I suggest.

'No. They can't miss out on their walkies!'

'Mr Mellifont's not going to know,' I protest. 'The dogs haven't got walkie meters on them!'

I'm protesting to the empty air. Squocka has hooked himself on to his team of dogs who drag him out the gate. He looks like Nanook of the North being hauled to the Pole by a team of Huskies. They just can't wait to get at that pole. My dogs get excited by the prospect that lies beyond the gate and off we go. As if I have any say in it.

There's no sign of Squocka and his hounds but I've got enough on my hands. They tug and spin as they try to go in different directions. The Great Dane fancies a coy Corgi and I have to drag him off, but get tangled up with a Kelpie. The Kelpie takes umbrage and goes to sink the teeth in, but I dodge aside and he only gets a bite out of my jeans.

The dogs drag me uphill and down, around corners and along busy streets where people say rude things to me. Some animals want to stop while the rest want to go on. At last, I make it back to the Doggy Hotel and note from twin drag marks in the gravel by the gate that Squocka is home too.

I put the dogs in their kennels and think of going to the office for a sit-down. Before I do that, I count the animals. Oh no! There are only thirty-five! I must have lost a couple on the way – or Squocka did, or we lost one each. Whatever way you sum it up, it's a disaster!

I do a name-check and work out that it's Angus and Hamish who are missing. Two Scotch terriers. A noble breed of well-behaved dogs, so quiet and peaceful I thought they were stuffed and had to poke them to get them to eat their haggis. There is nothing for it but to retrace my walkie route.

After an hour, there's no sign of them. Dejected, I return to the Doggy Hotel, thinking this is the end. Mr Mellifont won't trust us again. I surprise Squocka in the office nibbling a dog biscuit. 'Just want to see how they taste,' he says. 'For scientific research. If the Japanese can experiment on whales, I can do it with dog biscuits.'

I ignore this. 'Two dogs have gone. Hamish and Angus.'

'They checked out,' he informs me. 'Mrs McSporran took them while you were doing walkies.'

I tie him up with the leashes, then pelt him with dog biscuits until he begs me to stop. There comes a cough from the doorway and there stands Mr Mellifont, looking restored to good health. 'Having fun?' he says.

❦

Our week of free advertising is up and we return to the supermarket to see if we can keep our notice on the board a bit longer. Sad and jumpy Mr Briscoe greets us and the talk soon gets around to our babysitting business. 'I'd love to take my wife out,' he says. 'Trouble is, my boy Desmond's too much of a handful for any babysitter.'

Before I can sit on his head, Squocka goes, 'It's a piece of cake, Mr Briscoe. We just looked after a hundred dogs.' He points to our proud boast on the noticeboard: *We babysit anything.* I have a doom-laden feeling about this Desmond and try to wriggle out of it, but Squocka likes a challenge so he presses on.

Mr Briscoe brightens and says he'll give us a go. Could we come tonight so he and his wife can go to the movies? First time in five years. We agree.

The Briscoe front door boasts a big brass knocker and Squocka grasps it to sound a firm rat-tat-tat, but the thing comes off in his hand. Already it's not looking good and we're not even over the threshold.

Mrs Briscoe opens the door and takes the knocker from Squocka without asking what he's doing with it in his hand. If anything, she's even jumpier and more nervous than her husband and so keen on her night out that I feel sorry for her. This woman looks as if she could do with a six-month break away from Desmond.

Her husband arrives home and is relieved that we actually turned up. 'Thousands of babysitters haven't,' he adds.

'*Hundreds*, dear,' his wife corrects. She shows us where everything is, food, telephone, fire extinguishers. 'If Desmond gets hungry,' she advises, 'give him some baked beans.'

'He usually eats human beans.' Mr Briscoe's attempt at a joke only makes his wife cry. He ushers us into the sitting room, which looks like an explosion in a multi-coloured plastic toy factory. Of Desmond there is no sign.

'Um – where is the little lad?' Squocka asks hopefully. 'In bed? Asleep?'

Mrs Briscoe sighs and gives us a look as if to say, Oh, if only that were true. She says, 'He'll show himself soon enough.'

'When he's ready for you,' her husband adds.

After those chilling words, Squocka ushers them out, saying soothing things like no worries and have a nice time, leave everything to us. The idiot! We hear Mr Briscoe try to start the car, then comes a bang and the motor springs into life.

'That's a potato up the exhaust pipe,' a small voice comes from somewhere in the room. 'Works every time.'

We look around but there's still no sign of the child

although we can hear him cackle like a juvenile drain-pipe. 'Very funny, Desmond,' Squocka says, 'Now, where are you?'

I have already spotted Desmond and with a finger indicate an upwards direction. Six-year-old Desmond has curled himself around the blades of the ceiling fan. How he got up there is anyone's guess and we leave that puzzle for another day.

'I want a merry-go-round,' Desmond demands. 'Turn on the fan. Switch it to high and watch me go!'

'Better not,' I tell Squocka and have a vision of Desmond, the human missile, hurtling down High Street, catching up with his mum and dad at the traffic lights.

Flight of Flying Fancy:

Mrs Briscoe: *Was that Desmond, dear?*

Mr Briscoe: *I think so, love.*

Mrs Briscoe: *He didn't stop at the red light.*

Mr Briscoe: *He'll stop somewhere, love.*

We try to coax Desmond down from the fan blades but his preferred method is to drop on to the badly ruptured sofa, then bounce like a mad thing.

Squocka distracts him. 'How about a game, like pin the tail on the donkey?'

'Okay,' Desmond agrees. 'You be the donkey.'

'Let's see the pin first,' Squocka says cautiously, but Desmond is already looking for a blindfold. They have a heated argument over who should wear the blindfold

– the pinner or the donkey. Squocka wins by standing on a chair.

Since Desmond is the one who makes up all the rules, he sulks and bashes the sofa with a plastic baseball bat. This is when I discover Desmond's chemistry set. It occupies him for a while, until he wants to make a stink bomb, then set it off in the guest room which his mum and dad never use these days. I wonder why? Before I can stop him, Desmond starts mixing a whole bunch of chemicals together, so I leave Squocka to handle that one and go to the kitchen to see what's for eating.

When I return, there's no sign of them. I track Squocka down to a rumpus room, which looks like a battle zone with the wreckage of many a toy scattered around. 'We're playing a game from history,' Squocka tells me.

'Yes, it's William Tell,' Desmond adds. He gives Squocka an apple. 'Put that on your head and stand over there.'

Squocka is not familiar with this chapter in history so he does as Desmond asks. Desmond produces a crossbow and notches in a soft plastic arrow, then lets fly. Fwang! Luckily, the arrow has a suction cap so it sticks fast to Squocka's forehead. He drops to the floor and lies without moving.

There is a silence. 'M-mm,' I say. 'Looks like my friend is having a permanent lie-down.' I kneel to examine Squocka, who gives me a big wink then closes his eyes.

For the first time, Desmond looks doubtful. 'Is he . . . ?'

'I'm afraid so, Desmond.' I try to look like one of the fake doctors you see on television. 'This man is very dead.'

'Let's bury him in the garden.' Desmond becomes excited. 'With the budgie, the dog, the goldfish and next door's cat.'

'Not so fast,' I say. 'You pronged my best friend with an arrow, didn't you?'

'Yes, but we were only playing.' Desmond looks worried now.

'What you don't know is, Squocka was a member of a very tough gang – The Blue Meanies. You heard of them, kid?'

Desmond nods so hard his teeth rattle. 'I think so. They're blue, aren't they?'

'That's them. If anybody injures a Blue Meanie, he's in trouble.'

'You mean, they're coming for me?'

'Yeah, but I'll dump the stiff somewhere and give you an alibi.'

'Oh thanks, Wayne.'

'In return, you gotta clean up the sitting room, then go to bed. And be nice to your mudder and fadder for the rest of your life. Remember, the Blue Meanies are always watching.'

Desmond scampers past me as fast as he can go. Squocka opens one eye. 'Good one, Wayne!'

So we watch television with never a peep out of Desmond. All part of the service.

◆

Next morning Mum calls from the front door, 'Wayne, a postcard here for you from America.' Zoom! That's me going downstairs. The card's from Violet:

> Dear Wayne,
> I'm loving New York and have seen so many sights my eyes hurt – the Statue of Liberty, Empire State Building, Wall Street and Fifth Avenue. There is one amazing spectacle after another. You would never get tired of this place –
> Love, Violet. XXXX

My eyes glaze over, my heart beats faster; she has written: *Love, Violet* and added four Xs. But there's more. At the bottom Violet has written: *More information on Squocka's card.*

I skip breakfast and head over to Squocka's place but he's also skipped breakfast to meet me halfway. Hungrily we read each other's postcards. Silently I gnash my teeth, for she has written on Squocka's card: *Love, Violet.*

Then I study it again. On his card she only added XXX.

For a moment there, Violet had me worried.

Life just got better, Wayne. Violet Pridmore's back home.

As if I didn't know, Squocka. And looks like she needs my help.

Our help, as it happens.

With our plans, Squocka, we'll be famous in the USA.

Yep, they'll talk of us in Denver.

Sing songs in Santa Fe.

Of the show three Aussie kids put on.

For Amy Pastrami Day.

Can we take a bow, Wayne?

Not yet, Squocka. Better read the story first.

21 AMY PASTRAMI DAY

Big day in the life of Wayne Wilson. Violet Pridmore is home from America. All right, so I missed her. The last weeks dragged by like some kind of draggy thing during which I kept looking in the letterbox to see if she'd sent me a parcel. No luck. Postcard? Only one, but maybe there was a strike and she tried to send more. If time dragged for me, it crawled for Squocka who missed Violet too. But she's back this morning. Terrific!

Since this is a school day, and Violet will be resuming her education, the trick is to make sure I walk that way with her. So I linger by the curtains, looking out at the street until Mum spots me. 'Wayne, aren't you going to school?'

I expect this, and have an excuse ready – in one hand a shoe, in the other a rag. 'Gotta look neat, Mum.'

'Don't make me laugh. Your shoes long since died of polish deprivation.' Mum comes to the window and looks out, then immediately knows what's what. 'Oh, I get it; it's the old Lovelorn-Son-Needs-Reason-to-Dawdle. Waiting for someone, are we?'

'No, Mum,' I protest. 'Shoes need a good shine.' Rub, rub, rub.

316

'Oh, there's that nice Violet Pridmore.' Mum points out the window.

It's true! Violet is already walking past our front gate. Four seconds plus a quick sprint and I am striding along after her, my schoolbag banging against my legs, one shoe polished, the other not.

FLIGHT OF FANCY:

Wayne and Violet have not seen each other for many weeks. (Well, three weeks.)

Me: *Violet, I missed you. Really missed you.*

Violet: *Did you, Wayne? Well, I missed you too, your smile in the morning, your flashes of lively wit, your intelligence, having conversations—*

Me: *It hasn't been the same without you. The sun didn't shine, no bird sang, flowers failed to bloom and life was a downer.*

Violet: *Still the same old poetic Wayne. Don't ever change, will you?*

Violet leans her head on Wayne's shoulder and they go to school together. Sigh.

By the time I catch up in real life, I'm breathless. 'Violet,' I pant, 'fancy seeing you here.'

'Oh, hello,' she says. 'Now, don't tell me. It's – it's – *Shane*, am I right?'

'Ha, ha,' I laugh at her little joke, then change the subject. 'How was America?' Before Violet can give me exclusive details, I spot Old Squocka lurking on the corner, pretending to look in the window of a bottle shop, but he's really checking Violet's oncoming reflection. How obvious!

Squocka looks up. 'Violet,' he greets her, ignoring me, 'fancy seeing you here.'

'What is it with you guys?' She imitates our eager words, 'Fancy seeing you here.'

So we walk to school, a threesome. Not my favourite number. Violet has souvenirs for us. Squocka gets one of those little plastic bubbles full of water with a small Statue of Liberty in it. Give it a shake and suddenly there's a snowstorm inside. 'Gee, thanks, Violet.' Squocka shakes his bubble so much a short-sighted old woman across the street waves back and calls, 'Yoo-hoo, Percy. How are the hemorrhoids?'

It's a pretty juvenile souvenir because you don't get snow under water. Violet has one for me too – another plastic bubble except it's got a tiny White House inside with an even tinier US president out front making a speech about the urgent need to invade some foreign country. (That bit's a lie. So is the old woman/hemorrhoid bit.)

I look along the street and wouldn't you know it, there's Kevin Merry looking in the window of Douche-a-Rama, the bath and wash-basin shop. He sees us coming and calls, 'Violet— '

'Kevin Merry,' Violet gets in first, 'if you say, "Fancy seeing you here", I'll go the other way.'

'Wasn't going to,' Kevin tells Violet. 'Was going to say welcome back.'

Squocka and I hate him all over again. Then we're all going to school together, except Kevin wants to walk next to Violet, and uses his secretly aggressive elbow to assert his right.

Violet says, 'I had such fun in America.' She tries to tell us more but Kevin cuts in with footling questions, such as: do cars drive on the right side of the road, did you see any film stars, did you get mugged, how was Disneyland and have they got dollars and cents?

Squocka and I can't get a word in. But Violet's also fed up with Kevin going on and on. The bell rings and we file into class. First period it's drama with Ms Cook, so we sit at our desks and wait for her to show up. Kevin is a one-man FAQ and demands urgent answers. 'Do they have public holidays over there, Violet?'

'Heaps.'

'Such as?'

'Independence Day, Thanksgiving— '

Now that Violet's being nice, Kevin wants to keep it going and conversation's the way to do it. 'Any more public holidays you can think of?'

Violet's becoming impatient with him, only he doesn't see it. She starts inventing. 'They've got Al Capone Wednesday, National Pumpkin Tossing Day— '

Kevin is sucked right in. 'Fair dinkum? I'd like to toss pumpkins. Smash! There goes the dunny. Anybody in there?' He laughs.

At that wrong moment, Ms Cook shows up. She likes to make silent, dramatic entrances, so stands smouldering against the doorpost, her baleful eyes sweeping the room. Without seeing this, Violet gives Kevin another

made-up American public holiday. 'And *everyone* cele-
brates Amy Pastrami Day.'

'Amy whose day?' Ms Cook takes a sudden interest
and glides to the front of the class, her radar eyes going
swivel-swivel.

Violet is like a wallaby caught in the headlights of
a demented 4WD. Her voice is a whisper. 'Um – Amy
Pastrami Day, Ms Cook.'

Kevin speaks up. 'It's an American public holiday,
miss.'

When she sets eyes on Kevin, Ms Cook stiffens and
clutches the cameo brooch of Nicole Kidman at her
throat. 'Kevin Merry, why are you in my drama class?'

'I got slung out of metalwork, Miss. Said it was
dangerous. Told me to do drama.'

'To work off his aggression,' Squocka adds, 'but he's
not to handle spears.'

Violet is relieved. With the attention on Kevin, she's
off the hook, but no. Ms Cook swings back to her. 'Now,
Violet, you were saying about Amy Pastrami?'

Violet cringes once more in the gimlet headlights. 'It's
an American public holiday, Ms Cook.'

'Sounds fascinating. Tell me more.'

'Amy was a patriot.'

'What?' Kevin asks. 'Like a Patriot missile. Voom-
pah!'

'Kevin Merry,' Ms Cook snaps, 'another word and
you will go voom-pah. Right out that door.'

'Yes, Miss.' Kevin subsides. He's not happy. A few

minutes ago, he was having a nice conversation with Violet Pridmore, now he's in the far reaches of Outersville.

'Drama can be just as dangerous as metalwork.' Ms Cook warns, then returns to Violet. 'Now, Violet? What else?'

'She did something heroic, Ms Cook.'

'Women do heroic things all the time, Violet. Getting out of bed each day is a heroic act. But Brave Amy must have been *especially* heroic to have a public holiday in her honour.' Ms Cook scribbles the name on the whiteboard with a great flourish. The dot on her final 'i' is a little circle. 'And Violet will find out more about Amy Pastrami and report to us next lesson, won't you, Violet?'

When I glance in Violet's direction, she seems to have shrunk. Ms Cook begins the lesson. It is How To Act Horrified. Violet does it without the aid of a drama coach.

At lunchtime, her gloom continues. 'Guys,' she appeals, meaning me and Squocka. 'I'm trapped. How did I get into this mess?'

Squocka begins to count the ways, but I try to be more helpful. 'Why don't you just tell Cookie it was a joke— '

'Ms Cook's into tragedy, not humour,' Violet points out. 'And besides, it would hurt Kevin's feelings.'

'First you gotta find them,' Squocka says darkly.

Violet goes on, 'So you've got to help me, guys. Please.' It's the long, slow 'p-l-e-a-s-e' that does it, plus her eyes, brimming with hope and lots of other things. If Violet starts with the eyelashes, then I'm gone. Yep, there they go.

'Okay, what do I do?' I ask. For some girls it's that easy.

Squocka's ahead of me. 'Tell you what. Cookie wrote "Amy Pastrami" on the whiteboard. So what if somebody sneaks in and rubs it off? That way she'll forget. Out of sight, out of mind.'

'Squocka, you're brilliant!' Violet looks happy again.

Hang on, I make the noble offer to help, and who gets the praise? Next thing you know I volunteer to be the one who rubs off the name.

Problem: When I do my sneaking, Kevin Merry is already in the drama room, doing lines on the other whiteboard. *I must not act the fool until I get the part.* If I tiptoe in there and rub off the name, he'll wonder why. So I go to the sports store and find a lot of sticks that our super-enthusiastic PE teacher uses to mark out running tracks or something. In a few minutes, I join the sticks together with hairy string to make a long extension pole. With a bit of cloth tied on the business end, I am ready to reach in the drama classroom window and silently rub off the evidence without Kevin being any the wiser.

This plan is going well. Rub, rub, rubbity, rub. The name's almost gone. Then Kevin steps back to admire his commas. From the corner of his right eye he sees my bit of obliterating cloth. Kevin turns. 'Wilson! What are you up to?'

'Shut up, Kevin and get on with your punishment.'

322

'You and whose army?' Kevin grabs the end of my extension pole and we wrestle for it. There's a whirring overhead fan in the drama room. Somehow my tied-together extension pole gets caught up in the fan and there comes a horrible grinding and banging noise, then bits of stick fly out the window.

I report to Violet. 'Job's done. Name's gone.' She's delighted. My stocks are high.

Next drama lesson, Ms Cook is bitter. 'If you find it hot in this room, then blame Kevin Merry, who is going back to metalwork come hell or high water.' Everyone looks up at the ruined fan, wondering how it got that way.

As Kevin slouches in his seat, he points a dramatic finger at the whiteboard. 'She's gone, miss. The sausage woman. Amy Salami's gone!'

'What are you talking about, Kevin Merry?' Then Ms Cook sees the name is no longer there. 'Of course, Amy Pastrami. Violet, what have you found out since last time?' A quick scribble on the whiteboard and the name lives again.

With all eyes on Violet, Kevin sits up straight again as if he's been inflated with a pump. Violet says, 'Well, not a lot, Ms Cook. I need more time.'

That's where we come in, folks. After school Squocka and I turn up at Violet's place. There is a blank screen on her computer, just waiting for us to invent the life story of Amy Pastrami. Squocka says, 'She's a female pilot— '

'No, make it an astronaut,' I suggest, not wanting to be overlooked. 'She nipped out for a space walk one afternoon and got left up there.'

'Yeah, the guys forgot her,' Squocka adds. 'Until dinnertime. It was her turn to do the peas.'

'These are good ideas,' Violet encourages us. 'But I think Amy should be a patriot from the olden days.'

'From the backwoods,' I say.

'Or the front woods,' Squocka agrees. 'I'm easy.'

'She's out camping and something terrible happens.' Violet begins to type.

'She gets flu,' Squocka puts in.

Violet is already typing as fast as her flying fingers can get the words on the screen. 'It's garbage, but good garbage,' she goes on. 'If it gets old Cookie off my back, who cares?'

Next drama lesson, Violet reads from her report. 'Ms Cook, Amy Pastrami lived last century, way out in the backwoods when life was hard for a woman— '

'For some of us, things have not changed, Violet.'

'Amy lived in pioneer days when great herds of shaggy buffaloes roamed the wild prairie and the coyote howled all night— '

At this moment, Kevin lets fly with an animal howl. Ms Cook freezes him with a you-still-here? glare. He stops mid-howl with his mouth wide open.

'Buffaloes!' Ms Cook almost breathes the word. 'How dramatic. Huge, brown, rampaging beasts, with eyes like glowing embers, smouldering in the darkness— '

Since Ms Cook seems to know all about it, Violet sits down but gives me and Squocka a wink. 'Off the hook,' Squocka whispers to me.

Not quite. Ms Cook has another idea. 'Fellow actors,' she intones, 'we are going to study brave Amy's life story. I want all of you to find out what you can about Amy Pastrami – dates, costumes, the language of the period. So that's your project. Now, the lesson for today, How To Brood.'

At lunchtime, we're outside, practising our brooding. Squocka says, 'If we didn't have eyebrows we'd be stuffed.'

Violet turns up and she's brooding for a different reason. 'Guys, help!'

We line up in the library where all the encyclopedias are being used, but we find another book showing costumes and stuff. As we work, Kevin Merry enters and approaches the librarian, Ms Moise. 'Hello, stranger,' she greets him. 'Haven't seen you since Year 3! Have you still got that picture book, and can we have it back?'

'Got a drama assignment, Ms Moise. I'm looking for "Pastrami".'

'Mmm, shouldn't you try the deli?'

'It's a fair-dinkum assignment, only I reckon there's something fishy about it.'

'Not meaty?'

'This Pastrami ran about the prairie with a lot of buffaloes. And the backwoods. In olden times.'

Ms Moise is puzzled, but tries to help. 'Look, Kevin,

pastrami doesn't run around on four legs.'

'Buffaloes do.'

'That's true, Kevin. But not pastrami. Pastrami is dead.'

'So how come it's a public holiday?'

Squocka, Violet and I stay head down. We have a lot of inventing to do, so we keep our voices low as we discuss the plight of Brave Amy. 'What if Amy gets eaten by a bear?' Squocka suggests.

Violet objects. 'Getting eaten is not very brave.'

'Yeah,' I agree. 'All they'd put on her tombstone is "Not a fast runner".'

We're not getting anywhere and Violet loses her nerve. 'Guys, I'm going to confess that the whole thing was a joke.'

What? Give up? I have never been this close to Violet. If she gives up, we go back to how it was before. I rush to assure her. 'We can pull it off. We just create a bit more, Cookie gets us to write an essay and we're off the hook.'

Squocka is also not for giving up. He leans across the library table and tells us some of the story we will concoct. 'Amy's got two little kids, see, it's a dark, dark night. They're out camping in the backwoods. When suddenly, Amy hears a noise— '

Next drama lesson, Ms Cook listens keenly as Violet goes on with the story, 'That noise, Ms Cook, was a loud drumming sound.'

Squocka and I drum our fingers on our desks. Dara-dum-dara-dum.

Kevin Merry pipes up, 'It's the United States Cavalry. Going home on leave.'

'Be quiet, Kevin Merry. Go on, Violet, this is history.'

Violet puts on a dramatic voice. 'It was a herd of buffaloes, Ms Cook. Stampeding towards the spot where Amy and her two little boys were camped for the night in their flimsy tent.'

'Oh yes!' Ms Cook breathes.

Violet acts this bit. 'So brave Amy stood in front of the herd, making the buffaloes go on each side of the tent.'

'How could they see her in the dark, eh?' Kevin says in a got-you-there voice

'Be quiet, Kevin Merry. She must have had a lantern. Did she have one, Violet?'

'Definitely,' Violet agrees, giving me a swift frown because I forgot that detail. She finishes her story. 'So the children were saved, but poor Amy was trampled by the buffaloes.'

Ms Cook is in raptures. 'No wonder they have a special day in her honour!' She beams at us, then asks an innocent question, 'And when is Amy Pastrami Day, Violet?'

Kevin gets in quickly and makes a not-so-innocent reply. 'It's in a couple of weeks time, Miss. On the eighteenth.'

Violet looks puzzled by this, but what the heck. If we can invent stuff, what's wrong with Old Kevin joining in?

There's a lot wrong with it, especially when Ms Cook gets a faraway look in her eye. 'On the eighteenth? We must work quickly. Boys and girls, our drama class will celebrate Amy Pastrami Day.'

I die a little, but only on the inside. Violet keeps a straight face. What an actor she is. Ms Cook burbles on: she will write a play. Amy's story is full of wonderful multicultural implications. She rallies her faithful actors and behind-the-scenes persons. There's a lot to do! Violet is to be involved. Which means so are Squocka and I, because we got her into this, didn't we?

I write a song for the show, trying to weave in the word 'patriotic', but the only thing that rhymes is 'idiotic', which is about right. Violet tells us she's got to play the part of Amy. And guess who's to be her two small sons, Dwight and Abraham?

Kevin Merry gets to be a buffaloes and wonders how he'll attach his horns without glue or nails.

Rehearsals move at a great pace. Ms Cook issues our scripts, which is where the first snag occurs. The play sucks. Violet is to be dressed in a long white nightie while her two freckled sons, Dwight and Abraham, will peep from the flap of a small wigwam. We do a read-through, and it's no better than it was on the page. Violet holds aloft a lantern and declares, 'Behold my dear country, behold my future! But hush, what do I hear?' Violet cocks a hand to her ear. 'It is the trample, trample, trample of a thousand bovine hooves.'

Kevin watches from the sidelines, sorely miffed

because Ms Cook confiscated his home-made plastic horns and gave him more lines: *I must not gore my fellow actors.* Kevin sneers, 'So who wrote this junk?'

'I did, Kevin Merry, so be quiet.' This early in the production, Ms Cook is not ready to face the critics.

Violet ventures a small observation. 'Ms Cook, don't you think it's a bit old-fashioned?'

'Of course it is, Violet. After all, this story is from more than a century ago, not last week.'

I wouldn't be too sure about that, Ms Cook.

But on the rehearsal drags, the buffaloes enter in slow motion, which is not to Kevin Merry's taste. Ms Cook encourages them, 'Get in touch with your inner buffaloes.'

They take turns at making long, boring speeches about their absolute right to the grasslands over which they've roamed unhindered for centuries. But what with encroaching civilisation, things are getting crowded out there on the wild prairie. A spokes-buffaloes apologises for having to trample Amy, who stands between them and a patch of nice grass. It's nothing personal.

'Besides, we're not very intelligent.' Kevin gets to say that line.

Amy is heroically flattened, then the entire cast join hands to sing the Amy Pastrami Song:

> *Oh Amy, bold Amy,*
> *We salute your bravery,*
> *Oh Amy, sweet Amy,*
> *Out there in your nightie.*

You faced a herd of buffalo
And stood fast, firm and true,
Oh Amy, our Amy
You did what you had to do.

Oh Amy, brave Amy,
Congress honours thee,
It's sad that you got trampled
But at least you didn't flee.

We all bow low and Ms Cook tells us it has come together beautifully. A few rough patches, but it will be all right on the night. 'Break a leg,' she adds, 'and make sure it's yours, Kevin Merry.'

Violet, Squocka and I trudge home in silent and sombre mood. I'm the first to speak, 'Okay, guys, it's awful.'

'Terrible,' Squocka agrees. 'A clunker.'

'If anyone else comes to see it,' Violet moans, 'we'll be the laughing stock of the entire school.'

'Good thing it's just us, then,' Squocka adds.

'Hang on.' I hold up a brainwave forefinger. 'Violet just said it – laughing stock. Since it's only a play for our class, let's ham it up.'

'You mean— ?' Squocka's eyes are wide.

'We make it a comedy.' I say.

'With *our* dialogue.' Violet has a gleam in her eye. 'It'll be a hoot.' I've known this girl since Year 1 and never heard her hoot. 'Guys,' she points in the direction of her home, 'to my computer. Now.'

We faithfully follow. If Violet were a lady buffaloes, she could trample us any day.

Then comes *The Awful Tragedy of Amy Pastrami* and we three are excited because of the secret changes we've made to the script. Ms Cook has transferred the show to the gymnasium where there's a proper stage and more room.

Behind the drawn curtain there is such a buzz. Our teepee is set up centre stage and we are in costume, although I've never cared for dungarees. Then comes a crisis. There are twelve buffaloes, with eleven of them dressed in brown smocks and sporting neat sets of horns. The odd buffaloes out is Kevin Merry who wears a blush-pink smock and no horns. 'How come you guys got horns?' he demands.

'Got them in Mr Patel's Joke and Novelty Emporium,' Albert Pettigrew says. 'Gave us a discount because we bought so many.'

'Is that so?' Kevin demands just as Ms Cook comes backstage to check that we are all ready to perform. 'Ms Cook,' he goes on. 'They all got horns and I haven't. Plus I'm pink.'

'So, improvise, Kevin Merry. Be a pink, hornless buffaloes. Like the ones in New Zealand.' Ms Cook beams and turns to Violet. 'I have a surprise for you. Now, places everyone. Curtain up in two minutes.' Then she's gone.

Violet, Squocka and I look at each other. A surprise? We don't like surprises, especially not when we're ready with one of our own. Kevin Merry doesn't like not having horns and looking girly in pink. He sulks then decides to assert himself. 'Okay,' he says to the herd in general. 'I'm the leader of the buffaloes. So you guys, single file and follow me.

'We're supposed to make environmental speeches, *then* stampede,' Albert Pettigrew protests. 'Not do a conga line.'

Kevin engages Albert in a heated debate with a lot of shoving and making aggressive faces at each other. We three actors ignore them and wonder what Ms Cook's surprise could be. Squocka is full of hope. 'Maybe it's been cancelled?' Then from the other side of the curtain, we hear applause. Surprise number one: that applause comes from a lot of people, not just our drama class.

Then come some stirring American-sounding chords from the piano and we hear Ms Cook announce, 'Mr Principal, ladies and gentlemen, boys and girls.' Surprise number two: we didn't know the principal was going to attend. Then comes Ms Cook's third surprise: 'And this morning, Ms Shickenhauer, a representative from the United States Embassy, has joined with us to share Amy Pastrami Day.'

We make extensive use of our How To Look Horrified lessons. Then swish goes the curtain and we see the gymnasium full of students. Ms Cook is at the piano, the principal sits in the front row with a woman who wears horn-rimmed glasses, perfect teeth and lots of hair.

After a rippling chord, Violet steps forth with a worried look on her face. She adopts a listening pose, holding her lantern aloft. That's my cue, folks. I'm Dwight, so I let fly with our more authentic version of the dialogue. 'Mama, Mama,' I whine nasally. 'When will Dada come back from huntin', shootin' and fishin'?'

Violet responds as Amy, 'Hush up, Dwight, darlin'. I'm a-listening to some-pin' in them there backwoods.'

Squocka as Abraham gets in the act. 'Mama, ah shure am hungry. Do you reckon Dada will bring us back a skunk or a raccoon, do you figger?'

I catch sight of the principal and Ms Shickenhauer. Their jaws have dropped open. The rest of the audience is equally entranced, so it's gripping stuff.

Amy goes on, 'Now jes' you hush up, lil Abraham. Maybe Dada'll bring us back a bald eagle or a moose or some critter to gnaw on. But Mama's a-hearkening to this here noise which ain't no squirrel and it ain't no raccoon. It's some-pin' mighty heavy.'

Even I can hear it. In the wings, Buffaloes Kevin's protest over being pink and hornless has reached a climax with fists and elbows flying. But it's a noiseless dispute, like watching a silent film. Kevin's getting the worst of it. He's on the floor, being sat on by two brown-smocked buffaloes. Stick Kevin in a nightie and he could be a stand-in for trampled Amy.

At the piano, Ms Cook starts with some heavy, dramatic chords, supposed to represent the approaching herd of buffaloes. Dara-dum-dara-dum-dara-dum.

Amy peers into the wings and fearfully announces, 'It's a herd of buffaloes!'

Dwight and Abraham become alarmed. 'Mama, Mama, don't you go steppin' into that darkness.'

Amy Pastrami cowers. But the buffaloes don't come. Ms Cook bangs harder. DARA-DUM-DARA-DUM-DARA-DUM. Still no buffaloes.

'Mama,' Abraham warns. 'Them buffaloes sound mighty fierce.'

'And they're coming right for us,' I add. 'Oughta be here any second.' This bit is a lie. The buffaloes are still arguing the toss.

It falls to Violet to rush to the wings and bellow, 'Call yourselves buffaloes! If that's your best shot, then bring it on!'

'Mama, you sure are brave,' Abraham calls after her.

Violet's words have an effect. Albert gets up and adjusts his horns. 'Oh, are we on?'

'Yes,' Violet hisses. 'So come out here and *trample* me.' She retreats to the wigwam and becomes protective of her two sons. 'Now, chillun, get inside that tent there. Mama will save you.'

To Ms Cook's dara-dum music, on come the sheepish buffaloes. Amy holds her lantern high, Dwight and Abraham peer from the opening of the wigwam. The buffaloes forget their speeches and sweep Amy away with them over to the other wing.

Under cover of the surging buffaloes, Squocka and I litter the stage floor with bits of torn and bloody nightie plus a collection of meaty dog bones we got from Mr Smallgoods, the butcher. With the herd gone, I emerge from the wigwam and look sadly at the bloody remains on the ground. 'Well, Brother Abraham,' I say to Squocka, who is still inside. 'I reckon Mama jes' saved our lives and she gone to heaven.'

Squocka comes out of the wigwam, dragging a leg behind him. It is Kevin Merry's leg. The rest of him is tied up with hairy string and he wears a set of horns. 'Ah got me a buffaloes, Brother Dwight,' Squocka says. 'So kindle the fire and let's you 'n' me cook us a mess o' vittles.'

'Shure thing, Brother Abraham. Mama wouldn't want us to go hungry.'

Then comes the finale song. Squocka starts: 'Now all you good folk just listen here, to the tragic fate of our Mama dear.'

My turn: 'Who went for a walk in the pale moonlight, and now she ain't a pretty sight!'

Squocka: 'When them buffaloes started running free, Mama shoulda climbed the nearest tree.'

Me: 'But now she's flat upon the ground and this is the only bit we found— '

Squocka shows a large meaty bone: 'But life's like that, it just ain't fair— '

' – that Mama's fifteen metres square.' We bow low and the curtain closes, but before that, and for a split second, I note that the principal and Ms Schickenhauer are too stunned to applaud. I can't see Ms Cook's face but the rest of the audience clap wildly. They didn't understand it, but it was fun, plus a morning out of class.

The buffaloes and Amy crowd on stage for a curtain call, then it's all over.

Ms Cook storms backstage to lay blame. Who? Why? What? When and how? They're for openers. Kevin Merry has been freed from his string and demands an audience. The other buffaloes attacked him with their horns, he complains. Before long, other accusing fingers point his way. It's all Kevin's fault.

Meanwhile, Violet has to apologise to Ms Schickenhauer, who turns out to be a good sport. 'I really liked it,' she says generously. 'Now tell me, Violet, you picked up the Amy Pastrami idea during your visit to America?'

'Yes, but I didn't have a lot of information.'

'So you improvised?'

'A bit.' Violet crosses her fingers. She hates to lie.

Ms Schickenhauer doesn't seem to be offended. Ms Cook looks relieved, not to mention grateful. 'Um,' she suggests, 'maybe it had a few rough patches.'

Ms Schickenhauer smiles. 'Ms Cook, I can give you details of other public holidays.' She goes on, 'There's Frontier Heritage Day, Wagon Wheel Day, Charlie Chaplin Day— '

'Charlie Chaplin Day,' Ms Cook is impressed. 'You mean . . . ?'

'Yes,' Ms Schickenhauer agrees, 'bowler hat, big feet, silly walk.'

'This I like,' Ms Cook breathes.

'You could celebrate a different public holiday every week. Couldn't you, Violet?'

With a straight face, Violet agrees. But Ms Schickenhauer has to go back to the office. And since the American representative is so amiable about it, Ms Cook begins to look on the bright side.

And so ends the play. Got me closer to Violet, so it wasn't all that bad. Squocka got closer too, but you can't win them all. Ms Cook tries to send Kevin Merry back to metalwork but when she approaches the principal, he's not sympathetic.

Funny, that.

It had to happen, Wayne. It's the law of nature.

Yeah, Squocka, you grow up a bit, get body hair and a deep voice—

And meet girls.

Well, not so much meet them, Squocka. You sort of see them, and sigh.

Then get goose-pimples, Wayne.

We lost our heads. That's all we did, Squocka. It's all we did.

It's all you did, Wayne. I tried to warn you, but my tongue wouldn't work.

Well, it was summer time. Those long, carefree holidays, sunlight sparkling on the water, splashing about in rowing boats—

And rubbing them down with sandpaper! I've still got the splinters.

Then, comes the real thing. Genuine girls at last. I still see them, tripping lightly along a sunlit beach—

Then dragging us into a hamburger joint, yelling, 'Feed us, feed us!' I'm still paying off that loan.

Nature, eh? You can't beat it, Squocka. You can't fight it. So I reckon we should just accept it.

And next time go Dutch!

22 GOOSE-PIMPLES

t's a bit like that chapter in the Bible where they do all the begetting and begatting. One character begets another, then he who's just been begat begets somebody else and before you know it, you've read half a page of begettings. Where was I?

Yes, begetting, or one thing leads to another. Since Mum's made peace with Rupert's dad, I beget the odd bit of weekend and holiday work in his supermarket, stacking shelves and cleaning up the back store. Squocka helps too, so it's a good way of earning some pocket money. This is where another round of begetting begins. It's late on a Saturday afternoon and we're just winding up for the day when Mr Pringle comes in. 'Finished work, boys?' he asks.

'Yes, Mr Pringle, just doing this last bit,' I tell him.

The long and short of it is Mr Pringle has had a TV ad done for his supermarket so he's pretty chummy with the director who filmed the action. 'Tell you what, boys,' he says. 'The director's doing another ad tomorrow. Down at the beach. How'd you like to get some film experience?'

Our eyes and voices say, 'Would we ever!' So it's all

fixed. Mr Pringle will have a word, then all we need to do is turn up at Orchid Beach and we can take it from there.

'They like to start early,' Mr Pringle goes on, 'to make the most of the daylight, so get there at half-past five.' He goes off to see about counting his money or something, leaving us looking at each other.

We have just begat another job. But a half-past five start!

'Is that a.m. or p.m.?' Squocka asks, but he already knows the answer, which makes his gloom profound. 'It's winter, in case you've forgotten.'

'Yeah, but think of it, Squocka, we get to work on a film set. Plus we'll get paid.'

To get to Orchid Beach that early means getting out of bed at half-past four, or thereabouts. Mum thinks it's a great idea, not that she'll get out of bed to see me off or help me with breakfast. The night before she looks out an old duffle coat of Dad's and tells me to wear it.

'Mum, it's daggy. I wouldn't be seen dead in that.'

'You'll be seen dead without it,' Mum responds. 'It said on the news this morning they found a frozen polar bear at Orchid Beach, and two stiff penguins. Icicles everywhere.'

I try on the coat and Mum does up the toggles. I hate toggles, which are nearly as bad as woggles.

In my warm-but-uncool and badly dressed state, I go to Squocka's place to collect him. He nearly dies laughing when he sees me. 'You should wear a windcheater, like me.' He puts on a very annoying, superior-type laugh.

'It was Mum's idea,' I tell him as we head for the beach. But my scruffy duffle coat pays off in a spectacular and significant way. Read on.

At Orchid Beach in the half-light there's already a large bunch of people milling about on the loose, shingly sand. Everyone tries to be more important than the next guy.

FLIGHT OF FILMIC FANCY:

I'm more important than you.

No, you're not.

Yes I am. See, I've got a clipboard and a pencil tied on with hairy string, so there.

Well, I've got a walkie-talkie. Have you got one of them?

No.

There you are, then. Nerny-nerny-ner-ner.

Some people fuss around setting up big, round lights, while others drag out tripods and aluminium boxes full of microphones and cameras. There are spacious vans in the background with electrical wires running all over the place. It's impressive and everyone seems to know what they're doing, but where do we fit in?

Parked behind the vans is an old bus which has its windows painted white so nobody can see inside. 'Wonder what goes on in there,' I say.

The answer is not long in coming. The door of the bus glides open and one after the other, a team of stunning, sexy girls emerge. They're wearing colourful bikinis. Squocka starts to blush. 'Models,' he croaks. 'Bet this is a knicker commercial.'

There comes a sudden noise. It sounds like a female motor mower, but in reality it's the models going, 'Brrr' at the same time. To keep out the chill morning air, they huddle together and wrap their arms around their perfect persons. The girls look at each other with sad, longing eyes and think of last summer, which this is not.

One of the models lifts her lovely head and spots me all warm in Dad's hairy old duffle coat. She comes tippy-toeing across the shingle with her teeth chattering like Spanish castanets. 'Hello,' she says, 'I'm Jenny Dee.' Without bothering to ask, she undoes my toggles and snuggles inside with me, pulling the flaps of the coat shut behind her. Bet that never happened when Dad wore this coat. I'll need to ask him man-to-man some time.

As Jenny Dee squirms closer to me, I begin to steam gently. The top of her head is just under my nose and there's a sweet smell from her hair. Squocka is impressed by my good fortune. Jealous too. This I can tell because his eyes are out on stalks and his jaw hits the sand. None of the models rushes to join him inside his windcheater. Now who's laughing?

Meanwhile, I wonder if this is to be my job on the film set. Does it have a long apprenticeship? Will I be paid as well? But life can be cruel and just as I'm growing used to Jenny Dee making herself comfortable in there, a large, bossy woman comes on the scene. She's got 'authority figure' stamped all over her. 'You!' She means me. 'Get that female out of there.'

'Oh, wouldn't you know it!' Jenny Dee emerges from my warm interior. A cloud of steam escapes with her. She gives me a regretful look, then trips back to join the other models who go brrr, brrr in a lower key because they're running out of energy.

It turns out the bossy female is in charge. She is Lena Rieven-Steel, a film director of great renown, a hotshot of whom I have never heard.

'What's your name?' Her words come out like bullets. Easy to tell this woman doesn't like me. The old sixth sense is never wrong, especially about women. It's in their eyes, those little daggers of hate.

My tongue forms a reply. 'Wayne Wilson.'

'So, you're not the actor? Jeremy something.'

'No.'

'Actors always make trouble on my film sets,' she goes on. 'Throwing their weight around, forgetting lines, asking for special treatment. If we could do without actors, we would.' Lena Rieven-Steel looks as if she's about to declare war on some unfortunate country. Then she spots Squocka and looks him up and down.

'Good morning.' Squocka tries to appear intelligent. 'My name is Squocka Berrington.'

'Well, Squocka Berrington, you look like a useful man.' Lena Rieven-Steel actually smiles and adds, 'I bet you have a sensitive side.'

'Oh, well— ' Squocka gives a little nod as if to say it's one of his better qualities.

'I have just the job for you.' She curls a beckoning finger. 'Follow.'

As he passes, Squocka's face says it all, but he adds words. 'Nerny-nerny-ner-ner.' He has just begat a sensitive job.

Lena Rieven-Steel leads him to a small table where stands a box of odds and ends. She rummages briefly then produces a large tube of some sort of cosmetic cream. 'Now, Squocka, this cold weather brings the girls out in goose-pimples. Maybe you noticed.'

'Yeah, I did,' Squocka agrees. 'Some as big as cherries.'

'It doesn't look good when the camera starts to roll.' Lena Rieven-Steel hands Squocka the tube of cream. 'Take this goose-pimple cream and go over there and massage the girls with it.'

'Me?' For the first time, Squocka's face shows doubt. 'What if they object?'

'They can't. There's a no goose-pimple clause in their contract.'

Dongity-dong! That's Squocka's eyes popping out of their sockets to hang there going wibble-wobble on bouncy springs. (A little lie there.)

Lena Rieven-Steel puts on an encouraging smile and manages to look motherly and affectionate. Like a man in a dream, Squocka holds the tube of cream in front of him, then stumbles across the sand in the direction of the shivering models.

Some of the film crew stop work to observe this tender moment, whispering to each other. My keen ears tell me they're taking bets. Squocka reaches the knot of girls who open up to admit him to their circle. No one can hear what he says, but next thing you know, there's a combined cry of feminine outrage. 'Pervert! Rat-bag!'

Squocka makes a run for it, closely followed by fifteen girls. One of the film crew says, 'He only lasted eight seconds. Thought he'd have gone longer.' He collects on his bet.

Meanwhile, Squocka can recognise dire peril when it's chasing him. Small pebbles spurt from his shoes as he pelts along the beach. In seconds he executes a swift right turn, then finds a gap between sand dunes and soon he's lost from sight. Like a stream of avenging banshees, the models follow, hurling dire threats.

There is a sudden crisis. Jeremy something, the actor who is to feature in this TV advertisement has not turned up. Lena Rieven-Steel has declared outright war on him and his agent. 'Tosh and piffle,' she barks into her mobile phone. Everyone keeps out of her way as she storms around, kicking up explosions of sand. 'You're his agent,' she goes on, 'and I don't care if he has a broken leg, it's a sitting-down role.' She pauses, snorts, and says, 'Tell him from me he'll never work again.' With that she snaps her phone shut. Then she sees me and makes once more with the beckoning finger.

I ask, 'Me?'

The long and short of it is she wants me to fill in for the

missing actor. I'm about the same height, so it might just work. It's also a non-speaking role, but still I dither, which makes her apply some non-snarling charm. 'I'm sure you could do it. You have a strong, masculine face and body. You are born to acting and just what we need here.'

'Um,' I dither.

'And you'll be paid.'

Those are magic words. My dithers evaporate. The show must go on. There's no business like show business. Where do I sign and how much are we talking about here? I have begat a job in the acting profession, but before I get carried away with self-congratulations, I'm seized by two large, no-nonsense women. They are Dawn and Fay, from Make-up and Wardrobe. They whip me off to the bus with the white painted windows, where just my luck, there isn't a single lingering model.

Once inside, Fay rips off my duffle coat along with several layers of winter clothing. Soon I'm reduced to the saggy, grey underpants that common sense tells me I shouldn't have worn. My mother always checks to make sure my under-apparel is fit to be seen in public.

'Mum,' is my standard protest, 'no one's going to see my underpants.'

'They might, if you have an accident and get taken to hospital.'

FLIGHT OF FRACTURED FANCY:

Nurse: *Doctor, doctor, have a look at this patient's saggy underpants.*

Me: *They were fresh on this morning.*
Doctor: *How dare you come in here in that condition? Nurse, have the ambulance men return this dishevelled beggar to the scene of his accident.*
Me: *I thought you doctors and nurses cared about people.*
Nurse: *Not wearing underpants like that.*
Doctor: *So get off my operating table, you unkempt vagabond!*

But I needn't have worried. Dawn and Fay regard me with professional detachment. 'Isn't he pale?' Dawn reaches for a jar of tan-coloured cream then slaps a cold handful on my chest. Meanwhile Fay produces a pair of beach shorts in which I would not be seen on any of the free world's post-mortem tables. But since my shame is as high as my need for modesty, I grab the shorts and jam them on. 'Out of sight, out of mind,' Dawn remarks.

To complete my outfit I get a long black wig, a pair of thick horn-rimmed spectacles and a vivid yellow beach shirt. The look this season is geek.

Suddenly the bus door slides open and a man enters. 'Hello, my name's Rodney,' he carols, 'and you must be Wayne.' He catches sight of my outfit. 'Oh, I can see the talent already. Now, Wayne, my lot in life is to tell you what you are to do in this commercial we're making.'

'Rodney's the first assistant director,' Fay explains.

Rodney ushers me outside to the cold beach. 'This ad campaign is for Rippa Wrappa – the chocolate on every-one's lips. You've heard of Rippa Wrappa, Wayne?'

'Yes,' I respond. It's a chocolate bar that you hold

upright, then start ripping the wrapper around in small circles until it's all gone.

'Oh, good.' Rodney is pleased with my progress. He takes me to a part of the beach, surrounded by lights. The camera is ready and a bunch of serious-looking people stand around. There is a deckchair in the centre of it all, which is where Rodney seats me. It's freezing cold and I feel goose-pimples gather on my skin in knobbly clusters. A blind man could read me like a railway timetable and say, 'Dash, just missed my train!'

At that moment, the girls return, but with a difference. No longer do they shiver and cluster together for warmth. Their chase across the sand dunes has produced glowing and invigorated skin. They are flushed and smiling. Of Squocka, there is no sign. 'That trick works every time,' one of the crew observes. 'Warms them up a treat.'

A trick, eh? After our work experience, we should have guessed.

There is a beachbag beside the deckchair. I'm supposed to be a nerdy guy who suddenly has an urge to consume a Rippa Wrappa. When I produce one from my bag, the ripping noise attracts some bikini-clad girls who converge stealthily from behind. Rodney finishes his explanation, 'Do you think you could do that?'

'Piece of cake,' I tell him.

'So let's have a rehearsal, but on no account are you to look around at the girls, got that?' This part is simple. I take up a Rippa Wrappa, put on an expression of contentment then start the ripping action. Before I take a bite of the chocolate, Rodney calls, 'Cut!' He grabs my Rippa Wrappa and hurls it into a plastic bucket. 'Do it like that when the camera rolls and it'll be wonderful.'

Lena Rieven-Steel puts in an appearance, ready for Take One. The girls hide behind a sand-coloured canvas and we are ready to go. With a voice like a foghorn the director roars into a megaphone, 'Action!' Out at sea, two cargo ships change course. (That bit's a lie.)

As the camera rolls, my face shows a great urge to eat a Rippa Wrappa. I reach for one, then start to rip. The girls begin to lope towards the deckchair, then Lena Rieven-Steel yells, 'Cut! What about your expression?' she demands of me. 'You look like a caveman skinning a fruit bat.' The Rippa Wrappa ends up in a plastic bucket.

We do a Take Two, and that goes wrong as well. Something to do with me ripping too quickly. Take Three is a disaster because I stuck my tongue out. Takes Four to Nine are useless for different reasons. The plastic bucket fills up with discarded chocolate.

At this moment Squocka reappears, looking sheepish, but no one notices him. All eyes are on me. One thing I observe is that everyone is chewing Rippa Wrappas, that is, everyone but me. It's not long before Squocka has got into this particular bit of action, with a Rippa Wrappa in each hand.

We are up to Take Twenty-seven when disaster strikes. Not only is the take ruined, I happen to turn around and one of the models catches sight of me. 'Hang on! He's not Gregory!' she snaps. There is sudden confusion and I'm surrounded by girls who do not like what they see.

The long and short of it is that Gregory something, a real actor and member of the union was booked for this commercial. Lena Rieven-Steel has been trying to film with a non-union actor – that is, me. The girls get into a huddle, then decide to stop work. They shoot black looks in my direction. It's all my fault. I see Squocka enjoying this. Being chased across the sand dunes by a hundred models is nowhere as bad as what's happening to me.

Suddenly, there is a breakthrough. A small pink car drives onto the beach and a man gets out. The girls recognise him right away and rush to greet the newcomer. Rodney says, 'It's Gregory, come to rescue us.' The way they're carrying on, I guess this must be long-lost Gregory Claus, Santa's younger and more generous brother.

Even Lena Rieven-Steel changes her tune. She purrs when she sees him. 'Glad you could make it, Gregory, darling. Love your work.'

'And what's the score today, petals?' Gregory asks. 'What are we selling?'

'Chocolate bars,' Rodney says darkly, 'that's if this under-performing adolescent has left us any of them.'

After that it's easy. Fay and Dawn whip Gregory into the white-windowed bus, offering him the choice of which shorts to wear. The girls are a buzz of excitement. Squocka comes to observe these goings-on. 'Funny folk,' he says.

I give a petulant toss of my black wig. 'That's all you

know, darling!' My few seconds of filmed glory have to count for something.

With Gregory in the deckchair, the film shoot only lasts another hour. He does it beautifully, rips his Wrappa the correct way, manages to look furtive at the right moment before the loping girls surround him. At the end, Gregory gets to eat the chocolate bar and Lena Rieven-Steel smiles benevolently.

Then Gregory and the girls head for the bus together, which is when I remember I'm still wearing the make-up and geek gear. When I reach the bus, it's locked and laughter comes from inside, so I have to hang around until everyone comes out wearing scruffy jeans and sweaters with scarves around their necks. Two of the girls go off arm-in-arm with Gregory and no one gives me a second glance.

Our pay for the day's work is a box of Rippa Wrappas. 'Make sure you rip them the right way,' Squocka advises as he leaves me to get changed.

I get the bus to myself and wipe off some of the tan-coloured make-up, then put on my own clothes and the duffle coat. When I emerge, nearly everyone has gone. The crew are packing up the last of the equipment.

It has been a day of downers. But there's a ray of sunshine – two rays, if it comes to that.

One of the girls hasn't left the beach. She greets me as I trudge up the sandy path to the road. It's Jenny Dee. 'Hi, Wayne,' she says, and smiles. 'Just wanted to thank you for warming me up.'

'It was easy,' I say. 'I only provided the central heating.' It's a weak attempt at a joke, but maybe she sees that I need cheering up.

Jenny Dee gives me a card. 'That's my number,' she tells me. 'Give me a ring some time, eh?'

Oh, joy! I have begat a woman's telephone number. We walk away from the beach together, me and Jenny Dee. She gets my telephone number, which makes it twice as good. Since Jenny's an actor, she's into the 'darling' stuff and does things like take my arm as we walk along together. It's a nice feeling, until comes ray of sunshine number two.

Violet Pridmore is heading my way. She's been out shopping or something and can't help seeing me with Jenny Dee, who is laughing at something not very witty that I said.

I pass so close to Violet it's impossible for us not to greet each other.

'Hi, Wayne,' Violet says.

'Hi, Violet,' I respond, and that's it. We both move on, two ships that pass, and all that stuff.

How would you be? Spend my whole life trying to get close to Violet Pridmore, then when I *don't* want to see her, she turns up. Mind you, now that Violet's spotted me with a glamorous model, maybe it'll make her think.

But what'll she think?

23 BABES IN THE WOOD

The telephone goes 'brr, brr', reminding me of Jenny Dee and those shivering models on the beach. It's Jenny Dee's number I'm ringing, but she's not answering. Trouble is, I can't let the phone ring for long because it's the one in the hall at home where people come and go. Such as Charlene or my mother, who walks past and says, 'Who are you calling, Wayne?'

'Um, Squocka,' I lie and hang up quickly. 'But he's not answering.' Another lie.

'You need to give him more time to get to the phone.' Mum goes off humming, but stays within overhearing distance, able to eavesdrop on my shy and fumbling words. So how's a young lad to have a private conversation with the first woman to give him her telephone number? More than that, what's a young man to say to her?

I am just about to have another go, when Charlene pops out of the living room and catches me. 'Oh,' she cries in a tell-the-whole-world voice, 'Wayne's looking for some privacy so he can ring his girlfriend.'

'I'm not.'

'You are. I can see it in your face.'

So that's the problem. My mobile phone has gone on the blink and I'm not ringing from a public callbox. As soon as Jenny Dee hears the coins drop, she'll know it's someone terminally uncool calling her.

Maybe this is why men join the Foreign Legion or become monks and hermits and stuff. It's nothing to do with crime or religion but everything to do with their families never giving them the chance to do a bit of confidential talking with the woman of the moment. The poor guy either loses the notion or forgets the woman's name.

FLIGHT OF FANCY:

Wayne rings a number, knowing that a whole bunch of women live at that address.

Me: *Um, can I speak with Whosit?*

Girl: *No, Whosit got married last month.*

Me: *Then can I speak with Thingummy?*

Girl: *Thingummy doesn't live here any more.*

Me: *All right, last chance. Let me talk to the bald, ugly one with the spotty face.*

Girl: *How dare you? I do not have a spotty face.*

✦

Then in the last week of the school holidays I get home after a day of boring nothingness. The house is empty, so this is my big chance. With pounding heart I whip out Jenny Dee's card, which is grubby from all the handling it's had. I push the right buttons in the correct order, then the phone goes 'brr, brr', creating for me a mental picture of Jenny Dee gliding across the floor of a sophisticated apartment, wearing a long dress and a wide smile. 'Hello,' says her voice. 'You've reached Jenny Dee— '

'Hi, Jenny,' I say too quickly, then feel like a fool. It's her answering machine. Before I get a chance to wait for the beep and leave a message, the front door opens and Mum barges her way in with two armfuls of plastic bags from the supermarket.

'Give me a hand, Wayne,' she says. 'Oh, you're on the phone— '

'No, I'm not, Mum.' In two seconds, I hang up, then sprint to her side and take the bags.

'Who was it?'

'Nobody.'

Then Dad comes home, angry because he'd been called out to a blocked drain that magically cleared itself. 'Tea-leaves,' he snorts. 'Waste of an afternoon.'

Ten minutes later Charlene's home too, complaining that her Mini has got a dodgy sprangel-wongel and the man in the garage says it'll be off the road for a week. Conversation flies in every direction but mine.

Then the phone rings and Charlene says, 'That'll be for me. I'm expecting Rupert to call.' But in seconds, she's back in the living room with both eyebrows raised like flung-open upstairs windows. She announces, 'It's a girl. For Wayne.'

There's a silence, then Dad whistles and says, 'A girl, eh?'

'Yeah, well . . .' I make an apologetic shrug.

Mum says, 'So are you going to keep her waiting?'

I edge sideways to the hall, all the while conscious of three pairs of ears waiting to hear every word I utter. It's Jenny Dee on the phone. 'Hi, Wayne.' She catapults me back to that cold day when she came nestling inside Dad's old duffle coat.

'Hi.' My voice is hoarse.

'How are things, Wayne?'

'Quiet.'

'Same here. There's no work around.'

'Boring.'

'Wayne, if you're at a loose end, I've got something on tomorrow. Do you want to be in it?'

'Okay.'

Jenny gives me her address, then says, 'See you tomorrow, darling.'

'Yeah, bye.'

Clunk. Jenny Dee hangs up. 'Darling', eh? And something on. Definitely full of promise. Violet Pridmore never said anything like that, although writing 'love' on a postcard and adding XXXX is not to be sniffed at. Besides, I'm still feeling guilty about old Violet seeing me with Jenny Dee, as well as wondering what she'll think.

Back in the living room Charlene's eyes bulge with question marks. 'That was a tender conversation, Wayne.'

She repeats my words. 'Hi – quiet – boring – okay and, "Yeah, bye".'

Mum says, 'Charlene, don't tease. I can remember when you used to like some privacy as you talked with Rupert.'

I let it go because my mind is full of the something on that Jenny Dee has in store for me tomorrow. Once more my imagination runs away with my brain.

FLIGHT OF FEMALE FANCY:

Jenny Dee lives in a penthouse flat, which is decorated in white with muted gold toning. The furnishing is in excellent taste, the drapes hang with elegant understatement and the carpet is deeply piled.

Jenny reclines on a sofa, wearing white satin. By her side a darkly brooding pet cheetah is watchfully alert.

'Wayne, darling,' Jenny Dee greets me with a languid wave. The cheetah shows its teeth and claws but I am unconcerned because this is a dream and in dreams you are always brave.

Tomorrow comes soon enough and Jenny Dee's address leads me to a crumbling old part of town where birds don't sing and people leave their wheelie bins out all week. There are warehouses and factories mixed up with tumbledown houses and blocks of concrete flats. The building where Jenny lives is in keeping with everything else in this neighbourhood. It's an old brick two-storey place that was once Council offices but is now abandoned. Green paint peels from the front door and hangs off in loose flakes. The undercoat is pink. There is a bell push at the side but the press button is missing. Instead I knock at the door, which makes shards of dry paint fall around my feet.

My dream of Jenny has taken a severe knock. For a while nothing happens, then a man calls from an upper window. 'Whaddya want?' He shows a scowl and lots of hair.

'Um, looking for Jenny Dee.'

'Who wants her?'

Well, I do, you ning-nong. But since this guy could be a rival, I hold my emotions in check and give him my name. He withdraws and Jenny Dee appears. 'Hi, Wayne. Come on up. Just push the front door, but watch it. It's a bit tricky.'

After I give it a careful shove, the almost-green front door grunts. I lean my shoulder against it and press harder. With a slow groan the door falls inwards to crash noisily on the hallway floor. A huge cloud of dust flies upwards. I step in and find that the door was only held in place by the swelling dampness. Someone has removed the hinge pins, which is what happens when buildings get condemned. That and the wrecker's ball.

There's a crumbling staircase, with Jenny Dee waiting at the top. 'Hi, Jenny,' I greet her and start upwards. So far not so good. She's not wearing white satin, but jeans and a sweater and this must be the cheetah's day off.

Jenny leads me into a large room that was once painted

railway-station-waiting-room brown. Now it's not so sure. The shaggy guy sits cross-legged on a mattress on the floor, back against the wall, trying to tune a guitar. Twang, twang, it goes, then, t-w-o-i-n-g! He's not very good but raises a hand and says, 'Break a leg,' which is the jokey way actors wish each other good luck, as well as saying, 'I love your work.'

'This is Eugene,' Jenny explains.

'If he's staying,' Eugene mutters, 'I hope he brought his own beans.'

'Eugene's a sort-of actor,' Jenny says.

'What do you mean, sort-of?' he snarls.

'We're all sort-of actors,' Jenny Dee responds. 'We're not sort-of working, are we?'

'Oh, how you wound me!' Eugene takes a fit of the sulks and next thing you know, there's a big row between them. It's like a fast tennis match as they snarl and flare at each other, words flying in both directions. While this is going on, I take a look around the room. It is basic. A sink in the corner is full of bean-stained plates while at the side is a leaning tower of pizza boxes. They are empty, waiting for someone to take them out with the rubbish. There are also saucepans caked in baked-bean goo. I'm not staying to eat.

The row ends and Jenny drags me into her room, saying, 'Oh, I needed that little conflict, darling. Emotional laxative.'

'Yeah, right.' You have to say something.

Jenny's room is full of clothes which are piled

everywhere but mainly on a mattress on the floor. She kicks some aside, then folds gracefully on her bed and pats a place beside her for me to sit. 'Hi,' she says, as if we've met for the first time.

'Hi.' I sit nervously beside her.

'Thing is, Wayne,' Jenny Dee says. 'I've got a fight brewing and can't do it on my own.'

'Can't Eugene help?'

'No, he's into beans. This is marmalade, so he doesn't care.'

'Marmalade, eh?' My eyes narrow. I've stumbled into a madhouse with no way out. The windows have bars on them.

'It's this.' Jenny rolls over and produces a page torn from a magazine. She gives it to me. It's an advertisement for marmalade. Ralph Beamish's Rough-Cut Orange Marmalade. 'Do you see it, Wayne, darling?' Jenny's eyes are wide. 'Should we take them on?'

Take them on? Take who on? How do you answer such a question? Suggestions on a postcard please. Twenty-five words or less.

Dear Wayne,
Get out while you have a chance.
Signed,
A well-wisher and true friend.

'Marmalade's marmalade, isn't it?' I venture cautiously. That's the way; keep the conversation going, remain optimistic and avoid eye contact. That advice comes from the *Hostages Handbook of Negotiating Skills*. It's also a lie, but I'm desperate here. What is she going on about?

'Read it,' Jenny says. There's a paragraph, which I scan, hoping for some clue:

The Origins of Ralph Beamish's Marmalade

One morning in 1906, Ralph Beamish happened to visit the kitchen of his home where he found his young wife at the stove cooking something. Ralph tasted a spoonful and realised he had a success story on his hands. From that simple, homely beginning was born Ralph Beamish's Rough-Cut Orange Marmalade – the taste you've come to know and respect for a hundred years.

'Oh, yeah.' I nod wisely.

'Good.' Jenny Dee breathes a satisfied sigh and goes on, 'It calls for direct action.'

'Definitely.'

'A sit-in.'

'At least.'

Jenny rattles on, full of resentment and angst, which gives me an inkling of what's upsetting her. 'How dare he,' she fumes. 'His *wife* runs up a batch of marmalade, then into the kitchen tramples her overlord husband – bet it was the first time he'd seen the place, never even knew where his food came from – then he sells his wife's creation with *his* name on it.'

'He didn't?' I shake my head in disbelief. Before you

know it, Jenny ropes me into joining her in a protest at the head office of Ralph Beamish Fine Foods.

She starts to sing *We Shall Not Be Moved.*

'Can't we just save whales?' I suggest, but we're keeping that for later.

If we're to make a protest, we need placards and other things. Jenny gives me a list. 'Do you mind paying for them, Wayne darling?' She does things with her eyes. 'My cheque for the Rippa Wrappa shoot hasn't come yet.'

◆

I race through the streets, mentally counting my money. Not enough, but help is at hand. Squocka comes from the other direction. 'Wayne,' he says. 'What's up?'

'I gotta get some stuff, Squocks – urgently.'

'What? Bandages? Splints? First-aid kit? Intravenous drip?'

'Something like that,' I lie, then put on a worried face. 'Trouble is, I haven't got enough money— '

'Say no more.' Squocka delves a hand into his pocket, then hurries me on my way and calls, 'I hope everything's okay.'

It's going to be, apart from me lying to my best mate. I get the stuff on Jenny's list from a newsagent and a hardware store, then race back to Tumbledown Street. But around the first corner I run into Violet Pridmore.

'Hi, Wayne,' she greets me.

'Hi, Violet.'

'What's happening?'

'Nothing.'

'Boring, isn't it?' Violet seems to have something on her mind. 'Um, If you're not doing anything, what say we go out on our bikes?'

Violet, I think, of all the times to pick. You choose the one hopeful moment in my life when I telephone a girl and she answers.

'Great idea, Violet,' I begin. I don't get to the 'but'.

Violet reads me like a book. 'Oh well, maybe another time. Bye-ee.' She goes.

First lie to Squocka, then a follow-up to Violet. Not a bad morning's work.

❦

Jenny and I go to the protest venue by bus, with me coughing up for the fare. To make things worse, I hide a couple of cardboard placards up my sweater. They cut into my chin and force me to walk head up and stiff-legged, like I'm a Frankenstein monster, instead of just a teenage one.

'Isn't it exciting?' Jenny Dee asks. She takes my hand, which is nice but it's only to stop me running away.

The head office of Ralph Beamish Fine Foods is an impressive place and as we walk in the main doors, people ignore us. There are advertisements everywhere for Ralph Beamish's Chutney and Ralph Beamish's Emetic Sauce. Since he's a recipe thief I wonder what else he knocked off from his wife.

FLIGHT OF FANCY:

Ralph's in his shop one morning, nailing up a sign. His wife enters.
Wife: *Ralph dear, have you seen my hairpiece?*
Ralph: *Erm, no dear.*
Mrs Beamish leaves. Ralph stands back to admire his sign, which says:

> THIS WEEK'S SPECIAL. LADIES' HAIRPIECES.
> BUY ONE, GET A FREE JAR
> OF RALPH BEAMISH MARMALADE.

Jenny Dee leads the way into the main office where sit two dozen women working at computers. No one looks up as we enter. In a swift movement, Jenny sits cross-legged on the floor, hauls out the placards and at the same time produces a length of plastic chain, wraps it around the leg of a desk then snap-locks it on both of our wrists.

She holds up her placard.

> **THE ROUGHEST CUT OF ALL**
> RALPH BEAMISH IS A SEXIST THIEF!

Mine says he's an exploiter of women and a disgrace to marmalade. In the main office, one or two of the computer women notice us. I hope they can tell my heart's not in this.

'Ralph Beamish is a sexist pig,' Jenny chants, then whispers, 'Wayne, darling, join in.'

'Yes, he is,' I intone.

We don't even get in another word of protest before we're joined by a large official-looking man in uniform. 'Hello, children,' he says. 'Lost your mummy?'

'Don't patronise us,' Jenny snaps. 'This is a serious objection to sexist provocation.' She looks beautiful. Beautiful and unhinged, like that green front door I should have walked away from.

'I'm sure it is serious,' the official man agrees. 'But you're blocking the emergency exit. I mean, if we had a fire, how would all these young women get out? They'd be incinerated, then their mums, dads and boyfriends would have a protest to make.'

For the first time, Jenny looks doubtful. 'Phooey,' she says without much conviction.

'It may be phooey to you, but fires do a lot of damage,' the man goes on. 'Incineration's much worse than exploitation. And don't get me started on immolation.' With a tug and a snap, the man breaks the plastic chain, which cost Squocka seven dollars and sixty cents in the hardware store. 'And here's Mr Morgan from public relations. Why not make your protest to him?'

Mr Morgan oils up to us, beaming widely. His stock in trade is being nice to people. 'Hello, hello, what's this? A protest? Well, I do admire your concern and your social awareness. So why not come and let's talk about it?'

In his kindly way, he helps Jenny Dee to her feet and adroitly hands our placards to the man in uniform.

'Um, um.' I try to make a mini-protest of my own.

I could have used the other side of the cardboard for something.

Mr Morgan shepherds us into a room which has a large, polished table spread with advertising pamphlets and samples of the company's food lines. 'Now,' he begins, 'in 1906, when Ralph Beamish started in the food business, things were very different. It was a time when no woman – no *respectable* woman of Mrs Beamish's class – would even *think* about selling things. Women left that sort of thing to their husbands.'

'Did they?' Jenny sounds doubtful.

'They wouldn't have it any other way. For women, it was an age of elegance.'

'Yes, I can see that.' Jenny nods wisely.

'Nowadays,' Mr Morgan goes on, 'manufacturers fall over themselves to use women's names on their products.' He starts issuing to us some of the pamphlets on the table, advertising Mother McGinty's Savoury Pies, Sarah Dawson's Pan-Fried Fritters and Wendy Haddock's Salt-free Baked Beans with Triple-Grilled Bacon Niblets. 'If Ralph Beamish were alive today, of *course* he'd use his wife's name on anything she invented. Then it would be *Hermione* Beamish's Rough-Cut Orange Marmalade.'

I get into the act, 'Then why don't you change the name?' For this I receive an approving smile from Jenny.

'Good point.' Mr Morgan approves too. 'But it's difficult to change a name after it's been registered.' He turns to Jenny Dee as if she's the intelligent member of this protest group. 'You'd know all about that, wouldn't you?'

'Oh yes,' she responds firmly.

'So, there it is,' Mr Morgan smiles. 'Your complaint has been noted, but before you go, why not take some samples home?' He slides open a cupboard and produces two paper bags, heavy with Ralph Beamish products.

❦

Then we're standing at the bus stop, sorting through our bags of booty. 'That went well,' I say as we wait for the 493.

'Yes, it did, and we have made a difference, haven't we, Wayne, darling?'

'Huge.'

❦

Back in Tattsville, Eugene is pleased with our sample bags and rakes through them, discarding some tins and slavering over others. He's a vegetarian, so if he finds a triple-grilled bacon niblet in his beans, he'll spit it out. Look out, wall!

Jenny says goodbye to me on the street outside her condemned building with the front door still lying in the hallway showing its pink undercoat. She's preoccupied and gives me an absent sort of kiss on the cheek. The tip of her nose is cold.

Who cares that Eugene collared my share of the loot? I'm free to pursue my boyhood dreams with my own friends, and maybe patch up with Squocka and catch up with Violet.

Mrs Berrington tells me Squocka went out with Violet, and somehow that makes me feel better, but not a lot. It'll probably wear off in an hour.

*

Next day the phone rings at home and since no one else will answer it, I pick up the receiver. 'Wayne, darling,' comes Jenny Dee's breathless voice.

I cut in and try to sound like an answering machine. 'I'm not here right now but leave a message.' I go 'beep', then wait.

Jenny says all in a rush, 'Wayne, I think that PR man conned us with his talk of women living in an age of elegance. It was all rubbish and we were babes in the wood to fall for it. Can we make another protest tomorrow, only I haven't got the bus fare? Oh, and Eugene loved the beans. Bye-ee.'

Whew! I hang up just as Mum comes into the hallway. 'Who was that, Wayne?'

'Just somebody doing a survey, Mum.'

'What was it this time?'

'Marmalade.' It's another lie, but with this one I don't feel guilty.

24 MUTINY

In our fair town, Captain McCorkindale is a man renowned for having no sense of humour and a short temper. They say he became angry when he was a lad in Scotland, then spent the rest of his life getting better at it. He goes each year to the International Ill-Tempered Convention, held in Irascible, Ohio. Then he comes home and tries out his new techniques on his pet walrus. (That bit's a total lie, and possibly libellous, but he does have a bad temper.) He's also famous for being careful with his money, which is another name for tight-fistedness. It is those three McCorkindale features – unsmiling, angry and mean – that make wise people give him a wide berth. However, if you want to hire a small dinghy to go for a row, then you need to do business with the man. Reason: Captain McCorkindale operates a Rent-a-Boat outfit from a small hut and jetty on the river bank.

It happens one early spring Saturday that Squocka and I go for a walk in that direction because we know that Violet Pridmore often comes this way, sometimes with her friend Rosana Conti. On this morning there is no sign of either girl, but who should we see but Captain

McCorkindale leaning on his jetty rail sourly looking into the middle of the river. We spot that one of his hire boats has sunk out there with only the pointy bit showing above the water like a varnished iceberg.

As we stroll past, and before I can stop him, Squocka raises his voice to point out the obvious, 'Captain, one of your boats has sunk.'

Captain McCorkindale doesn't turn around, but tosses bitter words over his shoulder. 'Aye, I can see that for myself. I've been stood here twenty minutes thinking that very same thing. That boat is submerged, I thought, it's half under water, scuttled, come to grief, immersed, inundated, foundered, waterlogged, shipwrecked. S-U-N-K, sunk!'

'And stranded.' Squocka adds to the catalogue.

'Aye, so instead of telling me what I can very well see for myself,' Captain McCorkindale goes on, 'would it not be better to come up with a suggestion, like what I'm to do about it?' He turns around and for the first time we see that the man's arm is in a sling.

'Oh, you've got a— ' Squocka begins to point out even more of the obvious, until I clamp a hand over his mouth.

Captain McCorkindale reaches boiling point. 'So I can hardly row out there and fetch it back in, can I? Not with one arm.'

Since this is beginning to look like a conversation, Squocka keeps up his end. 'No,' he agrees. 'You'd keep going round in circles.'

370

'Squocks, let it go,' I whisper. My instinct is to drag him away, but my friend's in one of his helpful phases.

'We'll row out and get it,' he offers.

'First sensible word I've heard all day.' Captain McCorkindale nods approval and comes off the boil. 'Once it's back on the river bank, I'll see what the damage is.' He stumps off to his hut. I follow Squocka down to the shingly bank and help push one of the boats out. Captain McCorkindale starts brewing a pot of tea, carefully counting the tealeaves. 'One – two – three, och, I dropped one. Where's my tweezers?' (That bit's another lie, but he does make tea.)

The boat we've chosen for the rescue is called *Bounty*, and after launching it into the river and jumping in, we find it only has one oar. 'Maybe he's economising,' Squocka suggests.

'No, you ning-nong,' I snarl, taking a leaf out of the good Captain's *Manual of Condensed Irritability*. 'There should be two!'

'Then I bags it.' Squocka grabs the single oar and swings it over his head, just about felling me.

'Doesn't matter who bags it,' I growl as our boat floats further away from the bank. 'With only one paddle we're up the creek.'

At that moment a friendly guy trolls past in a power boat and stops laughing long enough to give us a nudge back to dry land where we collect another oar plus a bucket for baling.

Now properly equipped, we row out to the sunken boat,

where Squocka leans over the stern of the *Bounty* and starts baling the submerged one. I let him do it for a full two minutes until he sheepishly realises that he's baling out the river. We get a rope on the boat, then tow it back to the bank where it comes to rest, full of water and very wet. We beach the *Bounty* and Squocka grabs the bucket, then starts baling out the dinghy we've just recovered.

'Squocka, that's enough,' I hiss. 'Let's go.'

'Won't take a minute.' He carries on baling and sploshing.

I watch him work for ten minutes, then Captain McCorkindale emerges from his hut, fortified with weak tea. He calls, 'There's another bucket, lad. If you want it.'

Before I can think of a suitable answer, I find myself baling and sloshing with Squocka. My shoes and the bottom of my jeans are soaked. The waterlogged boat's name is *Limpet*, which is a kind of sucker. I know that feeling.

At last, *Limpet* is more or less empty of water and I think, Now's the time to get on our way, but no. Captain McCorkindale comes stumping down the shingle and looks at the dinghy as if it has personally offended him. 'What about the rowlocks?' he demands.

'They go in there.' Squocka points to the two holes where you insert the metal gadgets that hold the oars in place.

'I know that fine,' Captain McCorkindale snaps. 'But *where* are they?'

Limpet is full of river mud, so maybe that's where the rowlocks are, but I reckon we've done enough. Squocka grabs a bit of stick and says, 'I'll have a look.'

'Aye, you do that, if you like,' Captain McCorkindale mutters. 'That boat'll have to be dried out. I would not pay you to stand about idle.' He splashes off through the muddy shallows in his big sea boots.

'He said, "pay you",' Squocka's eyes go wide. 'The magic words. Looks like we scored a weekend job, Wayne.'

'Yeah,' I protest, 'but do we want it? What about catching up with Violet and Rosana?'

'They'll still be around. But just think, with a job I'll be able to afford the good things in life – fast car, rent my own pad.'

'It'll be a pad for kneeling on!' Bitterly I start scooping handfuls of mud out of *Limpet*. So far it has been a Violet-free zone and looks like staying that way unless Squocka gets this weekend job bee out of his bonnet.

We use river water to slosh out the last of the mud, then leave the boat to dry out.

❖

As the day warms up, more and more carefree, light-hearted young people come to hire dinghies for an hour or so. Guess who gets the job of pushing them out into the river? And beaching the boats when they come back in? That's right, us. Captain McCorkindale manages to use his good arm to collect the hire fee, so he's not totally out of action. Nor is his tongue. Since we are now employees, he finds things for us to do, such as sandpapering. 'To do it properly,' he advises, 'you need to put your heart into it.'

At the end of the day, when there's no more light, Captain McCorkindale orders us to collect all the oars and rowlocks and put them in the hut, then make sure the boats are secured for the night. 'All done, Captain,' Squocka says in his best nautical manner.

'Aye, well, I like an early start in the morning,' Captain McCorkindale says, then with a brief nod, he heads off.

'He didn't pay us,' I point out to Squocka.

'We'll get it tomorrow, Wayne.'

'Nor did he give us time off for lunch, or a tea break.'

'You don't drink tea.'

'It's the thought that counts.'

*

Sunday morning, we're back at work. The wind sweeps straight in off the sea and in this part of the world it rains horizontally. It stings my eyes because there are bits of iceberg in it. In weather like this, wise people stay home, and since Violet Pridmore is a woman of wisdom, there'll be no chance of seeing her.

Captain McCorkindale has already opened up his hut and simply gives a grunt, then stumps off to the shops. 'Going to buy a Sunday paper,' he says.

With the place to ourselves, Squocka decides to

impress our employer. 'Wayne, lets get the rowlocks and oars out.'

'Shouldn't we sort of wait— ?'

'Come on, mate. Initiative.' Squocka is off like the wind, grabbing armfuls of oars from the hut, then racing through the rain to the line of boats to put them in place. I follow suit with the rowlocks and we finish just as Captain McCorkindale returns with the Sunday newspaper tucked under his good arm. Is he pleased with our effort? Read on.

'What did you put the oars out for?' he snaps. 'Can you not see it's raining? I'll not have any customers.' He rants and raves, chewing bits off the jetty handrail and spitting them into the river. Not exactly true, but he rants and raves.

We collect all the oars and rowlocks and return them to the hut. There are squares of sandpaper lying on a bench in the hut, so with a sigh, we set to work rubbing down an old upturned boat.

The rain stops and the sun comes out, so we sprint with the oars and rowlocks just as the first hardy souls venture out for some fun and pleasure. At the end of that Sunday, there's still no sign of any pay. I nudge Squocka, and say with my eyes, Go on, ask him.

Squocka's lips, tongue and teeth move, but no sound comes out. I work out that he's saying, He probably pays fortnightly. I'll remind him next week. Okay?

So we go home without pay. As a boss, there's a lot wrong with Captain McCorkindale.

FLIGHT OF SEAFARING FANCY:

On board the good ship Iniquitous, *it falls to Seaman Wayne to complain to the captain. 'Aye, shipmate,' says Able Seaman Squocka, 'get him to see reason.'*

'Why me?'

'You're the one with the negotiating skills. The captain's that way.'

My knees go knocky-knocky and my teeth chatter as I approach the poop deck. 'Captain, sir,' I begin. 'The lads don't like your attitude and have asked me to have a chat with you, man to man.'

Next thing you know, I'm cast adrift in a small boat with only one oar. It is called Limpet *and I feel like one too. The ship sails on. Squocka waves and calls, 'Good try, shipmate.'*

I am alone in the vast ocean, but a mermaid pops up. It is Violet Pridmore. 'Hello, sailor,' she says.

'Get me out of this situation,' I plead. 'Please.'

'Who got you into it?' Violet shakes her lovely head, then disappears under the waves.

Mermaid Violet is right. Captain McCorkindale is a slavedriver with an attitude problem. But knowing that and doing something about it are two different things.

❖

At Squocka's urging, we turn up again next Saturday morning. After all, he argues, the man owes us two days' money. We work as before, and all day Sunday then in the evening when the sun goes down, Captain

McCorkindale says in a grudging fashion, 'Suppose I'd better give you loafers some money.'

Our eyes widen with gratitude and relief as he lays out two small piles of coins. As we scoop them up, the weight of them signals that he's not paid very generously. 'Thanks, Captain,' Squocka speaks for both of us.

'By rights, there should be a bit more,' Captain McCorkindale says. 'But I don't have it. Tomorrow is another day.'

'Tomorrow?' I echo.

'Oh, yeah,' Squocka says before I can strangle him. 'Tomorrow's a student-free day.'

'Oh, well, there you are then,' Captain McCorkindale says.

As we walk home, Squocka and I have a debate of great intensity. 'I'm not going back,' I say.

'But he'll give us the rest of our money.'

'I think we should call it quits,' I tell him.

At home, Mum sees me raiding the fridge because I haven't had a chance to stop to eat. 'What are you getting up to these days?' she asks.

'Oh, this and that.'

'Charlene says she saw you at the river, scrubbing one of Miserable McCorkindale's boats.'

'Oh, that? Well, I helped him out, a bit.'

'You've been at it two weekends,' my relentless mother goes on. 'I hope he's paying you.'

'Oh, yeah, I got paid.' The coins still jingle in my pocket.

Mum can read me like a book. She launches into a lecture about being exploited, not having my conditions spelt out, no holidays, meal breaks, toilet breaks, scratch-yourself-breaks, or compensation if I should get injured. 'It's a rort,' she tells me, 'a con, swindle, cheat, plus dirty work at the crossroads.'

'Yes, Mum. I'm not going again.'

'Just as well.'

Sure enough, next day, I meet Squocka whose ears are still bright red and burning.

'Mum cracked,' he tells me gloomily.

'Mine too,' I say. 'Went haywire. Full of common sense.'

'Who needs it, eh?'

Since we still have to collect the rest of the money we are owed, we turn up at the river bank where Captain McCorkindale greets us with a nod. Before we know it, we find ourselves getting out the oars and rowlocks, pushing out a couple of boats for early-morning rowers, then it's back to the sandpapering. This time we work on *Limpet*, which is now completely dried out. 'I didn't plan to do this,' I mutter.

'Okay, we collect our money then split,' Squocka says.

Suddenly, there is a change. No, it's not the weather, it is Captain McCorkindale. He turns nice and kindly and comes quickly across the shingle with a smile on his face. 'Boys, you've worked so hard, why not take a break?'

'A break?' I ask. This is seriously spooky, like when

the lion starts to purr and rub itself against the animal-tamer's leg. What's on its mind? What's on *his* mind?

'Aye, take one of the boats out for a row.' He goes to *Bounty* and even gets ready to push the boat off with his one good arm.

'Okay.' Squocka jumps in and grabs the oars. I join him and in seconds, we pull away from the river bank.

Captain McCorkindale smiles and waves. 'Have a good long row, lads. Take your time.'

'I bet he stops the hire fee out of our money,' I say.

'Wayne, you need to start trusting people,' Squocka tells me as he pulls on the oars.

'That's the problem,' I answer. 'I do.' Then I get to thinking, what caused the Captain's change of heart? Before long, I put two and two together, reach a conclusion, arrive at an answer to the conundrum and work things out, in that order. A tall man walks along the river bank, heading for Captain McCorkindale's hut. He doesn't look like a boat hirer; this man is dressed in a suit and carries a briefcase. Before long, he enters the hut and I see Captain McCorkindale greeting him. They both go inside.

'Squocka,' I say, 'let's try an experiment.' We change places and I take the oars.

'What sort of experiment? Navigation? Boat-handling?'

'You'll see.' In a few strokes, I slide *Bounty* back alongside the jetty and call, 'Ahoy, Captain!'

The man himself comes out of the hut and is not

pleased to see us back again so soon. He looks down at me. 'What is it?'

'I don't like these oars,' I tell him.

'What's wrong with them?' Captain McCorkindale struggles to be nice.

'They're bent,' I say, then whisper, 'as in – *crooked.*'

He takes an eye-swivelling pause. 'Then I'll change them,' Captain McCorkindale says at last, then stumps into the hut and comes out with another pair of oars and kneels on the jetty to lower them into the boat. The man with the briefcase looks on with interest. I see him in the hut, examining papers.

I keep my voice low, 'And we also need to be paid – like now.'

Captain McCorkindale frowns over his shoulder to indicate the man who is able to overhear things if anyone should raise his voice a decibel or two. 'Later, lads, I'll fix you up.'

By this time, Squocka has caught on to what's happening. The man with the briefcase is some sort of government official. It's obvious that Captain McCorkindale doesn't want us around acting like employees, which might give rise to awkward questions, not to mention uncomfortable answers. So we had to be got out of the way, and here we're back again. 'How about *now?*' Squocka says with emphasis.

With a face like a heavy squall, a thunderstorm and a cloudburst, our good Captain drops some notes into the boat, then with a smile I pull *Bounty* away from the jetty. Still keeping up his pretence, Captain McCorkindale calls after us, 'I hope that sorts things out, lads.' His eyebrows work overtime, heavy with hidden meaning.

Squocka grabs the notes from the bottom of the boat and counts them. 'Now I can put a deposit on that pad,' he says.

'We'll have a pleasant little splash about for a while,' I suggest, 'then dump *Bounty* and head off home, money in hand and a good day's work done.'

So we stooge around in the river for ten minutes, then who should turn up to make the day perfect but Violet Pridmore and Rosana Conti.

Since Captain McCorkindale is in such a generous mood, we push things a little more. All it takes is a swift pull back to the jetty, a quiet word with our ex-employer and next thing you know, Violet and Rosana are rowing out to join us in *Limpet,* courtesy of Captain McCorkindale.

'Hi, you guys,' Violet greets us brightly. 'How did you wangle a freebie from Mr Mean?'

'We have ways,' I respond mysteriously.

The briefcase man leaves the hut and walks off along the river bank. Captain McCorkindale comes out and leans on the jetty rail, surveying us. Ha! Suffer, I think.

'Violet?' There's a small, worried tone in Rosana's voice. 'Should there be this much water in the bottom of a boat?'

'You'd expect a *little* bit,' Violet says uncertainly.

Fortunately, that close to the bank the river is not

deep. I pull alongside leaking *Limpet* and say, 'How about you girls get in our boat?'

'No, thank you,' Rosana responds with a nose-high sniff.

The girls clamber over the side of their boat and start to wade ashore. 'There has to be a first time for everything,' Violet says. 'Go for a row with Wayne Wilson and end up walking home.'

The only one enjoying this is Captain McCorkindale. Who says he doesn't have a sense of humour?

25 GIRLS

quocka speaks without moving his lips, 'Wayne, I reckon we oughta make a move.'

It's deep in the summer holidays and we're sprawled on a warm, sandy beach with green surf to seawards and blue sky above. Women in bikinis fill our eyes and I have terminal sunburn but don't care. Squocka says he knows the technique of conquering the girls of our dreams, so there's no going home until I find out how to go about it.

'I'll say hello to Violet Pridmore,' I suggest. 'You go for Rosana Conti. She likes sophisticated men.' Our girls are not sunburned, but wisely seek shade under a beach umbrella a few metres away. They still haven't forgiven us for the boating escapade.

Squocka considers my suggestion, but 'Nah, I like a challenge,' he says. 'Reckon I'll go for the little one in pink over there.'

'She's number twenty-one.' I've drawn a map on the sand showing the position of every woman on the beach. Violet and Rosana are numbers twenty-two and twenty-three.

'Or I might check out the one in blue,' Squocka goes on.

'Twenty-nine.'

The one in pink gets up, shakes the sand out of her towel and heads off. She must have read Squocka's mind, which is not easy without the instruction book.

'She's gone, Squocks,' I tell him. 'Too bad, eh?' I smooth off the little pile of sand that was her spot on the map.

'That's her loss.' He flexes his muscles and looks around for a substitute. 'Could be the one in blue's lucky day!'

I put on my sin-glasses to check her out. Sin-glasses are great because you look as if you're staring ahead while you actually squint out the sides. Only drawback is you get a headache from too much eyeball-swivelling. The one in blue looks all right.

Squocka tells me to study his technique, then he rises and nonchalantly picks his way across the sand in the girl's direction, leaving me to wonder why I'm so tongue-tied in situations like this.

I lie back and pretend to doze, but a dark shadow falls on me. I look to see who is making it, hoping she's been unable to resist my youthful good looks.

FLIGHT OF FANCY:

I brace myself for the experience, for the onslaught of the woman's body as she flings herself upon me. Our suntan lotions mingle meaningfully and make a chemical reaction. Zap! Pow! Her Sophisticreme Sun Balm meets my irresistible Beach-Hunk Tanning Oil.

Romantic music swells on the sound track. Here ends the Flight of Fancy.

Truth is, Mum makes me wear Factor 93 Baby Bottom Lotion, plus a floppy hat and zinc cream on my nose.

Ploomp! A dollop of purple ice cream drops on my chest.

The shadow is cast by a four-year-old female small person who looks down at me. In one hand she has a bucket of sea water, in the other, a soggy ice-cream cone from whence came the scoop of boysenberry ripple. This is embarrassing. I am trying to attract a big one, only to end up with a small one. Privately, I hope none of the more mature women on the beach see what's happened, but already I am a marked man.

'Wayne's found a girlfriend!' sings a silvery voice with a little giggle attached to it. It is Violet Pridmore, wouldn't you know it! Squocka is further away, doing an imitation of the towering inferno, gazing manfully down at the one in blue who wears sunglasses so I can't read her eyes to see if she's noticed him. She hasn't moved, so she might be asleep.

'Go away,' I hiss at the child and wipe off her ice cream with Squocka's baseball cap.

'I can't,' she says. 'I'm losted.'

'Well, go and be losted somewhere else,' I tell her, looking away, hoping to assure everyone the child's not with me. By this time, at least three other women are sitting up taking an interest in the four-year-old who has the entire beach to be lost in, but has to do it in front of me!

There's a worse horror in store. The child dips into her bucket and produces, of all things, a crab. She holds it up and its pincers go click, click in my direction as if it can't wait to get at a human being. Under my sunburn, I turn pale.

The truth is, I do not relate to creatures with mandibles, claws and equipment like that. I don't even like them in seafood restaurants when they're stuck to the plate with potato salad and tartare sauce.

'Will you look after my crabby?' says the infant, then drops the beast on my chest. 'Her name is Miss Snappy because she's got a bad temper.' The crab scuttles across my bare skin and hides behind my left nipple, glaring at me with warlike pincers held high! One move and I'm doomed!

FLIGHT OF FANCY:

Coroner: *In your opinion, how did this man die?*

Witness: *He was attacked by a crab.*

Coroner: *A female one?*

Witness: *Yes sir.*

Coroner: *Go for the nipple, did she?*

Witness: *Yes sir.*

Coroner: *A painful death.*

The crab scuttles sideways to the right and lurks behind my other nipple, all ready for battle.

'She likes you,' says the child. Just my luck! A beach

full of females and the only ones I attract are Miss Snappy and Miss Nappy.

There's no way I'd put a finger near that crab, so the only thing to do is out-stare it. Just then, a vision appears. She's about my age, a sun-tanned blonde wearing a bikini and multiple golden bangles. With arms swinging loosely by her side, she steps across the sand to stop in front of me. This girl has long red fingernails and puts her hands on her hips. 'So, *there* you are?' Her words are silken. 'Found you at last!'

Oh joy! I wonder how long she's been looking. But it's not me she's talking to – it's the child.

'Hello, Ella,' the four-year-old greets her. 'I got losted.'

'Tanya, I hope you haven't been a nuisance,' Ella says.

I indicate the savage object on my chest. 'Your little sister's showing me her crab.'

'She's not my sister,' Ella tells me. 'I'm looking after her.' She takes Tanya by the hand and starts to drag her away.

'He took my crab!' the child yells. 'I want Miss Snappy!'

'Oh, all right.' Ella leans over and scoops the creature off my chest with her bare fingers, then drops it in the child's bucket. I am deeply impressed by this maiden who can handle crabs without fear. I am also transfixed by the touch of her fingers on my skin! When you first start on the Great Female Hunt of Life, you're grateful for the smallest contact. It all adds up.

'What else have you got, Tanya?' I rise from the sand to look in the bucket. It's full of shells and crawly things. 'Wow, aren't they amazing.'

Ella says casually, 'We're just along there, near the lifesavers' platform.'

This is a downright invitation if ever I heard one. 'I'll come over,' I offer nonchalantly. 'If that's okay?'

'Sure.' Ella heads off, taking Tanya by the hand. 'Come and meet my friend.'

A quick glance tells me that Squocka's still staring at the one in blue. She hasn't moved. I bet her mum told her to pretend to be dead and he'll go away.

This is how to do it, mate! I think. *This* is the technique! (Only I don't know what to do next.)

Then we're strolling across the beach together – Ella and Wayne or Wayne and Ella. Secretly, I try out the combinations and either way they sound nice. I tell her about my fictitious plans for university where I'll major in marine bionics, then study crabs, seaweed and things that get washed up on the beach. Then I see her friend. It can only be her friend. *Please* let it be her friend!

It *is* her friend, whose name is Yasmine. She's dark-eyed, black-haired and deeply tanned. When she smiles it's as if someone turned on lights or something. (I get this out of books in case you want to use the line yourself one day.) Wayne and Yasmine! That sounds nice too!

Ella sends Tanya off to a small rock pool where there are lots of other kids splashing around happily with floppy hats and zinc cream all over them.

Yasmine and Ella ask my name and I blurt out 'Wayne Wilson,' then flex my bicatreps and hope they're impressed. 'He had a *crab* on his chest, Yasmine,' Ella tells her friend. 'It was scuttling around amongst all the hairs.' (Go easy, girl! I've only got seven!)

'Yeah, well,' I lie modestly. 'It's just that – you know, I've always been fascinated by crabs. And lobsters.'

'What kind of lobsters do you like, Wayne?' Yasmine asks.

'Oh, thermidor ones,' I respond seriously. (I read that word in Mum's recipe book and hope it's right.) I tell you, this conversation stuff's a piece of cake. But just then I catch sight of the Spraying Mantis.

Now here I must tell you about this guy. His name is Tony Mantis and he went to our school, only he didn't actually learn anything like writing stories and deducting percentages. 'No worries,' was all Tony Mantis would say. 'I'll get by.'

Five summers ago he got the idea of spraying sunbathers with tanning oil, using a portable atomiser outfit. When he shows up on the beach, girls flock to let Tony spray them. A dollar a time, no worries. In the winter, he does designs and scenery on panel vans and surfboards. That's why he calls himself the Spraying Mantis.

Tony was such a success he got a lot more compressor units, then employed other guys to work the beaches up and down the coast. These days Mr Mantis, as we now call him, stays home and employs somebody to count his money.

Anyway, on this particular summer day at the beach, who should be doing the Spraying Mantis routine but one Kevin Merry.

As soon as Ella and Yasmine see Kevin, they squeal with delight and dash off with their dollars to be sprayed. Before long, there's a queue of sun-seekers waiting for the treatment. Kevin has a wall-to-wall grin on his face as he casually sprays them one after the other with long, slow, sweeping strokes.

The education authorities should see what a bad end Tony Mantis has come to! Him with his franchises and branches expanding everywhere.

Even Squocka's little one in blue joins the throng so he's left looking at the dimples in the sand her body left behind. He looks rejected, even though he was never accepted in the first place. I make with one of our semaphore signals – the ones you don't learn in the Boy Scouts. Seconds later, Squocka joins me. 'How'd you go with the one in blue?' I ask.

'Didn't,' he answers, 'so I just ignored her.'

'That's the way, mate. Treat 'em rough.' I indicate Ella and Yasmine who are waiting for the fish-oil procedure. 'I met those two. Ella and Yasmine.'

Squocka's eyes narrow and stay narrowed until the girls return to their spot on the beach, all a-thrill and coated in Kevin's sun lotion which is actually old peanut oil that Meals on Wheels throws out after they've done the chips. (That bit's a jealous lie.)

'Oooh! That was wicked!' Ella's every limb glistens.

'And what a hunk!' Yasmine breathes. 'Did you see him?' This is Kevin they're talking about.

'Yes, we're all proud of Kevin.' I try to share some of his glory. Immediately, the girls want to know who Squocka is, so before I stop him, he swings into his Portuguese teenage rock-singer routine.

'I am Raymondo Catarrh,' he says in a fake accent and makes a bow. This is a story we concocted in the hope of impressing girls, if ever we got close enough to one. Or two.

'Raymondo Catarrh?' Yasmine questions with a roll of her eyes.

'Sounds like a disease,' Ella adds.

'Issa my name,' Squocka insists. 'Und zis issa my ha-manager, Wayne Hunk.'

'Wayne Hunk, is it?' Yasmine's eyes appear over the top of her sunglasses.

I die a little on the inside and give Squocka a secret signal which means, *Belt up!* Thankfully he gets the message so sits and broods in what he hopes is the Portuguese manner.

For the next half hour, we sit and while away the time until Yasmine stands up and yells in the direction of the rock pool. 'Home time!'

Next thing you know, there's an avalanche of small girls and boys pelting up the beach as fast as their chubby legs will carry them. They mill around wetly with their sandy bodies and buckets of sea water. It turns out Ella and Yasmine help out at a child-minding centre by looking after the kids while the lady in charge takes delivery of a bulk order of desensitising pills.

'Aw, Ella,' the kids plead. 'Can we take our crabs?'

'No,' Ella says. 'They'll pine for the ocean.'

'Give them to Wayne Hunk,' Yasmine says. 'He *loves* crabs!'

At this, the kids push their crabs at me until I'm surrounded by claws, nippers and mandibles plus goggle eyes and mean looks. The kids can see through me and know I'm not really a crab-lover. They chase me past the queue of sunbathers waiting to be given the once-over by Kevin Merry and his Spraying Mantis equipment.

I've had better days. On top of that, at home Mum says the sunburn is my own fault, so I get no sympathy.

◆

Now that I've broken the ice, it's easy to meet Yasmine or Ella after work. It's also easy for Squocka, so we drop by together. He has dropped his Raymondo Catarrh persona.

Before long, it starts costing us a fortune in hamburgers and milkshakes because our girls like to be fed. Their boss gives them lunch every day, but she's into health foods and vegetarianism so the girls crave meat. Squocka suggests we catch up with them *after* they've been to the hamburger joint but I say that would make us look like cheapskates. 'Cheapskates or dorks,' Squocka says. 'Take your pick.'

I'm noble, so stick with being a dork.

The good news is they're a pair of funny girls and we enjoy being with them. We go for long summer afternoon walks, which helps them work up their appetite all over again and sometimes we go to the beach where the ice-cream man calls every half hour.

The girls tell us they've got bikes, so Squocka and I dig out our old ones so we can cycle along leafy lanes and down sun-dappled byways. Romantic stuff like that. I've grown too tall for my red BMX and get severe chafing of the ears because my knees rub against them as I pedal.

When I was small, my BMX was just the thing for attracting girls. They used to climb on the back without me even asking them to, but now it makes me look like a stick insect riding an eggbeater.

In our outings with the girls, whenever anyone says anything amazing or unbelievable, Yasmine has a habit of pretending to faint. Since I'm a sort of amazing and unbelievable guy, she does it at least half a dozen times an hour.

'Oh, hold me up,' she says, then pretends to keel over backwards, so that Squocka has to catch her. It's not fair – I make the swoon-inducing jokes while Squocka gets all the body contact. Meanwhile, I have to stand about laughing in a sophisticated way as if I'm above all that sort of thing. Well, I *am* above it, because I'm not getting any of it!

◆

But now it's time for the ominous dah-dah-dah-dum music. There we are, out for a late holiday Sunday stroll, all dressed up in our neat gear. Ella's sort of with me and Yasmine's definitely with Squocka. I wish Ella would make up her mind about me the way I've made up my mind about her. It's definitely love, I think.

Tick one kind of love from the following selection:

Unlucky ❏ **Ill-fated** ❏ **Doomed** ❏ **Jinxed** ❏ **Hopeless** ❏

We have fed our women hamburgers and French fries so that should keep them quiet until the next feeding stop, which is when we get to the bus station cafe. They're in a good mood. Yasmine is dressed in a cool, tight little dress that flows and swirls around her legs as she moves on her cute little high-heeled shoes. She looks a bit of all right and I am proud to be seen with her. *Nearly* seen with her, as she's walking with Squocka.

We stroll across the footbridge that spans the river, and when we are right in the centre, I make my big mistake by casually uttering something far out, unbelievably amazing and totally mind-blowing and since I do this all the time, I think no more of it than I would of blowing my nose. But Yasmine reacts, as is her habit, by pretending to collapse.

Only thing is, this time she doesn't fall over in Squocka's arms, as is her regular thing. For the first time, she swoons in *my* direction!

Body contact at last, you may think, but am I ready for her? Do I expect her to fling herself backwards at me? Do I open my arms to receive her bodily softness? I do not.

Next thing you know, old Yasmine's lying on the ground with mud on her dress while one of her high-heeled shoes flies over the rail of the bridge and splashes into the river below.

'Stupid lunkhead!' Ella snaps, and rushes to the aid of her friend.

'Oh, this is my sister's dress,' Yasmine cries. 'I'll never get the mud off.'

'Never mind your dopey sister's dress!' Ella snaps. 'They're my shoes you borrowed!' By this time, the item of female footwear is bobbing its way downriver in a little swirl of water.

'Em, em.' Squocka helplessly hops from one foot to the other while I rush with my clean hankie to wipe off the mud. Both girls hiss at me and say I've done enough damage for one day, thank you very much, Wayne Hunk. I knew they'd bring that up.

So, that's why the da-da-da-dum music and it's how our relationship came to a sudden end.

Squocka is also on the outer as *he* should have caught Yasmine. With his free hand, he should also have caught the shoe. They don't let us stay with them to help Yasmine limp home, or even let her lean on me.

We mope around the child-minding centre for a few days but the girls do not appear. At last, we decide to give it away, so that's that. But there is more. I am walking along the bicycle path by the river, a sad, pale lovelorn swain when – oh no! What do I see? Can it be true?

Three people are walking along, arm in arm. A boy

and two girls. Elegant Yasmine on the left and beautiful Ella on the right and in the middle, that well-tanned employee of the Spraying Mantis, Kevin Merry!

Yay, Kevin! Go for it, son! We're cheering for you, we want you to win, to show what you're made of, Kevin Boy. We want you to be a success!

But not *that* successful!

I am shattered and turn away in case the girls see me, but there's no chance of that with Kevin around. They'll end up with stiff necks from all the looking up they're doing.

At home, Mum sees my downcast face and doesn't rush to comfort me.

'Mum,' I say. 'I am emotionally shipwrecked!' (She'll relate to that. After all, it worked for Charlene.)

'What is it, Wayne?' she asks. 'More sunburn?'

'No, Mum,' I say. Tragic, tragic. 'It's more like heartburn.'

Dad gives me an indigestion tablet to suck. Later, I look up heartburn and find it's a medical condition caused by eating rich food, plus the pills were past their use-by date.

Sigh, sigh, tragic, tragic, mope, mope. I go off my food and do not ask for seconds. Nobody notices because I had a full plate first time around.

●

End of summer holidays and back at school, Violet Pridmore sits alone near the bike shed under the shade of our only tree. I think, hello, there's old Violet. Wonder if she's forgotten about that boating fiasco?

Violet raises her eyes and spots me. She smiles and pats the seat beside her. An invitation. She shifts along the bench to make room for me. 'Hi, Wayne.'

'Hi, Violet.' So far so good. I put my bag of books on the ground and Violet spots the new atlas that I bought in the holidays.

'Oh,' she says. 'You got the atlas. I couldn't find one.'

'You want to have a look?' I open the atlas and she leans closer. Her long hair falls on the map of Turkey. I push the stray lock to one side so Violet can read the rainfall figures, then suddenly I think, she's really nice. Really, really lovely.

This bit is not a lie, nor is it a flight of fancy. It's just a good way to finish.